Adelsverein: The Gathering

Book One of the Adelsverein Trilogy

Strider Nolan
PUBLISHING

Strider Nolan Media, Inc.
1990 Heritage Road
Huntingdon Valley, PA 19006
www.stridernolanmedia.com

Cover and interior layout and design by Booklocker.com.

Adelsverein: The Gathering

Celia Hayes

Although not quite a project created by committee, thanks and acknowledgements are due to a great number of people who contributed advice, feedback, editing, and all sorts of support to the writer of this novel, beginning with members of the Independent Authors Guild, most especially Diane Salerni, for editing, Michael Katz for technical advice and Al Past for the use of his gorgeous color photos. Text layout and cover design is by Angela Hoy and Todd Engel of Booklocker.com

Extravagant thanks are due to Barbara Skolaut and J.H. Heinrichs—generous patrons of the arts, literature and most importantly, genre fiction. Thanks also to local Friedrichsburg historian Kenn Knopp who kindly reviewed the manuscript in search of historical errors. Any which remain in are purely my fault. Thanks to Jim Berne, of San Antonio for a quick lesson in maintenance and handling of a 1836 Colt Paterson and to Jo Rudolf who read the early drafts and made many useful suggestions. Thanks also to my late good friend and computer genius, David Walsh. If I can only remember a portion of the computer and marketing knowledge which he attempted to pass on to me, I'll be doing very well.

And finally—the staff of the San Antonio Public Library, Semmes Branch. They managed to find many of those books on various matters to do with historical events in Texas which I needed to research this historical novel.

This book is dedicated with love to Mom and Dad, and to my daughter Jeanne—all of whom were supportive well and above the call of duty, especially as regards all that stuff that I 'forgot' to do because I was busy writing.

I will bring your offspring from the east

And from the west I will gather you:

I will say to the north, Give up; and to the south,

Do not withhold; bring my sons from afar

And my daughters from the ends of the earth

– Isaiah 43:5-6

Prelude – *Palm Sunday 1836*

Presidio La Bahia, Goliad, Texas

The Mexican soldiers marched the prisoners away from the old citadel on the seventh day after Colonel Fannin had surrendered under a white flag. His little command of volunteers and militia had fought doggedly and hopelessly for a day and a night, pinned down in the open just short of Coleto Creek, tormented beyond endurance by gunfire, thirst and grapeshot. It was the grapeshot that did it finally and Carl Becker, all of sixteen and a bit had stood in the ragged ranks of the Texas Volunteers, the Greys, Shackelford's Red Rovers and the rest, next to his older brother Rudolph. They silently watched Colonel Fannin march out of the ragged square under a tattered white banner made from someone's shirt. It was just sunrise, that hour when everything looks bleak and grey.

"What will happen to us now, Rudi?" he asked at last. He spoke in German, the language they spoke at home among the family but one of the other German boys, Conrad Eigener, who stood next to the Becker brothers laughed curtly and answered:

"With luck, take away our weapons and send us packing. To New Orleans, I think. They mean to break up all the Anglo settlements and throw the Yankees out of Texas. General Santa Anna means business."

"They said General Cos brought eight hundred sets of shackles with him last year, to drag us back to Mexico City in chains," Rudi answered with smoldering resentment.

Conrad spat, saying, "Well, that worked out real well for him. We kicked him in the nuts at Bexar and he went running home to Mexico City, squealing like a girl."

"That's why Santa Anna came back, breathing fire and swearing vengeance," Rudi answered, "He took it personal, Cos being his brother-in-law."

"What will they do to us, then?" Carl asked again. From the Mexican lines came the sound of a bugle call, and Carl could just make out another white flag, and the brilliantly colored uniforms of the men under it, advancing to meet Colonel Fannin and Major Chadwick.

"Nothing like what the Comanche would do, little brother," Rudi answered. Carl would remember always how he smiled, a flash of teeth in a face blackened with powder smoke. "They're real soldiers; they have rules they have to follow. We lost, fair and square, but they have to remember it could be them next time, and treat with us as they might wish to be treated then."

"All right, then," Carl answered, reassured. Rudolph was five years older, and almost always right.

At first it did seem like his brother and the other men were right. The men and boys who were still fit were ordered by their surviving officers to stack their weapons and form up. Carl let his old flintlock rifle go with a pang, but it was what Rudi said to do, and Captain Pettus and Colonel Fannin. Rudi had been telling Carl what to do for all of his life, Captain Pettus for most of the last year of it. As far as Carl knew, they were always right. Well, Rudi was always right and the captain was mostly right, but Carl had reservations about their commander, even before the fight at Coleto Creek.

Rudi gave up his own musket in a good temper, but scowled so fiercely at the Mexican soldier who took away his great long pig-sticker of a knife that another soldier menaced him with a bayonet. Both the soldiers laughed, as Carl pulled his brother away.

Rudi cursed under his breath, "Damn them! What's a man supposed to do without a knife?"

"I still have mine," Carl whispered to him, very low, "I saw what they were doing, and I slipped it into my boot-top without anyone noticing."

"Quick thinking, little brother!" Rudi murmured, his good humor restored as they followed after their discouraged comrades in Captain Pettus's Company, First Regiment Texas Volunteers. "We'll make a real soldier of you, yet!"

'If this is real soldiering,' thought Carl rebelliously, *'I'm not sure I think all that much of it.'*

At sixteen and not quite grown to his height, Carl appeared at first glance to be amiable and not terribly quick on the uptake. He and his brother had same broad, fair Saxon features, but Carl's heavy eyelids always made him look a bit sleepy, and so many people were deceived into thinking he was a dunce. He didn't mind letting them think so mostly, for he had found considerable advantage in that. He and Rudi had grown up, hunting together and otherwise running wild in the untamed country near the Becker homestead in a little settlement far up on the Colorado River. Rudi and Carl had spent many hours sitting quietly concealed in a thicket watching for deer or doves. It seemed quite natural for them to go off soldiering together in the fall of 1835 even before the harvest was done, for the situation with the Mexican government had come to a head and the American colonists had run clear out of patience. That was Rudi's idea, his little brother just followed along as he always had.

Carl liked to sit still and watch the sun dappling through the ever-moving leaves, the flash of a white-wing dove starting up from the ground, and he liked to watch people and sort out what they were thinking. He spoke two languages well, understood a third and even knew some of the Indian signing talk, but he was a quiet youth and not much given to putting himself forward. He knew how it rankled with some of the older men that Colonel Fannin hung back against all urging and advice. Colonel Bowie and all them were besieged in the Alamo fortress up-river in Bexar, still waiting for help after they sent messengers pleading for reinforcements three times.

The Mexicans marched their prisoners back to Goliad, to the old citadel; they did not mistreat them particularly, but they shut them up in the old garrison chapel building, the wounded and the fit all crammed together and left to sleep all crowded on piles of straw which became more soiled and bug-infested by the day. It was also very dim inside the tall stone chapel, for the shutters were fastened down over the few windows. Sometimes the prisoners were let out into the little yard during the day, but always strictly guarded. The two doctors in Fannin's command, Doctor Morgan and Doctor Shackleford, were taken away to tend the Mexican wounded in another part of the presidio. After a week of this, Carl was thoroughly bored. He had never before in his life had to spend a week inside walls, crowded in with three hundred other men.

"Did you hear? They've brought Colonel Fannin back from Copano," said Ben Hughes, excitedly. He was Captain Horton's orderly and possibly the only one of the prisoners younger than Carl. Carl was leaning against a sun-warmed wall in the chapel yard, trying to amuse himself playing cat's cradle with a long piece of stout string and he was glad of the interruption.

"What was he doing there?" he asked, as he wadded up the string and put it in his trouser pocket.

Ben answered, "Arranging for safe passage, I expect." He sighed a small and wistful sigh, "Say, I might be glad to see ol' Kaintuck again. I reckon we'll all have to make our way home again, if we're paroled. Where will you an' your brother go home to?"

"I dunno." Carl thought carefully. "Our Pa took a grant, near Waterloo on the Colorado. We've always lived there, since Pa was friends with the Baron an' came out from Pennsylvania. I don't rightly know where we'd go, if the Mexicans kick us out of Texas."

"There's always someplace," Ben said, cheerfully, and Carl thought about that. No, there wasn't; not if you had labored over a place the way that Pa and the family had. It was in your blood, your place, and no one had the right to take it from you, especially not a pack of fancy-dressed soldiers without so much as a by-your-leave, or a bunch of foreigners who only wanted to squeeze out of the settlers what they could in taxes and such. Carl knew about taxes and working the land, about Indians raiding and following a plow with a rifle on your shoulder. He knew about faraway governments and having to scrape for the favor of men with gold braid on their coats who could take away everything a man had worked a lifetime for with a wave of the hand. No. Such like that wasn't right, and it had no place in Texas. It saddened Carl to think that Colonel Fannin and Colonel Bowie and them had tried their best but looked to have failed to keep that from happening.

In the early morning, the word was passed to the able-bodied prisoners; gather up those few things they had left to them and prepare to march. "Hurrah for home!" said they, in jubilation at seeing an end to dank and filthy imprisonment. The Becker brothers stuffed what little had not been lost in the fight, or looted from them into their pockets. Rudi had been saving bits of bread and hard-tack and they had both been able to hold on to their water bottles. Only Rudy's was a real, regular Army water canteen. Carl made do with a dried gourd, a length of rawhide strap around the narrow neck.

"After Coleto," said Rudi determinedly, "I don't ever want to be without a full canteen near me, ever again." His little brother had his knife, still secreted in his shoe-top, a long coil of string and a lump of flint and steel tucked into one of the pockets of his roundabout jacket.

"Leastways, we can build ourselves a fire, tonight," he observed, "They're making us travel pretty light, aren't they, Rudi?"

"So's we can move all the faster," Rudi answered, cheerfully. To Carl, it made perfect sense. Rudi was always right.

Their spirits rose as they filed out onto the familiar parade ground of the old fort, into fresh air and seeming freedom. There was sunshine just breaking through the morning fog, a bell ringing from the chapel tower and a great company of Mexican soldiers in their fine parade-ground uniforms forming the prisoners up, into three groups of about a hundred men each.

"What day is this?" asked one of the others in same column as the Becker brothers and young Ben. Rudi smiled and answered,

"Sunday, I think—Palm Sunday." He looked at Carl and Ben, marching alongside towards the fortress gate, and began to sing.
"All glory, laud and honor
To thee, Redeemer King!
To whom the lips of children
Made sweet hosannas ring!
Thou art the King of Israel
Thou David's royal son . . . ."
Carl joined his treble voice to his brothers' tenor, until someone farther back said, "Is this a funeral, or something, boys? We're going

home!" and launched into "Come to the Bower!" The men around them laughed and joined in. Rudi set his arm around his brothers' shoulder, saying, "As long as we are together, we'll be all right, little brother."

Carl saw there were people at the gate, watching them march past; two well-dressed women and a little girl, with an officer and a sergeant attending them. The officer had more gold braid on his fine coat than any of the others, so Carl reckoned that he was one of their high officers. The younger woman looked very sad and distraught. She turned and spoke to the older woman and the officer and seemed to point at Carl and Ben. She looked as if she would weep and Carl wondered why. The gold-braid officer spoke to the sergeant, who bawled for the column to halt, and the officer came right up to the Becker brothers and Ben Hughes.

"You two . . . you are just boys, too young for this. Senora Alavez would have you stay. She insists."

At a nod from the officer, the Mexican sergeant took Ben by the arm and pulled him away from the column and would have taken Carl, but that Carl resisted, saying, "He is my brother, Pa told us we should stay together." And Rudi set his arm around Carl's shoulders and glowered at the officer. He looked at them for a long moment, seeming to chew on his mustache, before he said again, "It would be better for you to go with Senora Alavez, boy."

"I'll stay with my brother," Carl said firmly.

The officer looked sad and answered, "If that is your choice. Go with your brother, boy. Go with God." He nodded curtly at the sergeant who bawled at the column to move again. The last sight Carl had of Ben was of him standing between the two women, watching after the marching column with a bewildered look on his young face. The officer looked as if he too were about to weep like the younger woman, and Carl wondered why.

They went out of the gate, and turned left, a ragged column, two or three abreast, with a single file of guards on either side. It seemed like a lot of guards; there had not been so many when they were marched back from Coleto Creek into the old citadel. The American volunteers and the Texians were jubilant, the guards grim and unsmiling. They would not look directly at the men they escorted, or meet their eyes. When he was not very much older Carl would know how that could be, but the boy that he still was on that Palm Sunday morning only noticed without wondering why.

"This is the road towards Victoria," Rudi noted with satisfaction. "I recognize that brush fence, you can see the river though that gap. I guess they're going to march us all to . . . ."

There was a quick rattle of shouted Spanish, a command so quick that Carl didn't comprehend it at first, and suddenly the file of Mexican soldiers on their left faced right and shouldered through the prisoners, falling into line with their fellows on the column's right, who had faced about themselves, and raised their muskets.

To the end of his life, Carl remembered how very long the next moments seemed, as if time slowed to an eternity and suddenly every sight, smell and sensation was vivid and pure, etched in the crystal of memory. The smell of sweat and dirty clothing, of damp wool and wood smoke, the clear green odor of new leaves and turned earth, the clean scent of running water wafting up from the river. Cheerful voices and song, abruptly dying away . . . shock and sudden comprehension, musket-fire in a sudden cloud of black-powder smoke; Carl knew in a blinding flash why the pretty woman at the gate and the gold-braid officer with her looked so sad, why the Mexican soldiers wouldn't look them in the eye.

Rudi turned towards him in that instant of comprehension, spun the gawky, sixteen year old Carl around, pulling him away from the Mexican soldiers, shoving him towards the gap in the brush fence. For just that moment, Rudi stood between the black eyes of the musket-barrels and his little brother, just as the world erupted in a hell of point-blank fire and a cloud of powder-smoke and shouting.

He shouted, "Run, Carl! Make for the river, they're—"

And at that moment, Rudi's head exploded in a shower of blood and white bone, and his body fell lifeless as a sack of old clothes, falling as men screamed and groaned. A voice that Carl barely knew as his own was screaming too, screaming his brother's name, but he was already moving as Rudi commanded in his last breath, plunging through the gap in the brush fence and pelting across the meadow beyond, towards the line of green trees that marked the river.

The fence and the cloud of black-powder smoke screened him just long enough from the executioners. He fell down the steep and muddy river bank and lay gasping for a second, before scrabbling on hands and knees towards the water. He struggled to his feet in water that rose deeper and deeper around his legs until he flung himself into the current and let it take him, diving under and holding his breath until it felt as if his lungs would burst. He came to the surface and floated on his back, looking up at the sky, the blue Texas sky that Ma had always said was the exact color of his eyes.

He held very still, while the current drifted him around a bend and fetched him up by a thicket of rushes on the farther side. The river bank was steep there, impossible to climb, and a tree overhung it. He rolled over in the water and cautiously lifted his head. There was no one in sight, but there were Mexican soldiers shouting in Spanish, in the direction from which he had run. No luck climbing the bank without being seen, or swimming father down the river. The soldiers' voices sounded mocking and harsh like the crows wheeling and calling in the sky. He wished now that he had thought to smooth over the marks he had made on the bank, opposite. Anyone following with a bit of woodcraft in them would know at once that someone had come down the river bank and gone into the water. Carl crawled deep into the thicket, taking care to pull the rushes straight after himself, so no one would be able to see from across the river, or look down from the bank above and know that he had taken refuge there. He curled himself into as tight a ball as possible, knees to chin, soaking wet and covered in mire, sheltering in a hollow of black river-mud and rotting drift timber deep in the heart of the thicket. From there he could hear the regular crackle of musket-fire in the distance. No, not from where he had run from, but farther away towards the north and the road to Bexar.

The horror of realization chilled him, striking deeper in his bones than the chill of spring-cold river muck; three columns of Fannin's men, three roads away from the citadel, and three executions. With a clarity that struck him numb, Carl remembered also the wounded, the orderlies who attended them and the doctors, all left behind in the old citadel. Yet another execution, so they were all dead for sure; his mind could get no farther than that. His brother was dead and the other German boys, Captain Pettus and Lieutenant Grace and Sergeant James and all of them, shot down in a storm of shot and black-powder smoke by men who wouldn't look them in the eyes as they led them away. Dead and dead and dead again, three hundred and some times over.

For all that pretty young Senora Alavez and the high officer with gold braid knew of it and protested it or were appalled … it was happening, happening even as he huddled in the reeds and listened. At that moment Carl Becker knew two things with absolute clarity. He would never put any of his faith in a man who wore a fancy uniform. And he would never, ever again go into a fight where he did not absolutely trust the man who led him there not to surrender.

Also, for the very first time in all of his sixteen years, there was no one there to tell him what to do. Carl huddled in that thicket of rushes for an entire day, as women came down to the bank opposite to wash clothes from which the water ran red, while dragoons and foot-soldiers searched up and down both sides of the river, thrashing the thickets and prodding into the thick bushes with their lances, looking for him. He nerved himself to hold still, to stay as quiet as a deer fawn in the fragile fortress of the thicket, all the hours of that interminable Sunday. Towards the end of that day, he dozed and woke with a start, afraid that he had cried out, living again that awful moment when the Mexican muskets spat a storm of lead and black-powder smoke at Fannin's men. By the end of that day, he had thought over very carefully what he ought to do next. He took his time about it, for until that very day Carl had little experience of making decisions for himself. His father was one of those who had always considered him a dunce, especially compared to his older brother. All of them—Rudi,

Captain Pettus, his father—all those people had always told him what to do. He went along because he was of a calm and easy temper, not especially inclined to relish confrontation—and until this very morning, his elders had always seemed to be right about things anyway.

When it became full dark, Carl moved as stealthily as he could, from the thicket, on limbs that were clumsy and cramped from staying still for so long. He stood in the shallows, wet and cold, listening to the quiet ripple of water, the sounds of night-birds and the faraway howling of those shy little prairie wolves. He smelled smoke on the air, mixed with the smell of something like bacon burning. But he could not hear the voices of the Mexican soldiers, or the noises made by something large and clumsy moving through the brush by the riverbank. He was safe for now and almost for the first time in his life, completely alone. Never mind, Carl reminded himself; he had a knife in his shoe-top and string to make a snare. He had the flint and steel in his coat pocket, the river and the stars to guide him north. North. North to home, if home was even still there, if he could elude the Mexican soldiers and raiding Indian parties, the Comanche and the Karankawa. If he could keep himself alive, all alone. Well, Carl Becker told himself, as he set off wading along the river's shallow margin—*I might yet do better at that than anyone else had done so far. Sure as hell couldn't do any worse.*

For some considerable time, Carl Becker would not know there were other survivors, others among Fannin's men who had managed to escape from their murderers. In all the rest of his life he would only speak twice about what he had seen on that dreadful Palm Sunday. It took him nearly two months, moving slowly at night and hiding up during the day, to get to the Waterloo settlement on the Colorado, to get back to the place that he and Rudi called home. During that time General Sam Houston had finished falling back, and back and back, training and drilling all the men who had gathered to him, until he reached the San Jacinto River, far away in East Texas. Sam Houston turned and fought there. Santa Anna's grand army disintegrated, as Houston's men shouted "Remember the Alamo!", "Remember Goliad!"

But Carl Becker, sixteen and starving, stealthily working his way north with his knife and a snare made of string, a lump of flint and steel with which to make a small fire and hiding during the day like a wild animal . . . he would not know of that for many weeks.

He also did not know that once arrived at his father's homestead, he would leave it again almost at once and never think of it as home again.

Chapter 1 – *A Prince Among Men*

Eight Years Later: August 1844, Washington-On-the-Brazos
Formerly the Capitol of the State of Texas

Two young men sat in a quiet corner of a shabby tavern, a place full of good cheer, smoke and loud voices. They lounged with their backs to the wall and although at their ease and passing a bottle between them, they seemed ever watchful, their eyes wandering over the crowd. One or the other of them glanced at the door, every time it opened to admit another patron. They appeared to have just spent a couple of days hunting, dressed in shabby and travel-stained canvas trousers and work shirts. The taller of the two men wore a buckskin jerkin, and smiled often in mild amusement. He had light hair, bleached nearly white by exposure and deferred to his companion, extending a certain amount of respectful regard.

The second man was slight, and earnest of feature, appearing barely old enough for the need to shave. He bore himself with the demeanor of a school-boy of good family but both he and the other man carried a brace of Paterson Colt revolvers as easily as other men wore a pocket-watch and chain. Neither of them looked important at first glance or even a second, yet others seemed to keep a careful distance from the young-looking man and his tall, fair companion, the one with the weathered face of an amiable and not too shrewd ploughman.

The noisiest cluster of patrons in the tavern orbited around a splendidly uniformed gentleman in a coat hung with foreign decorations, tall riding boots and fine doeskin breeches which fit so tightly as to appear to have been painted on. The state capitol had officially relocated, but important men were still partial to doing business at Washington-on-the-Brazos.

"I was sorry to hear about your father," said the young-looking man, presently.

"Puts you into a small party," answered Carl Becker, without any particular rancor. "I was sorry myself, but only that he died before I could make a success of myself and throw it in his face."

"He sold off the property, didn't he?" The young-looking man asked, thoughtfully.

"All but the home place," answered Carl. He shifted restlessly and looked across the room again. He had been very long in the wilderness this time and still found an indoors place filled with other people to be fairly stifling, "I left it for my sister. Her man died of consumption and left her with four children. I still have my land certificates . . . just never found a likely place to settle on."

"Will you be back, when we're funded again?"

"Dunno." He looked across the room, and his eyes lighted once more on the splendidly uniformed gentleman.

"Who's the swell, Jack? He looks like a popular man."

"He's a prince," replied Jack and when Carl looked as if he would laugh, he added, "Didn't you hear of him? Genuine, all-wool and a yard wide, honest-to-god high-bred aristocrat."

"I've been out chasing Comanche along the south fork all these months," Carl returned, with an air of mild apology, "It keeps me from mingling in polite society, much."

Jack chuckled, warmly,

"Well, since that's what I sent you to do, Dutch and what you are paid so munificently for..."

"We get paid?" Carl put on a face of mock amazement and Jack laughed outright.

"In promises and the thanks of grateful citizenry! Pity you can't eat promises and thanks, but never mind. Be thankful the Rangers are supplied with ammunition, at least. The Prince has been a nine-day wonder. He landed in New Orleans last July, and has been making a lordly progress ever since. A bit like a circus, I'm thinking. Half the folk that come to meet him are coming to see a real live prince, like in the books and the other half are looking to see the elephant and the high-wire dancers."

"Did he bring along any of those?" Carl asked, as he poured himself another two fingers from Jacks' bottle of fine bourbon whiskey. Being that Jack was a gentleman, they were drinking it from cups.

"No, but he has two valets to help him into his pants of a morning," Jack answered, as Carl had a mouthful and choked when half of it went down the wrong way. "Kindly do not waste the finest panther-piss I can afford by spitting it all over the table, Dutch. It's the truth, and there are witnesses. He rides a white horse—"

"Bet the bugs eat the damn thing alive," Carl interjected, as Jack held up his hand. He was enjoying this,

"The Prince also travels with his personal huntsman, chef-du-cuisine and architect. He also stops frequently to lecture those who own slaves on the immorality of our peculiar institution."

"Tactless of him on that," Carl said only. "Especially round these parts." His opinion of the unnamed Prince was in equilibrium: approval of the sentiment warred with his disapproval of the arrogant tactlessness of expressing it. And he had never cared much for fancy uniforms.

"He also objects to sharing quarters and a meal with other travelers, spends money like water, dresses like a fop in a stage-play, conducts himself as if he is the aristo villain in every novel ever written, and has ambitions to plant a colony of German settlers on four million acres of land between the Llano and the Colorado."

"Good thing I didn't have a mouthful, then," Carl said only. "He's not serious, is he, Captain? The Penateka and the Jicaralla might have something to say about that."

"Like 'Come to the feast brothers, the table is laid'?" Jack nodded, with a flash of grim amusement. "Hans brought him here tonight so we could talk try and talk sense into him. Since you and Hans both still speak his lingo, I thought that might cut some of the ice, anyways."

"Why?" Carl asked, simply, and Jack looked across the room at the Prince, and his orbiting followers. Among them was another man in the same rough and simple clothes as the two of them. He met Jack's eye and nodded, and Jack said,

"He and his friends back in Germany have already gone a fair way towards that plan for a colony of their folk. He says they're going

3

to charter ships and bring them over by the thousands, single men and families both. Hell, they'll make every other impresario look like a rank amateur if they can pull it off. Which I most sincerely doubt, and you'll know why as soon as you've spent ten minutes in conversation with him."

"Straight from the Old Country," Carl remarked thoughtfully, "Into the country between the Llano and the Colorado. So, how many sharpers saw him coming, then?"

"Every damn one this side of the Mississippi for sure. Myself, I mislike the thought of what will happen to any that he does manage to bring over, if he doesn't get bored and drop the whole thing like a child with a toy he's tired of. He doesn't strike me as one with real leader potential, Dutch. Some of the rest of them may have what it'll take, but I fear he'll strand lot of greenhorns in the path of a Comanche war party unless he gets put into the way of a ration of sense."

Across the room, the man who had met Jack's eye spoke to the Prince and directed his attention towards the two men in the corner. As he turned towards them, Carl got a clear look at him, for the first time: a well-fed man in his thirties, with immaculately barbered whiskers, the whole of him as sleek and brushed as a pedigree horse on race-day, arrogance sitting in every line of his countenance. There was a sulky droop to his mouth, as if like a small child he would be capable of tantrums if thwarted. But now he smiled, like the same child presented with a wonderful and unexpected treat, and advanced across the room, all a-beam, with Hans Rahm at his elbow.

"Captain Hays! Such a profound pleasure, even in my home we have heard of the daring adventures of your Rangers; such astonishing feats of valor beggar the imagination. I am honored to join you, and to share your confidence regarding our great project." He sat down at the same table. Behind his back Hans Rahm briefly rolled his eyes.

Carl was privately amused to note Jack coloring up like a girl, saying dismissively. "Pretty exaggerated, most of those tales—I hardly recognize myself when I hear folk repeat them."

"But surely . . ." the Prince began, but Jack continued,

4

"Most of us, we do what is needful. Texas is a damned dangerous place, for all else you have heard about it. Folk struggle here as much as anywhere else, 'gainst the Mexes on one side, and the Comanche on the other, even before they get a living out of the land."

"But it is such beautiful land," the Prince enthused, "Your lieutenant Rahm has been telling me about the most beautiful place that he has ever seen, where springs of water come up out of the ground so forcefully, they form domes of water almost as tall as a man."

"Oh, the Fountains," Carl said, "Thirty miles from Bexar on the Comal. The Veramendis own it, I believe. And it is beautiful."

The Prince continued, as if he had not heard, "Such a romantic sight, in a beautiful valley full of trees! And such a land could be made even more fair and productive, with the settling of German farmers and craftsmen on our grant. The common settler sort here, so improvident... they do not even pull out the stumps of trees from their dooryards or even grow vegetables. No, we can do much better than that."

Carl kept his face straight, that mild and deceptive look that led folk who didn't know him into underestimation, but behind it he thought on how hard it was to clear the land and wrestle a crop out of it and wondered if the Prince had ever chopped down a tree in the whole of his privileged life. Or even if he had been up into the limestone hill country, above the rich coastal plains and piney-woods. It appeared not.

"So you might," Jack signaled the tavern-keep for another bottle and two more cups, "But it's just not gonna happen overnight. And my friend here is going to tell you why." He jerked his chin at Carl, "This is Carl Becker. He's one of my Rangers, just come back from a long scout into the Llano country. Carl, this is Prince Karl Solms-Braunfels, the head of the... what is it again, I can't never get my tongue around the whole of it. Too much of a mouthful."

"*Verein zum Schutze deutscher Einwanderer in Texas,*" Prince Karl said, rather huffily, "The Society for The Protection of German Immigrants in Texas. And I am not the chief, but rather deputized by the group to come to Texas and oversee the beginning of our great work here. Becker—that is a proper German name, are you one of us?"

"My grandfather was born in Kassel and served in the Landgrave's army," Carl answered, in German. He forbore mentioning that his grandfather was reputed to have deserted that army at first opportunity and switched back to English for his commanders' sake. "My father came to Texas as a young man. He was one of the Baron Bastrop's settlers, when Texas still belonged to Mexico."

"Splendid . . . so many of our people are here already, and have prospered," Prince Karl's enthusiasm was undimmed. "So many profitable enterprises, so many hard-working true-blooded Germans! This could be a veritable new German homeland, but a better and finer one, lighting the way for all."

"Not if you're still planning to send them all west to the Llano, it won't." Carl said, flatly. A cloud fell over Prince Karl's countenance.

"Why not?"

And Carl told him, unsparingly and in great detail; speaking in calm and level tones of depredations and atrocities, of the finding of bodies of settlers brutally tortured while still alive and mutilated in horrific fashion after death; of babies and their mothers killed out of hand, of children taken away and raised by the Indians, turned against their own. Carl left out nothing, not a single nauseating detail.

When he paused for breath, the Prince looked positively ill and said, "But how are they inspired them to such unnatural brutalities! Can you sure than in some manner—somehow you may have provoked them to such ferocities?"

Jack barely managed to veil his disgust. "They were doing all that to their tribe's enemies with great energy and enthusiasm long before we ever set foot across the Mississippi. Just ask some of our Lipan scouts about the days of their fathers, if you doubt it. The point is you'd be planting how many of your colonists right in the middle of that, hundreds of miles beyond existing settlements!"

"And hundreds of miles from Galveston and the coast," murmured Hans Rahm quietly.

"And sheltering . . . where? While they plant crops?" Carl added, and the Prince looked annoyed.

"But we have already considered all those matters," he sounded peevish, like a schoolboy unfairly reproved, "My associates are seeing hiring transportation of our people and to building houses for all! We shall see to everything, and the best of everything. We shall make our own port, so our people will not need to pass through Galveston and be tempted into idleness and the wasteful ways of the people there." He looked brighter, as if he had just thought of a splendid idea, while Carl considered the irony of the Prince lecturing slave-owners, while still speaking of German immigrants in such a possessive way and Hans Rahm again remarked quietly,

"Remember this, Prince Solms; Texas has a way of making equals of us all, however you might try to keep your grant a separate entity."

"We shall need to hire men to protect our people, of course. I would be honored if Captain Hays would advise me," insisted the Prince, with a mulish expression on his face.

"Carl might be free for a while," answered Jack, "And you couldn't do better, stake my honor on it, but the Rangers would be calling him back within the year."

"Splendid!" Again, Carl was reminded of a child given a longed-for treat, "We can offer a fine salary, and a generous grant of land—and we can fit you out with a suitable uniform or even my own household livery."

Carl shook his head,

"I'll do the work," he answered, "But I won't wear your uniform."

"But why not?" Prince Karl had that sulky-child look again, "There is honor in it; you would have authority and a future, in being associated unmistakably with the Adelsverein. Why not indeed?"

"Because I don't care for uniforms," Carl replied in a tone that brooked no argument.

"If it is your wish!" the Prince definitely sounded like a sulking child. He rose from the table, "We are in lodgings, at the moment. Make yourself known to my secretary in the morning, Becker." He nodded graciously to Jack and Hans Rahm, and excused himself from their table, leaving the three of them looking studiously polite at nothing in particular. When Prince Solms had rejoined his jolly circle of friends, Jack silently topped up Carl's drink and Hans growled humorously,

"Drink up, Becker. You're going to need it."

Carl drained the cup and answered, gasping slightly from the raw spirits,

"Jack, I'm only doing this because you favor the notion, god knows why."

"Because it'll give you a chance to associate with the high-born and the quality," Jack answered, his face alight with amusement, "'Sted of the riff-raff and rabble. Think you'll remember everything I tried to teach you about proper table manners?"

Carl answered, unprintably and Jack looked even more amused,

"There's more to it than just reminding us why we got shed of a British king and lords and nobles like that. Damn good idea, that was. Our fathers and grandfathers look more like men of sense, every day that I live!"

"My father always said that his father deserted from service under someone just like him. I get the feeling I am going to know chapter and verse, exactly why."

"That you are. Have another drink." Hans replied, but Carl covered his cup with his hand.

"Why this—and why me?"

Jack looked suddenly very serious. "Because you speak the language, and when folk look at you all they see is some back-country yokel who just stumbled off the boat. They'll forget themselves, and let something slip."

"The Prince has been indiscreet in his choice of friends and correspondents," added Hans Rahm, with a look at his commander. "And in an easy effortless way, he has made an annoyance of himself to practically everyone in the administration. But it is not politic at this time to say very much to the Prince himself, or his friends."

"Who has he been indiscreet with?" Carl asked idly.

Jack and Hans Rahm exchanged a long look before Jack answered, "Practically everyone who has an interest against annexation, including our old friends south of the Nueces strip."

Both of them watched his face for a reaction. They got none, other than an expression of thoughtful comprehension. When he finally answered, his voice was easy and light, "Not exactly the most tactful man in Texas is our Prince Fancy-Trousers, is he?"

"He's a fool with money and powerful friends," Jack answered, "which makes him about the most dangerous kind there is. Keep your cards close to your chest, Dutch—and your eyes open."

"I always do," Carl answered. "I always have."

In the end his employment with the Prince lasted barely five months and bored him immeasurably. Nothing ever came of it besides riding back and forth between Galveston and Bexar and Washington-on-the-Brazos and along the coast as the Prince looked for the perfect place to land his pet immigrants. Carl derived no small amusement from playing the silent and vaguely dangerous frontier roughneck to the Prince's entourage, especially his private secretary. All the Prince's German staff—and there were as many of them as Jack had claimed—were intrigued, apprehensive and condescending by turns and sometimes all three at once.

But towards the end of the year, a day came when the secretary explained with a look of hideous embarrassment that the Adelsverein line of credit was unaccountably overextended and therefore his wages could just not be paid. The Prince and his entourage had parked themselves at Decrow's Point, a little peninsula reaching out into the wide sweep of Matagorda Bay, begging hospitality of some new settlers there who fortunately for Carl turned out to be old friends from when he and Jack had first begun to run long patrols out from Bexar.

"A letter of credit, then?" Carl asked the Prince's secretary, who shrank back against the chair. Their hosts had given over several rooms and the breezeway of a rambling log house for the prince's use. The poor little runt looked absolutely terrified. Carl momentarily regretted having played up the dangerous roughneck. "Never mind, then. I'll be riding north tomorrow if anyone asks. It looks like Texas is going to be annexed after all, and that will mean trouble."

"Surely not," said the secretary, looking rattled and Carl sighed.

"How long have you been here? There's always trouble—if not from the Indians, than from the south and sometimes all together. I'll give my respects to Prince Karl and be away in the morning."

He had more than his usual disinclination for the merry gathering that evening around the Prince and his guests and their ever-patient hosts. The Somervell brothers bore up under the noble social whirl, but Sam and Mary looked to be quite weary of it all. Carl himself was fed to the back teeth by this time with the Prince and all his works and ways and deeply embarrassed to be associated with them, even if it were all at Jack's orders. Or close enough to an order. The Prince and his fancy retinue had no business being here. They were flashy and useless and arrogant and if they were out of funds, then that meant an end to the Adelsverein project. He could wash his hands of the whole mess and go back to the Rangers.

The Prince had that sulky-child look whenever his bored and restless gaze fell on him during that interminable evening. Carl guessed that the secretary had already told him that his pet frontiersman was fleeing noble employ with all dispatch in the morning. Wearing his blandest expression, Carl excused himself early from the revels and slipped away to his Spartan bedroll up in the loft of the Maverick's drafty stable building. While cold lodgings, it had the advantage of being quiet, save for the horses shifting restlessly in their stalls down below and the December wind whistling through the cracks. Early asleep and early waking to a quiet world wrapped in pearly grey fog, he dressed and padded silently to the outbuilding which housed the household kitchen. It was an island of warmth and firelight and the smell of good things cooking, sternly ruled by Jinny, the Maverick's ageless Negro cook. She moved like a calico whirlwind from stove to table, pausing momentarily to punch down bread on the rise in its trough, while her oldest child sleepily ground coffee beans. She wiped a floury hand across her forehead as Carl looked around the door, greeting him with frazzled good cheer.

"Good mawnin' to you, Mr. Dutch! You up befo' the chickens, this mawnin'!"

"That I am, Jinny. I'm riding out this morning, and I want to get an early start. I was hoping to beg some breakfast and a little something for the journey."

Jinny caught up the poker and rattled it in the stove firebox, stirring the fragments of red-gold coals, and answered over her shoulder.

"There ain't nothing near ready this very minute, Mr. Dutch, I am that sorry—nothing in the larder either, but some bread only fit to throw to the chickens! Miss Mary would be shamed to know I fed that to her guests! Them foreign fellows can shore eat, cain't they? They didn't leave but half a dried-apple turnover that Mr. Sam took for himself, f'st thing this mawnin'." She slammed the firebox shut, and wiped her forehead again with the corner of her apron. "He took hisself off for a ride, said he'd be back when breakfast was ready. You surely kin wait a bit, an' visit with Mr. Sam, cain't you? Miss Mary, too; she'd be wanting to visit, even feeling as poorly as she is."

"I surely will, Jinny," Carl answered, and he sighed a little. He had hoped to be away before sunrise.

"You do that, Mr. Dutch." Jinny looked at him appraisingly, as she broke eggs into a pottery bowl. "Do them good to visit with you. Do you good to eat a good breakfast, you near as skinny as Mr. Sam when he got hisself back from that Perote place. You an' those boys of Mr. Jack's don't hardly eat 'nuff to keep body an' soul together. Yore mama, she'd cry her eyes out, you go traveling up-country without a good meal inside yo' stomach to start."

"She'd never do that," Carl answered drolly. "She'd tell me to pick a hatful of apples from the tree, and get out from under her feet." Jinny's attempts to stuff Sam's bachelor friends full of food were legendary. She seemed to be convinced that they were all wasting away to bare skeletons, with only herself standing indomitably between them and starvation.

"You hush up that nonsense, Mr. Dutch!" Jinny dashed over to the stove again. "You leave out of here without no breakfast, Mr. Sam will send one of the boys straight after you, see if he don't. Could knock me down with a feather, you understandin' all that foreign jabber jabber jabber! Sounds to me like the crows squabblin'... but they be your folk, ain't they?"

"No." Carl shook his head. "No, my grandfather and some of my mothers' family came from the same place they do, but they aren't really my folk. I just understand their talk, that's all." Jinny seemed mollified, and he added, "I'll come back for breakfast, as long as I can avoid them. I wanted to talk to Sam in private anyway."

"He 'lowed as he was riding along the shore, eastwards a piece," Jinny answered. "Walk a little thataway, you likely meet him coming back,"

He had nothing better to do, and he did truly wish to avoid the Prince, or at this hour, his underlings. He always felt a little low in spirits at being reminded again that Jinny was a slave, that Sam and Mary owned her as surely as he owned his horse. That was one of those quiet things that Carl held to himself. He liked them both, they were kindly people. And Jinny was as bossy and managing, as if she were one of their blood family. She had stood between the children, hers and Sam and Mary's and a couple of Comanche fighters, in the aftermath of the Council House fight and seen them off with no weapon in her hands other than a great rock. Sam's own manservant, Griffin, had gone with the rescue force, following after when Sam was taken prisoner by Wolls' raid on Bexar a few years later. No, the Mavericks had the affection and loyalty of the people they owned, but Carl had been raised with the notion that it wasn't right to own folk. It wasn't right to own them, as if they were a horse or a cow. It was a contradiction that he had never been able to resolve; he suspected that if he ever did resolve it and spoke out loud, he would have few friends left. So he stayed quiet—that was just one of those things he didn't have to think about, out on a long scout in the Llano and just one more reason for wanting to be out there in the empty country, alone beneath the sky with the endless miles of the staked plain unrolling in every direction.

A light breeze had begun to shift the morning fog as he walked down towards the shore, towards the little waves lapping against the hard-packed white sand and crumbled shells. It made a noise like the rustle of a woman's starched petticoats. The sea was flat calm today, grey and gently rolling, as endless and empty as the Llano. He was restless, more than ready to leave, unwilling for some reason to merely sit and quietly wait. There was a sheltered inlet a little way along, out of sight of the house. He kicked off his moccasins and left his clothes on a ledge and walked into the sea for a swim, as good a way as any to kill the time and to avoid the Prince's people. He swam until he felt warm again and lay floating on his back, looking up at the sky. He had the obscure feeling that it was time, time for something to happen, but he couldn't put a finger on what exactly it might be.

When Carl returned to where he left his clothes, there was a small campfire sending up a thread of smoke into the morning air and a tin coffee-pot just close enough by it to keep the contents hot.

"I thought you might want some coffee. And one of these." Sam tossed him a coarse-woven huck-towel from where he sat cross-legged Indian fashion, contemplating the fire and the seashore and a tin cup of coffee. "Sea-bathing in December is a bit too much mortification of the flesh for me, Dutch. I'd never hear the end of it from Mary if I caught the lung-fever, for all that the water cure is supposed to be good for your health."

"It feels so good when you stop," Carl answered, hurriedly toweling himself dry and resuming his clothes.

"Washing off the stink of servitude, rather." Sam looked amused. He was a lean man about a decade older than Carl, with wrinkles of good-humor around deep-set eyes. "Jinny said you were leaving this morning. Here we thought it looked like you had settled into something permanent, at last." He filled another cup, and handed it to Carl as he settled onto the sand next to the fire. "They talk up this German scheme like it's a good bet—especially if you are in at the beginning."

"Whooo, that feels good!" Carl wrapped his fingers around the cup and considered how much of this he could tell Sam. "No, this was just another long scout."

"Devil Jack's notion?" Sam raised an interrogatory eyebrow.

"Of course." Carl drank some of his coffee and leaned on his elbow. "Who else? I think he thought as you did, about the Prince and his backers making an honest run at bringing over settlers to their grant. Me, I was just sent along to get a notion of how serious they are about it."

"Serious enough to have a ship full of them at Galveston," Sam remarked, and Carl shook his head.

"A couple of ships all full of settlers and they're already out of money. I can't see it going any farther, Sam. They're already tapped out, and Prince Fancy-Trousers is losing interest. He already guesses he's a laughingstock the length and breadth of the Republic . . . my God, they must have heard Somervell laughing all the way to Port Cavallo over the sight of the Prince being hoisted into his trousers of a morning."

"Not to mention his guards, prancing around with long swords and feathers in their hats." Sam added, with a broad grin, "And don't forget the tall boots and great jangling spurs. It's pretty clear they're not accustomed to conditions around here."

"That's for sure." Carl looked across the little fire at his old friend. Besides having ridden with Jack's company, Sam was a lawyer and had served in the legislature for a couple of terms. "If he was, he'd know better than to be making offers to the Mexes or entertaining their offers as regards his grants here."

Sam whistled, his face suddenly serious.

"You know that for sure? How?"

"Saw the letter," Carl answered, "as his secretary was writing up the fair copy. One of those little things I practiced—reading upside down."

"That's downright underhanded of you, Dutch," Sam grinned broadly. "Sneaky, ungentlemanly and dishonest; you ever thought about being a lawyer?"

"Not unless I have a skin-full, no. I saw just enough on this scout that I can assure Jack the Prince's scheme is about to collapse. Even if they scare up more money from their investors, once it gets around that they even thought of colluding with Santa Anna's government . . ."

"He'll be lucky not to be tarred and feathered," Sam completed the thought, grimly. "Did he truly have no thought for how much our folk loathe that butcher? Is he that much of a fool, to think that kind of double dealing would pass muster?"

"Most likely," Carl sighed. "He's like a child with toys. Do you think a child would think for a moment about how the toy feels? Or even care? Lucky for him, lucky for us too—he's getting bored with it all. Anyone who is fool enough to believe his promises would be better off staying in Galveston and setting off on their own or settling with Castro's Alsatians. At least, they've got a settlement built, of sorts."

"So what are your plans, then?" Sam cocked an eye at him over his own coffee. "Once you report to Jack, of course."

"Same as before, I guess." Carl shrugged.

After a moment, Sam ventured, "You ever give any thought to settling down? Following a regular profession of sorts? I wasn't entirely joking about reading law, you know."

"No schooling," Carl said, and Sam brushed that objection away.

"Not required; some of the best have taught themselves, or apprenticed with a practicing lawyer. I know you can read, and figure. What about surveying? You've been out with Jack and me often enough to get the hang of it."

"No, and I don't think I'm cut out to keep a store, either."

"What do you want to do with yourself, then?" Sam asked with genuine interest, "What did you apprentice to do, when you were a boy?"

"Farm," Carl answered. "My father had a farm up on the Colorado. It's what I know best—after ranging, of course."

"Well, there you go," Sam answered, sitting back with a great look of satisfaction, "Growing things; there's always a future in that. I should have my father write to you, then. He is always sending seeds and cuttings, and telling me to try this or that. According to him, we should be in the middle of a Garden of Eden, here. And," he looked over his coffee cup with a very purposeful look, "You might give a thought to courting, too. Mary could take you in hand, if you liked."

"You're getting too far ahead for me," Carl laughed, and emptied the last of his coffee. "Don't worry about me, Sam. I'll settle down when I am good and ready and not a moment before."

"Well, it's a pity that the Princes' settlement scheme isn't going to work out," Sam allowed, "You might have done very well with it, being a sort of go-between and all."

"Ah, well," Carl shrugged, "Bet anything you like. By the end of six months, we'll have heard the last of the Prince and his Adelsverein."

Chapter 2 – *Gehe Mit Ins Texas*

"Adelsverein!"   Exclaimed Vati, with enthusiasm burning hectically in his eyes behind his thick spectacles. "It may be the answer to our dilemma, the situation in which we find ourselves! Magda, dearest child, you must read this. It's all here. What they are offering. Everything and a new life and land, besides! Land enough for all of you children to have a decent and prosperous life, and I should not have to take myself away to the city."

"Yes, Vati," his stepdaughter sighed. "I'll read it most carefully, before Hansi and Mutti see it." She took the slim pamphlet from him, although she was already carrying his box of watch-making tools, as the two of them walked along the narrow village street, of which Albeck only had four, including the one which led to the city of Ulm. A late snowstorm scattered a few feather-like flakes around them, which whispered as they settled on the muddy and oft-churned ground. They stepped aside as a pair of bullocks pulling a sledge with a load of manure went past.

"Is that not Peter Frimmel already mulching his field?" Vati squinted after them. "It is early, yet, I think."

"It's March, Vati," Magda answered. She was a tall young woman with the ink-black hair and dark hazel eyes of her father, Mutti's first husband who had died when she was a baby. She had much of her mother's brisk manner and angular features wholly her own and thought to be too sharp and too forceful for beauty.

"Oh, so 'tis," Vati looked around him vaguely. He stood a head shorter than his step-daughter, a gnome-like and lightly-built little man of middle age, whose near-sighted gray eyes reflected both the gentle wisdom of years but still some of the innocent enthusiasm of a child. "I lose track of the days, in the shop and away from the land. And that is the problem, dear Magda. There is barely enough to support us now. How will you all live, when my share is divided between the boys and you have a dower-share as did Liesel when she married Hansi?"

"I don't care to marry," Magda answered with a toss of her head. "I don't care in the slightest for any of the eligible bachelors in Albeck, and I don't want to go elsewhere. Who would look after you and Mutti?"

"Even so. But you still should marry, my dear child. It would make your mother so happy," Vati said and looked at her very searchingly. "Don't you wish for it, in the least?"

"I don't know what I really want, Vati," Magda answered. "I would like a husband that I could talk to, as I talk to you. Someone who is kind, and amusing; if I could find someone just like you or like Uncle Simon, I think I would marry very happily. But there no one else like you in Albeck!"

"Alas, I am sui generis," Vati agreed somewhat smugly as they walked towards the gate that led into the Steinmetz holding, where a lantern burned primrose in the twilight of the cobbled yard and the range of fine timber and stone buildings surrounding it. "But still, my dear child, you should be caring for your own husband and children," he chided her, fondly. "Now, you see, there would be another reason for going to Texas. Besides three hundred and twenty acres of land— good rich land it is—for each family, there would be a chance for you to find a husband that would better suit you than a dull old farmer with his head among the cabbages. Some splendid young Leatherstocking hero or a bold Indian chief; would that content you, Magda?"

He looked teasingly sideways at her and thought she blushed slightly, even as she laughed and answered, "But it would mean going away from here, Vati—from everything."

The older man and the young woman paused in the gateway as if both of them had a single thought. This was the house where all of Friedrich Christian Steinmetz's ancestors had lived, where they had stabled their horses and cattle and gone out to tend their fields and pastures. Not an inch of it had known any but their hands for hundreds of years. Vati's, or any one of the previous Steinmetzes' hands alone had piled hay in the loft, repaired the tiled roofs of the barn, house, or chicken house, boiled cattle-feed in the great iron kettle. Their wives had born the next generation in the great bedroom upstairs, and their children had run out to chase chickens in the yard. Here were their roots set, generations deep. Although Magda was not truly one of them by blood, she had still lived here for nearly all of her life as Vati's much-loved oldest daughter.

"So it would," and Vati's eyes looked grave behind his glasses, as he opened the door into the farmhouse kitchen. "We could hardly take it all with us." They stepped into the little entry and from there into the warmth of the kitchen, scoured as clean as a new pin, full of the smell of food cooking and the yeasty scent of bread on the rise,

"Christian, my heart, my hands are all over flour!" exclaimed Magda's mother from beside the trough of dough. "You are early." Hannah Vogel Steinmetz did not look like either of her daughters: she was a plump little wren of a woman, brown-haired and rosy. Vati kissed her on the lips with a good enthusiastic smack before he was swarmed by his sons, Friedrich and Johann and granddaughter Anna, with joyous shouts of "Vati! Opa!" and a treble chorus of questions and accounts of what had been going on over the last few days.

The boys were twins of the age of seven, as alike as two peas for looks, having Vati's grey eyes and Mutti's fair to light brown hair, but very different in nature. Johann was serious and shy, Friedrich a daring scamp. It baffled Magda when people claimed they couldn't tell the boys apart. Friedrich's face was rounder, and he was the outgoing, happy-go-lucky adventurer. Johann's face was thinner; he was the more timid and serious one. Magda didn't think much of people who didn't notice those elemental differences. *Weren't they looking closely enough; how could they not see something so simple?*

Their niece Anna had serious dark brown eyes like her father, Hansi Richter, her mother Liesel's dimples and brown curls too short and wispy to be woven into plaits. A solemn-faced little mite, she could on occasion be brought to laugh, a happy little trilling sound almost like a bird. All the younger children addressed Magda as 'Auntie Magda', since she was so very much older than they. Now Magda set Vati's box of tools in the cupboard by the door and put the emigrant pamphlet into the pocket of her apron, for later.

"Children!" Hannah chided them, "Boys, you must behave!"

19

"No they must not—they are only children," Vati answered indulgently and swept small Anna up in his arms, whereupon a look of comic distress crossed his face. "Oh, dear, she has had a small accident ..."

"Liesel!" Hannah exclaimed, and Liesel, Magda's half-sister answered crossly from a chair by the fire:

"I'm nursing the baby, Mutti, I'll see to Anna when I can!"

"I'll do it, Lise," Magda said, taking her small niece into her arms, and Liesel said distractedly:

"Oh, of course you will!"

Magda and her parents exchanged a meaningful look, as Hannah murmured, "New mothers' nerves."

Magda shrugged and took Anna. Liesel was still in one of her black moods. She had always been that way, even before marrying Hansi and bearing her children. Vati had once observed, *"Annaliese is either on top of the tallest tower or in the cellar—nothing in between!"* When Hansi had been making fumbling attempts to court Magda—to Magda's hideous embarrassment, for Hansi had been her childhood playfellow, more like a brother than a suitor—Liesel had been serenely confident that he would be hers some day. She had adored Hansi since she was a tiny girl; Hansi—patient, stubborn and reliable with dark brown eyes so like one of his own oxen.

"He is only courting you out of courtesy, because you are the oldest, "she said then.

Magda retorted waspishly, "And Vati will dower me with the small field adjacent to his! I can't help thinking that is my most attractive feature in his eyes!" She could look in Mutti's little silver hand-mirror and acknowledge that she was dark and over-tall, while her sister was dainty and fair and everything considered beautiful. And Liesel had giggled, while Magda added, "He is just like all the other marriageable men in Albeck; he fumbles for words when he talks to me but his eyes follow you like a hungry dog!"

"Well, once he brings himself to speak of marriage, "Liesel consoled her, "you may slap his nose and say of course not—and then he will come to me and I will console him. And you both will sigh with relief and Hansi and I will live happily ever after and have lots of children, and you will marry a prince or a schoolmaster and come to visit us, riding in a grand barouche with footmen riding behind. You will live in a castle full of books . . ." She went on elaborating their fortunes until Magda had begun to laugh as well, for that was Liesel in her tallest-tower mood; merry and affectionate, and absolutely certain of Hansi's eventual affections. And so had it come to pass; Liesel's dark-cellar moods over the three years since had been infrequent. The worst one came after Anna's birth, and then again after Joachim, the baby. Magda supposed that the brunt of them now fell on Hansi, but he seemed well able to cope.

Now everyone, especially Magda put it out of their minds that he had ever courted her. Not an easy thing to do, when they all lived in the same house. But it was made easier by the fact that Hansi never talked of much beyond crops and his manure-pile. All very well because such matters put food on the table for them all, but Magda privately thought she would shortly have gone mad from a lifetime of sharing Hansi's conversation about them. She would rather go on living as a spinster under Mutti's authority and talk with Vati about his books and notions, than endure more of it than she did already. Now this talk of Adelsverein and Texas made her uneasy, as if something whispered in the corner, something from one of Vati's old tales that always gave her the shivers. She took Anna into the other room to change her sopping-wet diaper, and when they returned, Hansi himself had just come in from the barn.

"I think to start spreading the muck, as soon as the weather lets up," he was saying conversationally. Magda reminded herself yet again that he made Liesel happy and worked Vati's fields for him, and that's what counted.

After supper, she closeted herself in the little room at the end of the upper floor, the little room she had to herself since Liesel married. She lit a tallow candle and began to read. When she was finished reading, it was late, but there was still someone downstairs in the big kitchen, where firelight still gleamed warmly over the polished copper pots and pans and on the row of pottery jugs hanging above the fire.

Vati sat with his scrap album on his lap, in the chair where Liesel sat to nurse the baby, leafing over pages neatly filled with carefully-cut news sheet articles. He looked up at Magda

"Well? What did you think?" The firelight gleamed on his spectacles, like the eyes of some large insect.

"It's almost too good to be true," she answered thoughtfully. "They offer so much. I wonder what they are to get out of it."

"A colony, land, hard workers." Vati took off his glasses and polished them absently on his shirt sleeve, and Magda sat down on the bench opposite him.

"The Firsts have all that of the common folk, now," Magda pointed out, sardonically. "Hard working tenants who take off their hats when one them walks by. Would they expect that of us, in Texas, then? Might this be some clever means of skinning those who have managed to put a little money aside? All the gold should flow uphill, into the Firsts' money-bags, as they so kindly relieve us of the heavy responsibility of deciding what we should do with what we earn. They have so many better notions of what to do with it, after all."

"Such a cynic, my Magda!" Vati chided her.

She answered bitterly, "Such as you have made me, by allowing me to read your books and newspapers, and talking to me of important matters."

"Maybe they look for the honor of doing a good deed for the people. They are very forward thinking gentlemen, all of them."

"Perhaps; they are all but men and capable of shabby deeds as well as the noble." Magda became aware that her step-father was staring thoughtfully into the fire, his expression very serious. "Vati, what is it? What is it that you know that you have not told us?"

Vati tore his gaze away from contemplation of the fire and looked gravely at her.

"It might be well to think about leaving, Magda my heart, and soon, while we can still afford it. All of us; Liesel and Hansi, and the children. There is talk in the air—oh, there has always been such, but this is new talk, talk such as I remember when I was a boy and the Emperor Napoleon was on the march. Talk of conscription and war and repressions. I do not like it—not for myself, you understand.

There is no one's army would want a decrepit old clockmaker! But the boys—yes, they would want Friedrich and Johann in a few years, if it came to pass, and I won't have it. There is also the fact that business has not been good. So many factories, so much mechanization of things, so much change! And they will change, whether we wish to change or not. There will be new rules and repression of so-called dangerous thoughts brought down upon those of us to dare to think about such matters! What to do, Magda, what to do!"

"It is advised to take all that you can in a cart and sell the beasts that pull it at the port," Hansi answered decisively from the other end of the room. Startled, Magda and Vati looked up. Liesel's husband stood in the doorway for a moment, with Anna in his arms, half asleep. "And take apart the cart, and ship it with all your goods, since a good one may be hard to come by in the wilderness."

Magda regarded her brother-in-law with considerable surprise; how long had Hansi been thinking the same things as Vati? He strode across the room and sat himself down on the bench next to Magda, settling Anna in his lap so that she curled up, sucking her thumb.

"Anna couldn't sleep, and Liesel was nursing the little one," he added half-defensively, but he looked levelly at the two of them, all diffidence and talk of the muck pile set aside. "I heard you talking, so I came downstairs."

They looked at each other for a long moment, before Vati finally asked, "How long have you been thinking about emigration, Hansi?"

"A while," he answered readily, and there was firmness in his voice, and in his answer to Vati that Magda had never thought to see in Hansi. He wasn't impulsive; there was no dash to him. In a thousand years he would never do anything that his neighbors and family hadn't already done before, but there it was. He had been thinking long and seriously about emigration for that was the way Hansi did things. "Go with us to Texas." Hansi savored the words, much as Vati had, and continued, "Everyone is talking about it in Albeck these last few weeks. I thought about going myself, first before we married. Then I thought about the two of us going together, and then Anna was born and then the new baby. You are right, Vati. We should go now, while we still can."

"What about the fields?" Magda asked, the fields that he cared about to the exclusion of practically anything else, and Hansi shook his head, regretfully.

"It hurts me to say, but here is the truth of it. There's not enough. Not to grow enough hay for winter, not enough to grow what we need of beets or wheat or potatoes. There's just not enough, for all I break my back working at it and no way to get any more. The Adelsverein promises to send us all there, give us a house, everything we'll need for the first year—and three hundred and twenty acres." Hansi's face lit up in rapture as he said those last words. "Think of what I could do with that much good rich land. It's as much as all the fields around Albeck, almost."

Looking at the faces of Vati and her brother-in-law, Magda felt a chill around her heart, for it seemed to her that they were already decided, their feet all but set on that road.

Annaliese Richter was still awake when Hansi quietly returned upstairs with his slumbering daughter in his arms. She watched him through her eyelashes, savoring the very look of him, a solid square man, perhaps a little shorter than most, but a very rock for dependability. He moved quietly around the room, tenderly putting Anna in the truckle-bed at the foot of theirs and settling the covers around the child. She closed her eyes as he leaned over the baby's cradle, drawn close to her side of the bed. It was her secret pleasure to watch her husband when he didn't know that her eyes were on him. She never doubted that he would marry her, for she had adored him since she was a little girl in short skirts herself and he was a stocky boy more than a little taken with her clever older sister; Hansi, stout and stubborn and good with cattle. Steady and reliable, funny in a mild way when he felt like it.

It had always been a mystery for Liesel why her sister did not see or value those qualities in Hansi. Why had Magda not loved him? Magda with her head in books, Vati's favorite daughter, such a mystery! But exactly as Liesel had known would happen, Magda had come to her sister saying impatiently:

'That blockhead of a boy asked me if I would marry him! I told him not to be ridiculous, and to ask you instead! You worship the ground he walks on, anyway. Don't be a ninny—say yes to him, so he'll stop pestering me!'

Liesel did not mind at all that Magda had left him to her. It only proved that books did not tell you everything. Oh, no—books did not tell you anything about certain pleasures of marriage, certain things that she was privy to now, as a married woman. Magda did not know about that, for it was not a thing that an unmarried girl should know about; it wasn't proper. But she did, Liesel thought—there were things she knew that her clever sister didn't! She listened to the soft sounds of her husband undressing and climbing into bed to settle himself at her back. Her heart warmed with renewed affection; he took such tender care, quietly returning to bed without disturbing her, after seeing to Anna! Liesel knew that many husbands wouldn't have bothered. Tending the children was the business of their mothers, no matter how exhausted from nursing a fretful baby, or the work of the farm. Many another man acted as if once their wives had spread their legs apart for them, that was all they needed to do in regards to their children. But Hansi wasn't like that, not a bit of it. In his own quiet way, he took as much an interest in Anna and baby Joachim as Vati took in his own children. And for that, Liesel loved him all the more, if that were possible. She turned in the bed, reaching out as if half-slumbering, asking drowsily, "Are you just now coming to bed, Hansi? Whatever were you talking about for so long?"

He did not answer at once, but his arm curled around her. At last he answered, "We talked about going to Texas, Lise."

All thought of sleep was banished as if Liesel had been doused with a bucket of ice-cold water. She found her voice at last.

"And what did you say on that, hearts-love?"

He took a long time in answering, for he was a careful and considerate man.

"We ought to not let such an opportunity pass, Lise. We should go."

Liesel Richter did not sleep well that night, for those words echoing in her troubled dreams.

We ought not to let such an opportunity pass . . . we should go.

In the morning, she did as she had done all her life—she asked her sister what she thought, as they milked the cows in the morning darkness in the barn.

"What did you and Vati talk to him about last night?" she asked, leaning her cheek against the warm flank of a cow as her hands rhythmically squeezed spurts of milk into a pail. Magda was similarly occupied. "The baby kept me awake. When he came to bed, he said you were talking about going to Texas. I thought he was joking with me, Magda. He can't be serious!"

"Hansi never jokes," Magda answered, somberly. "He is serious, and Vati, too."

"What do you think of it?" Liesel asked after some moments of anxious silence broken only by the quiet hissing of milk breaking the surface in their pails. Magda was clever; Vati's daughter of the soul, if Liesel was his in blood. She always knew what to do.

"It might be rather interesting," Magda ventured at last, and Liesel's heart sank. "They promise us a new house. I expect it will be rather like the one in Herr Sealsfields' Cabin Book, in a wild and beautiful garden. Think on it, Lise—a house of your own!"

"But to leave here!" Liesel's voice trembled. How could they think to leave Albeck, everything they had ever known? "To leave everything behind and just go! I can't bear the thought of taking the children all across that ocean, going out to the wilderness! I really can't! How can he even consider such a thing, Magda!?"

"Nonetheless, he is, and Vati also," Magda replied, blunt and practical. "And he is your husband, Lise. If he says that he wishes it, you must obey . . . just as Mutti and I must obey Vati."

No. This was horrible. Vati could contemplate such a thing; he was a willow-the-wisp for enthusiasms, a man of books and the tiny gears of clocks spread across his workbench. Not Hansi, who never had a thought which had not already occurred to his ancestors.

"But you have Vati twisted around your finger," Liesel pleaded, already knowing that she protested fruitlessly against the inevitable. "He would not make you go if you did not wish it."

"But Vati does wish to take the Verein's offer, "Magda sighed, from the other side of the cow. "He has already convinced himself that it would be for the best for us. He reads books and talks to people, Vati does. He sees that things are not good and growing worse." As Liesel watched, her sister deftly squeezed out the last rich drops of milk from the cow's udder. She stroked the creature's flank with brisk affection before moving her milk-stool and herself on to the next cow. She looked sympathetically at Liesel as she did so. "Lise . . . dear little sister, I think our father made up his mind long since. He just waited upon the opportunity, and now the Adelsverein have given it to him. He and Hansi will sign the contracts, no matter what you and Mutti will have to say about it."

"Oh, and Mutti will have plenty to say," Liesel predicted with gloomy relish, hoping against hope as she did so that perhaps Mutti might prevail against this insanity. "And she will weep tears by the bucket!"

"To no effect," Magda answered. "In their hearts, Hansi and Vati are already there, running their hands through rich soil and counting ownership of more land than either of them ever dreamed."

"What shall we do then?" Liesel asked. Her sister turned her head and smiled at her.

"Think on those things which we value the most, and contrive some means of taking them with us," she answered. "Tears will avail us nothing, Lise. Smile and be brave."

On the day of their leaving, a bright and clear September day, Mutti cried as if her heart were breaking in two. There was a small gathering in the farmyard, clustering around the Steinmetzs' and the Richters' carts: Hansi's older brothers Joachim and Jurgen and his parents, Mutti's friends and a scattering of younger women, Liesel and Magda's contemporaries. Auntie Ursula, the sister of Mutti's first husband and her husband Onkel Oscar had come out from where they lived in Ulm on this momentous day. There were not too many other men, for it was harvest-time and most had already gone out to their fields. It felt very strange to Magda, for them not to be at work themselves, not to be gathering their own harvest, filling the storerooms and larder in the old house. It was as if they were already strangers.

At the moment when they had finished taking the last of their things from the house, Vati's friend from Ulm, Simon the goldsmith, came rushing into the yard with a small package in his arms.

"I was afraid I would be too late!" he gasped, as he and Vati embraced. "This is for you," he added, thrusting the package at Vati. "A quire of fine letter paper and ink and pens enough for two or three scriveners, all to encourage you to write to me, as often as you can. I shall want to know every detail of your venture, Christian!" And he beamed at Vati, while Vati thanked him effusively.

"My people are given to travel widely," Simon gracefully waved off the thanks. "But so far, I know few who have ventured into Texas! I will look forward to your letters with great interest." Simon smiled warmly at Magda, the skin crinkling around his wise old eyes, and added, "You must remind him to write, Miss Margaretha, since we both know how forgetful your father may be. I shall miss his company very much; letters will be a poor substitute."

"I won't forget, Uncle Simon," Magda answered. He smiled again, but did not embrace her as he did her father. Such was not the custom among his people, for a man to touch a woman not his wife, for all that Simon and her father were so close, close enough that they all called him their uncle.

"Good!" Simon looked at their carts, laden with all but the last few little things. "I see you took my advice about traveling with only the essentials. And all your papers are in order?"

"I have them right here." Vati patted the leather wallet, tucked into the inner pocket of his coat. It held all the necessary permits, visas and certificates; everything that the Verein had requested of Vati and Hansi to have in order before signing their contracts. "Don't worry, Simon—Magda shall see that I keep them safe. We arranged the sale of everything that is not in the carts," Vati added cheerily. Perhaps that was why Mutti wept in the arms of her dearest friend,

Auntie Ursula, now that the moment had come to leave behind everything that had made her home so comfortable and welcoming. "We expect to live like gypsies, at least until we get to our new homes in Texas. Did I tell you they had assured us each a house, built on our own lands? It will probably not be as solid as what we leave behind, but I expect we shall prosper, none the less." Certainly that was what Hansi expected. Even if Liesel seemed as apprehensive as Mutti about leaving, she always believed what Hansi said.

"If you have any need of help once you reach Bremen," added Simon, his eyes beginning to overflow, "call upon my cousin David. I have written to him already. A safe journey for you, a safe journey and a golden future, my friend!"

"To be sure," Vati answered happily, as he wrung Simon's hand again and consulted his pocket-watch. "It is time, my dears. Now let our adventure begin with a smile, Hannah-my-heart . . . Magda, boys ..." He deftly detached Mutti from Auntie Ursula with many determinedly cheerful words and handed her up into the first laden cart, where she sat with her shawl pulled tight around her elbows and her cheeks wet with tears. She reached down to grasp Auntie Ursula's hand while both wept mournfully.

". . . so far away," Auntie Ursula choked out, through her sobs, "Such fearful dangers, robbers and brigands! We will never see you and the children again!"

"Of course you will see us again," Magda said roundly although she did not believe it herself. She picked up her skirts and scrambled up to set next to Mutti. She worried that Mutti and Aunt Ursula's tears might frighten the children, especially Anna. They were leaving the only place they knew, bound to be frightening enough for them, especially if Mutti carried on too long about it. She put her arm around her mother's shoulders. The horses shifted restlessly in harness, and the twins drummed their heels on the sides of the wooden chests upon which they sat, until Magda turned and told them to stop.

"Are we leaving now, Auntie Magda?" asked Friedrich, excitedly.

Magda answered, "As soon as Vati is finished talking to Uncle Simon, Fredi."

On the other cart, Liesel had the baby in her lap. Anna sat prim and wide-eyed beside her. The moment had come. Hansi's brother Jurgen slapped his shoulder, and his mother hugged him too her one last time, ruffling his hair as if he were still a small boy.

"Go with us to Texas," he said jauntily. "I'll write and let you know when it's safe, Jurgen," and his brother Jurgen jeered half-enviously, as Hansi climbed up and picked up the reins of his team.

"Away with you," Jurgen called cheerfully after Hansi's cart, as it creaked slowly towards the gateway and the road beyond, "and have a care for the wild Indians!"

Vati embraced Simon one last time, clambered spryly into the cart, where there was just enough room for the three of them, and chirruped to the horses. Auntie Ursula walked beside it, still holding onto Mutti's hand and both of them sobbing uncontrollably until they reached the gate and passed out into the road with a lurch and a bump.

"Goodbye, goodbye!" the boys shrilled from the top of the pile of boxes and chests lashed to the cart, "Goodbye! We're off to Texas! Here we go, we're away to Texas!"

Magda silently handed a handkerchief to her mother. They squeezed elbow to elbow on the narrow seat. Hannah dabbed her streaming eyes with the handkerchief and blew her nose. Vati looked across at her and smiled, as happily as his sons, saying, "The open road calls us, Hannah-my-heart. Can't you hear it?"

"Nonsense," Mutti snorted. "All I hear is Peter Frimmel cursing because he has stacked the hay too tall and it has fallen off onto the road."

They passed the last buildings of Albeck, dreaming under a deep blue autumn sky. Out among the meadows, and golden fields of wheat and barley still bowed heavy-laden and un-harvested, or lay in neatly mown stubble. One or two of their neighbors, already hard at work, waved cheerfully as Hansi and then Vati's carts passed by on the little road that led to the bigger road that would take them towards Wurzburg and the north, to Bremen on the sea where waited the ship that would take them away. At a turning in the road, Hansi's cart halted, and Vati said, "What can be the matter already; did one of the horses lose a shoe?"

But ahead of them, Hansi was standing and lifting Anna in his arms.

"Look," he called to them all, "Look back, for that is the last sight of Albeck! Look well, and remember—for that is the very last that we will see of our old home!"

Magda's breath caught in her throat. She turned in the seat, as Hansi said and looked back at the huddle of roofs around the church spire, like a little ship afloat in a sea of golden fields. All they knew, all that was dear and familiar lay small in the distance behind their two laden carts. Really, she would slap Hansi, if that started Mutti crying again. Even Vati looked sobered; once around the bend of the road, trees would hide Albeck from their sight, as if it had never been a part of them, or they a part of it.

Magda lifted her chin bravely and said to Vati, "Really, I wonder how suddenly Hansi got to be so sentimental. We should drive on, Vati. There's no good in dragging our feet like this. Texas may wait for us, but the Verein ship won't."

"Right you are, dearest child." Vati slapped the reins, and the horses moved on again. Only Mutti looked back, her face wet again with fresh tears. Many years later, Magda would wonder if that were an omen.

* * *

Letter from Christian Friedrich Steinmetz: Written on 2 November 1845, from our lodgings in Bremen, to Simon Frankenthaler, Goldsmith of the City of Ulm in Bavaria

My Dear Friend: I write to tell you that we are departing very early on the morrow with the other families recruited by the Adelsverein, on the brig Apollo. After a review of our papers and signing the contract, we waited in lodgings provided by the Verein for the ship to be properly victualed and outfitted for the crossing and to have our many belongings stowed in her hold. The Apollo is a German-built ship, stoutly fitted, which seems to be a reassuring omen for us. We wait in company with many other families who have gathered from across Germany to venture our fortunes in a new land. We are grateful many times daily for the assistance of the Verein, without which we would otherwise fall to the importuning of the many scoundrels who prey upon those wishing to take ship for the Americas. I shudder to think on how we would have had to thread our way between perils, not knowing whom we could trust, aside from your cousin David in a place we know not! Son Hansi insisted that our two sturdy carts be disassembled and stowed with our other stored belongings, over the quartermaster's objections. Hansi was most determined upon this and prevailed. Our carts, in which we and our goods traveled from our old home, may prove to be of such stout service in our new one, on the other side of this grey ocean. You will be relieved to know that we now have seen the advantage of your wise advice to convert much of our goods into cash.

My dear Simon, I must confess to some apprehensions at this juncture. It seemed to be a very logical and necessary venture, sitting in the comfort of our late home, or the warmth of your little shop to consider all the reasons in favor of immigration and to boldly decide on them. But at this moment, as we are about to take that great step, all the uncertainties and dangers arise to torment my imagination. Can our situation in my ancestral home really have been so harsh? Should not we have attempted some other resolution, other than immigration? The perils and discomforts facing us on the morrow seem altogether more momentous when we are about to take that last irrevocable step, turning our backs forever on the ashes of our forbearers and the altars of our gods.

Hansi and all the children are anticipating the morrow with great excitement. My dear wife seems to be of an apprehensive and heavy heart, as does Annaliese, but they put on a cheerful face. Margaretha remains ever stoic; as always my stoutest and best support. I will write again, when we reach the port of Galveston, which we are anticipated to reach in *some seven or eight weeks, a fair wind allowing. Until then, from your old friend,*

C.F. Steinmetz

* * *

"It looks so small," Magda kept her voice low. "Surely that one ship can't be meant to carry all of us?" Behind her, the boys were jumping down from the coach, packed with families who had shared their lodgings. Vati reached up to help Hannah down from the step. From the look of horror that flashed across her face, Magda knew that her mother shared her own apprehensions.

"This way, this way!" The Verein representative in Bremen bustled along the stone quay, shouting to be heard above the crowd of people, thronging the space between warehouses on one hand, and the serried ranks of tall ship-masts on the other. Above them, seagulls dipped and whirled, crying their desolate, mewing call. A bitter-cold wind came off the sea from the north, and Magda pulled her thickest and heaviest shawl close around her. Another carriage clattered in from a narrow alleyway, disgorging more immigrants with their unwieldy bundles and boxes.

"It's larger than it looks, Magda, my heart. There would be three decks and a hold below," Vati replied, cheerily. "Here, Hansi, I'll take that." From the top of the coach, Hansi and the driver were handing down their own luggage; a great roll of blankets and bedding, a large provision-box, along with bags of clothing and necessities for the children. They joined the jostling, slow-shuffling mass of men, women, and children. Hansi and Vati carried the heavy box between them. Hannah and Magda walked with the twins between them, and Magda held Anna's hand as Liesel followed with the baby. Magda wished she could herself have held her mother's hand, for Hannah looked very grey and fearful.

"All here for the *Apollo*!" shouted a sailor through cupped hands from above the place where a stout plank was laid from the quay to a little gate in the ship's rail. He stood on the deck rail, bracing himself against the gentle sway of the ship with an elbow looped through what looked to Magda like a many-stepped rope ladder, which extended from the side of the ship to the mast, far above. "Step lively, now, step lively! All for the *Apollo*; go with us to Texas, otherwise it's a damned long swim!" Another sailor stood by, helping people down the short step from plank to deck. The plank shifted slightly, scraping on the stones, as the Apollo shifted with the water's movement.

A ship's officer in a fine braid-trimmed coat had a list in his hand, standing on the quay by the Adelsverein officer in Bremen and another man, very grandly dressed. A crowd gathered close around them, ever-shifting, as men and families were counted off from the officer's list and crossed over to the Apollo's deck, even as more gathered from along the quay, taking their places.

Hansi turned his head and smiled at the women. "Smells like snow," he said.

"More like dead fish," Magda answered. "And dirty old privies."

"Imagine the reek on a hot summer day," Hansi pointed out, solemnly. "How can people bear to live in cities? I'll take my manure pile, any day." He and Vati were nearly up to the officers and the fine-dressed man.

"Your name?" bawled the officer. He spoke as if he were more used to bellowing at people a fair distance away and in a howling gale.

"Steinmetz and Richter," Vati answered.

The Adelsverein officer read from his list, "Steinmetz, Christian Friedrich, wife Hannah… daughter Margaretha, aged 22, sons Johann and Friedrich, aged seven."

"Boos-Waldeck," said the fine-dressed man, shaking Vati's hand with great enthusiasm. "You bring honor to us all in this venture. I commend your spirit. It's a beautiful country! We shall all find a great reward in building new lives in it."

"Baron!" Vati returned the handshake with the liveliest interest. "So we shall, so we shall. Now, about the country—is it all wooded?"

34

But the ships' officer was saying,

"Now, step careful now, one at a time," and the Baron was already turning towards Hansi and Liesel as their names were read.

"Hans Richter, wife Annaliese, daughter Anna aged three, infant son Joachim."

The Baron beamed down at the baby, and chucked Anna's cheek, "Here's a fine little Texan!" He shook Hansi's hand. "Don't let the little ones forget where they were born, hey? You are serving a great venture, you and your family."

"Allow me." A burly sailor took up the heavy box from Vati, balancing it on his shoulder as easily as if it were nothing at all, and stepped lightly over the gangway plank. "Now you, sir," He jumped down to the deck and turned around. "The ladies next; one foot in front of the other and best not to look down."

Vati looked everywhere but down, craning his head to look up at the tangle of ropes, rigging and canvas. Magda held her breath as one of his feet strayed perilously close to the edge of the plank.

"Keep moving, keep moving!" the ships' officer bawled again.

"You go now, Mutti." Magda nudged her mother. "Go on then, I'll hold your hand. Look ahead, look at Vati. He'll help you down." One step, two steps, three, and Hannah reached down for Vati's hands, and the waiting sailor lifted her down in a swirl of skirts. "Now the boys." Johann and Friedrich needed no encouragement or help. They stepped eagerly out on the gangplank with never a look down at the narrow wedge of water between the wooden swell of the *Apollo's* hull and the steep stone quayside.

"Now, miss. Just step onto the plank. Don't look down." Magda looked straight ahead, as a sailor took her elbow; two steps, three steps.

"I'll take that for you, miss." A sailor took her bundle, and Vati swung her down to the deck, which swayed slightly under her feet. He handed her back the bundle, and chanted "Straight on down the companionway. Families one deck down, single men two decks down. Move along then, this way, then." And as if there were any chance of being confused, another sailor stood by what looked like a pair of double doors. A pair of short stairs led upwards to a higher deck level on either side of it.

"Down the steps, miss . . . mind your feet . . . lower your head, sir . . . mind the beam."

The way into the *Apollo's* lower deck was a stairway so precipitously steep as to be more of a ladder. It led them down into a windowless cave only slightly less cold than the outside air. Magda came down to the bottom of it with a thump, nearly blind in the sudden darkness below deck.

"Single men, down one more, families on this deck . . . just walk straight ahead and find yourselves a bunk, and stow away your clobber." Another of the steep staircases opened at a turn. "Come along, miss, Captain Feldheusen wants to catch the tide."

Magda stepped forwards a little way, hesitating while her eyes adjusted to lantern-lit dimness. A baluster enclosed the steep stairs to the lower deck, but otherwise it looked to be just one large room, with slightly angled walls that curved together somewhere in the shadows ahead of her. Three rows of great roughly squared pillars marched at regular intervals the whole length of it, from which hung lantern brackets. It seemed that those lanterns accentuated the darkness, rather than shedding light upon it all. As her eyes adjusted, she made out the regular shapes of two or three immensely long tables with benches on either side flanking the center row of pillars, which stretched the length of the deck. There was some little space on either side of the table and benches, then another long series of bunks built between the other rows of pillars and the ship-wall, like two levels of nest-boxes in a henhouse, just barely wide enough for two people to sleep in it, side by side. There was a long, continuous bench along the lower level. At her back, Hansi remarked in a determinedly cheerful tone, "God in heaven, we'll have about as much room as my oxen did in their stall in the old barn. We'd better hurry, Magda, if we want a space where we can all be together."

"We want that?" Magda looked around in horror.

"We're family." Hansi took her arm, "We'll have to endure each other; strangers don't have that luxury."

Halfway along, Mutti was sitting on one of the bunk-side benches as if she could go no farther. She had an arm around Friedrich and Johann, huddled one on each side of her, as Vati stood irresolute in the narrow aisle between the benches. Mutti's voice was low, almost frantic. Magda caught the tail of it.

". . . not endure! We cannot live like this, Christian, not for two months, not for two days! Oh, please let us go home, forget this madness!"

Hansi sighed patiently, and stepped in front of his sister-in-law.

"Mutti, we cannot return to Albeck. The house and lands are sold. We have already deposited the fees to the Adelsverein and signed the contracts, and there is nothing for us to go back for. Think how it would look to everyone, if we came crawling back."

"The die is cast, my dearest," Vati recovered his voice. "Hansi is right. We have burnt all of our bridges behind us. Think of the future before us, Hannalore, my heart. As we live in hope of the everlasting joys of heaven, think of this brief time on the *Apollo* as our time on earth, before we ascend to the bliss of the everlasting. Endure, with the hope of heaven before you, I beg!"

"And you call yourself such a free-thinker!" Hannah snorted derisively. She seemed to have recovered, and Magda sighed, inwardly. Vati could always talk her out of a black mood,

"Thinking to cozen me by quoting doctrine!" She took Vati's hands and looked up at him. Magda thought that her mother truly looked frightened. She firmly quashed her own distaste and horror at the thought of living in—as Hansi said it—a space hardly larger than a cattle stall, for the next few months.

"Dearest Christian, I shall endure, but I confess to such apprehensions!"

"Truly natural and understandable, my dearest." The lantern-light caught Vati's glasses again. Magda thought that perhaps he was himself a little taken back at the very spare condition which they must now endure. Dear Vati, with his head in the clouds always; no, this was not entirely his doing. Hansi, so dull and plodding was as stirred by the promise of land as Vati, with golden promises on the other side of the ocean.

"Mutti, let us choose our own space, before too many more come aboard," Magda spoke calmly. "We wish to be all together. We can hang blankets between the bunks. We shall need . . ."

"Two spaces, above and below," Hansi spoke firmly. "Liesel and I, and you and Vati, with Anna and Magda and the boys above."

Mutti looked around and above where she sat despairing and answered, "Well, this shall do as much as any other, I suppose." Her chin lifted, the brave housewife reclaiming her territory as meager as it was; the space between two beams and a long table, to be their home for the duration of their voyage.

Vati and Hansi pushed the heavy box underneath the lower bunk.

"At least they have put in fresh straw," Mutti said.

Magda, standing in the bench and investigating the upper bunks answered, "We are expected to sleep on this, like animals in the barn?"

"Thank god, we have brought our own beds," Mutti sighed, as another family shouldered by her, carrying their own bulky roll of blankets and beds. "Excuse me, I am sure!"

"Vati, may we go on deck again?" Johann asked. He was wriggling with excitement.

"No, you may not—you'll be in the way of the sailors. Help Magda make up your bunk." He and Mutti unrolled the bedding with some difficulty as other travelers kept walking down through the space, seeking an empty bunk for themselves. Baby Joachim began to cry, a thin fretful complaint.

"He's hungry," Liesel said, desperately casting an eye around for a place where she could sit down, and unbutton the front of her dress to nurse him.

"No help for that, Lise. Look, we'll hang up a blanket here and you can sit in the bunk." Magda hopped down from the bench with a sigh, and set to work. Her head ached, from the noise around her, the fumes of cheap tallow candles and another heavy smell she couldn't identify, which seemed to permeate the whole deck.

A sailor with a collection of buckets, carried with the aid of a pole over his shoulder thrust through their bails walked the length the narrow aisle. He put down a bucket on the floor by every couple of bunks, and Magda asked, "What are those for?"

He looked at her with a knowing air and answered, "You'll find out soon enough, I'm thinking."

Chapter 3 – *Voyager*

Thinking on it much, much later, after a long and eventful life, Magda Vogel would remember crossing the Atlantic on the emigrant ship *Apollo* as one of the most horrific experiences of her life; a long purgatory of darkness and misery, jammed together with her family and dozens of others in the reeking 'tween-deck, and only let above-decks when the weather was fair and they would not be in the way of the sailors.

It had not seemed quite bad at first, settling into the Steinmetzes' crowded little corner, once Mutti had got over the shock of seeing where they were supposed to live. They spread out their bedding in the four bunks, and screened them with blankets for an illusive speck of privacy. Other families streamed down the companionway from the upper deck, pushing past them, searching for their own; a stout Swabian farmer and his wife with six children trailing after, an older man in clerical black, he and his wife both clutching bundles. Presently the traffic from above ceased and not a moment too soon, Magda thought. The place between the curving wooden walls was packed with families, all settling themselves into the shelf-like bunks. A sailor came halfway down the ladder-stair, shouting, "The captain orders everyone to stay below, while we're casting off. As soon as we're underway, we'll let you on deck, by turns - as long as you stay out of our way!"

New and strange noises came from overhead, the rattle of chains, and sailors chanting, and Magda gasped as the deck underneath her feet swayed with a wider motion. Mutti sat down heavily on the bench, her eyes suddenly wide and dark and the older man in clericals took his wife by the hand and declaimed fervently, "So the Lord said to Joshua, 'be strong and of good courage, for you shall go with this people unto the land which the Lord has sworn to their fathers to give them …it is the Lord who goes before you, he will be with you, he will not fail or forsake you, do not fear or be dismayed.'"

"I think rather it is the "*Apollo's*" figurehead, going before us," Vati remarked. "Superstitious nonsense." The old cleric looked at him, very sternly.

"You reject the consolations of faith, my good sir?"

"Frequently and with great vigor," Vati answered. "As a free-thinker, I can do no less."

Magda met her sisters' eyes—well, at least Vati hadn't made his usual remark about organized religions being a pustule on the buttocks of humanity. He would seem to have remembered they would have to spend eight weeks in close quarters with these people.

"Than I shall pray for your immortal soul," the cleric replied keenly. "And I hope that we are never in such straits as to lead yourself to seek such comforts, for then I know that we all shall be in great peril."

The *Apollo* then gave a great lurch, and there was a shout from above; and it seemed to Magda that the ship now canted at a decided angle. Yes, the lanterns hanging from the central beams now seemed to tilt. Vati's eyes lit up, and he said happily, "We have cast off from the quay, children! May I introduce myself, since it seems we are to be close companions, reverend pastor? Christian Friedrich Steinmetz, clockmaker of Ulm in Bavaria."

"Pastor Bernard Altmueller, Doctor of Divinity and late of Gersthofen near Augsburg." Pastor Altmueller was a little older than Vati, a gangling figure in clerical black, with cadaverous features and an expression both wry and worldly. "Hearing all this talk of immigration and the Verein plans, I obeyed a calling to minister in a new land and to travel with my flock. Our own children are grown and settled. It all was most providential. We did not wish to set ourselves apart, but travel as humble pilgrims."

"Humble it is, indeed," Vati agreed with great good humor. Magda and Mutti exchanged a fond and commiserating glance.

"My husband would be content in a lions' den, if he only had someone to converse with," Mutti said to Mrs. Pastor Altmueller, who agreed graciously that it was so with her husband. She was tiny and round-faced, the very opposite of her husband, but also had the same wry and worldly sparkle in her eyes.

"Please, call me Mrs. Helene," said Mrs. Pastor Altmueller. She was briskly tidying away hers and Pastor Altemeuller's bundles and bedding, as calmly as if she had set out for America every day of her life.

"Magda, when can we go up to the deck?" Friedrich asked, impatiently. He and Johann sat, swinging their legs over the edge of their upper bunk. "We want to see something . . . the sailors . . . Vati told us they climb high up to the top of the tallest mast to work the sails."

"This is the very biggest boat we have ever seen," Johann added seriously. "I do not see how the wind can move it, Magda, truly I don't."

"I shall ask one of the crew to explain it to you, boys," Vati said, fondly. "It is certainly possible; the force of the wind pressing against the great area of the sails is very much greater than the force of water pressing against the area of the wooden hull. The hull of the ship is designed, you see, to slip through the water while the sails are designed to catch as much of the wind's great force as possible." His eyes were alight with wonder and interest. "It's a wonderfully complex mechanism, boys; every tiny piece of it serves a purpose." Vati expounded at length, until they were allowed to come up to the deck, into the freshening breeze as the *Apollo* left the Weser estuary farther and farther behind. The shore was already a blue shadow behind a scatter of buildings like children's toys. Over their heads, canvas cracked in the wind like sheets billowing on a clothesline. Sailors climbed impossibly high amongst a dizzying tangle of ropes. They had left the last pearlescent rags of fog behind. Full sunshine sparkled on the tops of all the little waves all around the Apollo and the water looked more blue than grey.

Magda leaned her elbows against the carved wooden rail, watching the coastline diminishing gradually as the Apollo painted a gentle wake across the sea. The land seemed to melt, dissolve into an insubstantial blue shadow. Already it seemed like Albeck was merely a dream, something that had happened a long time ago to someone else entirely. And being young, and naturally optimistic, she thought on the future. What would Texas be like, and what kind of life would they all be able to build for Anna and the baby and for her half-brothers? She looked over her shoulder; yes, Vati had buttonholed one of the ships' crew, who was good-naturedly explaining how the sails were worked. The boys looked enthralled. They had no interest in looking back, only forward, and Friedrich was already loudly voicing his desire to be a sailor when he grew up.

"Will they remember the home we leave behind?" Hannah came quietly up to the rail, beside her daughter.

"No, Mutti, I think not." Magda considered for a moment. "Friedrich and Johann will think on it only a little, as something long ago and far away and only when we remind them. Anna and the baby will not even remember it at all."

"And so," Magda saw her mothers' eyes fill, and spill over, "so fortunate for them. I have lived the greater part of my life in one place and will always be reminded of it. So greatly do I pray that Christian will be happy in this choice that he has made . . . for I am so filled with apprehension and I fear that I cannot entirely hide it. I put a brave face on it all, Margaretha, but I am so fearful."

"I am sure Vati knows." Magda put her strong young hand over her mother's work-worn one; what was this, Mutti always so brisk and self-assured, almost despairing. "And he understands—after all, it was his father's home before it was ours, and his father's father, before that." Upon reflection, she rather thought Vati probably hadn't noticed her mother's apprehension, so filled was he with optimism and enthusiasm for the journey and its many diversions. Best not to say, outright.

Hannah smiled, seemingly comforted and answered, "He is a saint, such a dear, dear man. I came to love him so very much, after we married. Such a surprise! I did not think I could ever love another man as I did your father."

Magda was herself diverted: Hannah talked about her father about as often as she herself thought of him, which was to say little and rarely.

"What was he like, Mutti?" she asked and Hannah smiled, fondly.

"Oh, so dashing! Tall and dark and gallant. We were so happy, and then he was gone so suddenly. He fell ill and died between one day and the next, before they could even send for me. He was gone, like a candle-flame blown out, and I never had a chance to say goodbye. I thought my heart well-broken. You and I went to live in Ulm with his sister—your Auntie Ursula. She was very kind. Her husband's house was near the old marketplace; I would often walk past the clockmaker's shop with you and that is when your stepfather first began to notice us."

"How old was I, then?" Magda thought she must have been very small indeed, for she could recall nothing of this.

"A baby, just old enough to walk. He would come out of the workshop and speak to us; he was also very kind. I thought of him as nothing more than a friend, but a very gentle and amusing one. Such a funny little man, nothing at all like your father, but he made so much of you. And then one day, he asked me to marry him and I thought I might as well, for I had no life, no home of my own. I had to provide for you. And if I had to be married, it may as well be to a friend. I only grew to love him later. In all those years, I never had cause to be unhappy until now."

"We shall be happy in Texas." Magda lifted her chin. "For I think Vati was right about the farm, and the boys. You are only sad now, Mutti because we have gone ahead and cannot go back."

"Perhaps," Hannah sighed, and her eyes went again, longingly to that last blue shadow of land. "Perhaps. Magda, I think I will go below. The ship rocks too much, and I do not feel well."

By the time the *Apollo* edged into the North Sea, under canvas bellying full from every mast, every one of her passengers realized what the buckets were for, although the children seemed to be least affected. Magda realized that she felt better immediately upon venturing into the open air, even if it were so cold that the spume flung by the wind from the tops of waves seemed half-frozen and everyone but the children had retreated to their shelf-bunks. She spent every minute on the Apollo's modest middle deck that she could when the weather was fair and passengers allowed to take the air, tasting the salt on her lips and keeping an eye on her brothers and Anna.

Poor Anna, baby Joachim took up so much of Liesel's attention, just when Anna had begun to develop her own character. Magda wasn't much interested in babies. She thought of babies as helpless little boring lumps who made a lot of noise at one end and horrible messes at the other. A child who had begun to think and talk and notice things around her; to Magda that was far more interesting.

The ship's carpenter constructed some swings for the children and hung them from a boom over the lower deck so that the smaller children had something to play on. On one fair, cold day some three or four weeks into the voyage, Magda pushed Anna in the swing, chanting:

"All my little ducklings, swimming on the sea; their heads are in the water, their tails are all you see!"

Anna gurgled with laughter and Friedrich demanded, "Where are the ducklings, Auntie Magda? We don't see them at all! Is it just a story?"

"Yes, it is," Magda whispered, "but don't tell Anna."

"Vati says that there aren't any birds in the middle of the sea," Johann remarked, seriously. "He says the sailors told him that the birds only appear near to shore. Is that true, Magda?"

"If Vati said so, then it is most likely true," Magda answered.

"So, when we see birds again … that's how we'll know that we are almost there," Johann persisted.

"I expect so," Magda answered again, but Friedrich had already moved on to another worry.

"Magda, how will Father Christmas find us to bring our presents, when we are in the middle of the ocean?"

"How can you be sure that Father Christmas isn't bringing you a switch and a lump of coal, then?" Magda answered teasingly, and had to laugh at the expression on Friedrich's face, a transparent mixture of calculation and guilt. "Fredi-love, Mutti says that you should be spanked every day. If she doesn't know the reason, she is sure that you can think of one!"

"But what about Father Christmas?" Johann looked particularly woebegone. "He can find us, can't he, Magda?"

"I'm sure he can," Magda reassured them, "He is a saint, and saints can do miracles."

Both boys seemed reassured and Magda thought, 'We *shall really have to think up a good story for them. I suppose we could ask one of the sailors to be Father Christmas. I know Mutti will have something hidden away for the boys and Anna. Mutti always plans ahead.'*

But two days after that the *Apollo* encountered first one storm, which kept them all below, and then another and far worse, which sent everyone to their shelf-bunks, terrified and racked by seasickness. Mountains of white-streaked grey water rose on either side of the *Apollo's* fragile rails and washed across the deck. A great sheet of seawater cascaded down the companionway to the lower decks, mixing with the stink of vomit and the contents of the upset privy-buckets, washing back and forth across the floor as the *Apollo* rolled. The sailors were all aloft among the ropes and acres of canvas, fighting for mastery over forces that could smash the ship as easily as a man smashes a nutshell, too busy to see to the aid of passengers too sick to care for themselves.

At the height of the storm, Magda braced herself against the violent tossing of the *Apollo,* wedging her body crossways in hers and Anna's bunk, her back against the rough boards of the bunk side and her feet and one arm braced with all her strength against the cold-sweating bulwark that was the *Apollo's* hull. The ship plunged into a storm swell, shuddering as she rolled with a loud wooden groan of agony. With her free arm, she held Anna against her, grasping her tightly to her own body, sheltering the child against that violent tossing. The front of her shift and dress were soaked with vomit, her own and the child's, and Anna's fearful tears. She knew Anna was crying still by the jerk of her body against Magda's own ribs. The sound of her sobbing was lost in the cacophony of misery around them; groans and weeping, the sound of people being wretchedly sick, of gasped-out prayers from the mortally fearful. A woman screamed from the rank of bunks across the deck . . . or she would have been, but for that she had been screaming since the storm began hours ago. Her throat was scraped so raw that the only sound emerging from it was a harsh croak.

Magda's arms ached. Her whole body hurt as if she had been beaten, but she still clutched Anna to her and knew absolutely that everything she had ever been told about Hell was wrong. Hell was not hot, filled with the shrieks of the damned. Hell was cold and dark, where people moaned and vomited with terror as the ship tossed end to end. The very timbers moaned as if the *Apollo* was about to crack apart and drop them all down into the cold black water. Worst of all, there was no end to it. Not a moment of surcease and comfort wherein to draw close all the cherished memories of Albeck dreaming under a mild summer sky, of Vati telling stories by the comfortable fireside, nor even to sit and talk with the others about hopes of a new life under another sky and beside a fine new fireplace.

No, there was only the now, in the cold Hell of the *Apollo's* lower deck and Anna in her arms, thinking that death might be welcome because there would be an end to suffering in that case. Death would hurt for a few moments—but it would be such a waste for it to happen now. Magda set her teeth. No, she wanted to live.

Amid all the noise, the screams and the groans, the roar of the storm all around, someone sang bravely in the dark. Magda braced herself anew against violent shuddering of the ship and strained her ears: a fine baritone voice, Herr Pastor Altmueller. Curious that such a rich, powerful instrument lived in such a lean and cadaverous old man! She caught a few words:

"*... fortress is our god ... defense and weapon ... frees us from distress and need, that has us now o'ertaken ... Our ancient evil foe ...*"

A mighty fortress—the Reformer's defiant hymn and talisman against evil and defeat. A scatter of voices joined, strengthened against the misery and fear that washed through the passenger deck like the watery sewage rolling back and forth under their feet; Hansi's pleasant tenor, a scattering of other voices:

"*... can aught be done ... we'll soon be lost, rejected... but for us fights the Valiant One...whom God Himself selected...*"

At her breast, Anna hiccupped; poor mite, she had nothing left in her to be sick with. Magda held her close and said, "Anna, sweeting, listen to them singing! Can you hear that? We are safe in Gods hands always, never forget. No matter what happens, we'll be safe ... and we are together, always."

Magda fell into a doze shortly after that, exhausted and aching as the storm roared on, with Anna still locked against her. Sometimes when she swam up to the surface of consciousness, it seemed that the *Apollo* was not tossing so violently. Was it hours or days? Magda was not entirely sure of anything, only that the misery seemed a little less acute and that she and Anna were still alive and vaguely surprised to be so.

"You should drink a little water, children," remarked a voice at her back. Groaning, Magda let loose her hold on Anna. Her legs cramped as she straightened them. "The storm is over, praise be to Him."

Pastor Altmueller stood on the bench, peering in at the two of them and bracing a bucket of water between his body and the side of the bunk. It was not so dim. Someone had lit the lamps. As she rolled onto her back and sat up, she saw Vati with another water-bucket, also going from bunk to bunk. Pastor Altmueller filled the dipper and held it towards her, as she and then Anna drank greedily. Behind him, one of the *Apollo's* sailors carried a huge trug filled with—what was that? Magda squinted at it: slices of fat salted bacon. She could smell it. Oddly enough, it made her hungry.

"How are you feeling?" Pastor Altmueller asked, anxiously.

"Sore. As if I had been trampled by a mad cow!"

"That was a right proper storm and no mistake," said the sailor cheerily. "But a good little bit of salt pork will settle the stomach, right enough." He held out a piece and she ate it greedily, while Pastor Altmueller moved on with his bucket. "Swab out the mess, you'll feel as right as the rain."

Magda groaned again at the thought of that work. It revolted her that she had been lying for days in filth, that hers and Anna's clothing and blankets were crusted with old vomit and urine. At least, the dirty water washing around on the deck had drained away. She swung her legs over the side of the bunk and scrambled down. Her knees nearly buckled under her. Hansi crawled out of his bunk, moving as carefully as if he were an old man and crippled with arthritis. Liesel still slept, the baby a small lump in the blankets beside her. He caught Magda's eye and grinned like a boy.

"Well, we'll know what to expect in the next storm! Anna sweeting, come down to Papa, don't sleep the day away."

He lifted Anna down from the bunk, grimacing slightly as he did so. "Liesel is still sick and so is Mutti. I guess it's up to the boys and us to clean things up. Not such a pleasant way to spend a morning, hey?"

"You're very cheerful," Magda answered, sourly.

"We're alive, and it is morning—what's there to be glum about?" he answered jauntily, as Pastor Altmueller came to refill his bucket of water from the cask at the foot of the stairway, which the sailors always kept full.

"That is the proper spirit," the old cleric remarked, approvingly. "The purser said that he could make some fresh hay available, too. But salt water is all there is for the washing, which is most unfortunate."

"It will not make things truly clean again." Magda straightened her shoulders. "But it will have to do! Friedrich! Johann! Come help me with the blankets, boys. We shall need to wash everything." She felt like groaning again, thinking of the labor of washing all the blankets in a wooden tub. Friedrich fairly bounced with excitement. He and Johann were quite recovered.

"Magda, shall we do what the sailors do for their laundry? They do the funniest thing … they throw it overboard!"

"What?" she exclaimed.

Johann said, seriously, "We watched them, one day. They tie their dirty things to a long rope and drag it after the ship for a while, until they are clean."

Hansi laughed, "Me, I wish they would drag me after the ship until I am clean again, too," He tickled Anna until she squirmed and giggled, "And Annchen also, my little piglet."

"Texas had better yet be a paradise." Magda pulled the bedding down from the upper bunks and made a pile of it on the bench, "Anything to make this all worth the trouble of getting there!"

"If it isn't," Hansi replied jauntily, "it will be by the time that we are done with it. And Joachim will have as much land as he can attend to, and not have to split his inheritance with his brothers."

Fateful words, as Magda remembered long afterwards, sitting in the parlor of the house that her husband had built for her, watching the shadows lengthen over the long pasture which reached from the white clouds of apple-blossom in the orchard, all the way down towards the riverbank. Little Joachim was fated never to reach Texas and never to share an inheritance with Hansi's other sons, even the one son who wanted no part of it.

Just before Christmas, passengers began falling ill, at first complaining of chills and fever, lying listlessly all day on their beds. And then the fever burned through their bodies, so hot they seemed to be on fire, their skin burning red with a crimson rash. Most recovered, although very slowly. But Liesel and the baby fell to it, followed by Mutti. Even Hansi complained of a headache for many days. Vati sat for hours at Mutti's side holding her hand, distraught and bewildered, almost like a child himself. They grew to dread the entry of the ship's boatswain's mate into the passenger decks, accompanied by a couple of ordinary sailors bearing a roll of canvas and a length of chain ballast or some such, especially if they all looked terribly solemn. It meant that someone had died, and the sailors were there to sew them into a canvas coffin.

"I daren't fall sick," Magda said through her teeth, when Pastor Altmueller chided her, mildly observing that she looked pale and ought to rest herself. "I cannot. Who would look after us, then? Don't tell me that God will provide. He is up there, and we are down here, leaving me with all the details."

"Margaretha, child, we are never sent more than our shoulders can bear," Pastor Altmueller answered sorrowfully. "So … I will sit with your father and your sister for a while. Take the little ones onto the deck. It will do no good to kill yourself with work, as if that would make some kind of bargain with Him. Go!" he made a shooing motion at her.

Vati lifted himself out of his lethargy to say, "Yes, Magda, the boys need sunshine and fresh air—go on then."

"I'll sit and keep you company," Mrs. Helene said firmly. Overruled, Magda lifted Anna onto her hip. The two women followed the boys up the steep ladder to the open deck where Mrs. Helene spoke to her of books and embroidery patterns, and even teased her gently about her marriage prospects.

"It seems that many of the young men have realized they can double their land-claim from the Verein by marrying," Mrs. Helene pointed out.

Magda answered, "Fine—then let them marry each other." She was not in a good temper, in spite of Mrs. Helene's conversation. She was half crazed with worry and exhaustion, with the closeness of the passenger deck and the constant noise. There was never a moment when she was alone, when it was quiet. Even in the middle of the night people talked; they moaned in their sleep or chattered to their children or argued in fierce low voices with their husbands or wives.

"We are never alone!" she said to Mrs. Helene. "The noise batters me as much as that awful storm battered the ship."

"It is a very great trial for us all," Mrs. Helene agreed, with something a little less than her customary serenity. "I try and imagine myself in the parlor of our house in Gersthofen. A spring day, with the windows open, and the roses outside in my garden all abloom."

"For myself, I would kill to be alone for ten minutes," she said fiercely, as Anna laughed and reached up her arms to be picked up. Magda sighed, and hugged the child to her, so dear and alive. "I would like to sit by a river in a green field, and listen to the birds singing."

"That sounds like a lovely dream to hold on to," Mrs. Helene said, and Anna looked up at her face and asked with interest.

"Birds?" Magda thought fondly that Anna could talk very well, for a three-year old. "Ducklings?"

"Yes, my heart, ducklings and dogs and deer. We will sit by a river in a green field, and watch the ducklings and dogs and the deer … and never, never have to set foot on a ship again!"

But Magda was wrong about that, for she would indeed set foot on a ship again to cross the Atlantic. But then she would spend her days in an elegantly paneled stateroom fitted out with an electric bell to call a steward and sleep at night on a fine spring mattress with a silk coverlet. She would call on the services of a stewardess and a lady's maid and drink coffee from a fragile china cup, poured out of a silver pot, while sitting on a private promenade wrapped in fur. And all the while, she would morn anew the loss of the one man who would have shared it with her and been enormously amused by the lavish luxury of it all.

"Magda, wake up." Someone shook her arm. She turned—a lantern, the light of it dazzling her eyes for a moment. Voices murmured from the bunks around them, like chickens disturbed at night. Mrs. Helene in her nightdress, and wrapped in a fine Turkey-work shawl. Her face was in shadow and but her voice reflected deep sorrow. "Magda—the baby has died. Your sister won't give him up."

From below her bunk, the tangled voices of her sister and Hansi, of Vati and Pastor Altmueller.

". . . no, he is only sleeping . . . you cannot take him away, he needs me, he will be hungry soon. . ."

"Annaliese, give Joachim to me. You need to rest. We will take care of him!"

"No . . . you cannot! Please, Hansi, he is only asleep!"

"She is delirious with the fever," Mrs. Helene murmured quietly to Magda. "And your mother is still so terribly ill; I think your poor father is quite distracted."

"Give him to Hansi, Annaliese my heart's love. Your mother is asleep. If the baby starts to cry, then he will wake her."

"Yes, yes, he will begin to cry . . . he will be hungry, then."

"Let your sister hold him for a while, then," Hansi sounded pleading.

He, and Vati, and Herr Pastor Altmueller clustered around Hansi and Liesel's bunk, Liesel crouched as far as she could get from them, a tangle of blankets around her. Her hair flew around her face. She looked a madwoman clutching the baby to her. Magda was horrified to see that one of Joachim's little arms curved stiffly outwards. He must have died some hours ago, with Liesel unknowing in her fever.

"I made her a hot drink," Helene whispered to Magda. "I put laudanum in it, to make her sleep, if you can only get her to swallow it."

"Lise," Magda took the pottery mug cup from her and sat on the edge of the bunk. She made her voice very calm and gentle. Hansi moved a little way aside to make room for her, his coffee-dark eyes frantic with worry. She moved closer towards her sister.

"Lise, listen to me ... you fed him just a little while ago. Let me take him to my bed, so he can sleep with Anna. You need to rest. You are sick and we need you to be better, for the children." She gestured impatiently to the others. All but Hansi withdrew a little apart. She went on talking, kindly and soothing words, as if everything were utterly normal. As if they were girls again in Albeck, and Liesel had a toothache, or a nightmare or some such childish ill, and Magda the comforting elder sister. "I'll bring him back to you, as soon as he begins to fuss, but he'll be quiet, he is ever such a good baby."

"Yes, he is a good baby," Liesel agreed; she seemed calmer and Magda held out the cup.

"See, we put your medicine in a hot drink. You should drink before it gets too cold. Give Joachim to me. We'll smooth out the blankets so you can lie down and get a good sleep. "

Liesel hesitated, and Magda's heart seemed to stop. Almost, almost. She cooed, approvingly, "There, take it in both hands, lest the ship rocking make you spill any of it. I'll take the baby ..." Liesel took the cup uncertainly in one hand and Magda gently took Joachim away. "There's a good little lad. He's fast asleep, Liesel. I'll just tuck him in beside Anna."

The baby was cold, his flesh rigid, stiff and unyielding. Life fled with breath, many hours ago. Magda wrapped the blanket around him as if he still lived and stood up. She nodded to Hansi, who took her place, murmuring soft encouragement and smoothing down the blankets. Vati and the Altmuellers huddled at the table which ran the length of the passenger deck, a few steps away. Vati looked at her pleadingly and she slowly shook her head. Helene Altmueller sighed.

"Oh, Magda - I will help with the laying-out, if you like." She stroked the baby's head with her well-tended fingers. "Such a little mite!"

"Burial at sea," Pastor Altmueller sighed. "I had hoped not to have to conduct another such a service. It does not seem right, somehow."

Hansi quietly joined them, saying, "She is asleep now." His cheeks were wet, but his voice steady. "Thank you, Magda. I don't know what came over her. I'll take … my son now. I suppose we must tell the purser so they can make arrangements."

"'Tis a very great grief to lose one of your children," Mrs. Helene murmured, sympathetically. From the look which she and the Herr Pastor exchanged, Magda comprehended that it was a grief they both knew very well. When she slipped into her blankets beside Anna, much, much later, she wrapped her arms around the child, sleeping deep and breathing regularly, as if the feel of the living flesh of her would banish the remembrance of the baby's unresponsive limbs. She cried a little herself, for guilt that she had not much interest in little Joachim and regret that she would never see him grow into a child like Anna or the twins.

Liesel slept restlessly, tossing in a fever-nightmare for many days. She was not able to come up for the sad little rites on the mid-ship deck or comfort her husband.

"So little, so little!" said Hansi as the tiny canvas-wrapped corpse of his son vanished with hardly a splash. Suddenly his solid composure shattered and he wept unashamedly, racked with grief.

Magda impulsively put her arm around him, as if they were still children themselves. He turned towards her and bowed his head to her shoulder, while Vati wordlessly held them both. Magda wondered why she had been so impulsive; still and all, they had known each other all their lives. And he was a good and loving father, nearly as good a father as Vati.

But greater grief was yet to come and it had become plain by the time that Liesel woke to consciousness around midday, two days after little Joachim's burial. She opened her eyes and looked calmly at her sister, saying only, "Joachim is dead, isn't he?"

"Yes," Magda answered simply. "And Mutti is dying."

Hannah Vogel Steinmetz's fever burned through her, for all that they could do. No remedy from their own stores, or provided by Mrs. Helene, or out of the ship's medical cabinet had any effect. Nor did Vati's long vigil, sitting at her side, holding her hand and talking of old times in Albeck, or what a grand future they would have when the Adelsverein granted them a new farm. She smiled a little for Vati and Magda and spoke a few words when she still had the strength.

"You look so like your father," she said drowsily to Magda. A little after that, she smiled at Vati with great fondness. Then the fever took her; she never opened her eyes or spoke again. She lay hardly breathing for three days and nights, while Vati and Magda hovered and Hansi and the Altmuellers came and went as quietly as they could. At the end of three days, the thready pulse in her wrists and temple simply faded away. It was the middle of the night, when all of life's tides are at lowest ebb. Her chest ceased its slight movement. Herr Pastor Altmueller brought out a small mirror and held it before her lips and nostrils as Vati watched him. He crossed himself and said heavily, "Into thy hands we commend thy dearly beloved servant, Hannah. She is with our Savior now, Christian. It was a gentle passing, thanks to be Him."

"Gentle indeed," replied Vati. "I don't know what manner of thanks is due to him, though." He took off his glasses and scrubbed at his eyes, while Pastor Altmueller patted his shoulder. He was a kindly man, less offended by Vati's free-thinking than Vati himself assumed.

"Should I wake Margaretha… and your son-in-law?" he offered, and Vati shook his head.

"No, let them sleep a little longer. They are tired, both of them and Liesel is much weakened. Let them rest. In any case, I should like to sit alone with her for a while."

He sat so for many hours, until bells sounded for the change of watch. The passengers began to stir. Magda sat up in her bunk and saw him sitting quietly below. She climbed down silently, not wanting to disturb Hannah or her sister. Just as she opened her mouth to ask after her mother, the boatswain's mate and two sailors came clumping heavily along the deck. Magda's heart grew cold behind her ribs; there was no need to ask. Vati's devastated face held all the answer she needed, that and the boatswain's mate, saying with clumsy sympathy, "I'm sorry, sir … we must take her away then. You understand how it is."

Hanna Vogel Steinmetz was buried at sea, a canvas-shrouded corpse who vanished into the water over the *Apollo's* side as silently and as uncomplaining as she had departed this life. Vati wept openly, a bewildered and sad-faced man who looked more like a gnome than ever. The bewildered twins clung to Magda, herself overwhelmed with the unreality of it all. Surely, Mutti was not gone: this was all some hideous dream.

She would wake up in the morning and Mutti would surely be there, brisk and bossy, clattering the pots in her kitchen. But when she woke up in the dark of morning on the passenger deck the day after that strange and unceremonious funeral, she knew it was true. Mutti was gone, taking the heart out of her family and out of Vati, too. Liesel was ill and Hansi grieving silently over his own loss, and that left Magda to look after them all. She clung to her vision of resting by a quiet river, the green meadow star-sprinkled with flowers, and bird-song among the leaves overhead. It became her talisman of hope against the nightmare present, a vision that never wore thin, as she hugged Anna against her going to sleep at night.

That very day, they saw the sea-birds again, great white creatures circling the *Apollo* and dipping down into the wake thrown up afterwards.

"We must be close to land again!" Johann said hopefully. "Look, Magda - there is another one!" The boys counted three or four and one of the sailors told them that he thought they would be able to see land in a few days, and so they did, but they were all chased below again immediately that happened, so that the sailors could run up their rope ladders into the sails. They needed to move the ship about to another heading, to go west, for they had seen the shoreline a long way off. It was a thin line just at the edge of the blue ocean, tan below and green above, gradually growing more distinct, above the rolling blue water. When they were let up again, they climbed the companionway with the greatest excitement and lined the carved wooden railing in company with most of the fit passengers.

"It's very green!" Friedrich said, excitedly. "Vati, is that where our land shall be?"

"No, children—I think it shall be farther inland. This is just the coastal plain."

"It looks quite beautiful," Magda said. "But now, I think that any dry land looks beautiful to me." She wondered if there was such a river just as she had imagined, running past a meadow covered with flowers, and thought probably not, for she had built her dream around what she knew, and this Texas was a new place entirely.

"It's supposed to be quite tropical," Vati said, with a ghost of his old enthusiasm. "A veritable paradise. I shall have to begin my second letter to Simon."

Chapter 4 - *The Landing Place*

Letter from Christian Friedrich Steinmetz: Written on 24 January 1846, from the port of Galveston in Texas, to Simon Frankenthaler, Goldsmith of the City of Ulm in Bavaria

My dear friend: I wished to write you with good news of our safe arrival, but alas; although the children and I are in good health, and Annaliese's husband and little Anna also, my beloved wife and Liesel and Hansi's baby son perished from ship- fever some weeks ago. To our very great grief both my dearest Hannah and the baby were buried at sea. Annaliese remains in poor health. The Reverend Doctor Altmueller, who is accompanying us on board the brig Apollo, performed the appropriate services for them, and for other members of the company who also were taken from us in so cruel and final a manner. Altmueller attempts to console us by dwelling on the ineffable glories of heaven and being with Our Savior... and also by reminding us that we are so very much closer to our new home and lands. He means well, but such thoughts have all the savor of dry sawdust, now that I am bereft of the company of my dear Hannah. I had so anticipated her happiness and contentment in a new home . . . alas for that which will not be!

We were met by agents of the Adelsverein, including their commissioner in Texas, Baron von Meusebach. He made us a most gracious welcome and saw that we all were conducted to various hotels and boarding houses in the city . . . such a strange city it is, at once elegant and modern, but all built of wood and seeming insubstantial, like a very new world Venice. It almost seemed, looking on it from the deck of the Apollo that we were above the level of the city and looking down. The city is itself constructed on a sandy barrier island, with a great lagoon (which is the main harbor) between itself and the mainland, appearing barely above the level of the sea. The Baron, who modestly wishes to be known in this country only as plain Mister Meusebach, informs us that we must take a further sea journey very shortly, by smaller ship along the coast westwards to the Adelsverein's own established landing of Karlshaven, where we will be met by wagons and transported inland. In the meantime we will rest and recover from the sea passage, and fortify ourselves against the rigors of the continuing journey. At the same time we will acquaint ourselves with the conditions of the land we will now call home. Such a curious medley of folk throngs the streets of this city! There are of course sailors from many lands much as there were in Bremen. But there are so many others, many of an exotic and picturesque appearance and every color imaginable, from ebony-colored Africans to native Indians the color of cinnamon and painted in diverse other shades. Then there are Yankee businessmen as sober as any good bourgeois of Ulm, and Texian frontiersmen in calico shirts and buckskin trousers, and also many military officers. There are fears of war with Mexico, since Texas has now voted to join the United States. Mr. Meusebach has tried to relieve our fears in this regard. War is only threatened, as it has threatened frequently along the border; it has not happened yet.

A curiosity I have noted is that most of the native-born ... that is, those who have been many generations in this country, are taller on average than more recent arrivals; taller and more robust. And universally, even if they appear in rags and seemingly of the meanest degree, they bear themselves well and treat each other with perfect princely courtesy. It is almost as if they are all grandees in the guise of beggars. One must beware of taking the measure of a man based solely on his appearance here, for they are careful of their honor and sensitive to apparent slights, resorting to offense with whatever weapon is at hand, just as the noblemen of old and of more recent date!

I find myself able to understand written English with perfect clarity, but alas, I have had so little practice in speaking it . . . and moreover, there is such a multiplicity of accents, I confess with considerable embarrassment that I am at a loss in making conversation in other than the most simple exchange of pleasantries.

Addendum: 29 January—It appears with the threat of imminent war, Mr. Meusebach is experiencing much difficulty in obtaining sufficient transportation for all of us newly arrived. My son-in-law, with great foresight insisted on bringing his two farm-carts, disassembled, in the Apollo's hold. He sought out Mr. Meusebach and made him aware of this, whereupon the latter was greatly pleased and ventured an offer of hire. He intends to charter a great number of wagons and teamsters to convey us from Karlshaven into to the north where the Adelsverein grants are located. We and some small part of our company shall depart on the sloop Adeline, all but Hansi, who will go with Mr. Meusebach and his party by land. I shall write again, as soon as I may.
    Your old friend,
    C.F. Steinmetz

* * *

"He seems to be quite distracted," Magda observed, as the crew of the *Adeline* made ready to cast away. This operation did not seem to be as complicated as it was on the *Apollo*; at any rate, those who wished it were allowed on deck as the space of water between the dock and the sloop's hull widened gently.

"Who does?" Vati said, distractedly.

"Mr. Meusebach, the baron with the red beard. He is not one of those arrogant 'Firsts'. His eyes look haunted, and I do not think he sleeps well at night."

The new commissioner had come to meet them when the Apollo docked. It was hard not to notice him, surrounded always by a clamoring crowd; a slender man of ordinary height, a great beaky nose, and a hairline retreating from above an already high forehead. A grand banner of flaming red beard rather made amends for that particular withdrawal. He had greeted them all, made his deputy in Galveston known, and welcomed them to Texas.

"No," Vati answered. He had talked with Meusebach on several occasions and discovered that they had many correspondents and mutual interests. "He is one who feels the obligation of leadership and loyalty to his friends very deeply. He takes the place as director here of Prince Solms—who had grand ideas, but not much of a head for business." Vati shook his head, pityingly, "I have been talking to some of the others. The Prince left affairs in such arrears and confusion that poor Mr. Meusebach has been months untangling them. They say also," and Vati looked as sly as an unworldly man could, "that the Prince had ambitions for political advancement in an independent Texas, and the annexation ruined them. And that also, having given offense by his arrogance to so many of the public men here, all the use he could still be for the Verein was to return to Germany where he might raise more funds, and leave Mr. Meusebach to make such repairs as he could."

"How did you discover such gossip, Vati?" Magda asked, and Vati blinked at her in gentle astonishment.

"Oh, I merely asked and seemed interested. Most people are cheered to find that someone is interested in their businesses, and to talk about them at length. And everything is so different here. So new and fascinating ... compared to my little workshop. I had heard everything that my friends there had to tell me years ago, all down in a rut with the cabbages . . . ahh, look there, Magda! Is that a pelican? What a splendid specimen it is!" He pointed at a great brown bird, swooping down to water-level and skimming the surface. Then it angled upwards and landed ungracefully in the top-masts of another ship as they glided past. "They are supposed to be the emblem of self-sacrificing mothers," Vati added, regretfully, "tearing open their own breasts to give nourishment to their young. Such sacrifices have been made, to bring us so far. Magda, my dear," and he looked at her mistily and polished his glasses, "I so hope that if any other such sacrifice is demanded of us that I shall be the one chosen for it."

"You are such a pagan, Vati," Magda answered lightly, although she felt a cold chill clutching at her heart at the thought of losing Vati as well as her mother. "It was the ship-fever—besides, what should we do without you? You have a useful trade, at least. Hansi is a farmer, and how many farmers are here already?"

"You would get on," Vati patted her hand, comfortingly. "You should be able to find a handsome husband with a good trade of his own! Then you would not have to fear losing your creaky old father."

"Creaky!" Magda snorted, scornfully. This was another sore point: having been afflicted since landing with an astonishing number of marriage proposals made on very short acquaintance from some of the single men who had signed Verein emigration contracts. "I saw you playing ball with the boys today! Besides which, you are the only one among us who understands English."

"Which reminds me, my dear; I wonder if any of the crew will have time to make conversation later? I need to practice speaking and listening. "

"I expect they will, if you ask them and look interested, Vati."

He patted her hand, and said, teasingly, "And especially if you are nearby, and they wish to impress a pretty young maiden by being kind to her doddering old father."

"Vati, you are incorrigible—you do not dodder!"

"I can pretend!" Vati answered with great good humor, but it seemed to be not necessary, for Magda observed him later, deep in earnest converse with the sloop's first mate, in a mutually satisfactory cloud of pipe smoke.

The sloop was never far from land; Magda found the sight of it always to be comforting over the next three days as the *Adeline* coasted west. Although the below-deck of the *Adeline* was very much smaller and consequently more cramped than the *Apollo*, it was broken into a number of tiny cabins. Magda, Liesel, and Helene Altmueller shared one with Anna, while Vati and the boys shared another. The rest of the passengers were young men, who arrived on another Adelsverein-chartered ship some days before the *Apollo*, and several of Mr. Meusebach's assistants, accompanying a shipment of foodstuffs.

"It seems almost like a lake," Magda remarked to Vati and the boys, one morning. "The water is very gentle, not tossing us about at all. Is it always like this?"

"Mr. King, he says that they have storms, horrible storms that come through . . . but yes, it is very mild, right now." That was Vati's friend the first mate. "But he tells me that this winter has been stormy and cold, and there has been some sickness at Karlshaven. He advises that we find shelter as soon as we can. And that if it weren't for waiting for Hansi, he says that we ought to leave from there as soon as we are able."

* * *

Letter from Christian Friedrich Steinmetz: Written on 1 February 1846, from the port of Karlshaven, Texas, to Simon Frankenthaler, Goldsmith of the City of Ulm in Bavaria;

My Dear Friend: I am starting this letter so soon after sending my previous missive in order to provide you with a complete account of our travails. We are encamped in miserable conditions, awaiting the arrival of Mr. Meusebach and the wagons. Many of the Adelsverein settlers have been here for months and have begun to despair! Mr. King and some of his men very kindly carried our goods ashore, wishing us good luck, and then took their departure. We were most particularly advised by Mr. Meusebach to procure some canvas for tents, and additional blankets and food sufficient for the short stay we would have at Karlshaven, but we were not prepared--- although there is little which would prepare one--- for the shock we encountered. Mr. Meusebach's deputy at Karlshaven is one Lt. Wilke, a young Prussian officer from Colberg. He is able and willing, but quite overwhelmed. There is also a Pastor Ervendburg... "

* * *

There was nothing at Karlshaven but a few rough houses and a dozen tents, set up on the hard-packed shell and sand back of the shore. A crude wooden jetty had been constructed, reaching like an arrow into deeper water, where the *Adeline* tied up. Around the houses and tents stretched a scattering of rough shelters made from trunks and boxes, roofed in blankets and tattered strips of canvas. Magda looked around; she had Anna by the hand and an arm around Liesel's waist. Anna was cross; she sucked her thumb, and Liesel drooped. She was still quite weakened and spent most of the time lying down. Even slight exertions left her grey-faced and faint. The sun shown warmly, but the breeze held the threat of chill in it as well as an evil smell blowing from the land. Vati and his family, the Altmuellers and the young men—all the new arrivals hesitated as they clustered around Ludwig Wilke and his handful of men, bewildered and horrified at the waste and spectacle of human ruination before them.

A great quantity of furniture and broken wood lay abandoned and half-buried in drifting sand, close by the landing place. There were a scattering of people there, ragged folk who stared at young Wilke and the new arrivals with hollow eyes. They snatched the supplies distributed by Wilke and his assistants and ran away carrying their meager rations like animals scuttling back into their holes. Those who did not merely stared at the new arrivals with hollow eyes, until one man among them ran up and embraced Pastor Altmueller, weeping.

"He is Peter Engelke, from my old parish," Herr Pastor Altmueller said, as the man began to speak, brokenly. "He is angry at the Verein, at the Baron Meusebach, at all of them. They have sickened, all of them who have been here all this time. They hardly have strength enough to bury the dead deeply enough to keep the animals from digging them up again. There was one caravan gone to the north under Prince Solms' direction but none other since. Captain Buchel talks of taking a company of men to take service with the American Army. They'll go to fight in Mexico just so they may leave this place of death!" Pastor Altmueller looked genuinely appalled. "This is not good; this is not what we were promised. Conscription into a war we had no wish for? That was an evil which we thought to leave behind!"

"It is not what we signed contracts for," Vati answered grimly. "But it is not the fault of Baron . . . Mister Meusebach. He is doing his best. Tell him rather that my own son-in-law is to meet us here within days with a convoy of wagons."

Liesel drooped against Magda's shoulder and Vati hastily steered her to sit on the smallest of their trunks.

"I would like to lie down," she whispered pitifully to Magda. "And it is so cold!"

"We'll find a place soon," Vati promised, while Pastor Altmueller drew aside with his old parishioner. The other young men from off the Adeline looked around, uncertain and worried.

"The tents are too crowded," young Lt. Wilke said, quietly. "And there are too many sick among them. I hardly know how to advise you." He looked nearly as harried as Mr. Meusebach. "Perhaps I can beg of some of the families nearby. But they are few and so many are sick, I cannot extend much hope on that account."

"I have the utmost confidence that we will not remain here long," Vati said firmly. Wilke sighed, a harried expression on his face.

"So we have all hoped—but every week more arrive! We are stranded here until the rain stops and the road to the north becomes a little less of a marsh. The Prince himself was here at Christmas, but I would not suggest that he ever come this way again. He would be torn apart, like Acteon by his own hounds. I am sorry, Steinmetz, truly I am; we are overwhelmed, quite overwhelmed. You have brought canvas? I will send some men to help put up a tent of your own. It is all that I can do. Just come to the storehouse, over there, when you have found a place for your family." Wilke nodded and walked away. As he went, Magda saw that his shoulders slumped, as if he held off discouragement while he talked with them, but had not the strength to keep it at bay any farther.

Peter Engelke straightened, seeming to recover his composure. "You bring welcome news; we are despairing of ever leaving here! Johann Schwartz built a house for his family but he had enough money for it. He sent for a load of lumber from the city. The rest of us," Peter shrugged, hopelessly. "We have nothing but what we brought with us and promises from the Verein, damn them."

"So do we all," Pastor Altmueller answered calmly. "And they shall be fulfilled, in due time. But in the meantime . . ." He looked around, thoughtfully. "What manner of place is there for lodging? We had expected to find some shelter here."

"Verein promises," Peter Engelke laughed, bitterly. He might have been a young man, but he looked old, starving and ill, with his eyes sunk into his skull. "There are tents but I do not advise them. The wind blows cold at night, especially when it comes from the north. Another hollow Verein promise, Pastor Altmueller - this is no tropic paradise."

"My daughter was ill of the ship-fever," Vati spoke up, "and she is still not entirely recovered. Might you show us where we might be sheltered for a few days?"

Peter Engelke frowned. "There are some people who have gone north; they were living against a steep bank, which gave more shelter from the north wind. If no one else has moved in, you may as well take it for yourselves. I will show you, if you like. It is not far."

"We'll wait here with the boxes," Magda said. She took out a blanket and wrapped it around her sister. Sitting down beside her, she took Liesel's head onto her lap, "Will we be safe?"

"Safe?" Peter Engelke laughed bitterly. "As if you are in church! Everyone who might be a danger to you is sick, dead or gone!"

At that, Liesel began to cry softly. Magda commanded, "Vati, go with Pastor Altmueller, and find this place - boys, you go with them, too." She gathered Anna to her side, safe under her shawl. Liesel's eyes were shut, the lashes lying across her pale cheeks. Vati, the boys and the Altmuellers followed Peter Engelke away from the landing, around the makeshift huts with sand drifting against their sides and weathered grey shrubs. There was a slight rise of land crowned with stubby trees some little distance away. They might be a while, even so. Magda hummed softly to Anna, and sang, "Sleep, baby, sleep, Your father is watching the sheep, Your mother is shaking the little tree, Sweet dreams fall down for you and me, sleep baby sleep!"

"Mutti used to sing that to me." Liesel opened her eyes, "And I used to sing it to Joachim. I was dreaming about them, just now. Such a pleasant dream!" Her eyes filled, "It doesn't seem real, that we are here and that they are both gone, Magda. Being awake is such a nightmare. I wish I could just sleep and sleep, and maybe when I wake up again, it will be better."

"You are still sick, Lise. You can't just sleep and hope for things to get better of themselves," Magda answered, firmly. "Who would look after Anna and Hansi? They need you to be well, and so do I."

"Do you?" Liesel asked, miserably. "You do everything so much better than I can. Anna follows you everywhere. Mutti always praised your work, and Vati talks to you, really talks to you ... everything of mine is always second best. If I should die, then Hansi should again ask you to marry him!"

Surely that was just the black cellar mood talking, and Magda cradled her sister's head on her lap. How ridiculous, when she had always hopelessly envied Liesel's pink cheeks, neat figure, and curls! Everyone had admired and petted Liesel when she was a child, so like a doll. They paid no mind to Magda, who knew she was skinny and plain to everyone but Vati. With her straight black hair, she seemed destined to be the ugly older sister in one of Vati's fairy stories.

"Lise, don't be a silly! I used to be in tears because everyone made so much of you," Magda answered, bracingly. "And I couldn't think of marrying him—we have known each other for too long! He is like a brother, only not a pest the way Friedrich is."

"Truly?" Liesel sat up, reviving somewhat like a wilted flower placed in water. She looked searchingly at her sister. "I always thought you were so brave and clever, you could have any suitor you wanted."

"Too clever to want most of them," Magda snorted. "You are down in your black cellar Lise, with this talk of dying. Hansi prefers to have someone to look at him as if he is the most wonderful man in the world, and I could never do that! You are like Mutti, wanting nothing but a tidy little house full of children and to make jams and make it look pretty and welcoming for him."

"I do," Liesel answered, as if this was something she had just now realized was true. "Remember that morning in the barn, when we were milking the cows, and I told you I didn't want to leave Albeck and make this awful journey? I was perfectly happy back home. Hansi promised when we married that he would buy out his brothers when his father died. I would have liked to have had our own little house, but you told me that Hansi and Vati were set on it. I listened to Hansi. He was so excited about all this talk of Texas. So I pretended to be excited about it too, because it made him happy. But really, I would have been just as content to have stayed in Albeck." Her eyes filled again. "Oh, Magda . . . what are we going to do? It's a desert here. It's full of savages, and they don't speak German and I hate it!"

"Shhhh . . . now that we're here, we mustn't say a word of complaint," Magda answered, practically. "Well, not to Hansi or Vati, anyway. Or to the children, even. You should think about the house that you will help him build. Think on how you want the rooms to look, and what you want to see outside of the windows, and where you want everything to be. Tell Hansi exactly what you want in your house, when he has his fine Texas land." They sat for a moment, while Anna quietly sucked her thumb.

"What would Mutti have wanted her house to look like?" Liesel asked, finally.

"I don't know. But Vati would have hardly noticed anyway. I expect she would have liked something as much like the old house as possible . . . oh, look, Vati and Pastor Altmueller and Friedrich are returning. Good, that means we have not to walk a long way."

Vati was smiling, although the smile appeared a little forced.

"It is not so bad," he said breathlessly, "It is a sheltered cove, hollowed out of the little cliff – out of the wind. All it lacks is water. I'm afraid you girls must come to Wilke's storehouse for water. There is even an adequate hearth, built into a natural chimney. We'll set up our canvas over the top and pile up our trunks in front, and it will be big enough for us and the Altmuellers. Mrs. Pastor Altmueller and Johann are sweeping it out. There was much filth left behind. I am afraid your dear mother would not have approved."

Liesel and Magda's glances met, in perfect communication: *No, she wouldn't have, but it's not like we had much choice!*

Magda said in forced cheer, "Then show it to us, at once, Vati. Liesel is very tired and Anna did not have her proper rest today."

Well, thought Magda philosophically, sometime later, *at least it does not roll up and down. And it is dry— drier than the Apollo.*

She met Helene Altemeuller's eyes and knew that she thought the same thing. The men had already spread out the canvas tent which Mr. Meusebach had suggested diffidently might be a good thing to purchase in Galveston, all the while apologizing for the fact that the Verein had not been able to properly organize matters at Karlshaven. At least, he had given them some forewarning. It gave her the shudders to think of staying for months as so many others seemed to have done. With the boys' help, she and Vati and Pastor Altmueller stacked their trunks and boxes two and three high, a little way out from the cove to make a walled enclosure, roofed with tent-canvas.

"Quite the nomad's snug little den," Vati pronounced cheerily as he and Magda walked a little way along the shore, searching for firewood. "But still, I shall be glad to see Hansi and his carts... though we may not sleep in any more comfort on the road. Here, let us chop some of this stuff, to cushion our beds against the hard ground. You know, my dear Magda, I have read so many accounts of adventures such as this and they all leave out the very important things—like how one finds comfort sleeping on the ground, and what a chore it is to cook simple food over an open fire."

"I am glad one of your books made mention of bringing a hatchet, Vati," Magda answered, as she chopped small limbs from the branches of a wiry grey shrubs, one of those which grew thickly on the low hills inland of the sand.

"Oh, but it was not in a book," Vati answered. "I made conversation one day with a workman in Galveston to practice my English, of course. I asked him to talk to me, to tell me how one built something in this country and he explained to me how to build a cabin of logs. He said one or two men could build an entire house themselves and every stick of furniture and item of comfort within it, using just a simple hatchet, only." Vati blinked earnestly." It was

69

quite an enlightening lecture. He said many times that a hatchet was the best thing you could have, other than one of those patent-revolving pistols. He insisted that I should purchase one at once. He even took me to a shop."

"Vati, he was probably a tout! And the shop belonged to his brother, or something. You know how Mr. Meusebach and the others warned us, how people would try and take advantage of us."

"Do you think so?" Vati took off his glasses and polished them, "It is quite a fine hatchet. And I was not over-charged. I went to two other stores, just to be sure. And he really was a workman."

"How could you tell?" Magda asked. Really, just when you thought Vati should not be allowed out without a keeper, he confounded you with some clever insight.

"His hands, Magda. Very rough, callused all over - and his clothes were full of sawdust. I do not think a tout would take such trouble."

"Probably not," Magda slipped the handle of Vati's precious hatchet through the waistband of her apron, and caught up the corners of it to make a sack, so she could gather a double load of the wiry branches. "Here, just pack them in and then if you can carry the bigger branches . . . Vati? What is wrong?"

"I am not sure, Magda. I thought I heard one of the children crying."

"Are you sure?" Magda listened. No, she heard nothing but wind and surf, washing gently against the shelly beach. Even the voices of those in the camp were as faint as the cries of seagulls, wheeling in the salt-tangy air as the sun began to slide down into the hills to the west.

But even as they gathered up their loads of wood and brush and walked back towards their camp, Magda noticed that Vati still lingered, turning his head this way and that, listening still for something which she could not hear.

Pastor Altmueller met them as the threaded their way through the trampled dunes,

"Stay where you are," he commanded harshly, holding up his hands, when Magda and Vati were about twenty paces removed from him. "Don't come any closer to me. I have been looking for my other parishioners among all the tents and shelters. There is great sickness here, and I have been among it. I dare not spend a night in the shelter with you until I have burnt the clothes I have on and scoured myself clean. Even so, I would best spend a couple of nights apart, until I am sure that I am not sickening myself. Please, do not come near me. Tell Helene to bring me a change of clothes, and some blankets - but not to come near me, I beg of you all. I would not risk your lives or hers."

Vati came close to dropping his armload of firewood. "Please, do not say such things! Let us leave some of these branches; at least you will have a softer bed. Are your folk truly in that bad a condition, Bernard?"

"They are," Pastor Altmueller replied, grimly. "And I will not countenance any argument on this matter. The Baron and his wagons had best arrive soon. Even so, some of them will be traveling no farther than the nearest burial ground. Tell my wife - tell Helene I shall make a small camp for myself and to fear not, for I shall be in His hands, always."

They returned to their shelter in a sober mind and relayed his message to Helene Altmueller. In her quietly capable way, she and the boys had already built up a fire and sorted out bedding enough for everyone. The tiny shelter appeared to be reasonably cozy, now as the sky darkened and the wind's chill became more evident. She calmly wiped soot off her fingers saying only, "I feared as much - from the smell, as much as the appearance of Peter and the others. I would think that many have been afflicted by the ague and intermittent fever, or perhaps the flux. Much different from the ship's fever."

"Scurvy, also," Vati said. "That would appear from the loosening of the teeth. Did you notice? It is caused by a deficiency in diet." He was talking to himself, for Helene Altmueller had already wrapped a set of clean clothes for her husband in several blankets, taken a half-burnt branch from the fire, and departed, slipping through the blanket hung over the opening. "Oh . . . I will take Bernard some food later." He tilted his head, listening for a moment.

"Did you hear it? I thought I heard a child, crying still. Strange—it does not seem to come from the direction of the main camp."

"I don't hear anything, Vati," answered Magda.

"I heard it, when we were looking for driftwood," Johann spoke up. "I thought it might have been Anna, but it wasn't."

"Now it's gone; the winds have shifted," Vati said. "Well, boys, how do you like this adventure, hey? Sleeping on the ground, like a true Roman soldier!"

Leave it to Vati, thought Magda; he could make it all sound as if it were a thrilling and novel escapade. Within a few minutes Helene Altmueller returned, calm and serene as always and saying, "Doctor Altmueller has found a little sheltered space farther on, and built a fire. He tells us not to worry for him. He has seen nothing which might be the cholera,"

"God in heaven, never that!" Vati might have turned pale, but the dim firelight in their cave and canvas shelter cast strange and flickering shadows. "How does he fare, Mrs. Helene?"

"Very well, actually," Helene Altmueller smiled fondly, although her expression was rather strained. "He has found a broken chair and is sitting in it by the fire, reading his Psalm book as best as he can. Really, I have no worries for my husband—as long as we spend no more than a few days in this place."

"I have the utmost faith in Mr. Meusebach," Vati answered, jauntily, "And Hansi . . . of course, I know my son-in-law rather better. I do not think we shall spend more than three or four days living here."

Magda devoutly hoped not, for little icy drafts crept into the shelter, seeping in through the cracks between the canvas and the cliff-face and little showers of sandy grit constantly fell from the walls, onto their bedding and clothes. She entirely sympathized with Mr. Schwartz, sending for a shipload of boards and building a cozy house, straightaway. Lucky Mr. Schwartz—luckier Mrs. Schwartz that they had managed to hold onto some money! While Vati had taken Uncle Simon's advice and sold much of what they might otherwise have brought with them, Magda did not think he had enough to build a house; he had paid some of Hansi's fees to the

Adelsverein. Until she went to bed, sharing the blankets with Liesel and Anna sleeping like a little mouse between them, she did not feel entirely warm. She fell asleep, wondering exactly how much a shipload of house lumber might cost.

In the morning, she and Johann and Friedrich set off with Vati's hatchet, to explore inland and look for firewood.

"I think a lot of people come this way, Auntie Magda," observed Johann. The shore around a vast, reed-grown lagoon was trodden into deep mud as it spread out into a marsh and drained away into sand at the ocean's edge. The breeze from the north blew keen and cold, rattling the tall dried rushes with a sound like bones. Still, it was not as cold as it would have been in Albeck, that day a year ago when Vati showed her the Adelsverein pamphlet.

"We'll go as far as we need to find as much as we can carry," Magda decided, so they followed the lagoon-shore inland, skipping between stones and clumps of rushes, until they could no longer smell the stink of the camp and the smoke of fires was just a dirty smudge.

"It is not as pretty as the woods around Albeck." Friedrich balanced on a stone and hopped to the next one. He missed the next one with a splash and was up to his ankle in mud.

"Have a care, now you have gotten your shoes all wet," Magda said. "But nothing looks pretty at the end of winter like this, everything grey and brown and dead." They went as far as they dared, past where they could see other footprints and where small branches had been broken off the bare grey shrubs. With reassuringly heavy bundles they set off on the walk back. Halfway there, they met Vati, who was looking off to the north and frowning in perplexity.

"I hear that child crying again," he said. "Mrs. Helene heard it also. It worries us, to hear it still crying. I am walking a little way along the beach . . . no, you need not come with me; Mrs. Helene and Liesel are waiting for firewood. I'll be back, in a little while."

So, they carried their precious wood back to their camp, where Liesel sat in a patch of sunshine, out of the wind, with Anna in her lap.

"Mrs. Helene has taken some bread to Herr Pastor," she said. "And to fetch a bucket of drinking water from Lt. Wilke's water-cistern - did you see Vati? He went to look for that crying child. We all heard it this morning; I do not think Vati has imagined it." She looked critically at the armloads of cut brush that Magda and the boys carried. "Will that last us long? It's very cold, and the wood burns very fast."

"There's plenty more wood on the beach, but it's all wet!" Friedrich pointed out.

Magda said, "Then go and gather some of it! It will dry soon enough! Make use of those sharp eyes of yours!" Friedrich made a face, but Johann pulled him away. They had hardly been gone a few minutes before they returned, stumbling over each other in their haste.

"We saw Vati!" gasped Johann, "He is coming along the beach in a great hurry!"

"He is carrying something!" Friedrich added.

Behind him, Mrs. Helene exclaimed, "God in heaven—the poor child!"

For it was indeed a child that Vati carried as he stumbled awkwardly towards their camp, a child wrapped in his coat who appeared a little younger than Anna, and who clung frantically to him.

"She was alone, there were none left alive," Vati gasped. His face was grey with horror. "A man and a woman . . . they have been dead for many days . . . a little camp, far from all. . ."

"I will fetch my husband," Mrs. Helene said, firmly. "At least he may advise us, from a little distance. Could you tell of what they had died?"

"I could not," Vati shook his head. "I could not bear to look closely, though. She was sitting in the middle of filth in her nightgown . . ." that fact announced itself to all their noses. "I do not think she is sick, herself."

"Any child who could cry for a day and a night is too strong to be sick," Liesel observed.

Magda added, "Anyway, we must wash her, and decide what to do next. Here, let me take her." But the child clung frantically to Vati, turning away from Magda and squeezing her eyes tightly closed.

"She's frightened, poor mite," Vati hugged her close and rocked her gently, chanting, "A rooster and a hen, the sermon will begin. A cow and a calf, and that is just half. A mouse and a cat . . ."

Magda sent the boys for more water, telling them to hurry and it didn't matter if it were so clean, just enough to fill the laundry tub, set close to the fire. Liesel produced a clean towel out of their own luggage and a dress which Anna had nearly outgrown. By the time the boys returned, the Altmuellers were there, too. Mrs. Helene searched out a little tub of soap, and between the two of them and with much gentle soothing, she and Magda coaxed the child into sitting in the washtub, although she did not let loose of Vati's hand. The three of them knelt around the tub, while Magda and Mrs. Helene scrubbed her clean and Liesel sat with Anna in her lap and watched.

"I will take Peter and some of the others, and go out to that camp where you found her," Pastor Altmueller said, heavily. He stood just outside the shelter, watching through the makeshift door. "There must be something there to tell us her name. Can you tell her age, Helene?"

Mrs. Helene shook her head.

"Between eighteen months and two years," she answered. "Too young to talk, although she might recognize her name." Magda poured a scoop of water over the child's head, and massaged a little soap into her hair.

"The color of strawberries and gold." she said, "Someone must remember hair like this, if she had it from one of her parents."

"There is some advantage to this," Vati said, sorrowfully. "She will not remember any of this horror."

"More to the point," Magda added, "will any remember her, and claim her for their family?"

Vati blinked, thoughtfully, "Well, I shall, of course—if she has no family among the camp that we may find. I don't imagine there is anything such as an orphanage . . . cruel places, for so young a child." Liesel and Magda looked at each other, utterly taken back. Vati continued serenely, unaware of their shock, "Your dear mother and I had hoped for more children after the boys." And he looked most impishly at Magda, "You see, this way, you may allow yourself

75

to be courted away, without worrying that there shall be no one to care for me in my old age. Three daughters shall be able to share that onerous burden very nicely."

"You know nothing of this child," Pastor Altmueller said, warningly.

Vati replied, "I know that whoever her parents might have been, her father signed a Verein contract. And she will not let go my hand; that is sufficient for me. This is our little Texas rose, found growing by the wayside." As he said that, the child looked expectantly at his face. Magda said, "Vati . . . I think . . . "

"Ah!" Vati beamed, his face brightening. "Rose… Rosalie. If it isn't her true name, it's close to it and will serve well enough."

"Anna will be eaten up with jealousy," Magda said, well aware that Anna intently watched every move of the strange new child and how everyone was fussing over her. "She sulked for weeks when her little brother was born."

Mrs. Helene answered, "Oh, no, not this time, my dear." She lifted Rosalie out of the tub, swathing her in a towel. "She is old enough to be a help." She raised her voice, slightly and called, "Anna, sweeting, can you fetch my comb from my little bag, and come here? We need your help."

By the time that Anna returned with Mrs. Helene's fine ivory comb, Rosalie was dressed, although Anna's old dress fell well down to her toes. Mrs. Helene had rubbed the last water from her red-gold hair, exclaiming in admiration, "There's the lovely Rosalie, cheeks like pink roses!" She was a beautiful child, with eyes the dark blue-purple of pansies, set in a heart-shaped face. Mrs. Helene fastened the last button and said to Anna, "Anna my heart, this is Rosalie and you are now in charge of her. She is your baby; do you understand? You must take care of her. She needs to have her hair combed, and to have her breakfast fed to her. Can you do that?"

Anna nodded and Mrs. Helene said briskly, "Then go take her to sit on your bed, and comb her hair." And to Magda's astonishment, Anna took Rosalie firmly by the hand and led her over to the bedrolls. Rosalie followed unresisting, while Mrs. Helene watched with satisfaction and whispered, "It does not fail. The little ones like to mother the littler ones. And it is better so, to compete with you to be a mother, than to compete with the smaller child to be a baby still. Set Anna to care for her, in little ways; it will do them both good."

* * *

4 February 1846, from Karlshaven, Texas: Today, the much-anticipated arrival of the wagons, to bear our party north on our continued journey. We rejoice at being able to leave a place which has become a sad graveyard for many of us who ventured forth from our homeland with such high hopes... such as our dear child Rosalie's parents. We were not able to find anything identifying them in what was left of the camp where they had perished. We could not tell if it was because they had been left with little upon arrival, or if such meager items which might have identified them were taken by others. No one claimed to recognize her, or know anything of her parents. My dear Margaretha insisted that she be properly baptized as my daughter which our companion Altmueller did, albeit with many forebodings. But she is the dearest child and plays so sweetly with little Anna. On the morrow, we embark on the next portion of our journey. I will continue this narrative upon arrival . . .

Chapter 5 – *Weeping and Remembering Zion*

Such a welcome sight, the unaccustomed noise and business-like bustle the Adelsverein-hired teamsters brought to the haunted beach landing when they came wading and lurching through the muck and mud to the landward side of the landing-place. They had come bearing more supplies and a quantity of lumber and tent-canvas. It was intended, explained Mr. Meusebach, to try and build better shelters for those who were too sick or worn down to make the long journey by wagon. Magda noticed how he looked cheerful at first, but following a long and quiet-voiced consultation with Lt. Wilke, the Verein's commissioner looked as harried and as ill as before.

"We are to leave tomorrow," Vati related, joyously that evening, as Hansi and two of his new friends came to carry most of the Richters' and the Steinmetzes' belongings and load them into Hansi's carts. Mr. Meusebach was there, also.

"They were a Godsend, the Baron said so himself," Hansi slapped the side of his cart, and Mr. Meusebach sighed and patiently asked them one again to refer to him as plain Mr. Meusebach, not Baron Meusebach any more.

"There are no First ones here," he said again, as he stood with Hansi and his friends who were rapidly disassembling the wall of boxes and trunks which had been the front of their home for a little while. "We have come through the water and fire, and are born again."

"Washed clean in the blood of the lamb," said Pastor Altmueller earnestly, although Vati snorted. Magda knew that he liked teasing the straight-laced Altmueller who wore his piety so openly, but he was also the only one of their current companions who was as learned as Vati and had the same taste for long philosophical discourse. And he had volunteered to remain and tend to the spiritual needs of those of his parish unable to travel. Both Vati and Magda made their farewells of Pastor Altmueller and Mrs. Helene with sorrow and regret.

They set out at the beginning of March, leaving behind the horror of the landing camp, winding their way north along the river in a great caravan of wagons, guarded by a handful of Verein troopers: gallant looking men who wore cock-feathers in their hats and sword-belts over their fine grey tunics.

"Banditti and raiding Indians everywhere," Vati reported with enormous relish.

Magda said in exasperation, "And if they should happen to raid our company, Vati . . . you think they would allow you to look at them as if they were actors in a play?"

"No, dear, I suppose they wouldn't." He blinked vaguely and apologetically, adding, "Still . . . it would be most interesting," as Magda rolled her eyes.

Liesel and the little girls rode, but Vati and Magda and the boys walked, rejoicing in the freedom and the open air. The heavy-laden wagons set a gentle pace, once they were past the muddy swamps immediately inland. A fresh breeze blew from the north, blowing away the stink of the camp and the salt-smell of the sea, rustling the stands of reeds along the inlet and the river which ran into it, as if they were whispering secrets to each other. The sun shone every day out of a sky of such a clear blue that Magda wondered if she had ever really seen the sky before. Clouds like drifts of pure white un-spun wool drifted in it, their edges glittering as they passed in front of the sun which light seemed to fall on them with a gentle benison. Although it was March, it already seemed summer-mild. They camped in tents or underneath the wagons almost every night, when the teamsters drove them into a great circle with the team animals corralled inside.

The teamsters whom Mr. Meusebach had hired and the Verein troopers who accompanied them were all in the habit of breaking travel at noon, for several hours.

"Custom of the country," explained Mr. Meusebach, and Hansi as well. Magda and the others found it a good one, since it permitted a lunch and a rest after a good five or six hours travel, especially welcome for those on foot, and by the children who had a chance to play.

Magda was finishing the tidy-up after the meal, and Vati was snoozing in the shade with a calico handkerchief over his face. Rosalie curled up in a nest of blankets beside him on one side, and Liesel on the other. Nothing short of actually picking up and carrying Rosalie away could induce her to go very far from Vati. Only Anna could take her firmly by the hand and do so. When anyone else tried she screamed and kicked so violently no one had the heart to attempt it more than once. Liesel still looked exhausted and grey, her face thinned down to bone, all the bonny pink and white prettiness faded. This was how her sister would look when she was old, Magda realized with a pang.

They had come across a wide, grassy plain, veering away from the coast, and fetched up along another river, which Mr. Meusebach assured them would lead all the way into the first way-station which Adelsverein had established. They were, he said, a day's journey or so from a town called Victoria. The wagons drew up into a meadow between the road and a loop of the river, where it ran shallow with a narrow lip of sand beach. Friedrich and Johann ran off to play, taking Anna with them. She thought that Hansi was watching them, but when she straightened up from re-packing the basket with the plates and ends of bread and butter, there was Johann, standing there with a look of frozen panic on his face, tears trembling from his eyes.

"Auntie Magda. We've done something."

"What is it, hearts-love? It can't be that bad."

"Yes it can, Auntie . . . but we didn't mean it!" and Johann began to cry in earnest, gasping out between sobs and pulling at her hand. "We built it with the wood we found . . . on the river . . . we didn't mean...oh, come quickly!" Magda, torn between the urgency, and knowing how the twins were such good lads at heart, followed that tugging hand, followed her half-brother down to the river, little believing that the boys could have done something that bad. Johann, after all, was the sensitive one. He always over-reacted. But Friedrich met them on the riverbank and grabbed her other hand. Her heart sank; where was Anna? Friedrich looked nearly as tearful as his twin.

"What have you done with Anna?" she demanded, sternly and both boys quailed, Johann bursting into fresh tears.

"Sh-she-s in the river!" he gasped out, between sobs. Friedrich pointed downstream.

"It went out into the current." he said woefully. "It's not our fault, Auntie Magda, it got out of our hands."

"What got out of your hands?" Magda shouted, and now Friedrich also dissolved into remorseful tears. They pulled her along the river bank, stumbling over rocks and mud as they gasped out their terrified and guilt-stricken apologies.

"We didn't mean it . . . it just happened . . . Auntie Magda, please don't tell Vati!" Around the lower bend of the river, where the water swept wide, deep, and smooth around a knot of trees, there was a white-bleached tree-trunk fallen and wedged against a line of boulders. It lay a fair distance out from the shore, nearly to the middle. Perilously wedged half-against it was a tiny raft of driftwood, bound together with rope and willow-slips, almost sinking under the weight of a child. Anna. She was a stoic, unlike her uncles, or maybe too young and trusting to recognize her own peril. Magda sized up the whole situation at a glance.

"Of course I shall tell Vati!" she shouted, shaking her hands free of the twins. She cupped them and turning towards the camp, screamed for help, screamed again and again, until Johann pulled at her apron and pointed wordlessly at the tiny raft, which now tilted to one side, tugged by the current. Anna now truly looked frightened.

"Auntie Magda?!" she called, pleadingly, and Magda knew she must go to her, this instant, now matter what the risk to herself. She screamed again, crying, "Anna! Keep still, I'm coming!" She ran out into the water, plunging into it knee-deep and staggering against the current bewildering her steps, wrapping her skirts around her legs. She stumbled over rocks, sank into the boggy bottom at every step, deeper and deeper into the river, thinking of nothing but Anna and the terror in her eyes.

Until something, something thin and hard as an iron bar closed around her, lashing her arms to her sides, pulling tight, and jerking her backwards with great force into the muddy shallows. She was aware of something large storming past her, but she was under the water, fighting to breathe, fighting to find her feet, to free her arms. A pair of strong hands reached down and helped her to stand. Magda came up from the river, gasping, furious and frightened. A young-looking man, at least she thought he was young until she noticed the lines around his eyes, stood her upright. He was saying something to her, something she couldn't understand in tones of voice meant to be reassuring. He was also taking something from around her . . . a long length of rope? Magda blinked; how had a loop of it come to be around her? Behind the young-looking man, other men on horseback lined the riverbank, all rough-looking Americans in travel-worn clothes, bristling with weapons; knives and guns, both long and short. None of them were those hired by Mr. Meusebach to guard the train. Another man on horseback plunged out into the deep water, the water threshing around his horses' legs. Was that what had passed by her, as she struggled in the water? At that moment, the fragile raft tipped finally to one side and Anna slid with a desperate tiny cry into the current. The man in the water dropped his reins, flinging himself from his saddle and dove after her.

Magda felt the man holding her up, the young-looking one with the old-looking lines around his eyes, take a sharply indrawn breath, although what she could see of his face was impassive, emotionless. Before he could let it out, two heads appeared above the flowing river, a fair head and a small brown one with the water streaming off them; the horse swam strongly, borne by current towards the bank a little farther downstream. The man with Anna under his arm swam powerfully, even with that burden. With a few strokes he was in water shallow enough to stand up. He waded out of it and dropped Anna into her arms as water ran from their clothing. Anna thrashed feebly, coughing and spitting water, crying more from astonishment than anything else, while her rescuer said calmly, "She should be all right, madam. I reached her before she was under for more than a few seconds."

Magda nearly dropped Anna from astonishment; she had understood every word. Surely that could not be happening; was this some kind of magic spell? She clutched the child as Anna clung to her frantically with arms and legs, and looked up. Here was other cause for astonishment, a man that much taller than herself. Saxon-fair, with calm blue eyes the color of the sky; she said the first thing that popped into her mind, "You talk like a man of Hesse."

"My grandfather," he answered serenely as if they were anywhere else than knee deep in a river and dripping wet. "Sorry about the lariat. The bank drops off quite suddenly, under water. And the current is very fast. You can't swim, can you?"

The young-looking man with the old-looking eyes standing at her back said something in English, and all the men on horseback around them laughed genially, even Anna's rescuer, as she answered, "No, of course not."

"Then why were you going out into the river, if you can't swim?" he asked, looking at her as if he was intensely interested in the answer.

"She is my niece, and she was frightened to death," Magda answered helplessly, "I couldn't not try!"

"That was silly," commented the blue-eyed man. "Brave, but silly." He was still looking at her, half smiling as if he were amused.

Who were these men? She wondered. They were a savage-looking lot. She saw now there were really only seven or eight of them, all dressed like common laborers albeit very well armed ones. One of them brought up the reins of the blue-eyed man's horse, a raw-boned grey beast with black feet and a shaggy black mane, while another retrieved his flat-brimmed hat from the river-bank, leaning down from his saddle to scoop it from the ground as if he were doing an equestrian trick and tossing the hat to its owner with a remark that made all the others laugh.

"Anna! Magda...what has happened!" Vati and Hansi shouted breathlessly, as Mr. Meusebach and a crowd of the folk from the caravan came rushing from the camp. The old-eyed young man handed Anna's rescuer a wide leather belt with two long pistols hanging from holsters attached to it. He was strapping it around his waist again, as Magda hugged the sobbing Anna to her.

83

"Magda, my heart, what has happened!" cried Vati, "Why are the boys crying?! What has happened, that you and the little one are all wet?"

Anna began howling in earnest. Hansi took her from Magda's arms and looked belligerently at the strangers crowding close.

"The boys were playing by the water," Magda answered. "They built a raft and began to play on it with Anna, and then the current took it away. These gentlemen heard me calling for help."

"Screaming like a wild cat being skinned alive," added the blue eyed man with deep and appreciative amusement. "We were coming along the road towards Victoria. We weren't told about any Comanche raiding parties with captives along this way, so Captain Jack made it our business to come and see what all the fuss was about!"

"Don't you dare make a sport of this!" Magda stamped her foot, not remembering she was still knee deep in water. It made a nice splash. "Our Anna was about to drown in your horrible river!"

"My river?" he answered. "It's not my river, it's a Texas river." He jerked his chin at the boys and his voiced turned very serious. "Look, you two . . . there is enough out here that will kill you dead if you turn your back on it. It's not like you have to go searching for it by doing something stupid."

At that, Magda's last shredded nerve gave way; to her horror she found herself trembling like a leaf in a gale. Vati put his arm around her and led her from the water, saying, "Magda, there, the little one is safe, calm yourself. The boys—I must think of some suitable punishment! They are safe too."

Hansi looked perfectly furious, and began speaking, but his words were cut off.

"Where did all you come from?" That was Anna's German-speaking rescuer again, "What on earth are you doing here."

The Baron—No, Mr. Meusebach answered calmly, "These people are immigrants under the auspices of the Society for the Protection of German Immigrants, bound for our way-station at the town of Neu Braunfels, then into our grant in the Llano country. I am John Meusebach, their commissioner in this country."

Anna's rescuer said something in startled English to the old-eyed young man. From Vati's momentary stillness, Magda knew that he had understood it.

Now Vati said formally, "I am Christian Friedrich Steinmetz. May I present my daughter, Miss Margaretha Vogel, and my son-in-law, Hans Richter? You have rescued my dear little granddaughter, Miss Anna Richter, and I regret that these two bad boys are my sons, Johann and Friedrich."

Vati frowned most severely at the boys, while Magda asked quietly, "Vati, what was it that he said in English, just then?"

"Something silly," Vati murmured quietly, while the clamor of exclamation around them covered his voice. "He said—I think—'Good God, Prince Fancy-trousers pulled it off!'" Vati shrugged, "I have no notion what they meant by this."

"Carl Becker, Sergeant of Rangers." The blue-eyed man who spoke German half-bowed, with equal formality and gestured towards the boyish looking man with the old eyes. "This is Captain Jack—but he is now Colonel Hays, who commands us." Becker looked bemused, as if the whole situation was a great fuss over nothing. His eyes kept wandering back to Magda in a curious manner. But Mr. Meusebach wore a look of awe and began to speak in English to him; apparently Colonel Hays was someone of prominence.

Vati said, "We are in your debt, entirely, Sergeant Becker. Might we repay your kindness by loaning you some dry clothing? We could not let you go on your way without offering at least that much of our hospitality, slight as it is." To Magda, he murmured, "He is taller than Hansi, but not so broad across . . . only until his own things are dry. You should change to dry clothes also, my dear, before you catch a chill."

"I would be grateful," Sergeant Becker answered and spoke quietly to his officer in English. What he said sounded humorous, for Colonel Hays chuckled and so did the other Rangers. It seemed that Mr. Meusebach was also offering the hospitality of the Adelsverein camp.

Vati said, with his arm solicitously around Magda, "Then… please to come with us. May I ask how you came to be here on the same road with us?"

"We were coming from Goliad, just west of here," Carl Becker replied, walking easily alongside, with his horse clumping obediently after led by his reins. "Colonel Hays is forming up a battalion of Rangers to serve with the Army."

"Conscription! God in heaven, isn't that one of the things we left behind?" Hansi's countenance lit-up angrily, and Carl Becker looked a little puzzled.

"No, that is not the way of things. Not here, and not with the Rangers. We don't fight our wars with press-ganged men. We're volunteers. The Rangers are chosen from the best fighters. Jack Hays sees to that."

"You had business in Goliad?" Vati asked. "You know it very well? Was that place not the scene of a most dreadful incident when General Santa Anna . . ."

"Yes," Carl Becker answered simply. There was a momentary stillness about him, although the expression of his face did not change, or the timbre of his voice. There was nothing more that he would say on that matter, Magda sensed. Fortunately so did Vati.

"Magda, my dear, did you know that Colonel Hays is quite famous, even as far as Bavaria? He is the scourge of Indian marauders throughout Texas, yet he appears to be hardly older than Johann and Friedrich!"

"And are you famous as well?" Magda asked of Carl Becker with a touch of malice. His description of her screaming still rankled and so did the way he kept looking at her.

He only smiled serenely, as the jibe went sailing past. "I am famous, but only in Texas, as the Ranger who was scouting a raiding party of eight Penateka Comanche around a campfire built in a little draw down beneath. The bluff-edge gave away under me, and I slid down twenty feet straight into the middle of their campfire."

"What did you do then?" Vati was openly fascinated. Magda thought sourly that he might be teasing them again.

"Shot my way out, of course." He looked vaguely apologetic, "and then put out the fire. My clothes were burnt. The others still talk about how I had to ride bare-arsed all the way back to the Clear Fork. Your pardon, Miss Margaretha, for mentioning that . . . but you did ask."

There was a glint of laughter, deep in those very blue eyes, and Magda thought wrathfully, '*That wretched, provoking man, he is teasing me again, how dare he!?*' while Vati and Hansi laughed, and then appeared vaguely embarrassed.

"You killed them? Those Indians?" she demanded.

He answered mildly, "That was our purpose, Miss Margaretha, hunting them in the Llano country. They had killed and taken captives. I will not tell of what they had done to those they took, but among them were a woman and her two babies. We did not get them back alive. Not after what had been done to them."

Vati patted her hand and said only, "Not every exploit is worthy of a verse in the Iliad, my dear."

They had reached their little portion of the camp by now. Liesel and little Rosalie were awake, Liesel demanding to know why Magda and Anna were all wet, what had happened to the boys, and who was this tall, wet, and diffident stranger leading a horse? Magda simmered with suppressed fury and embarrassment. Fortunately, Vati was equal to explaining it all, and Liesel bustled away to find some of Hansi's clean shirts and trousers. Sulkily, Magda opened her own bag, took out her one clean, best dress and a set of petticoats and withdrew to a tiny space in Hansi's biggest cart. When she emerged, the men were gone. Liesel was capably wringing the last drops of water out of Sergeant Becker's clothes and shaking her head over their condition.

"We'll hang them over the back of the cart—give me your things, too, Magda. I think everything will be dry by tonight. He does not have a wife, I think," Liesel added impishly.

"How do you know that?" Magda asked, as she squeezed water out of her petticoat. Anna's little dress already hung from the cart-tail.

"I'd think shame to let my Hansi go about, with his shirts in this condition. On the other hand, she might be a slattern when it comes to mending."

"I can't imagine why you should think I care," Magda snapped.

Liesel replied peaceably, "He saved Anna's life, of course—and maybe yours, too. You cannot swim! What would have happened if the current swept you both away?" She took the damp dress and petticoats out of Magda's hands and brushed her cheek with a light kiss, "What would we do if we lost you both, then? Be nice to him, Magda, for our sakes if not your own. Or at least be less prickly. Even better than that; mend his shirt for him."

"And why should I do him that particular favor?" Magda asked, and Liesel looked amused.

"If you don't know why, I am almost afraid to tell you. I have enough of my own mending to do—that is all."

Presently, Mr. Meusebach's teamsters called for hitch-up, and their daily march resumed. Magda and Vati walked with the boys to one side of the lurching wagons, out of the haze of dust ground up by their wheels. Vati sternly insisted that Friedrich and Johann remain under his eye, as punishment. They looked longingly after Mr. Meusebach's mounted guards, who patrolled up and down the length of the wagon-party.

"Might we have horses when we have our farm?" Friedrich pleaded. "No one walks here, Vati! Everyone rides a horse."

"I do not know if you would deserve something as fine as a horse," Vati answered, sternly. Magda calculated that he would be strict with the boys for perhaps the rest of the day at best.

"Look, there are the Rangers," Johann said; and it was indeed Colonel Hays and his men and Mr. Meusebach, cantering by in a great rush of hoof beats.

"They ride like centaurs," Vati's eyes followed them, almost wistfully, "as if they were one creature. I must remember to write to Simon about this. Do you see? Mr. Meusebach, he is a gentleman, and has been carefully taught how to sit on a horse. But the others; they ride as if they were born on horseback and have barely ever dismounted."

The last rider gallantly tipped his hat as they swept past, Carl Becker's blond head as distinctive among them as that checked white-and-blue shirt of Hansi's. Magda silently fumed; did he do that to make a mock of her again? Vati and the boys didn't think so. But she suspected that behind that bland face and those disconcertingly blue eyes, he was amused and laughing at her all the same. Never mind, she told herself and lifted her chin, I will be most crushingly polite to him.

When they made camp at the end of the day's march, she sat herself down with her mending-box, threaded a needle and set to work on the shirt as Liesel had suggested. She had the distinct feeling that Vati and Liesel and the others noticed, but wisely forbore to comment, observing the thunderous scowl on her forehead as she worked. Vati was reading a novel to the boys and Rosalie, attempting to teach them a little more English.

Really, it was as if the man never noticed that half the buttons were missing and those remaining were all odd. Magda picked out a rough darn made with glaringly mismatched thread, repaired it with tiny stitches and searched through her little square wooden mending-box for better buttons and some dark calico to patch the worst-worn portions. When she was finished, she folded it together with Carl Becker's other clothes and said calmly, "Vati, Sergeant Becker's clothing is dry. Did you see where they had camped this evening?"

"By the Baron's wagon, a little way along the river bank," Vati answered, distractedly. "Do you wish me to accompany you?"

"No, it is only a short way, and I shall be in sight of our campfire."

She did not particularly fear being offered any insult, rather she dreaded that Vati or another one of her family might witness her being teased, or made a jest of. She walked past Hansi's carts . . . one, two of the stores wagons, the spring-wagon that was Mr. Meusebach's and down towards the river-bank where the Rangers picketed their horses for the night. The men themselves lounged around a small campfire: no tents or comforts, merely a number of rough Mexican blankets and saddles scattered about. She hesitated; he was not among them, but Colonel Hays met her inquiring gaze.

"I am returning Sergeant Becker's clothing," Magda said, firmly. She didn't understand what he said in reply, but he pointed along the river-bank. One of the other men laughed in a coarse and knowing way. Magda lifted her chin and looked at him scornfully. Then she stalked away, along the way that Colonel Hays had pointed out. This was the second time that day she had walked along the riverbank. This time she was alone. Not running in a blind panic, led by hysterical children. This time she was calm, resolved. She walked around a clump of trees dipping their knobby knees in the river and a thicket of willows, and there he was, sitting and looking out at the river as it swept around another bend in a wide, shimmering reach.

He sat with his back to her, a double-barreled shotgun propped against a current-scoured dry branch. As she came closer, she saw that he had a dirty bit of canvas at his side. He was cleaning those two great pistols of his with bits of flannel soaked in oil. The pistols were disassembled, a profusion of matte metal components, all laid out in careful array, the empty holsters and gun belt laid on the grass close by, along with a lumpy haversack.

"I have brought your clothes," she announced. He didn't look around until she spoke, but he was not startled or surprised in the least.

"Thank you, Miss Margaretha. I am most grateful."

"You should be. Whoever does your mending, it is a disgrace."

"Ah." There was the amused mockery again. "There is no one to do my mending, unless it is my sister. Her name also is Margaret."

"Your sister?" Magda meant only to set down the bundle of clothes and leave, but this caught her attention. "You have a family here in Texas?"

"Of course. Margaret keeps a boarding-house in Austin. It was our home-place, once. We came there when I was very small. I don't remember living anywhere else."

He bent over his task again. Magda would have taken her leave then, but she looked out over the river and recalled the word picture she had painted for Anna, aboard the *Apollo*.

I would like to sit by a river in a green field, and hear the birds.

Here was that green field and the river, and birds alive and cheeping in the branches over their heads: a vision such as she had hoped to see, sea-sick and fearful in the dark and reeking passenger deck of the Apollo. At that moment Carl Becker asked curiously, "What was it like—your home-place in the Old Country?" He was as sincere as a child and she thought for a moment of how curious it was that he could speak the language, but still know nothing of his ancestral country. She carefully sat down on the grass, close enough to talk yet far enough for propriety and straightened her skirts.

"It was very old," she answered, thoughtfully. "Vati's family had lived there for hundreds of years. When Vati was a boy, he once found some old silver and gold coins as he was following the plough. They just turned up, in the dirt, those Roman coins. Someone lived there, or passed through in ancient times. There was a stone threshold to the main door into the farmhouse. But so many people had passed in and out that there was a hollow worn into it by their feet."

"That old?" he asked, and she nodded.

"Everything was perfect or so my mother said. Over the years, everything had been done that could possibly could be done to my father's house to make it more comfortable."

"It can't have been that perfect," he said. "You came here, after all."

She nodded, acknowledging. "Not enough land. Vati and Hansi wanted more land, enough to farm and keep us all. And they were afraid of conscription, when my brothers were old enough. Hansi was made to serve, for a little while. He hated it. But mostly, it was for land."

"Land," Carl Becker observed. "Everyone comes here for land. It's all that Texas has, but I am fairly certain there are no Roman coins buried in any of it . . ." He hesitated as if he would say more, but decided against doing so. But he was still looking at her, as if he wanted to ask a question.

"Why do you keep looking at me?" Magda demanded, bluntly.

"When I first saw you in the river," he answered, "I thought sure you were a Mex or an Indian. The black hair, you see."

"If that was a compliment, then thank you very much!"

"Those high-born Mex women turn heads, sometimes," he said solemnly, but his eyes had that half-hidden amused expression. "And there are some right pretty young Indian girls around."

"Then you should be giving your compliments to them, if that is how your favors run!"

"Oh, I would," he assured her, "but they often have very watchful fathers. Or brothers." The amused look broadened to an outright grin. "Husbands, even."

She didn't like the flustered feeling she had when he stared at her that way, but she couldn't think of anything proper to say to that. And then he asked, again with complete sincerity, "What was it like? In the ship, I mean."

"It was dreadful," she answered bleakly. To her horror she could feel tears starting in her eyes. With an effort, she forced them back. "A waking nightmare, we despaired of our lives, then. So crowded, and so dark and it smelled! People sickened and died! I pinned my life on a vision of sitting in a meadow, by a river like this. I can't tell you how much I longed to sit in the quiet by a river, and listen to the birds," and all the words spilled out. Mutti and little Joachim dying, burial at sea and the landing camp; of all of that and when she ran out of words, Magda found herself sitting beside a stranger on the bank of her dream river, hugging the bundle of clothes in her arms with tears running down her face.

Carl Becker handed her a bit of cloth, rather less grimy and reeking of tallow grease than the ones he was using.

"My mother died also. But I was not there. And it was no longer my home. My brother . . ." he paused, with that same stillness as when Vati asked about Goliad. Magda dabbed at her cheeks with the revolting cloth,

"You have a brother, as well as a sister?" she asked.

"No longer. But he also liked to sit out in the woods or by the river. Our father's farm was near the Colorado River. We would tell our parents that we were hunting, but more often we were just watching. I had my life saved once, by jumping into a river, but not this one."

"What is this river called, then?" Magda asked. "My father and Hansi have read so much about Texas and talked with the others, but sometimes I think that they do not know anything for sure. Nothing we have seen so far is anything like what we expected. Sometimes we hardly know who or what to believe; will our grants be in lands that look like this?"

"No, not much like this," Carl Becker answered, mildly. He finished reassembling one of his long pistols and gave it a last polish, before replacing it in his holster. "This is the best of the lowland country, you understand. Most of it has already been settled. You should know there are really three parts to Texas. This part is the first: flat and rich, with many rivers and easy to farm. This is shaped like the palm of a hand, with rivers for fingers, running down through it. Then there is the second part, the hills where those rivers begin. Just north of San Antonio de Bexar, it begins: a line of hills like a palisade, a curving wall. Limestone hills with forests of oak trees - meadows in the spring that are nothing but wildflowers, blue or red, or pink. I think myself it is very beautiful land but not so good for farming as this first part. That is where the Verein way-station is, where they are sending you for now. And then behind the hills is the last part, where the big Verein grant is to be. They call it the *Llano Estacada*. In Spanish it means 'the Staked Plain'."

"Why do the call it that?" Magda asked. "Have you been there?"

"Of course. I have been into it many times. It is an empty plain covered with short grass, mostly. It is not quite flat, but it looks as if it would go on to the ends of the world. There is also a sort of bush growing there, with leaves like the points of a spear. It sends up a single flower stem, taller than a man; that is what looks like stakes, for miles and miles. I do not think it would be good farm country. All the land can grow is grass—too harsh, too dry, even if it were not for the Comanche."

"The Indians?" Magda asked, "What have they to do with it?"

"They hold it," Carl Becker answered, simply, "Your Prince Solms may have a grant to part of it, but that is a piece of paper only. The Penateka, the Apache—they own it in reality. They raid as they will, and take what they please. There may not be any Roman coins buried in the ground here in Texas, but there is blood. Lots of blood spilled on it." He finished reassembling his second pistol and wrapped up the cloth and his cleaning tools: three little brushes and picks on a ring, and a strange little thing as long as her hand, with one bulbous end and a flat-leaf-shaped end. He held the heavy pistol in his hands for a moment, turning it over and over as and stroking the polished wooden grip if it were something he was just now seeing for the first time. "And that is why the Rangers are supplied with these. Jack Hays saw to it that we have a chance to match them in a fight when we take it to them." Magda felt a chill at his words, right down to her bones; Vati's gossip had not included this sort of bad news. Carl Becker looked sideways at her face and added, somberly.

"Prince Solms was warned about the Indians and the danger of sending settlers to the Verein grant in the Llano country. Colonel Hays told him. I was present and warned him also. We thought he had then reconsidered but Mr. Meusebach told us otherwise. I think Prince Solms did not want to hear anything that contradicted what he wished to believe. He wished to believe that all of Texas was like what he saw. He did not venture into the Llano."

"What shall we do?" Margo whispered, almost to herself. Carl Becker looked very grave.

"You have three choices, you Verein people. The first one is to go back. Not to Germany, unless you wish it. Somewhere else, more settled."

"We can't," Magda said, despairingly. "Most of our money went to pay the fees. And our home is sold. There is nothing to go back to, even if I would willingly set foot on a ship again. What are your other choices?"

"Make peace with the Indians one way or another," He answered simply. "Or this. Hold out your hands." She did so, holding her hands cupped together and he put his pistol into them. She nearly dropped it, from astonishment and from the weight. "Learn to fight, with this or something like it. This one fires five shots without needing to reload. Be careful with it, Miss Margaretha—it's loaded."

"So," she said with bitterness, "Those three choices—I do not think much of them, Sergeant Becker."

"They are all the choices there are," he answered obliquely, taking back his pistol from her. He replaced it in the other holster and picked up the roll of canvas with his tools. But before stowing them in his haversack, he took a couple of small apples out of it and a slender knife from his boot-top. "An apple, Miss Margaretha? These came from the trees that my father planted, when he and my mother first came to Texas. My sister picked these, the last of the season and stored them all winter in a barrel of sawdust." He gravely peeled and quartered them both, and handed an apple quarter to her. She ate it and took another; a little withered from storage, not quite as crisp as it would have been newly harvested but still something to savor after a long winter.

"Not quite an Eden, this Texas of yours," she remarked.

"And it was Eve who tempted Adam with an apple," he answered, giving her another piece. His hand brushed her fingers and lingered as if he would have liked to touch her again. "Still, I think my notion of paradise is an apple orchard."

"Perhaps you will plant one of your own some day," she said as he ate the last of his apple.

"Maybe - when I find the right place for it." He stood up, holding a hand down to assist her. "I hope that the Verein has found the right place for your family and you can make as good a place of it as you left behind. But you should remember," His eyes looked grave, sympathetic; how could she ever think he was laughing at her? "Texas makes equals of us all, remember that."

"If it doesn't kill us all first." she answered as she stood. Again, she thought how odd it was, speaking to a man that much taller than herself. "Thanks to you, it didn't kill Anna or me today—for which we are grateful. Loaning you some dry clothes and mending your shirt seem like very small things in return, but that is about all that we could do in our present circumstances."

He took the bundle of his clothes from her, saying "Well, it's more than what we usually get in the way of thanks, Miss Margaretha. I shall bring back the things that you loaned me, later. I probably will not see you after that. We must ride, very early in the morning."

"To the—what is it, the Llano country, to fight the Indians?"

"No," his eyes were unreadable, "South to fight the Mexes."

"Oh." That was an unsettling thought for Magda; a war, one that was not supposed to be happening which had nothing to do with them. "We shall pray for your safety, then—for all of you."

"Thank you, Miss Margaretha. We shall probably need it. Jack Hays would ride straight into Hell if he could, and we would all follow him most willingly."

"And you have a good reason for that?" Magda asked on impulse.

"One very good one—he'll never surrender." He tipped his hat again to her, adding, "It is nearly sundown, Miss Margaretha. Should I walk you back to your camp, then?"

"It is not necessary. I can find my own way," she answered and walked away before he could offer any more uncomfortable advice or gallantries. For her part, they were almost as disquieting as if he were still laughing at her.

* * *

Continuation of letter from Christian Friedrich Steinmetz, to Simon Frankenthaler: . . . we continued our travel towards the Verein establishment and way-station of Neu Braunfels, founded in a beautiful river valley, much reminiscent of our own beautiful hills and forested lands. We had made the acquaintance of a young man who seems to look on my dearest Magda with much favor. He has lived long in Texas, since childhood but is of a German family, and has given us much good advice about the countryside. It seems that although

Prince Solms had secured a vast tract of land for eventual settlement, times are not propitious for our people to settle there! Alas the many rumors of war between Mexico and the United States turn out to be a harbinger! Mr. Meusebach had contracted with diverse parties to transport our people from the landing camp on the coast, but with the expected hostilities to commence shortly, they have voided their contracts with the Verein. Our friends such as the Altmuellers must find their own way. Mr. Meusebach is only able to make such limited provisions as are within his own control, establishing another way-station settlement in the hills to the west, and hiring men such as Son Hansi to travel back to the coast with a small party and transport others of our people hither . . .

Chapter 6 – *Sophienberg*

Letter from Christian Friedrich Steinmetz: Written on 15 March 1846, from the town of Neu Braunfels on the Guadalupe River, to Simon Frankenthaler, Goldsmith of the City of Ulm in Bavaria.

My dear Simon, I write to inform you that we have arrived safely in the town recently established by the Adelsverein to serve our needs and to support our further ventures. Alas, I must tell you that our journeying days are not yet ended! It is still a very new town, although carefully laid out in a most beautiful situation with many fine houses already under construction. To my great joy there is a school established for the children, also a church and many other useful enterprises. I have made the acquaintance of Mr. Lindheimer, who has traveled widely in this part of the country. On political matters we are much in accord, and he is also extremely knowledgeable about native flora. He has collected a vast array of botanical specimens, which he has been very kind to show to me, and also has introduced me to many of his friends.

I should be happy enough to remain here but alas for our purposes, Neu Braunfels is already full to bursting. My family is once again crowded into one room, a small cabin built of timbers stood on end and roofed with branches, over which is piled a great layer of mud; such is called a "Mexican hut". Although it provides shelter from the cold weather, alas, of rain it is somewhat less effective. There are no farm plots left nearby, and son Hansi is extremely disparaging in any case.

* * *

"We passed up better farmland on our way here," Hansi observed, bitterly. He shifted Anna to his other knee. For lack of room and the darkness inside the little hut, which had housed the family upon whose town lot it sat until they had completed a finer, bigger log house, the Richter and Steinmetz families sat outside on crude benches and rounds of log set on end to make stools. Here in the hills it was cooler of an evening than it had been on the plains, almost as chill as it was on the coast. Enormously tall trees, with stately silver-white trunks stood in groves, holding up their bare branches to the sky where the sun was setting in a smear of orange and gold. A few stars pricked the dark velvet sky in the east.

Warm golden lantern light spilled from the windows and porches of those finished houses, including the sprawling log house at the top of the hill called the Sophienberg. Mr. Meusebach lived there, when he was not off on business, doubtless working late into the night trying to untangle the affairs of the Verein. He looked as haunted and harried as ever, Magda thought. War had broken out between Mexico and the United States. All of the Verein contracts to transport the German settlers from the desolate landing place had been broken. Hansi had made several trips with his carts and returned from the last of them shaking his head in despair. "The dead and the dying are scattered all along the roadside between Karlshaven and here. The sickness follows them. Pastor Ervendburg has gathered up enough all the orphans to his house. God knows, I don't want Anna to be one of them. We should leave here as soon as we can."

"But it is a beautiful place," Vati answered, almost pleadingly, "as beautiful as the Black Forest, or the hills of Switzerland. And with springs of water welling up from deep within the pools! Is it not the most amazing sight to behold?"

"You can't eat scenery," Hansi pointed out with considerable bitterness. "Prince Fancy-Trousers indeed! It doesn't surprise me that he picked this place. He was no farmer. I'd be surprised if he could tell one end of a cow from the other. What were they thinking? Were they all so dazzled with his title and fine clothes as to take his word alone on where to plant our futures?"

Vati chuckled wryly, "Hansi my son, you talk now like a republican and a radical. It does my heart good, it does. Until now I thought you had no interest in such dangerous political philosophies."

"I'll speak my mind freely then," Hansi replied, "since here we know there is no one listening to every word and running to denounce you to the police. Thank God Mr. Meusebach is not cut from the same idiotic cloth. He might have been one of the Firsts, but at least he is one of the useful ones. Vati, I think we should accept his offer."

"For his new settlement?" Vati sighed, "Another journey!"

"Vati, they promised us lands," Hansi scowled. "They promised us land and a house, and a year's worth of supplies until we brought in a crop. There is no way for them to fulfill that promise here. Sergeant Becker spoke well of the hill-country, did he not? He struck me as one who would know farming."

"He said the valley lands were good, the hillsides less so," Vati answered cautiously. He was happy here, with his friends and the boys in school; he did not mind living in the mud hut.

That evening, when the Ranger came to return Hansi's clothes, he had stayed and spoken long with Vati and Hansi, sitting by their fire and patiently answering a volley of questions. His eyes strayed often towards Magda, who had pretended not to notice. She was confused, and unsettled in her mind. He was unlike any other man she had met, teasing her gently one minute, and listening to her like an old friend the next. She had been putting off clumsy attempts at flirtation from other men who had come with the Verein since they had taken ship at Bremen. His attentions were altogether different. She finished the washing-up and amused the children with a few games before sending them off to bed, always aware of his regard. They had not spoken to each other again, save for when he took his leave, saying, "Good night, Miss Margaretha," as if it were a love-poem. Liesel, preternaturally aware of any possible romantic attachment, had looked between them both and seemed much amused.

"He is smitten," she had announced in a whisper, as they undressed for bed that evening, and Magda had snapped, "I can't imagine what would make you think that!" Liesel had only looked even more amused. No one had dared mention Sergeant Becker to Magda's face after that. In the morning, Colonel Hays's little company was gone, the dust long-settled in the tracks of their horses on the road north. And Magda could not decide if she were relieved or disappointed, although for many days she had looked twice at any

man who rode past on a grey horse with black feet and a black mane, and then chided herself for doing so.

"I would take his word on that," Hansi declared, firmly. "The word of one who lived all his life in this country—not leave it for one of the Firsts to decide, even one as useful and well-intentioned as Mr. Meusebach. But I will accept his offer to go to the new settlement. We must go forth with this party, or we will have to accept only leftovers."

Vati's eyes wavered towards Magda. He would, she realized, have asked Mutti what she thought of this, looking to Mutti to support him. But Mutti was gone, the burden fallen to her. She wrenched her memory from the picture of Mutti's canvas-wrapped corpse sinking under the waves. She ordered herself to think of the meadow and the quiet-rippling river, birds squabbling cheerfully in the branches above, Carl Becker's calm blue gaze and level voice:

Limestone hills, with forests of oak trees, and meadows in the spring that are nothing but wildflowers, blue or red, or pink. I think myself it is very beautiful land." You can't eat scenery, thought Magda, despairingly. *But the other land, the land which Prince Solms had consigned them to, against all good advice - that wouldn't do either. "They call it the Llano Estacada. In Spanish it means 'the Staked Plain. I do not think it would be good farm country. Too harsh, too dry even if it were not for the Comanche.*

"I agree with Hansi," Magda answered firmly. "Mr. Meusebach himself selected the place for this new town, over others which he has himself seen. He is sensible and careful, not like the Prince." Vati's face fell, almost comically tragic. "I am tired also of wandering and living in caves and stables, Vati. But I think we should go with his first party." She looked at her sister and added, "Don't cry, Liesel - it will be just this once more." But she sighed as she said it, cuddling Rosalie to her, the child curled half-asleep in her lap and drowsily sucking her thumb.

"Out into the wilderness!" Liesel looked crushed. "Among all those savages, just when we were about to settle down!"

"There are too many of us packed in here, my heart," Hansi reasoned, patiently. "And the best lands hereabout are already dispersed to others. It will only be a year or so before the new town will be as far along as this."

"I own, I am looking forward to mending clocks and watches again," Vati said, regretfully, "but I may do it there as well as here. We shall let Mr. Meusebach know of our intentions in the morning."

* * *

...my daughters and the boys and Hansi, all of us have agreed. We shall depart next week, with our recent acquaintances the Arhelger and the Lochte families, and some others, all fit and adventurous, with a dozen mounted Verein soldiers to protect us, and all things necessary to at last begin our new lives. We will be under the direction of Mr. Bene the surveyor: an able and energetic person charged with carrying out this particular enterprise. (I have heard a rumor that he was once a Prussian officer who was asked to emigrate under a cloud of scandal, having stabbed a man in Koln. Such are the people one meets here!) I have used a little of my money to buy seeds to plant a garden, and Mr. Lindheimer has promised to send me more. Liesel has procured a fine hen with a clutch of eggs from one of the established families, which she hopes to have hatch, so that we may start our new farm with a fine flock of chickens. She is much taken with the well-being of the hen, and keeping the eggs warm, and son Hansi has made a small crate lined with hay and lint for them. So may this endeavor prosper, and serve as an omen for others!

* * *

Twenty heavy-laden carts, the clumsy Mexican kind with solid wheels, a couple of large wagons and Hansi's light and useful farm carts stood assembled with their teams and drivers in the open ground before the Sophienburgs' deep porch. In the chill of an early April, the breath of the oxen and the folk clustering around made fine clouds of mist in the air before their mouths and nostrils. Magda hugged her warmest shawl around her, pulled over her head like a peasant woman. Her fingers were cold; oh, her hands were always cold in this country! But not her toes, clad in stout new shoes from the Adelsverein stores. Pastor Ervendburg had just finished blessing them all, followed by a wandering missionary priest, Father Dubois, who offered a blessing in Latin, and an unkempt little man who claimed to be the Methodist lay-preacher. Mr. Meusebach stood patiently by until the lay-preacher had exhorted them for perhaps five minutes and Vati muttered irreverently to Magda, "If such exists, the deity must be bored out of all patience with this kind of mummery. Were we not supposed to have an early start?"

"Shusssh!" Magda hissed, but Mr. Meusebach also seemed impatient. When the lay-preacher drew a breath, Mr. Meusebach thanked him courteously but in a tone that brooked no argument and stepped to the front of the porch.

"My friends, I do not propose to delay the start of your journey for much longer, not with such a task at hand as this. Virgil said *Tantae molis erat Romanam condere gentem*—with such great labor was built the Roman people. The labors you are embarking upon today will, I am certain be great, but they will not be fruitless. You will be doing your part to build as great a nation . . . even a greater nation than Rome. You are the first to take up this endeavor but you will not be recorded as being among the least. And as you stride forth into the wilderness, know this: you bear with you our hopes and our prayers for your safety and success."

Mr. Meusebach nodded towards Mr. Bene and the little band of soldiers and stepped down from the porch. He went from family to family, quietly saying a few words as the first carts began creaking slowly down the hill towards the muddy track leading west, into the blue-shadowed hills, following the small troop of mounted Verein troopers. He spoke to the tall Lochte boys, and their mother and father, and then he approached Vati and his family. He shook Vati's hand and then Hansi's, saying, "Ah, Richter, I regret you could not make another trip to the landing for us. A good wagon-master is above price. Thank you for your work, and the best of luck… Steinmetz… there will be work for a man of your skills, never fear, even if it is only keeping those imps of yours out of trouble." Anna and Rosalie sat in Hansi's cart with Liesel, both of them already half asleep, sheltering under the folds of Liesel's shawl like chicks under the wings of their mother. Mr. Meusebach gallantly tipped his hat to them, and added quietly, "Miss Margaretha … you will keep your brothers away from playing with boats, then? Unless there is a dashing rescuer at hand, of course." Magda blushed furiously.

"Alas, our most reliable rescuer is off to fight in Mexico!" Vati answered. "A pity, but not a waste, if he only impresses the enemy there as much as he has impressed the boys! Well, come along, Magda. Our great labors await us." He took Magda's arm, and they followed Hansi's cart with the boys, picking their way down the hill, and avoiding the worst of the mud, while Magda silently wondered for how much longer she would have to endure jests about rivers and dashing rescuers.

In two days, they had crossed over the first range of hills and begun descending into the valley beyond, towards the course of a small river. It was empty country, of forests of oak trees cut with ranges of hills and outcroppings of limestone like the bones of the land. The carts moved very slowly, jolting over the ruts and rocks, following the faint track into the west. Such an empty land is this country, Magda thought, as empty as the very beginning of the world. Not even any roads, but what they made for themselves, shifting rocks out of the way, and filling in the little watercourses so that the wagons could cross over.

In Albeck, one could scarcely go for a walk in the woods without seeing some little reminder that people had lived long and left many marks on the land. There was hardly a hilltop not crowned with a ruinous tower, or a field not edged with an ancient stone wall or hedgerow. Stone terraces framed the fertile hillsides, and there was no such thing as an un-bridged river. It had been thousands of years since where they came from had been a wilderness such as this. Everything around Albeck was the results of many lifetimes of work, and sometimes Magda quailed at the thought of all the work necessary to make this empty land even one-quarter as fine and comfortable as their old home had been.

Their ox-teams plodded so very slowly, and to ride was such a jolting discomfort that nearly everyone preferred to walk, it being no great effort to keep up. In fact, Magda often found herself and the little girls walking faster than the carts, with very little exertion and then having to wait for them to catch up. They camped at night, setting up tents and brush bowers in whatever green meadow Mr. Bene and the troopers had selected for them.

As Helene Altmueller had predicted, Anna took her responsibility for little Rosalie with great seriousness. She combed her hair and fastened the back of Rosalie's dress, attentively seeing to her needs, much to Liesel and Magda's amusement. Little Rosalie bloomed like her namesake and looked nothing at all like the frantic, filth-caked orphan that Vati had rescued from the desolate camp on the coast.

"She isn't anything like the baby," Liesel confessed, sitting on the ground at their camping place, with Rosalie gathered into her lap and her chin resting on Rosalie's red-gold curls as the child clung to her with exuberant affection. "But I find that I am not grieving for him quite so much. Strange, isn't it?" Magda sat with Anna in her own lap, quietly marveling over how Anna did not seem the least bit jealous of Rosalie and answered, "No, not at all . . . she seems to love everyone and in turn, everyone loves her." And so they did, for Rosalie had become a beautiful, sweet-tempered child with a ready smile and a happy way of making friends once she was less inclined to cling to Vati.

"It is good that she does not remember very much," Magda added.

"I remember!" Anna spoke up stoutly, from around Magda's collar-bone.

Magda asked affectionately, "What do you remember, Annchen? Do you remember the big ship?" Anna nodded her head firmly and Magda persisted, "Do you remember Albeck? Do you remember our old home? What do you remember about it, Anna?"

"The doves . . . they flew away. And Opa reading by the fire." She screwed up her little, serious face. "He read to me and Ros'lie."

"But he couldn't have, Annchen—that was before we found Rosalie," Magda answered gently, but Anna insisted.

"He did . . . he read to me and Ros'lie by the fire."

Liesel's eyes met hers, over the heads of the little girls, and Magda laughed a little.

"Not to wonder; sometimes I must remind myself also that we have not always had a little sister."

"Leave it to Vati to arrange another child, without Mutti's help," Liesel agreed.

During the evening of the second day as they made camp, a lone Indian strode out of the nearby woods bearing a fresh-killed deer across his shoulders. This created a small commotion amongst them all, especially the women, although the nearest Verein soldier, a quiet man named Conrad Merz, did little more than just watch warily as the Indian walked up to the Steinmetz's campfire.

"Looks like a Delaware," Conrad offered softly. "An eastern tribe, pushed out of their lands. They're friendly enough. And the Baron ... Mister Meusebach, he has made agreements with them. We have nothing to fear."

"I hope you're sure of that," Hansi answered, just as softly. Magda regarded the lone Indian with some apprehension and no little curiosity: there had been Indians in Galveston, but those seemed to be sad, degraded specimens. This Indian was a wiry man, a little less than medium height without a bit of spare flesh on him, and so weathered from exposure that he could have been anywhere from Magda's age to a patriarch of Vati's years. A trickle of blood from the deer carcass ran across his bare chest. He carried an ancient flintlock and a small leather bag on a strap that crossed his body from one shoulder, and when he reached the edge of the campsite, he dropped the deer and looked at them.

"What does he want, then?" Hansi looked up from where he was mending a bit of harness, although he, like Conrad, glanced quickly aside to assure himself that the old carbine that he had bought to protect himself on his forays to the coast was within reach. The Indian, who seemed to perceive their bafflement, took the little bag from around his body and shook it; it rattled.

"Ah," Conrad said, with an expression of enlightenment. "I think he wishes to trade the venison for shot and powder for that antique shooting-piece of his."

"What do you advise?" Hansi asked.

Conrad answered, "Do so . . . the Delaware are friendly enough and almost civilized. Not Comanche, anyway. And it's a fat-looking deer. Just don't give him enough for his whole damned tribe."

Hansi measured out a half a handful of shot, and a generous quantity of powder twisted in a paper quill. The Delaware hunter nodded briefly; obviously, that was an acceptable trade. He loped away into his woods, vanishing silently into its depths like a spirit of the wilderness.

"Supper!" remarked Conrad, eagerly. "Who has a knife then? We shall have a fine supper tonight!"

"It was my powder stock and bullets traded for the deer," Hansi pointed out. "So by rights, the deer belongs to me, and my family."

"Right then," Conrad answered. "Then am I invited for supper? If he comes tomorrow, we shall trade out of the Verein stocks."

"Just repay me for what I gave to the Indian and you and the others may take of it as you like," Hansi answered.

Magda added, "And if you could skin and dress it somewhere that we won't have to look at the mess?"

"But of course, Miss Magda!" And Conrad capably hoisted the deer onto his own shoulder and carried it a little way from camp. They dined well on it that night, although the bread which Magda contrived from the maize flour provided to them from the Verein stores tasted like dry sawdust.

"It is coarse stuff," she said distastefully. "I believe they grind flour from the harvest when the pigs won't eat it."

"Most curious, " Vati set aside his share of it, "I have read that American maize is a most useful and delicious commodity and capable of being prepared in many delightful ways."

"We had best find out exactly what they are," Liesel added, "before we break our teeth on it. What I wouldn't give for a good loaf of rye bread!"

"All in good time, my heart," Hansi said, jauntily. "Say, two years at best." He wiped his mouth of grease and savory juice from the venison and mused, thoughtfully, "Juniper berries . . . venison with juniper berries."

"Men—you all think with your stomachs!" Magda tossed her portion of the bread into the fire. Liesel giggled, murmuring quietly,

"When they're not thinking with something else! It was a good attempt, Magda. Maybe we should try boiling it. Surely there is something to do, to make it fit for humans!"

"I think it is good!" Friedrich piped up and Magda laughed.

"Bravely spoken in defense of my cooking, little brother, but between the two of you growing boys, you'd eat everything down to the legs of the table."

"That's it!" Hansi slapped his forehead in mock amazement. "A use for Magda's bread! She could bake a big enough slab, and we could carve a table out of it. As hard as the finest oak and very durable—think of the polish it would take!"

"You are being silly!" Magda began, bursting into laughter as Vati guffawed and Friedrich began miming eating such a table.

"See... here's me, carving it up with a knife and fork!"

Even Anna and Rosalie began to giggle, although it was only because everyone else was suddenly struck by the same ridiculous picture, and Magda laughed until the tears came, only thinking afterwards, as she curled up in her blankets, curving her body around the sleeping Anna and Rosalie: *That was the first time since we left Albeck, the first time since Mutti died that we have laughed so hard...all of us at some silly imagining, as if there was not a care in the world. How nice to know there is still laughter in the world.*

But tragedy still had the ability to reach for them: the next morning, as they reassembled for the day's journey, one of the soldiers dropped his pistol. As it fell on the ground, the hammer caught and it fired a single bullet. Magda and Friedrich were walking close by, with Mrs. Lochte. Magda flinched at the sound of the shot, and at Friedrich's almost simultaneous cry of shock and pain.

"Oh, my god," Magda looked down at her little brothers' foot, gushing blood from a tear in his leather shoe. "What has happened?!"

"The poor child," cried Mrs. Lochte. "The bullet stuck him just there!"

"Here, Fredi, lie down!" Vati came running up, paling at the sight of the blood.

"It doesn't hurt," Friedrich insisted, although he had tears in his eyes, and his face was pale. Together, Vati and Magda eased off his shoe, as Mrs. Lochte capably gathered him into her lap. By misfortune, the bullet had grazed Friedrich across the top of his foot. Although missing the bones, it scored a bloody gouge across his flesh. The soldier picked up his pistol and looked as near to crying as Friedrich did.

"Miss . . . Sir, I am so sorry, it was an accident . . . truly I had no intention . . ."

"What can we do, Vati!" Magda asked, "There is no doctor among us. What kind of medicines do we have, to treat this?"

"It does not look so bad," Mrs. Lochte said comfortingly to Magda. "My boys had worse hurts, when they were small! Oh, such worries I had for them! But it all worked out well." She patted Magda's hand, and Magda for a moment felt like throwing herself into Mrs. Lochte's arms and crying for gratitude for her cheerfulness. Mrs. Lochte was a handsome and indomitable matron, the mother of two grown sons, each more strapping than the other. She scandalized Liesel by wearing men's trousers under her skirts. Of all the women in the wagon party she was the most adventurous and seemed to take the whole matter very much in the same spirit as the men did.

They could doctor poor Friedrich with nothing but the last of a bottle of whiskey, brought out by one of the teamsters with somewhat of an embarrassed face. Conrad Merz sponged some it over the wound, while poor Friedrich bit his lips and tried not to let a sound emerge. He held Magda's hand so very tightly that she had bruises by the next day. They bound up his foot with cold-water compresses and made a place for him in the largest wagon, thinking and hoping that would be enough.

"After all, we cannot go back," said Mr. Bene, who had been summoned from scouting the day's march, ahead of the train. "Although if it begins to mortify, two of us shall put him on a horse and make all speed back to New Braunfels to put him in the care of Doctor Koester. That is the best we can do, Mr. Steinmetz."

"My son is young and healthy," Vati answered, optimistically. "He has taken injury before and recovered; I don't expect this to be much different."

But by afternoon when they made camp, the edges of the wound were red and swollen, and Magda felt her heart begin to sink within her. She felt his cheeks and forehead; he was already in a low fever. She sent Johann to the brook by their campsite to soak the compress in cold water, to wring them out and bring them back, cool and soothing. When he returned, there was a shadow at his heels: the same Indian from the night before, again with a dead deer on his shoulders.

"Oh, give the man some powder and shot," Magda said, distractedly. "Can anyone think of a way to tell him to go away?"

But the Indian dropped the deer carcass close by the fireside, as lordly as one of the Firsts, confident that his payment was assured. Distractedly, Vati took up Hansi's belt-pouch, and measured out a half handful of shot and another of powder, but the Indian did not accept them and go away. He came closer, examining Friedrich's foot. He stood over them first, and then even closer, stooping over the wounded foot, close enough to take a sniff of the inflamed flesh. Then it seemed to Magda that he looked at them with an impatient and exasperated expression and loped off into the woods.

"What was that in aid of?" Liesel wondered, and she and Magda exchanged puzzled looks over Friedrich's feverish head. "Magda, all I can think of to do is to go on with the cold compresses.

Poor Fredi; this must be the very first time ever that it was not your fault in the least."

Magda went to wring out the compress cloths in the brook, but when she returned, the Indian hunter had emerged from the woods again. He carried a handful of green leaves, some kind of fern, Magda thought. He squatted, and crushed several fronds, kneading them until the leaves were bruised and giving up some of their juices. Then he pressed the green pulpy mess into the reddened and puffy-edged gash on Friedrich's foot. The remainder he stuffed into his leather bag, and he made a gesture with his hand, a circling gesture. When Magda looked baffled, he took one of the compress cloths out of her hand with an impatient gesture and wrapped it tightly around Friedrich's foot, pressing the leaves well into the gash. He nodded once and swept a hand from horizon to horizon overhead and stalked away into the woods.

Both Vati and Johann observed with great interest.

"I believe he was administering some kind of native medicinal substance," Vati said. "How most peculiarly kind; I own we were not given to expect this sort of charity from them. Quite the reverse, in fact."

"I wonder what they are... those leaves," Johann appeared fascinated. "If we only knew what they were and how to find them!"

"And what they would be useful for, aside from open flesh wounds." Vati's face lit with interest. "My herbarium would be so useful in determining what it might be..."

"It is packed, deep in the wagon with your other books, Vati," Magda reminded him, "Fredi, how does your foot feel, now?"

"About the same," Friedrich answered, woefully. In the morning, Magda thought he did not seem feverish and when they opened the compress, the edges of the wound did not appear to be so puffy, or red.

"Although, I am not sure it is just my imagination, seeing what I wish to see," she said to Vati, who answered stoutly:

"It is not worse than last night, I am absolutely certain," He tousled Friedrich's head, affectionately. "See, Fredi, you will get better, I am sure of it."

To their very great astonishment, the lone Indian appeared that evening, as they set up their camp for the night. He strolled through camp as if he had been invited, so perfectly at ease that no one had any thought of alarm. When he came to the Steinmetz's campfire, he sought out Friedrich, and crouching down, unwound the compresses.

"What is he doing?" Liesel asked, in astonishment.

Hansi replied with much amusement, "My heart's love, it looks for all the world like a doctor's house call."

Their visitor sniffed critically at the wound, but seemed to approve progress, for he did not seem as impatient as he had the night before. He tossed away the limp remnants of the herb he had applied the night before. He took then a fresh handful from his little pouch, bound them against Friedrich's foot and stalked away into the woods, just as before.

"I wonder if our friend is going to turn up every evening," Vati wondered, with intense interest. "How wonderful it could be if we could only speak his language."

"I suppose he must be following us," Magda offered. "Did not we read about how shrewdly the Indians track game and such?"

"Well, it's no great chore to track us," Hansi answered. "With our wagons and stock and all of our people? We might as well have a brass band."

"I wonder why?" Vati searched around on the ground, until he found a few of the leaves the Indian had thrown away. "Ah-ha! I shall save these! If I cannot work out what it will be, I shall send some to Simon. His nephew is a doctor and botanist; terribly learned. What a wonder it would be, if it is a useful plant unique to these hills and valleys! I wonder if I have a small container…" his voice trailed off, as he bustled off towards the cart with their stores in it.

Hansi watched him go, with a smile of wry affection and said to Liesel and Magda, "Do you know, Vati will never be old; he may age, but he'll never be old."

"Hansi, you would have never have said something like that, back in Albeck," Magda observed. Hansi looked startled.

"It would have never occurred to me," he said, thoughtfully. "I don't suppose I looked at things, much. There was no point, really.

Everything was always the same. Here things are so different; one must pay the greatest attention. Something might be important, something that we should consider, even though it might seem of little consequence."

The train made little progress on the next day, for it rained during the night, a heavy downpour that ran through their tents and soaked the blankets of everyone lying on the ground. In the morning, the only possible route for them led across a muddy, boggy tract of land. It was necessary to gather rocks and gravel to pack into the worst places, to make a firmer footing for the heavily-laden wagons. It slowed their progress and left everyone exhausted and covered in mud, so they did not make nearly as much progress as expected. But that evening, the lone Delaware hunter appeared again, unwrapping Friedrich's foot and applying another handful of his herb remedy. Conrad Merz silently paid out a handful of shot to Hansi, for they had made a bet on the Indian appearing yet again. Hansi triumphantly offered half of it to the Indian, who seemed to shrug and accept it.

"He does not need it," Vati commented, fascinated. "I think he only accepted out of courtesy. How amazing, to need only such few things, living in harmony with the woods and meadows."

"A Garden of Eden, Vati," Magda noted dryly. "He appears very weathered. It must be rather a taxing existence, all things considered."

"Possibly," Vati agreed, his eyes shining with interest and curiosity. "But think on the appreciation of nature and all its glories..."

"Glories best appreciated from under a strong roof and behind a fine glass window, I think." Magda replied.

"Magda my heart, you have no poetry in your soul," Vati chided her.

"Probably not," she agreed. "Dearest Vati, you think too much of Rousseau and his savage nobility. The life they lead in reality must be very hard, indeed. I don't think it is very elevating to the character at all to sleep on cold ground, and have the rain running into your bed."

"No, it isn't" Vati answered, looking momentarily downcast, but then he brightened and said, "But it all is so interesting, isn't it?"

"Yes, dear Vati; it is that."

In the afternoon of the day after, which dawned fair and clear, their wagons followed a gentle bend in the little river towards higher and less boggy ground. Mrs. Lochte walked back along the line of wagons and carts, leading the Strackbein girls, Elizabeth and her little sister Christine by the hands.

"Magda, Liesel—you must come with us, there is the most wonderful sight up ahead! It is like the most beautiful garden you can imagine," Mrs. Lochte said, enthusiastically.

Magda reflected that Mrs. Lochte, like Vati, would age but never be old. She lifted Rosalie to her hip, and asked, "What is it?"

"Something more beautiful than I can describe," answered Mrs. Lochte. "You really must see it for yourselves." So they went with her, walking faster than the plodding oxen, ahead of them all, to where Conrad Merz and Mr. Bene and a couple of the other Verein soldiers stood with their horses, on the crest of a low hill, seemingly struck to stillness contemplating the glorious view beyond. A fair green meadow opened out at their feet. The nearest trees were at some distance, and all the space between was thick with dark-blue flowers. They grew in clusters, tipped with white, but so many and so close together that they almost hid the grass and the farthest reaches appeared as a solid carpet of blue.

"Aye, that's a fair sight, that is," remarked Mr. Bene. "There was hardly a one of them in bloom when we returned by this way last month."

"Oh!" said Magda, breathlessly. So it was as true as Carl Becker said, about meadows of nothing but wildflowers. "He said it was beautiful, but I didn't really believe him."

Overhead, clouds as fair as drifts of new wool drifted across the sky, and their shadows followed them across the rippling grass and the glorious flowers. Rosalie wriggled to be let down, and she and Anna and the Strackbein girls ran, laughing joyously into the meadow, wading into that waist-high ocean of wildflowers.

"Ah," Vati appeared at her side, polishing his glasses. "I would not have believed myself, hearing tell of this. Are they common, do you think? I should like to dry and press some, between the leaves of a book. Simon would find this of such interest. Who was it told you of beautiful meadows such as this, Magda my heart? Was it that young man whose name we barely like to mention, since you betray certain feelings whenever that happens?"

"I do not!" Magda answered indignantly, but Vati only smiled. "But...yes. He did. We talked for a little and he was very kind."

"When he came to our camp that evening, I think he wished to speak more with you," Vati said. "Not Hansi or I, although he was most civil in answering our questions. I noticed that he kept looking towards you. Why did you not encourage him? I think he would have welcomed your interest."

"Oh, Vati, I don't know," Magda sighed. "I was embarrassed. I thought he was laughing at me, at first. But then he listened to me talk about our old home, and the ship, and how horrible it was. I felt that he was being very kind, even though he paid me the oddest sort of compliment. But then he was so quiet, as if he didn't want to say anything more but warnings and advice. And besides that," she added firmly "he was going off to fight in Mexico. I don't suppose we shall ever see him again."

"Too true, I suppose," Vati admitted, sadly. "Such a waste— for I really think he would have suited you, being of complimentary tempers. You should be married, Magda; your mother would have wished so. And there are so many likely young men among the Verein settlers. It worries me that you do not seem to consider any of them seriously."

"I would wish to be the reason for any of them to double their land-hold, instantly? When they look at me, all I can think is that they are picturing a larger farm. I would not ask for tempestuous romance, Vati, but I would like something that is not a matter of cold calculation."

"I think we all wish for that, when we are young." Vati patted her hand, comfortingly. "And I would almost be willing to say that young Becker would offer you romance, perhaps not of the tempestuous sort. I do not think it would be in his nature. But enough of that, my dear; shall we go and pick some flowers for Simon? I shall feel very silly if there are other meadows like this along our way. Conrad says we shall be another three days, crossing into the next valley, and then following that river to where our town has been marked out."

"There will be other meadows like this," Magda answered. "He said there would be all colors of flowers."

"Oh, good, I shall pick some of those for Simon as well." Vati looked very sympathetic, and added, "Do not despair of seeing him again, my dear. I think he will return. He had the look of a very determined man."

"I don't know if that counts for anything, in a war, Vati," Magda replied. Vati sighed and let the subject alone after that. She gathered an armful of flowers, as did the girls.

When she climbed back into the cart to show the flowers to Liesel, she discovered many thorny little burrs clinging to the hem of her dress and Anna and Rosalie's also, which drew blood from her thumb when she began pulling them loose from the fabric.

"Everything here has barbs, or stings, or is poisonous," said Liesel, in exasperation as she bloodied her own fingers helping her sister. "It's hardly worth going to admire something beautiful, if it draws your blood in penalty!"

"Perhaps that is its price, here." Magda sucked the pinpricks of blood from her thumb. "Every beautiful thing ringed around with thorns, just to keep it safe and to make sure we appreciate it! What are you smiling for, Lise?"

"Nothing," Liesel answered. "Roses and thorns, sister, roses and thorns."

Chapter 7 – *Into the West*

Letter from Christian Friedrich Steinmetz: "Written in haste, 10 May 1846 in the wilderness west of Neu Braunfels, to Simon Frankenthaler, Goldsmith of the City of Ulm in Bavaria.

My Dear Simon: I am sending this short letter with one of the Verein soldiers, Conrad Wehmeyer. He has instructions to post it to you. (I also enclose some very interesting pressed flowers and leaves which we have found on our journey.) We arrived with much rejoicing some two days since, after a journey of two weeks...

* * *

They crossed over the last range of low hills and descended into a wide, gently sloping valley. A river the color of green-bottle glass flowed down through it, down the center of a wide expanse of pale tumbled stones and white gravel. They sent up camp on a knoll overlooking that small river, and Mr. Bene jauntily told them that they had nearly reached the site of the new settlement.

"One more day . . . not even that. We'll cross the river in the morning."

"Such good news," Vati enthused, over supper, "and Fredi's foot is so well-healed, that we have not seen our Indian friend today."

"So it is," Magda remarked. "I almost miss his presence, he has been so regular in attending on us. I do wonder why he did so?"

"I guess it must be rather dull during the winters," Hansi shrugged. "Perhaps we were as much interest to him, as he was to us."

"Tomorrow," Liesel said softly to Magda, as they washed dishes, after supper. "I can hardly believe it! Only one more day." She sighed, happily. Looking at her in the glow of the campfire light, Magda thought that Liesel might be finally recovered from her sickness on the Apollo. She looked as blooming and as pretty as she had ever been, as if the whole ghastly sea-voyage had only been a bad dream. Dear Lise, out of the cellar and on the highest tower once more.

"Have you planned out your new house?" she asked.

Liesel giggled, happily, "I have. Poor Hansi thinks that he will have to build me a palace, but I have it all worked out in my mind. A little stone house of four rooms, nothing less . . . or maybe fachwork; it depends on what is to hand. But stone floors and windows looking east and south to catch the morning sun. And always a bowl of flowers on the windowsill."

"You might not have it right away," cautioned Magda.

Her sister answered, firmly, "I know that. But I will have it. And as soon as we have our land, I will mark out exactly where it is to be."

"You sound very sure," Magda said. "You have Hansi wound well around your little finger," and Liesel giggled deliciously, as she always did.

"Yes, sister, but it's not my little finger." Seeing Magda's look of puzzlement, she added knowingly, "Oh, you'll understand when you marry that handsome soldier of yours; the one who rescued Anna from the river."

"I cannot imagine why everyone seems to think that!" Magda complained bitterly. "First Vati and now you. It is really quite vexing, how everyone seems to assume! I've barely had ten minutes conversation with the man and that including being dragged out of a river!"

Liesel merely smiled, and Magda wondered by what means her sister had come into so much wisdom about men. Perhaps being married had something to do with it. "Perhaps I do assume. But a man whose eyes followed me like his followed you; I could make him do anything, if I cared to."

"Well, I didn't care to," Magda snapped.

Liesel only answered mildly, "Well, you should have! He was certainly very handsome and he spoke so well! I thought sure he would make some excuse to speak to you again."

"He did not!" Magda said, with a sense of injury. "Why would that be? Tell me that, since you seem to know so much?!"

"Truly?" Liesel frowned thoughtfully, "I think he might have been a little afraid that you would snap his head off. But mostly, I think he was shy and knew little of women. I would guess he has spent much of his life among men, since becoming a man himself. But that is my guess, only. Some of the other men here in America, they seem the same. Elaborate courtesy and longing with their eyes, but all uncertainty underneath. Such men as that need encouragement at first."

"He spoke of a sister, with fondness. He told me a little of his family and how they came to Texas . . ." Magda straightened herself, and added briskly, "But then he was off with his colonel, to a war that is none of our business. If he were truly that interested, I think I would have heard more!"

"Perhaps I was only reading into things." Liesel sighed, and like Vati, added wistfully, "Anyway, for you, sister—there are more fine fish in this sea than there ever were in Albeck."

"Then I will have all the more work to avoid them!" Magda observed, sourly.

In the morning, they broke camp with great excitement, but when Mr. Bene and soldiers returned from their morning scout, they appeared unsettled. Conrad Merz rode back along the length of the assembled train, pausing briefly and speaking to each teamster and man. When he came to Vati and Hansi in turn, he said in a low voice, "There is a great camp of Indians in the valley just ahead where we must ford the river. Remain calm . . . they are mostly Delaware—and friendly. Their chief was one of those who helped us to find this place. It's a great worry; we must cross at exactly that place and there are more of them than there are of us. Captain Bene says to stay calm and close to the wagons. Don't do anything to provoke them. There are many more than we have men."

"Oh my," said Vati. The only weapon he had to hand was the hatchet he had bought in Galveston.

"They are friendly," Conrad repeated.

Magda said, "Vati, dear, you would need your glasses, to tell an Indian from any of us."

"You are right, Magda," Vati polished them on his sleeve and put them on again and tried his best to appear fierce. Magda and Conrad exchanged an exasperated look, as Vati said, "Of course, we should remember that one of them came to our camp to look after Friedrich. They cannot be truly hostile to our presence."

"They don't need to be truly hostile," Conrad said, as he rode on. "There are enough of them to be a danger even if they are only in a bad mood. It might be best for your daughters to ride in the cart today, too."

"I don't think that one Indian will want to hurt us," said Friedrich bravely. "After all the trouble he took over my foot."

"None the less, you boys climb into the cart with me, at the first sight of them," Vati ordered, as the front of the train began moving away, with a great crackle of whips and shouting from the teamsters.

The train moved slowly that day, skirted by the handful of armed Verein troopers. Tension radiated from every line of their bodies as they patrolled the length of the train. Magda hugged little Rosalie to her, perched uncomfortably on top of their bedding in the second cart, which was itself piled on top of their crates and trunks. The child had unerringly sensed the nervousness of those around her, for she sucked her thumb and hid her face in the front of Magda's dress. Even the draft oxen seemed to sense it; only Liesel's laying hen seemed immune, clucking gently whenever the wheels went over a particularly rough bit in the track.

"We're almost there," Hansi called to them. "The ford is just ahead. Do you see anything yet?"

High up, on top of the cart's load, they could see farther, over the tops of willow and beds of tall rushes lining the river banks, and those few stunted trees, with their roots firmly gripping the gravel and rocks in its bed.

"The first wagon is just going into the river," Magda answered, as her heart sank. As they moved slowly on, it looked to her as if the trees parted in the manner of a stage curtain, revealing first a handful of conical skin tents, or small arbors built out of brush and then gradually more and more. "It looks like a whole city of them," she whispered, and in truth so it was. Hundreds of fires dribbled smoke up into the sky and there were folk coming and going about their own business as there would be in any city; women bringing skin buckets to the water, children playing here and there, men tending to horses.

A few of them looked to be watching the cart train with mildly curious interest, sitting on their haunches on the riverbank to watch. Otherwise there seemed to be no alarms, no hostility. Vati and the boys hastily scrambled onto the cart ahead, so she knew they must have seen the Indian encampment too.

The sound of a single gunshot cracked the tense stillness and Liesel whispered, "Oh, God, surely they are not attacking us now!"

"I knew it, Liesel, your beautiful eggs! We should have eaten them for supper last night!" Friedrich called back comically. He and Johann and Vati were perched on top of a pile of freight.   Magda began to laugh, as someone ahead of them shouted, "Quickly, help me! Bring a knife!"

"What is it, what is it! What do you see?" Hansi called up to them. Two Verein troopers were converging on a thicket, across the river. There were no more shots, and the wagons ahead of them continued to move slowly into the water.

"I don't know! I think there was something in the thicket. The Indians don't seem to be taking any notice," Magda answered.

Presently, Conrad Merz rode up, beaming from ear to ear. "Schmidt shot a great black bear, just on the bank. Killed it dead with one shot! There'll be meat for supper tonight and Schmidt will have himself a fine black rug! Take care in crossing over, Richter. The water is about four feet deep in the middle for a little way, but the bed is all gravel and there is a little bit of a current."

They waited, while the cart ahead, with Vati and the boys, edged into the water. Conrad and another trooper urged their horses in on either side of the laboring oxen. In a little time, it reached the other side, and Friedrich turned around to wave cheerfully at them. And then it was their turn to edge down into the fording place. Hansi looked back at them and called encouragingly, "All ready, then? Here we go!" as his team waded farther and deeper into the clear green water. Hansi spoke soothing words to his ox-team. They snorted a little, tossing their heads nervously as the water rose towards their bellies, and the current made a deep "v" in the water on the downstream side. Hansi turned his head and called cheerfully, "It's cold enough—I shall want some dry clothes as soon as we are through!"

Conrad and the other trooper splashed towards them, close on either side, almost near enough to touch hands.

"They're doing well, Richter, doing well," he called. The water now reached to the middle of Hansi's chest, and he gripped his lead ox's yoke for support against the current. A wheel passed over a rock and dropped with a jolt into a hole in the river-bed. Liesel gasped, and Conrad sang out again, "Doing good, doing good… almost there, that was the worst part." The water streamed from his horse and his clothes; they were already in shallower water. Magda forced herself to smile cheerfully at Liesel as the cart bumped through the dry part of the river-course and up onto the level ground again.

"I do not like crossing over the water," Liesel whispered. "I so fear what would happen if the cart tipped over."

"We should learn to swim, then," Magda said, "until they have built bridges in all the places which need them."

"Are you all right, back there?" Hansi looked over his shoulder at them, smiling exuberantly, although soaked to the skin, and Magda waved, to reassure him.

"We're all right," she called, "Even the hen is happy!"

They moved along at a brisk pace after crossing the river, as if anticipation put wings to their feet and those of the animals. With no little relief they left the Indian encampment behind although there was one more fright, caused by another gunshot.

"I wonder if someone has shot another bear," Friedrich wondered, but no; Conrad overtook them, laboring up from the river crossing. He had the body of a huge wild cat, hanging limp over the back of his saddle. His horse pranced restlessly, looking back at it with the whites showing nervously in its eyes.

Conrad exclaimed with happy enthusiasm, "I tell you ladies… Richter, this is just the country for hunting! One shot, and it lunged towards me! I thought I might have to re-load in a hurry but then it dropped dead in its tracks!" Liesel looked as if she were about to faint. Seeing this, Conrad added, "Nothing to fear, ladies, you shall always be protected!"

Magda suddenly recalled the weight of Carl Becker's heavy revolver dropped into her hands and the certainty in his quiet voice as he advised *'Learn to fight; with this, or something like it'*.

They followed the line of the river all the rest of the day, spirits rising unquenchably, as the crossing and the Indian camp were left farther behind. Magda climbed down from the cart with the girls and walked, with a swinging step as a gentle breeze fluttered her skirts this way and that.

"We're almost there," she encouraged Anna and Rosalie, "Almost there... run, my little rabbits, run." And she took their hands and began to sing:
'Rabbit sat in the grass so green
Rabbit thinking what does this mean?
Isn't that the hunter's gun?
And it's time for me to run?
Rush my rabbit, rush
Into the thickest bush!'
Anna began to sing with her, and Rosalie laughed a happy little gurgle of a laugh, her purple-blue eyes alight and her red-gold curls bobbing around her head, as if she knew the end of their long journey was actually almost in sight.

The sun had begun to sink low in the afternoon sky, that time where everything was touched with gold, when they forded a small creek and came at last into a vast grove of great oak trees. Bars of sunlight slid between the branches overhead, gilding the edges of the new green leaves, and scattering spots of themselves like golden coins in the leaf-mast at their feet in those places were there was not a thick undergrowth of brush. Huge tangles of wild grapevines festooned the lower branches, already hung with dusty green bunches of grapes.

In the very middle of this forest Mr. Bene and his advance party had made a place where those bushes had been cleared away. A half-built log blockhouse stood in a little space of trampled mud and wood-chips. Mr. Bene's troopers were dismounting, the teams from the first wagons already unhitched.

"We're here!" Friedrich exclaimed, "Oh, Vati, it's beautiful!"

"It's a wilderness," said Liesel bleakly, while Hansi looked first delighted and then puzzled, as he lifted her down from the cart. Vati beamed in frank delight.

"It is like the Black Forest! Such trees, my dears! Of such beams were the roofs of the cathedrals built . . . and does it not seem very like a cathedral? So hushed and dim! "

Friedrich suddenly struck Johann's shoulder and shouted, "Catch me! Bet you can't catch me!" And the two of them went running off among the trees. Excited, happy voices rose around them; the Lochte boys were slapping each others' backs and Mr. Strackbein embracing his two daughters, while Mr. Bene strode among them, beaming.

"Just as we left it! Shall we have a celebration and feast tonight, hey? What do you say about that?"

". . . storehouse to be finished. . ."

". . . sleep under the trees tonight. . ."

". . . already surveyed the town lots, the farm tracts will be done later. . ."

". . .to be named after Prince Friedrich of Prussia, so I was told."

Hansi lifted Anna into the air, over his head and said, "Annchen, we're home at last! Isn't it beautiful?"

She laughed delightedly, saying "But Papa, where is our house?"

"In your mother's head, is where it is!" He set her down and embraced Liesel. With an impish look on his face, he lifted her up and whirled her about until she began to giggle and beg to be let down.

"I don't want a house; why can't we live in a skin lodge like the Indians?" Friedrich asked Magda.

"Because we don't," Magda answered, decidedly. "We're not Indians." She picked up Rosalie, and spun her around, as Hansi had done with Anna, until she began to giggle. "We're home, Rosalie! Home, although it doesn't look like much yet."

"Magda!" Friedrich said, excitedly, appearing breathlessly at her side. "We have found a brook—with fish in it. Enormous fish! Come see!"

"I'd best go see," Magda said over her shoulder to Vati, "and make sure they have not built a boat!"

"Magda, we wouldn't!" Friedrich protested, looking rather wounded. "Not after last time!"

"If course you wouldn't," Magda answered briskly. "And to make sure you are being good, we'll take the water-buckets with us, and put the time to good use."

She followed Friedrich down a well-trodden path through the trees, thinking that this must be where Mr. Bene and the survey party had come for water. Here and there were sharpened pegs sticking out of the ground, with bits of cloth tied around them, or a blaze cut in a tree trunk, but it seemed utterly fanciful to see this place as a town, with streets and gardens, and fine stone houses. The waters of the brook Friedrich led her towards were deep and clear, gliding over a sandy bottom with barely a ripple, edged with tall rushes and willows. Bright dragonflies, like living jewels, hovered over the surface. A handful of grey doves, their wings edged in white, exploded out of the undergrowth as they came out into the last of the sunshine along the grassy bank. Something lying in sinuous coils on the grey trunk of a tree fallen half into and half out of the water slithered off it with a faint plopping noise and vanished, leaving only some widening ripples on the brook's surface.

"Did you see that?" Friedrich demanded. "A snake, a huge snake!"

Magda shuddered. "I did not, and please don't say anything about so-called snakes to Liesel! She's on the point of believing everything out here stings, bites, or has thorns, and it's all poisonous and all dangerous!"

"Well it does, doesn't it?" Friedrich said. "That's what he said. That man on the grey horse who spoke German to us—Vati's friend, Sergeant Becker."

Johann pointed up into the sky, where a fierce-looking large bird with long reddish wings wheeled slowly and dropped silently onto a high perch in a tree across the brook.

"That doesn't. It's an eagle."

"It's a hawk," Friedrich answered. They quarreled amiably over it while Magda filled the water buckets and suddenly recalled how the Verein troopers had killed both a bear and a large cat, at the water's edge that very morning.

The sound of axes and the crash of falling timber brought them back to where they would spend the night and begin building their new town, their new lives. Already Mr. Bene's troopers had begun cutting more wood while the wagons were emptied of the goods they had brought with them and carried into the blockhouse for safe-keeping.

That night, the men built one great campfire in the middle of the clearing, and they brought out the meat from Trooper Schmidt's bear, and Conrad's cat, and some fish that the Lochte boys drew from the creek, which they all set to roast. Mrs. Lochte, and Mrs. Strackbein, Liesel, Magda, and the other women baked soda bread, for there was no time to let yeast bread properly rise. Mr. Bene brought out a sack of potatoes to bake in the coals and many large stone-ware bottles of beer for the men.

While the women cooked, the men finished unpacking the wagons and setting up tents and brush-arbors for shelter. They set a number of rough-sawn planks across some tree-stumps still sticking out of the ground to make a couple of tables, and brought out chairs and blankets to sit on, and rolled some fallen logs close to the fire, as darkness fell and shadows lengthened between the trees.

"It is like the ancient tales of Teutonic warriors in their forest home, feasting after the hunt!" Vati remarked, delightedly, "All we would need for a perfect picture would be swords and shields, mead-horns and a bard with a harp, to sing of our glorious triumph!"

"Somehow, I don't think Mr. Arhelger's concertina will strike the right note," Hansi said dryly and they all laughed.

126

"Do you realize, Vati . . . it has been a year, almost to the day, since we decided to follow this road?" Magda noted, wistfully.

"Why, so it has," Vati answered. He looked around at them all, smiling in wonder: tired and dirty, wearied from their long travel that day, but all of their company exultant in having finally arrived and eager for the Verein promises to be fulfilled. "Sometimes it hardly seems like any time at all, and sometimes it seems an age has passed since then!"

Laughter echoed through the trees, and music, as some of the older men began to sing:
"By the fountain near the portals,
There stands a linden tree.
I dreamed beneath its shadow
So many dreams of thee.
I cut into its bark there,
So many a word of love ... "
"Ah," said Mrs. Lochte, fanning herself, "It does one such good to hear them singing! It seems so much more like home—oh, listen to them now!" and she began to sing softly along with them,
"Must I then, must I then
From my town go away, town go away
And you my love stay here?
When I come, when I come
When I come back again, come back again
I will come to you, my dear ... "
She looked at Magda, smiling and saying robustly, "Nothing like a good melancholy song, for making you feel better!"

The smell of roasting meat came from the fire, and Magda's mouth began to water hungrily. Good smells also rose from the round iron ovens set into the fire with coals piled upon their lids. That, so said some of the Verein troopers who had been a little longer in Texas than the rest, was how bread was baked by an open fire. The flames leapt up, gilding the wearied but merry faces of those around it and sending odd shadows flickering between the tree-trunks.

Back amongst the trees, two or three of the Verein troopers stood watch, although Mr. Bene insisted that they were safe enough, on the high ground between two creeks and the river they had crossed that afternoon.

"We may as well have this to celebrate!" Mrs. Lochte brought out a jar of honey. Liesel and the other women ransacked their own stocks for other treats. Mr. Bene thought for a moment, and then slapped his forehead and asked one of the troopers to bring out a crock of pickles from the blockhouse stores. When the long makeshift table fairly groaned under a generous load of platters and dishes, Conrad began slicing off pieces of bear meat onto the largest platter, so that all could help themselves. For the first time it seemed like they could eat their fill and they had the appetite to do justice to such a feast. Magda sat with Mrs. Lochte; they apparently had been nominated to oversee the table and keep it heavy-laden with food.

"We came so far and it's been so long, I can hardly believe we're finally here at last."

"Believe it," Mrs. Lochte beamed fondly at her sons, eating heartily with their hands beside the fire with the other men. "The lads have so many plans. They will make a paradise of this. Have you seen the soil by the creek? As black and rich as you could hope for! My Fritz says he could sink his arm into it up to the shoulder without any effort at all. Of all those Verein promises, this is the first one to better expectation."

"My father says this is like a cathedral," Magda remarked, "with the tree-trunks all around like they are."

"Stone, timber, and water," Mr. Bene waved a tankard cheerily. "It's what the B … Mr. Meusebach wanted. All of that within a short distance; he ordered it, and so it was done!"

"All thanks to him!" Mrs. Lochte affirmed stoutly.

Magda added with a sigh, "My brother-in-law doubts that any of the rest of them could tell one end of a cow from the other."

"It would have saved a great deal of trouble for us, if they had put him in charge from the very first," Mrs. Lochte said, roundly, "and I'd tell them that to their faces!"

"So you would, madam, so you would!" Mr. Bene tipped his head back for a generous drink. "And now we have music and revelry, to follow the feast!"

On the other side of the fire, Mr. Arhelger brought out his concertina, and there was a fiddle, too, scraping out a merry, rollicking polka. Conrad Merz appeared out of the shadows and caught Mrs. Lochte's hand. "Dance with me, madam!" he commanded and, pulling her to her feet, whirled away with her as she whooped with laughter and not very strenuous protests. Magda watched in amusement: Vati twirling around with Rosalie in his arms, Hansi smiling down at Liesel and Johann solemnly stepping through the figures with Anna as his partner. Even Friedrich, looking terribly nervous, was dancing with Christine Strackbein, who topped him by at least a head.

"There are so many more men than there are women." Fritz Lochte caught her hand. "You dare not sit out a dance, Miss Magda!"

And then it was one of the Arhelger boys claiming her hand and Conrad Wehmeyer the trooper after that and another of the Arhelger boys, until she was breathless and giddy. While she had not intended or expected to, Magda enjoyed herself, celebrating the end of that long and heartbreaking journey. She put aside the worries and apprehensions, stepping though the complicated figures of dance with Conrad or one of the Lochte brothers, while the campfire sent sparks skywards and the sound of music echoed among the pillar-trunks of those huge oak trees. Here would be home, and it would be as fine a home as Vati had promised and in a land as fair as Carl Becker had said it would be. The soil was rich, the Indians would not molest them, and the Verein would see to their needs and their protection.

She did wonder for a brief moment, what it would have been like to dance with that tall, diffident man, Saxon-fair and such a good horseman; of course he would be a good dancer. Would he laugh as uproariously as Conrad at something which amused him, she wondered? And then she reminded herself very firmly that he was doubtless fighting in Mexico, following after his Colonel who would never surrender. It might be best, after all, to put him away from her mind entirely.

Annaliese Richter smiled at her husband across the fire. He turned his head from talking to Vati and smiled in return, a private smile meant only for her, his eyes dark-shadowed in the firelight. Hansi sat with Anna in his lap, the little girl half-asleep and yet seeming to listen to her father's and grandfather's conversation. Liesel and her husband had danced together this evening until she was breathless. She could still feel the print of his arms around her, the pressure of his fingers on hers, and now she savored the vision of her husband and her daughter in the firelight, loving them fiercely with all her heart. Liesel knew herself to be not the least bit clever, not in the way that Vati and Magda were. She could see things plain about those she knew best, including her own self, though. In her own heart, she knew that she was timid and fearful. She hated the desolate wilderness all around her, the huge emptiness of the sky overhead. Everything about this place that they had brought her to made her want to hide under something heavy, with her fingers in her ears and her eyes tight-closed. But she trusted Vati and Magda and most of all, her husband. She could endure this place for the love of her husband, who knew what was best.

When Magda told her going to Texas was for the good of them all, Liesel had made herself bottle up her fears and put on the best face of it for the sake of the children. She tried to copy Magda, to lift her chin bravely, to pretend that she was happy also. Hansi was her husband, after all, and it was her duty to obey, even if this sudden, reckless spirit had sprouted up almost overnight, like some sort of weed in the smooth and straightforward garden of their lives.

Here was her plain, stubborn, trustworthy husband, suddenly deciding to leave his ancestral fields, everything which they had ever known. Liesel still couldn't fathom how it had happened, could scarcely believe that she sat in a wooded clearing in the farthest wilderness and would sleep under the trees tonight. How could that have happened, she wanted to cry to the very heavens.

Everyone knew that Vati was a dreamer, an impractical, clever man, full of ideas and books. But how could he suddenly act upon them and drag the stolid and practical Hansi along? How had that happened? Liesel still had no idea why her husband chose to partake of this insanity. She wanted to have him at her side, strong and practical; no not more dancing, not tonight. Liesel wanted the other, the bedding thing that married folk did with a sudden fierce intensity that turned her bones weak.

Their gazes met again, struck sparks. It was late, but not too late, for many of the others were still dancing, merry and joyous in the firelight. Hansi stood up carrying Anna, asleep in his arms and bid Vati good-night. Liesel moved around the tables and the knot of dancers, towards her husband and daughter, as slowly as if she were moving under water, meeting them just at the edge of the firelight. No words, just moving together as if they were still dancing. He shifted Anna to his shoulder and put one arm around Liesel's waist. They walked into the darkness together, silent except for the sound of each other breathing and the delicate little snoring sound that Anna made, almost like a kitten purring.

A little moonlight sifted between the leaves of the huge tree that Hansi and the boys had placed their things under; building a little arbor made of brush and canvas under the shelter of those leaves, a shelter as fragile as a breath. Anna stirred a little, when Liesel unfastened her little dress and shoes and put her into Magda's bed, where she curled up and dropped soundly asleep as soon as Liesel put her down.

So quiet it was, under the tree, with everyone still at the campfire. She took off her own shoes; the grass felt like silk, cool under her bare feet. Liesel tucked her daughter in, smoothing the blankets over her. She felt her husband's fingers on the back of her neck, unlacing her dress. She waited until her dress loosed entirely, before she turned around and let it drop, let it drop and her petticoats with it, a pool of fabric around her feet. Her turn: the buttons on the cuffs of his shirt…

"You're missing one!" she whispered, the least sound in the quiet, in the brush arbor, just a breath over his breathing, his hands on her, warm on her skin through her shift.

"Meant to tell you." His lips close to her ear, affectionate humor in every word, seeking her own lips, while her hands dealt with the complicated business of braces and trouser buttons. The night air was chill, but his hands were warm, as if they left a left a trace of fire on her skin. She shivered suddenly. Hansi embraced her, held her close. Oh yes, he was ready for this, her very bones felt as if they had dissolved into water from desire. She kissed him, knowing that he was smiling at her in the dark from the shape of his lips under her mouth. He drew her down into their blankets and she lifted up the front of her shift; oh, yes, this was the ritual dance of married folk. She welcomed Hansi into her own body, pulling the dear familiar weight of him down onto her, pressing her against the blankets and the springy branches which softened their bed. She looked first into the moon-shot darkness over head, and then closed her eyes. *'Love me, my husband . . .'* Liesel begged silently. *'Worship me with your body, start another child growing in me this night... protect me with your strength, for the sky here is too large and the wilderness too vast... love me, and help me not to fear . . . '*

* * *

. . . and celebrated under the trees with a communal feast. Trooper Merz had shot a bear, the flesh of which we roasted over a large fire. Mrs. Lochte sampled the head of the bear, to our very great amusement, for she said then it was most delicious! The town has been roughly surveyed and marked out, but can hardly to be seen for all the trees! Mr. Bene who has been deputized as our leader had buried a great store of tools next to the half-built house, which is to serve as a blockhouse and storage. He has directed the construction of a large enclosure to shelter us, and a fenced garden plot, at which we all willingly bend our backs.

Alas, there are fewer of us to share this labor than we had expected, for after quickly erecting some tents and brush arbors to shelter us against the weather, Conrad Merz and his troopers and twenty teamsters made ready to return to Neu Braunfels. We are told they are needed, in conveying more settlers hence, but in the meantime those few of us remaining are left to see to our own survival.

Those of our party so inclined held a service of thanksgiving under the trees after our arrival, and formally named our new home Friedrichsburg, after the Prince of Prussia who is one of the patrons of the Society. I wish as a stout republican, that we could have named it after someone else, but it is felt politic, and properly flattering.

Written in haste from your old friend
C.F. Steinmetz

Chapter 8 – *The Home Place*

A dazzle in his eyes and a roar of noise in his ears: Carl Becker swam up to consciousness and a rough hand shaking his shoulder . . . the uninjured one. Even at that, pain stabbed up unto his skull, harsh as the Mexican lancer's blade striking him down in a cavalry skirmish outside of Monterray . . . how many days ago?

"Rudi . . . is it the soldiers coming for us?" he mumbled in German. The hand shook him again, as a voice commanded, "Speak English, you blockheaded Dutchman! Are you fit enough to walk out of here?"

Carl squinted against the light of a lantern held above his head and focused against his blurred vision on the face of the man holding it. Big Bill Wallace ... Jack's lieutenant. Sometimes he had thought Jack had been there, looking down at him with a worried face. But such was the power of fever-dreams that sometimes it was not really Jack's face, weathered and lined with responsibility, but the boy he had been when they first made each other's acquaintance. Sometimes Trap Talmadge was also there, grimacing and cursing under his breath as Rip Ford dug an Apache arrow-head out of his flesh with a hot knife-blade . . . no, that was wrong, that was after...

"I feel like dogshit, Bill," he mumbled in reply, and coughed painfully. Bill Wallace set down the lantern carefully, and checked the blood-caked bandages on Carl's left shoulder.

"There ain't no bubbling coming out of the deepest cut," he remarked, with professional assurance. He was a tough as nails, as tough as they came and right good with rough surgery and the sort of practical medical knowledge that had allowed him to survive harsh imprisonment at the hands of the Mexicans at Mier. "The sawbones says that bastard of a lancer missed your lung by a squeak, but you got the lung-fever or the ague sure enough, and a busted collar-bone to boot. You ain't gonna get any better in this-here cesspit. We got some of the boys heading home, now that their enlistments are up, and a courier going with them. Jack says there's a place in an empty supply wagon for you, if you can walk to it. You got a home, they can take you to?"

"My sister's." Carl gathered his thoughts and his strength. "They can take me to my sister in Austin. Mrs. Margaret Vining. She keeps a boarding house. There's a row of apple trees in the front yard. Anyone there will give directions."

"Best place for you, then." Wallace assisted him to sit up and steadied him while his head swam. "Tell you what, Dutch, we sure as hell gonna miss you. There's many as is as good a shot, but not above two or three that keep cool in a pickle. Talk about a rumpus when we reach Mexico City . . . I think Gen'ral Scott, he's gonna keep all the fun and glory for hisself and his blue-coat boys."

"He's afraid we won't leave anything but picked-over trash." Carl forced his eyes to focus. "M-mm saddle. I'll take my saddle and things ... if you can carry it, Bill."

"Pity about your horse. That big ol' grey of yours, he was something prime. Look, Dutch—I got your arm strapped up, so the bones don't grind together. How's that feel?"

"Fine." Carl gritted his teeth until the agony in his shoulder stopped sending shooting stars in front of his eyes. "My coat...it's c-c-cold."

"Jes' slip your good arm into the sleeve." Bill draped the rest of his buckskin coat over his bandaged shoulder. "I'm gonna take your traps out to that Dearborn, make sure there's a place in back for you to lie down. You just wait here, half a tick." He hoisted up Carl's old worn saddle and the belt with his Colt revolvers, while Carl leaned his good elbow on his knees and thought very hard about standing up. He tried to keep his teeth from chattering together; oh, he had the ague and shivers right enough.

Poor old Hellion, thrashing on the ground with two broken legs after the lancers charged them. In the thick of it, Carl had wrenched Hellion around, throwing him against the Mexican's lighter beast, but the bastard had a lance and would have speared Carl square in the chest with it, but for Carl catching him at point blank range with his Colt. The Mexican had his lance in a death-grip, though. It went into Carl as the horses crashed together, high in the hollow of his left shoulder, glancing off bone, slicing through flesh and sinew, throwing him down as Hellion fell. He thought he could still hear the sound of it, like a cleaver slicing through meat, and the agony coming after, like thunder after lightening. He hoped someone had shot his horse, afterwards. Or maybe he had. Who could endure the sound of a horse screaming? Could have been a man screaming, the way they had screamed and cursed before the Mexican soldiers cut them down outside the Goliad on a spring Sunday morning. No, the fever had everything all muddled up in his mind. Carl could not bring to mind anything happening after the lance blade, save a flash recollection of someone handing him a bottle and saying, "Half of this in you, and half on you, if you please, so's I can get to work. And make it quick, I don't have all day." And then looking over his shoulder to someone in the shadows, ". . . and bring me some of that damnable moldy bread. We can't eat it, may as well get some good out of it."

Oh, yes, long ago . . . in that time before, Ma used to use moldy bread to stop up blood. The moldier the better . . .

"You ready, Dutch?" Wallace's scuffed and dusty boots appeared in the range of his sight. "I had the boys put down some nice fresh hay in the back of that there Dearborn, and a couple of blankets. You'll ride as comfortable as if you were a babby in your mothers' arms. Now, then—one, two three—hupp!"

A mighty effort got Carl to his feet, and the room spun around him. He thought he might have fallen, but for the big man hauling on his good arm. One, two, three steps across the dusty floor; they stumbled like a pair of drunks and he closed his eyes to keep the place from spinning around. The light stabbed his eyes again, when he opened them, even though it was barely dawn. Oh, the dusty farmyard outside Monterray. They had been quartered in the wrecked and looted stables off and on for weeks.

A nightmare stagger across the farmyard towards the Army Dearborn, the teams of horses hitched to it shifting impatiently. Voices and other willing but clumsy hands helping him negotiate the tricky business of climbing. Was one of them Jack? He thought he heard him say, very low-voiced:

". . . not good, Bill. Are you sure about this?"

". . . tough as old boots . . ." Bill's voice, also very low. " Kill 'im for sure to stay here . . ." And then louder, cheerfully urging him up into the Dearborn. "Up you go! Here—goddamn Daniels! Easy on his arm! Break it open again, the sawbones 'ull hunt you down personal and geld your clumsy ass. Look here, if you can, give him some of this quinine bark tincture—should keep the ague down to a dull roar, 'til you get him to his sister's house. Right you are, Dutch— they'll look after you."

Mercifully, Carl could lie down, lie down and hug the blanket around him, with his head pillowed on his saddle. He could let the world go whirling away for the agony went away with it, although not the nightmarish dreams, the faces and memories spinning through his mind without any order or reason, merging into each other with a queer logic of their own. Cushioned on a deep bed of straw in the Dearborn against the jolting of the ruts in the road to the north, he was heading towards home, or at least as close as he would ever get. Home.

That was where Trap Talmadge had tried to send him, drawling scornfully in his cracker-Carolina voice, "Looky here, boys, this ain't no nursery, and I sure as hell ain't no wet-nurse. You two git along home. Colonel Smith is plumb out of sugar-tits this morning!"

Old Trap had been lean and stringy even then, tobacco-juice staining his raggedly drooping mustache, one of those men who suddenly became middle-aged early on and after that never changed much at all. Ten year gone, he was one of old Deaf Smith's sergeants in the company he had been charged to raise for General Houston. That was in the fall of the year that Texas had won independence, the fall of the year that Rudi and Ma died.

There were a good few men waiting to see Colonel Smith where the Army was camping in a straggle of trees at the edge of town. Word had gotten round that he was recruiting for a big company, a company that would be paid by the legislature. Carl had come all the way to Columbia from Waterloo on the Guadalupe, on the strength of that word, carrying an old British-made musket that his father took off a dead Mexican soldier after the San Jacinto fight. He lingered at the edge of the crowd, very well aware that there was only one other who looked even younger than he did, a slight and delicate looking boy with rather heavy eyebrows.

"They say they're having a regular Army officer inspect everyone's weapons and horses," said the boy suddenly to Carl. Carl was startled; he had been looking at the other volunteers and wondering if his musket was good enough to qualify him. Everyone else seemed to have more than one firearm and enough knives to outfit a hardware store, and all he had was the little one he kept out of habit in the top of his brogan.

"That musket of yours looks like you found it at the bottom of a well. But your horse looks good enough," the boy added, thoughtfully and Carl took another look at him. No, Carl realized that the boy was older than he looked. He spoke and carried himself with more of a man's assurance. Carl answered, "I won him playing cards."

"Did you?" The boy seemed quite impressed. "You must be very good at that."

Carl shrugged and answered, "So-so . . . it was more them underestimating me." The boy grinned, approvingly, "And I'll bet you gave them every reason to do so! Why didn't you play for a better weapon, while you were outfitting yourself?"

"I might have, but no one was betting anything but that paper Republic scrip."

"Where did you learn to play cards?"

"In the militia," Carl explained. "We sat around in garrison a lot."

And that was when Trap Talmadge came up to them, looked them both over with a great show of disgust, saying, "Looky here, boys, this ain't no nursery, and I sure as hell ain't no wet-nurse. You two git along home! Colonel Smith is plumb out of sugar-tits this

morning!" And he spat on the ground, as Carl's new friend answered
firmly:

"*I think you must have mistaken my friend and me for someone
else, sir. I came to volunteer for Colonel Smith's company. I have a
letter from General Houston recommending me to him, and I served
with General Rusk all this last spring. And,"* the boy added with
perfect assurance, "*this last spring, I put a bullet into a bully from
Nacogdoches who thought I looked like an easy mark."*

"*Indeedy?"* And Trap Talmadge looked him up and down with
grudging interest, while Carl kept his face expressionless. He'd heard
a lot of big talk in the militia and somehow that didn't sound much
like it. "*No brag, boy?"*

"*No brag,"* he answered, evenly. "*He knocked over my drink
and tried to pick a fight. No one objected much when I gave him what
he wanted."*

"*I'll certainly hand it to you,"* Trap chuckled rustily and spat
again. "*You are one touchy sumbitch. Who are you to Sam Houston,
then? What is the moniker you go by?"*

"*He's a distant connection to my family, back in Tennessee,"*
answered the boy., "*I'm John Coffee Hays. But most everyone calls
me Jack. My friend..."* he hesitated slightly, "*my friend here was in
the militia, and he's looking to volunteer, too."*

"*Don't he have nothin' to say for hisself?"* Trap looked towards
Carl as he bit off a plug, and chewed rhythmically. "*Who are you,
boy and what was your unit?"*

"*Carl Becker, First Regiment, Texas Volunteers,"* Carl
answered, "*Captain Pettus's company."*

There was a very long silence, as the scornful look eased off
Trap's face. His voice almost sounded respectful as he said, "*Your
pa—he'd be Alois Becker? That Dutchman with a place on the
Guadalupe, up Waterloo way?"*

"*That's the one,"* Carl answered quietly.

Trap looked thoughtful for a long while, before saying, "*Well,
leastways you're used to living rough. I just can't see that musket of
yours passing muster, though."*

"If it don't, I'll be back again." Carl answered, "I'm not going home."

Trap spat on the ground again, "It ain't up to me. But I'd advise you to have something better to show the inspecting officer." He ambled away, leaving Carl standing with Jack, who was himself looking very thoughtful.

"I bet you're very good at arithmetic—sums and things," he commented. Such an unexpected observation, and when Carl looked puzzled, Jack expounded, "It's one of those things; people who are good at cards tend to be good at numbers, or so my father said once. And very good at noticing little things." He sized up Carl, in one of those quick, assessing glances that Carl would come to find very familiar and seemed to nod to himself. "I'll loan you my carbine, if that's what it will take to get you into the company. Just give it back when you've gotten a good one of your own."

"Why would you do that?" Carl asked.

Jack had shrugged evasively, "I just think you'd be a good one to serve with. That's all." He looked off into the distance, as if he were looking for something very far away, and added very softly, "General Rusk . . . he had us bury them all decently. The Mexes just left them all lie."

"I know," Carl answered, in a voice that gave nothing away. "Remember Goliad."

"Remember Goliad." Jack echoed. That was all that he needed to say, and all that he ever did, for which Carl was grateful. There were some things that didn't need to be said between true friends.

An interminable time later, that roaring world of pain and wracking fever finished with him and spat him out, limp and weak as a half-drowned rat. He lay with his eyes closed at first, sorting out where he was, obscurely fearing that he might open them to someplace unpleasant, dirty, and dangerous. No, that was not straw that he lay on, but cool linen sheets. A wooden, regular creaking sound came from close at hand; not the Dearborn's incessant swaying. No, he was somewhere else. The creaking sound ceased, replaced by the rustle of fabric, a woman's skirts, and a cool hand on his forehead.

"Open your eyes, little brother. I know you're awake." Margaret's voice, calm and fondly stern. He obeyed, profoundly grateful to find himself in a bedroom he didn't recognize, but in what must be the old Becker home place. It would be Margaret's house now; a whitewashed room and plainly furnished, but neat as a pin. Mid-morning sunshine spilled into it through the French doors leading out to a veranda, and moving leaf-shadows speckling the scrubbed oak floor.

"How did you know I was awake?" he asked. His voice sounded to his own ears like something rusty, disused, and Margaret smiled.

"I've been watching, and I know you very well, little brother." His sister had the same calm, observant blue eyes as he did and hair of the same pale wheat color, woven in a neat coronet of braids around the top of her head. She had a vast apron tied over her morning dress.

"How long . . ." he coughed, and Margaret brought him a cup of bitter-tasting liquid, and deftly helped him to drink. "Have I been here for very long?"

"Your friends dropped you on my doorstep like a load of dirty laundry two weeks since. They said you took that wound in the fighting before Monterray. This is the first time you have been sensible. Doctor Williamson has been attending you every morning and evening."

"Very dedicated of him," His voice sounded less rusty.

Margaret smiled. "He's one of my boarders. Nothing is too good for our heroes of Monterray, although I suppose I shall have to discount his rent in courtesy. Shall I help you to sit up? You should, if you feel strong enough."

"I've enough of looking at the ceiling, Margaret."

"Very well, then." She lifted his head and shoulders and capably slid a couple of pillows underneath, before letting him sink down again. Margaret had cared for an invalid husband for several years before he was finally taken by consumption. "Let me know when you've had enough." Now that he was propped up, he could see more of the room. Definitely not familiar; he didn't even recognize the furniture.

"This is new. You have built on another wing?"

"Yes, six rooms downstairs, three up. They had just begun building it when you were here last. I had meant to rent these three, but they have such a pleasant aspect, I have kept them for the family. You should come home more often."

"Home." He smiled very wryly. "It's that place, that when they dump you on the doorstep like dirty laundry, they have to take you in."

"So true," Margaret agreed sweetly. She seated herself in her rocking chair again, and took up her mending from the sewing table beside it. "As it is, you turn up every couple of months with your clothing in rags and fit only to be burnt and a beard like a wild man, saying very little of where you have been and what you have been doing, save that it was at Jack Hays' bidding. This last time, I thought you were working for that Prince Fancy-Trousers—oh, my, the stories that went around about him—at least the ones the boarders would tell me." She shot a very shrewd look at Carl, adding, "At least this time you found someone to mend your clothes for you. You should tell me about her, little brother."

"Her? Why would you think that, Margaret?" She couldn't read much of his expression under the beard, but his voice sounded very bland.

"I unpacked your saddlebags and for a marvel, found a shirt in it which wasn't in rags. In fact, it was mended very neatly and folded up with great care. I have met men who can tell one end of the needle from the other, and even make stitches with it, under extreme duress, but never as neatly or as small as a woman does. I was not born last night. You either have a pet mouse whom you have taught to sew, or you have met a woman in the last year who thinks well enough of you to do your mending. Who is she, Carl?"

"She thinks well of me because I pulled her niece out of the river," Carl answered, morosely. "It's a long story."

"You should tell it to me, then," Margaret set aside her mending. "I have an idea. You shall tell me about her as I shave off those dreadful whiskers—really, you look so much a stranger with them and I can't bear it. Don't laugh, little brother, I used to barber

Mr. Vining all the time, when he was too weakened. We used to have some of our nicest talks, then."

"Well of course, you were the one holding the razor," Carl pointed out.

"Don't be provoking," Margaret answered briskly. "You'll feel much better without all that awful bristle. It makes you look too much like Pa, anyway." As she bustled out of the room, to fetch a bowl of warm water and the other necessities, she thought she heard her brother murmur:

"Hell with my back broke, than go 'round looking like him!"

Margaret felt her throat tighten. *Oh, Pa,* she said to herself, *you never had the slightest idea of what you did to Carl, did you?*

She took her time, settling the kettle over the fire, and trying to remember where she had put away Horace Vining's strop and razor, before calmly appropriating her oldest son's shaving soap and brush. Young Horace was at least two years from having a serious need of them anyway and wouldn't mind his uncle having some little use, she reasoned. The kettle barely stirred over the fire. Margaret had long since bought a patent iron stove but the kitchen was in the oldest part of the house, that part of it built by their father, Alois Becker, with his own hands, back in that time before. That part left standing, when Alois and Margaret and her husband and her children had returned after the terrifying scramble of the "runaway scrape".

Margaret still shuddered, thinking on the nightmarish terror of those days. Santa Anna and his terrible army, on their way to wreak bloody vengeance on the Texas settlements; Pa and Mr. Vining answering the call to Sam Houston's ragged little army, her brothers already gone south with Colonel Fannin's militia. She and Ma had to load her little sons into a wagon, with what little they could carry and flee east with the other refugees.

They had come home in dribs and drabs. Margaret and her husband found their own house in Gonzales, and her husband's little school all burnt to the ground. Horace Vining was already sickening with the illness that would kill him within a few years. Ma had died of the bloody flux in a ragged camp near Harrisburg, where they had heard of how Colonel Fannin's men had been massacred at the Goliad. When they all returned, there was no place to go but the Becker homestead. In a way, Margaret thought, it was as bad for herself after the San Jacinto victory as it had been before: her brothers assumed dead with Fannin's butchered garrison, a sick husband to care for, and a father half-mad with grief.

Too late in the year to put in a crop; everything that Alois Becker and his family had built, or planted, or stocked was wrecked, looted or trampled into the ground, all but the apple trees. A week after their return, before they had even managed to patch the roof over this very room, Margaret heard a scratching at the door, a scratching like a dog would make, begging to be let in. Margaret unbolted the door and opened it to her youngest brother: gaunt, ragged and half-starving, all but skin and bones. He had made his way home on foot, hiding during the day like an animal.

She had thrown her arms around him, crying his name joyfully, crying 'Pa, *Pa! It's Carl, come and see, he's alive!'*

But when Alois Becker came to her side, he looked past his younger son, looking out into the darkness behind him, as if he looked for someone else, asking only, *'But where is Rudi, then? Carl, why you leave your brother?'*

Margaret still remembered how her brother had flinched, and the terrible look in his eyes, as if he were seeing hellish things. He pulled away as if he had been struck, tearing himself out of her arms and ran away, ran away from the doorway and their father. She called after him, and finally took a lantern and went out to search.

Alois Becker had only said impatiently, *'That young blockhead— he'll be back when he's hungry enough. Leave him sulk, Margaret.'* But Margaret went out anyway, and eventually thought to look in one of those places she knew that her brothers had loved best: a place on the riverbank some distance from the farmstead, a sheltered hollow between the knees of a great sycamore. He had been curled into a tight ball, knees to forehead, arms wrapped around his knees, not making a sound.

'Come back to the house, Carl,' she had begged, setting down the lantern. *'You know Pa doesn't mean anything . . . Rudi is just his favorite, that's all.'*

'Rudi is dead.' His voice was muffled; he was speaking to his knees. *'They killed us all, but Rudi told me to run away. I think some others ran. There was a pretty woman and an officer, they tried to make me leave Rudi, but I wouldn't go. I hid in the bushes across the river and watched their women washing the clothes they took from them afterwards until the water ran red.'*

Boiling water purred in the kettle. Startled back to the present, Margaret took a cloth and carried it, together with a large basin and a number of clean towels into the sickroom. She was calmer now. This had been a comforting ritual with her husband, a ritual remembered with great affection: laying out the towels, mixing a lather of soap, deftly stropping the razor, all to the tune of fond and intimate conversation.

"So," Margaret sat on the edge of the bed. "I think I will clip off the worst of it first. Tell me about this girl. You rescued a child? Of course—all the sentimental novels have something like this. What is she like?"

"A very spirited filly," her brother answered, thoughtfully. "She's tall with good lines, and totally fearless. Looking at her was like looking into a whole corral of horses, seeing just that one and knowing that is the one you want, no matter the asking price."

"Oh, dear," said Margaret, busy with the scissors. "Never tell her that, little brother. A horse, indeed; not the most romantic thought. You should think of something more gallant."

"I can't," replied Carl, crossly. "She's like a fine thoroughbred that I want for my own, and that's all. Pa always did say I was a dullard compared to Rudi."

"Oh?" said Margaret, with some asperity, "So he did. And did you take it so to yourself, thinking it was true? Pa loved Rudi, over and above you and me; live with that, little brother. Should what Pa thought and said stab you so to the heart?"

"We loved him too, Margaret. He was the best of brothers."

And afterwards, Pa made Rudi into a perfect plaster saint, thought Margaret. *Being dead and perfect is not easy to match. Easy enough for Rudi, being one of the noble martyrs of Goliad! Not so for Carl, having escaped by chance and Rudi's last gesture. Perhaps Ma might have made Pa see that, made him soften the things that he said all unthinkingly to my imperfect but very much alive little brother.* Aloud, Margaret said, "He was that, indeed. What I have always remembered most was how he loved pranks and practical jokes, and making people laugh. There wasn't a shred of malice in him, either. Even the people he pranked were always laughing, afterwards . . . hot towel, little brother. Hold still and think about what you are going to tell me about this girl of yours. Who is her family, and where did you meet them?"

"One of Prince Fancy-Trouser's settler families, come from the Old Country to take up a fine land grant they know nothing of," answered Carl, indistinctly from behind a hot, damp towel swathing the lower half of his face. "Jack and the rest of us saw them this spring. nooning by the riverbank on the road from the coast to Victoria . You could have knocked us down with a feather when they told us who they were."

"Mmmm," said Margaret encouragingly. The soap lathered up nicely. His eyes were closed, with shadows like bruises under them. He was tiring; she would have to hurry this along. "Now, I was told that your Prince Fancy-Trousers had to skip the country shortly ahead of a pack of creditors. His replacement needed first thing to bail him out. I have heard that he is a more sensible man; sensible enough not to play the nobleman around here, but at his wit's end nonetheless."

"Meusebach—that's his name, by the way. I'd take a bet he don't know whether to piss himself or go blind." Carl muttered. Margaret took the towel away and began swabbing lather on his jaw, while he continued, "He was securing his grant, getting credit from his investors and see that thousands of greenhorns move safely from the coast to their holdings, all on a shoestring. Jack and I, we both agreed afterwards, we're damned glad we don't have his job."

"Hold still or you'll get a mouthful of soap," she commanded, as she deftly scraped away with the straight razor. "Perhaps I should tell you some of my own thoughts now . . . listen and hold still, you should not talk during this next part."

"You have a very sharp razor within an inch of my throat. That ensures my complete attention, Margaret," her brother said only, but his eyes looked amused. Margaret settled herself more comfortably on the bed.

"Well, I am considering marriage again—to Doctor Williamson. He has asked me so, several times and I am inclined to accept. I do not need to marry, but I enjoy his company and think I would relish more of it. And also the boys like him. Really, little brother, I should cut your hair, as well. Remind me on this . . . Anyway, I am considering his proposal with all care. Do not think I would neglect securing my own interests and those of the boys. I have not rented rooms to lawyers and legislators for nothing! I think if I appealed to certain of my boarders, I could get a bill passed for my exclusive benefit!" As she talked, Margaret worked away with the razor, turning his face this way or that with her other hand. Carl listened with his usual quiet attention, irregardless of the razor. "It is not as if the boys need a fatherly example, as you would be if you visited more often. But I like him, and relish his presence without being particularly set upon it. So, tell me now. What do you think?"

"I should have to meet him, while in my right mind, of course," Carl answered, as she rinsed the razor. "Other than that, just be certain of your own interests, in letting him control your property."

"I have already seen to that," Margaret answered serenely. "Half of this is entailed in your name. It is only right, even though I know you want no part of it, but I have named you as guardian for the boys, in any case. I am well protected against any fortune-hunters. Now, hold still, this is the tricky part... there. Now I am finished. You can talk to me and tell me true. You met this party of folk from the Old Country. Who are they and how did her niece get into the river?" She rinsed off the razor, and studied her handiwork carefully.

"Steinmetz . . . Christian Friedrich Steinmetz," Carl answered. "He makes clocks, but he farms a little on the side. He had a wife but she died on the boat coming over; he now has two sons, a son-in-law and three pretty daughters."

"Sounds like one of Ma's old fairy tales." Margaret dabbled away a bit of foam with a towel and wondered if she dared risk too many more questions. "I suppose it is the youngest and prettiest that you have charmed."

Carl let out a great laugh that turned into a coughing fit.

"The youngest and prettiest is all of two years old," he gasped. "Oh, damn, it hurts when I do that! And the middle daughter is the married one. She has a little girl - the one I pulled out of the river."

"So, you have set your heart on the oldest daughter . . . hold still again." Margaret made neat work of last bit of stubble on his cheek. "Lift up your chin, now, I am nearly finished. How does she regard you, little brother?"

"I don't know." He sank back onto the pillow. With the beard gone, he looked very wan. "They were very kindly folk. They made much ado about loaning me dry clothes. She brought my own back to me . . . and we talked for a little."

Of course, no doubt about the way that he said "she". This was more than calf-love for a pretty neighbor girl on the part of the boy that her little brother had been. Now he was a man grown and yearning after a woman. And if he hadn't been so ill, Margaret very much doubted that he would have been brought to speak of it. Quiet and soft-spoken as a boy, as a man he was practically a sphinx.

"Is that when you began to like her?" Margaret asked.

"No, that was when I saw her heading into a strong current after the little girl, even though it looked like she couldn't swim a lick. Not a chance in hell, but she tried, anyway. Cold nerve—that's what I liked. I talked later with old Steinmetz, and Hans, that's the brother-in-law. It was very agreeable, passing the time with them." He added wistfully, "Almost as I remember it being before, when Ma and Rudi were alive."

Ah, thought Margaret, in a flash of illumination. *It's not only the girl he desires, but the company of her family as well; her sisters and brothers, and the clever, kindly father— whom I do not think plays favorites with his sons.*

"What were you planning to do, then?" Margaret asked, "I think I should take away the extra pillows and let you lie down again to rest."

"I wasn't thinking so far ahead," he answered, "And I'm too tired to think about it now."

"I shouldn't have had you sit up for so long," Margaret said remorsefully as she tidied up the towels and the bowl of water, "Now that you are home, perhaps you can send a message to them. No doubt they think of you fondly," but even as she spoke, her brother had drifted into sleep again; not the restless and fevered slumber of before, but a healing, quiet sleep. Margaret resettled the quilt around him, thinking that he appeared just now as she had always thought of him, as a boy hardly older than her oldest son. In her mind, Carl was always about sixteen, gawky and not quite filled out, the way he had been when he left for good.

Another sorrowful memory for Margaret: the summer day that the man from back East came to the Becker home place, just after the War for Independence had been won. He was, he told them, writing an account for an eastern newspaper regarding the heroic death of Colonel Fannin. He had heard from others, he explained politely, that Alois Becker's younger son had been at Goliad, had been one of the survivors. Might he speak with Carl?

Margaret had herself gone and found him cutting summer hay, swinging a scythe in the lower hay-meadow, the field that was now sold off and built over. He came willingly enough, albeit not enthusiastically. Carl had his full share of questions when he returned, had answered most of them briefly or not at all. Other people had suffered appalling tragedies during the war; it seemed to Margaret they were inclined to be understanding of his reluctance to speak of his particular part in one.

Margaret listened to them from the kitchen, as they talked in the parlor; Pa's gruff voice interjecting once or twice, the newspaperman's occasional deft questions, but mostly Carl's light, uninflected tones. He recounted the whole dreadful story dispassionately, as if it had all happened to someone else: occupying the Presidio, of Fannin's fatal indecision, of Coleto and surrender, the aftermath, his escape to the river and his torturous journey home on foot.

And at the very end of it, as Pa was showing the newspaper writer out of the parlor, he shook the man's hand and said, in Carl's hearing, *'Oh, but you should have known Rudolph, my oldest son. He was such a promising boy, worth three of this one any day of the week.'*

Margaret always thought the newspaper writer may have been at least a little taken back. She herself was so horrified at her father's words that she could hardly bring herself to look at Carl who stood in the middle of the parlor. He looked blank, just as if he had been struck so hard that he couldn't feel any pain at all. He walked calmly out of the parlor and went back to scything hay without a word to Pa, or to Margaret.

In the morning he was gone, taking only an ancient musket that Pa had brought back after San Jacinto and borrowing a horse and saddle from a neighbor. Sometime later they heard from the neighbor, who had gotten his horse returned, that he had gone to Columbia to join Colonel Smith's Ranger troop and was off on a long scout to the borderlands. Margaret occasionally got word of him through friends, but he did not return for nearly two years. When she finally saw him again, he had filled out, grown tall and hard-muscled, no longer a boy but still silent. He stayed a day or so at the homestead with them, saying nothing much to Pa but the bare courtesies and then went off again.

Sometimes Margaret heard talk or read in the newspapers of the exploits of a company she knew her brother was riding with, and she felt a cold chill, wondering if his most recent visit would turn out to be the very last time she would ever see her little brother. The only thing that changed during that time had been after Pa died. Carl's infrequent visits became a little longer in duration, then.

Margaret emptied the basin into the slops jar and gathered up the damp towels. She looked down at her brother and thought, *He is too shy to tell me your name, clockmaker's daughter from the Old Country. But treat him with kindness; that is all I ask of you. Just because my little brother will not show his hurts, doesn't mean he doesn't feel them.*

Autumn days waned and shortened into winter, and a bitter wind banished the leaf shadows dancing on the scrubbed pine floor. Carl slept and woke, and slept again, sometimes to see Margaret keeping vigil in her rocking chair, other times to hear her footsteps in the next room or in the hallway. There were other voices in the house, other footsteps, but with the lassitude of illness he could not bring himself to care very much. Margaret brought him cups of strong beef tea and delicate little messes carefully arranged on a china dish to tempt an appetite and cut up so as to be easy managed with one hand. He ate obediently; it would take too much energy to refuse.

Doctor Williamson proved to be a burly, strong-featured man of middle age, carelessly dressed but possessing astonishingly gentle hands. He probed the discolored tangle of scars and half-healed flesh and bone that was Carl's upper chest and shoulder, and said thoughtfully, "About the best I can say for whoever patched you up is that there are no signs of mortification - he certainly has no calling as a surgeon."

"Our Lieutenant," Carl felt obscurely moved to defend Bill Wallace. "And the army surgeon, using good whiskey and bad bread. They didn't do too bad, considering that I'm still alive."

"Tell him in future when you see them again, to stick to doctoring horses," answered Doctor Williamson. "The breaks . . . here, and here, are knitting well. At least he knew his trade in setting bones."

"It aches like hell, still."

"Permanent condition, I'm afraid. But you'll be able to predict changes in the weather, now. Let me listen to your lungs. Mrs. Vining thinks you are coughing too much." Doctor Williamson frowned thoughtfully as he listened to Carl breathe in and out. "You are at a risk for lung fever, especially with this harsh weather. I would advise remaining convalescent for a while longer."

"Since I can't take two steps on my own without falling flat, I might as well."

"Good," Doctor Williamson said, kindly. "Really, you are coming along remarkably well, considering. I shall tell your sister— Mrs. Vining so." He looked almost shy when he said Margaret's name. "She has been much concerned, these last few weeks. I would so much like to relieve her mind. A fine woman—I have the deepest respect for her, of course." Now he looked even a little flustered and looked around the room in vague confusion. "I seem to have misplaced my coat."

"Hanging on the hook, on the back of the door," Carl said, with dry amusement.

"Oh, so it is." The doctor gathered up his bag, and his coat, and went to give the good news to Margaret, although he did have to come back later for his spectacles, left on Margaret's sewing table.

"And so what is your opinion of my suitor?" Margaret asked that evening, when she brought in another of her dainty little invalid meals, "Now that you have made his acquaintance in your right mind, of course."

"He seems well-intentioned, but passing absent-minded."

"Oh, he has no mind for anything but medicine," Margaret answered, fondly. "He comes to dinner reading some foreign medical journal and props it against the cruets. We are all quite used to him returning from a day of house-calls and forgetting where he has left his coat, or his hat, or even his horse."

"Then you should accept his suit, if you wish it and if it would make you happy." Carl set down his fork. "He's too absent-minded to even remember that you have property, let alone where he left his own traps. Might I have a little more, Margaret?"

"You are hungry?" Margaret sprang up from her chair, "That is a good sign, indeed. Yes, of course." She took the plate from the tray on his knees.

As she did, he said, "Her name is Margaretha."

"Oh," said Margaret thoughtfully. She stood for a minute, in the pool of lamplight. "If you please, I shall talk to some of my friends and see how we might find out where to find her family. But only if you would like."

"Yes . . . if you can. Thank you, Margaret."

She bent down on impulse and kissed his forehead as if he were one of her own children, and replied. "Don't mention it, little brother."

Chapter 9 – *Forest Home*

Letter from Christian Friedrich Steinmetz: Written 15 August 1846 from Friedrichsburg, to Simon Frankenthaler, Goldsmith of the City of Ulm in Bavaria,

My Dear Simon: Such a series of events which tax my poor pen to describe! We were left alone in the wilderness, as I described in my previous missive to our devices under the direction of Mr. Bene, and with only such items and supplies as we had transported with us, or that Mr. Bene had left on his previous visit. We had first to finish the storehouse to safeguard our supplies, and a large compound of logs within which we would be secure at night, to which labor all male persons willingly applied themselves. We also needed to construct shelters for ourselves, for the weather has proved to be very changeable! We were struck by a spell of cold weather and a violent storm, with our shelters being yet half-built. It became so cold that a newborn child perished of exposure, despite being sheltered with his mother under a thick feather-bed. The boys and I and son Hansi have bent every effort towards providing shelter for ourselves. We have experienced some few unfortunate deaths, mostly of disease that strike when we poor humans must live without shelter and in primitive conditions. As my dear daughter has pointed out to me, the life of a noble savage is likely to be devoid of comforts that we cherish, and we suffer accordingly with their lack! All these events increase the urgency we feel towards bettering our overall conditions of life. There is so much to be done; I have little time to write to you of our various projects! (We are currently without a doctor; Mr. Meusebach is endeavoring to provide us with one.)

Mr. Bene directed that a large plot of ground be cleared and fenced for cultivation immediately, in order to supply vegetables for ourselves. Scarcely had this work been accomplished on the community garden, when another cart train of settlers arrived from Neu Braunfels with several wagons of supplies. Among these new arrivals were our very good friends, the Reverend Doctor Altmueller and his wife. We received them with much joy, as you may imagine. We also have another reason for rejoicing; the disposition of town lots has been made. Son Hansi has a very fine lot on Creek Street, or what will be called Creek Street when there is rather less Creek and rather more Street. He has already built a small shelter there, of the rough kind called a "Mexican hut," and planted a garden. My own lot is on the crossing of Market Street and San Antonio Street, a short distance away. The Indians come often, to trade meat or nuts and wild fruit from the woods as they find it, for such trifles as we can spare. Between their offerings, the stores issued to us by the Verein commissariat and our own hard work, we are very well fed. We still live very simply, a little above the level of the gypsy-folk. It is reasonable to expect our lives to continue in this manner for a year or two yet. It is very hard for my daughters, though, to cook over a campfire, and bread is a very scarce commodity. To earn more money, many of the younger men are taking work elsewhere and leaving their families here. . ."

* * *

"I think I shall have to take up the Baron's offer," said Hansi quietly on a summer evening, in the voice of a man who has already made up his mind. Liesel's heart sank within her, but she listened quietly; her husband was not clever with words, not like Vati. He was careful; he thought things through and came to a decision long before he ever spoke of it. "He sent word that he needs teamsters and wagon-masters again. We need the money that the Verein would pay to build us a proper house, hearts-love."

They lay in bed together, spoon-fashion, with Liesel tucked into the curve of his body, and his arms around her. Anna had long since gone to sleep, curled like a kitten in her little bed. The chickens clucked sleepily in their hutch, built against the wall of standing logs that made the four walls of their little house.

"When?" asked Liesel after some moments. Her throat hurt, she could barely say that one word.

"As soon as I finish thatching the roof," His arms tightened around her, comfortingly. "This is not the house I have promised you, I know. It is just shelter for now."

"We have only been living in it for a week . . . why do you need to go?" It was bare and crude, the floor was swept dirt, the roof leaked in a heavy rain, there were gaps between the logs that it was built of, but it was hers and hers alone, the first house they had ever possessed of their own and lived in together.

"Because I can best be spared now," Hansi answered, patiently. "The garden is thriving . . . I know that we planted very late, but you and Anna should be able to tend and harvest yourselves. Vati and Magda can help, as well."

"I'd rather live in a hut that I shared with you, than a mansion alone!"

Liesel began to weep and he said, reasonably, "You would not be alone. You have Vati and Magda close by, and the Altmuellers. And it's not as if I would be away, really. I would be traveling back and forth between here and Karlshaven and Neu Braunfels, just for the rest of the summer and into autumn, helping to move those of our people still waiting there. The war in Mexico has made it nearly impossible to hire teamsters this summer. They would rather work for what the Americans can pay, than what little the Verein can offer. So we must see to our affairs ourselves, Lise. Think of what the Altmuellers told us. Our people die, waiting for help—for help that only we can provide!"

"I remember very well what it was like," Liesel answered, "and I shall not forget it . . . but there is another reason I want you with me." She took his hand in hers and placed it on her belly. Although nothing showed as yet, she could feel that difference within her already, that sense of something planted solidly and already growing strong.

"Ah." He comprehended almost at once. His arms tightened around her. Not for nothing was her Hansi a farmer, a good stockman. He knew well the changes in flesh, the sense of new life springing up and the tender care it would take to see it grow strong and vibrant. "When?"

"After the New Year—February, I think. Think of it, Hansi! I hope for a boy, a brother for Anna."

"All the better reason for me to take this work that the Baron has offered," he answered, firmly. "This is no place for my wife and my children to live. I have promised you so much better, and you will have it. Or if not that, at least a proper floor."

And with that, Liesel knew she had no hope of dissuading him. She turned, under the blankets pulled over them both, and buried her face in his shoulder, crying just a little as he held her close and murmured comforting endearments.

What a difference that a couple of months of hard work had made, thought Magda as she walked from Vati's town lot towards Hansi and Liesel's hut. And still, there was so much remaining to be done, as she reminded Vati whenever he seemed more inclined to set aside his tools and engage in some entrancing matter of the intellect! She picked her way along the edge of a long cleared space adorned with many tree stumps and the ruts of iron wagon tires. Mr. Bene had assured them cheerfully that it was to be called "Market Street" although nothing else was much in evidence yet to support that assertion save for piles of shaped timbers being made ready for building cabins and houses. Since their arrival in spring, much of the underbrush had been cleared away, turned into firewood and rafter poles or rough pieces of furniture. A number of the great post oaks still stood bravely, those tall, straight-limbed trees which reminded Vati of cathedrals and which had sheltered them in their first days, although many were slated to be felled for timber. But they would go on sheltering them in another manner, for their houses were being built of them.

Vati himself had decided to keep the two largest oaks which stood towards the middle of his property, but otherwise there still there remained a forest of stumps. One of the recent arrivals, a man of Vati's age, had taken it as his special responsibility to up-root those in that area that had been marked out as the main square, one by one. Magda waved to old Mr. Wahrmund as she and Rosalie walked past where he was laboring with a shovel and an ax. She carried two buckets and led Rosalie by the hand; they were on their way to the Baron's Creek for water. Vati had grand plans for a well in the back of his new house. Magda still liked the excuse of walking down to the creek and visiting with Liesel and Anna.

With the underbrush and the sapling trees cleared away, it was easier to see where the surveyor's marks denoted the boundaries of the town lots and the straight angles of the streets. Mr. Bene had mapped out generous avenues, and straight regular corners. Passage of many wagons, coming to and fro made their purpose manifest with deep ruts. It was now possible to see all the way down Main Street, past Mr. Kiehne's forge towards the Verein blockhouse, the storehouses, and the adjacent walled compound. Indeed it was possible to see them for a good distance now in any direction. What was left of the oak-wood echoed with the tap-tap-tap of hammers, the scrape of saws and the deep and regular thud of axes chopping them down, one by one. Mr. Kiehne had set up his smithy forge under a huge post-oak along Main Street, and the music of his hammer and anvil added to the symphony of their new town, growing up in the wilderness. Others had already begun cutting stone and burning lime in a makeshift furnace, to make plaster.

Most folk, like the Lochtes and others, chose to begin with a hastily-built brush arbor, or as Hansi did, with a Mexican hut, built of logs with their ends sunk into the ground, and roofed with canvas or thatch, wanting some kind of shelter for their families, no matter how ramshackle. But Vati had blinked vaguely at his town lot and said firmly, "Your dear mother would never have wanted this for you. No, I shall do it properly from the start. Besides, I must have a proper workshop and a place for doing business."

He and the boys, with the help of the Arhelger brothers, had built a tiny cabin at the back of the town lot and roofed it with tent canvas well pegged down. It had taken them only three or four days, once the timbers were cut and rough-shaped. Then William Arhelger, skilled as a carpenter, had cut the intricate corner notches while Vati and the boys helped lift them into place, side by side. It held out the breeze about as well as a sieve, what with the cracks between the logs.

"Green wood," said William, apologetically. "Sorry, you'll be patching cracks for the next couple of years, until the timber cures."

"We shall have our house finished well before then," Vati said serenely. "And then we can use this for another purpose." Fortunately the summer was mild, even at night, so Magda and her brothers did not mind overmuch. As Vati saw it and reminded them often, the building of the cabin left room enough at the front for building the new house, and in between there was space enough for work under the trees and a garden for vegetables.

"We really shall have to fill the cracks with plaster if we are still living here come winter," Magda said.

Vati polished his glasses again and answered, "I would rather put our efforts toward the house, at least until summer ends. I have an advantage, my dear Magda, since I was able to sell our old farm and the freehold of my little shop for so much. There is sufficient, if we are careful, to hire others. And that would serve their needs as well, since then they can earn enough to build their own houses without having to leave and earn it elsewhere, like Hansi, and we may have the use of our house all the much sooner."

"I wonder that you did not offer to help them with their house," Magda said, and Vati shook his head.

"I did suggest so, but he was most adamant in refusing. He had already arranged to take work with the Verein. It is a matter of pride for Hansi that he should care for your sister and Anna and the new little one himself, rather then depend on the whim of another. He has promised Liesel a house, and a house she shall have, built with his own hands or from the fruit of his own labor."

By midsummer, timber framework for Vati's new house had already gone up: four rooms on the ground floor and four rooms upstairs. Vati had thought to make two of the rooms his shop and workroom, with a separate door to the outside on San Antonio Street, a little way down from the door to the rest of it.

"Really," Vati said, "I may be able to rent that portion to others, at some time in the future. What a thought, that I should become a land-lord!" Magda looked every evening at the looming skeleton-outline of it, from the doorway of the meager little cabin across an oceanic litter of wood-chips and crude forms for casting the mud-brick which would fill in the sides in between the timbers. She relished the sight of what had been accomplished that day. Every day the neat stack of bricks grew taller, as did the pile of shingles which Vati cut from rough-squared short bolts of oak left over from cutting the main timbers.

And that very day, Vati had hired a pair of stonemasons, the Berg brothers, newly-arrived from Karlshaven and the Old Country, to construct the staircase and the fireplaces. Vati hoped that there would be enough of the house finished by winter so that they could move out of the drafty little cabin.

Magda turned towards the right at Creek Street, where Baron's Creek itself touched upon the road. These lots had been much prized and sought after, for the richness of the soil and proximity to water, although they were at the very edge of town, right where the farm lots were to begin. As she and Rosalie followed another stretch of ruts and stumps, she could see Liesel and Anna at work in their vegetable garden beside the tiny thatched hut. When they were close enough, Liesel stood, and pressed her hands against the small of her back and Anna came running towards them.

"Auntie Magda, come and see! We have ever so many eggs this morning!"

"How many is ever so many?" Magda asked, and Anna held up four fingers.

"As many as that? That is four, a fortune in eggs, dear heart."

Liesel's precious flock of chickens were allowed to pick and scratch as they pleased, but at night they were shut into their own little house, built of stout scraps of plank, against the side of Hansi and Liesel's shelter. Anna and Liesel guarded them with great care during the day against the hawk which still nested in the great trees by the creek and hunted by day, soaring almost motionless in the air, and the native foxes that boldly crept out during the night.

"I think we shall eat them," Liesel remarked, as she hugged her sisters in greeting. "We have as many chickens as we can take care of, now."

"You should, for yourself and the baby," Magda advised. "Do you need anything from the storehouse? I was going to draw our own, after I bring the water."

"No. We shall walk there ourselves, when I am done with weeding." She took off her flat straw hat, and fanned herself with it. "Do you want some vegetables? I would like to thin out the carrots, and there are some squash just begging to be eaten."

"Only if you don't want them for yourself," Magda answered. Liesel shook her head.

"I have eaten so much I think I should be as fat as a pig. My stomach must be making up for spending two months rejecting everything that I put in my mouth. I am so glad to have that over with! I feel so splendid now, as if I could go and climb up mountains." She laughed, and amended it, "Well, small mountains anyway." Magda looked at her closely: she looked blooming, pink-cheeked and happy as she had been always before. Hansi may have gone here and there with wagons to the coast and back again, but he came home often enough to keep Liesel content. And she had the new baby to look forward to.

They talked for a little, admiring the way the garden thrived, while Anna showed Rosalie how to scatter dried corn for the chickens.

"She is a dear child," Liesel said, watching the two little girls throw handfuls of corn at the importuning chickens and Rosalie shriek with surprise, as they all came running. "It's as if she was given to us as a gift, like the little folk left her in a basket by the door." Liesel looked a little saddened and added, "I just hope that she will not be taken away from us so quickly, as if they who gave her to us would want her back again!"

"You say that as though you were thinking of little Joachim," Magda said with concern, but Liesel smiled after a moment and answered:

"No, it was only an odd fancy! Come and pick your carrots and squash, then!"

Magda took her buckets to the creek bank, and drew them up, well filled. She let Rosalie carry the fresh-picked vegetables, and they walked back towards Vati's town lot.

Vati and the boys had been hard at work since sunrise, under the pair of huge oak trees which dominated the middle of his lot: Vati industriously slicing rough shingles with a froe and mallet, and Johann and Friedrich combining work and pleasure by mixing clay, and straw and horse dung to make brick, in a vast wooden trug.

"It is every boy's delight to be given permission to play in the mud," said Vati with satisfaction. "I am almost sure, also, that most of it is indeed finding its way into the moulds. Do you know, I think I should have a barn . . . or at least a coach-house, or a stable of some kind—built at the end of the house, but with a gateway and a covered passage between for convenience, just as it was in Albeck? What do you think?"

"I do not think that will be necessary," Magda answered thoughtfully. "After all, it does not get so cold here; if last winter is anything to judge by. And if it is as warm every summer as it is now, would we really want the stable so close to the house?"

"Oh. I had not thought on that," Vati looked slightly crestfallen. "At any rate, Mr. Berg is here. Such a clever young man, quite the artist. He is looking over the house, I thought you should tell him where the fireplaces should be . . . no, no, Rosalie my dear. Leave the finishing knife alone. It's too sharp; you'll cut your pretty little fingers."

Magda swung Rosalie up onto her hip, not quite trusting the child to safely navigate the tangle of hazards presented by a building site on her own feet: sharp tools, carelessly stacked beams, and the delights of mud. She herself stepped carefully around the crude wood frames packed tight with rough clay and yesterday's production of bricks, turned endways to dry and cure.

Their new house would be one room deep and shaped rather like an "L"; kitchen and parlor, with a staircase in a corner of the parlor to the rooms upstairs, and doors which gave passage from the back yard, a front door on Market Street and another into the shop and workroom. Magda picked her way through the jumble and into the parlor from the back. To the left would be the kitchen, to the right Vati's shop, one great square room at the very corner, with his workroom in back. Timbers for the bottom floor had been cut and allowed to season for a few months, then mortised and pegged together, top, bottom and corners, and cross-braced at the angles. Today, they had begun work on the upper floor. To her surprise, there had already been a number of rafters laid over the space where the kitchen would be. A slight, clever-looking young man was walking around in the space, carefully studying the wall-timbers.

"Miss Vogel? Good day to you. Peter Berg." He bowed briefly over her hand. "Your father said you would best know about situating the fireplace."

"There." She pointed to the end wall, opposite the door in the wall between kitchen and parlor. "So that in summer, the heat from it will not make the parlor unbearable. It would be well to have a bread-oven also built into it, also, and a warming cupboard, if possible."

"And have it extend all the way across, from here, to the back wall, yes?"

"Of course." He nodded, and she asked, "Aren't you going to measure, or write anything down?"

He shook his head. "It is not necessary for me. I have a good eye. And this floor will be all in stone, cut to fit?"

"Yes. And a stone staircase in this corner, to the upper floor, but with a wooden banister."

"Very well. It shall be done, as you ask." He nodded abruptly. "I shall speak to your father regarding the arrangements and make up a design with your specifications. Good day, Miss Vogel."

"Good day, Mr. Berg." He left through the front, dodging a falling shower of sawdust and a length of sawn-off peg-end, dropping down from where William Arhelger was working on the upstairs.

"Willi! Have a care, that's the stone-mason! Try not to kill him until after the stonework is done!"

"Your pardon, I am sure!" Willi called down. "Didn't see him!"

She hoisted Rosalie a little higher on her hip and called from the place where the windows in the back would be, "Vati, I'm going to see the storehouse to ask for some flour!" Vati waved, and Magda set

163

off on her second errand: along the edge of Market Square to Main Street, and east towards the Verein storehouse to see what she could get of the Steinmetz family ration. She had to wait her turn, for Sophie Ahrens and her mother were there ahead of her and an impatient young man drumming his fingers on the counter while he waited his turn. He wasn't one of the Germans, but rather an American. He reminded her somewhat of Carl Becker, as he possessed the same open face and air of capability. She was amused to see that the American kept looking towards Sophie Ahrens, who had pink cheeks and very curly dark hair. The Widow Ahrens, her two daughters and son-in-law, along with a whole constellation of relations had come from Neu Braunfels with one of the later parties.

The clerk at the storehouse was not someone she knew. There were so many people coming into town from Neu Braunfels and the coast, it was hard to keep up with all the new faces. Every day seemed to bring more, like the young American. This clerk was a wiry young spark with lively blue eyes and an engaging grin, a little older than Magda. His face looked sun-burnt, and there were lines around his eyes as if he had spent many hours looking into the sky in all weather. No, he had spent time as something other than a mere storehouse clerk. And he talked to the American in English, as if the two young men were well-acquainted. It even sounded as if the clerk was jesting with the American, who stared after Sophie Ahrens as she and her mother went out from the storehouse. Finally it was her turn.

The clerk greeted her pleasantly and looked up their account when she told him their family name. By a miracle he produced not only a bag of flour, but a little quantity of tea and some fresh cheese.

"We just finished unloading the supply wagon last night, Miss Vogel," he remarked cheerily and then he reached over the counter and appeared to take a small silver case-watch out of Rosalie's ear.

"That's a strange place to keep a watch, little Miss," he said. "Looks like there is something else in there, too!" With great aplomb he appeared to remove a small ink-bottle, a gold coin and five whole pecans from the same place. Rosalie, much puzzled at first, began to laugh as the succession of unlikely objects appeared. Magda watched with frank delight.

"You're a conjurer!" she said, admiringly.

"I am a man of many skills," He began deftly juggling the five pecans, until he missed one. All of them promptly went skittering all over the counter and floor.

"Oh, bravo!" Magda applauded, while Rosalie wriggled to be let down to hunt for the pecans.

"Somewhat less practiced at some of them," he confessed and bowed, very correctly. "C.H. Nimitz, at your service, Miss Vogel. Born Karl-Heinrich, but in this country, Charles Henry; Charley for short. My family came from Bremen, while I was serving on a merchantman as supercargo and clerk. They settled in Charleston, but I came here."

"Why here?"

"Why not? I heard that the Verein offered land and thought, if it's going to rain oat-porridge I may as well have my bowl right-side up. Besides, this is about as far from the sea as I can get without running the risk of being scalped by a wild Indian or eaten by a bear."

"You did not care for seafaring?"

"Hated it, profoundly," Charley confessed with a shudder. "I can't describe to a lady the vileness of certain experiences, such as trying to get a good nights' sleep in the forecastle after the crew has dined luxuriously on beans. Not to mention a winter gale in the mid-Atlantic. They were all interesting experiences, which I abandon gratefully to those who have a taste for them. Since I do not... best to move on and sample some of life's other delights. Square holes, round pegs and all of that."

"I was only the once at sea," Magda confessed, "when we took ship at Bremen to come over here. It was horrible, a nightmare. I still don't like to remember it."

Charley shook his head most sympathetically. "They say, and I can confirm from my own experience, that the only thing that smells worse than an immigrant ship after a long voyage is a slaver." He brightened and added, "I suppose you did not linger long in Bremen. I was born there and would have stayed, but there was no work except for going to sea."

"So - what do you look for, here?" Magda asked.

Charley Nimitz looked around, wryly sizing up the interior of the Verein storehouse and replied, "More than this, Miss Vogel; much more than this! And I shall have it. We must put up with these conditions for the present, but there is nothing that says we must put up with them for long."

"My father is of the same mind," Magda said. "He wanted to build a proper house as soon as possible, so he may open his shop again."

"We might yet have all which we need in the way of comforts, and sooner than we think," Charley said. "You saw my friend—the gentleman I was speaking to in English? He is thinking of coming here and starting some kind of enterprise. It shall have to be something really superior, to meet with Mrs. Ahrens' approval."

"Was he truly trying to flirt with Sophie?" Magda asked with amusement and Charley laughed.

"John cannot speak German, and she can't speak English. I can just picture myself, reduced to translating all sorts of loving endearments. Perhaps I should just give them each a dictionary and let them alone, eh?"

"And another dictionary for Mrs. Ahrens, for she must chaperone her daughter," Magda suggested. Charley laughed again at that. After a few more pleasantries, and Charley admiring Rosalie very much—and appearing to find a piece of hard-candy in her ear, which he gravely presented to her, Magda walked out into the street with her basket and Rosalie. This was a good start to a day. Charley - Mr. Nimitz lightened the whole world around him with his wit and good cheer.

"You like him, don't you, Rosalie?" she asked Rosalie She had begun to be in the habit of talking to her so, even though the child barely understood one word in four. "He makes you feel that you yourself are clever and excellent company, rather than puffing his own self up, like a big frog."

"Frog!" Rosalie giggled and blew out her cheeks. She swung their linked hands back and forth, as she skipped alongside Magda. "Froggy, Charley, Froggy, Charley!" She made a chant of it, while they walked back down Main Street. When Magda and Rosalie returned to the frame of Vati's house, the boys had finished packing mud into about half the brick moulds and gone to dig more clay from the creek-bank. William Arhelger, a wheelwright as well as a skilled carpenter, had built them a hand-cart to haul small burdens.

"They gave you the rations as readily as that?" Vati asked, doubtfully.

"There is a new clerk, in charge of stores," Magda answered, "He seems very pleasant and cheerful. He did magic tricks for Rosalie and gave her a piece of candy. He's from Bremen, and said he was a sailor until he got tired of it. He seems very clever. And there was an American there, in the storehouse; we thought he was trying to flirt with Sophie Ahrens. He'll have his work cut out getting past Mrs. Ahrens. The American, not the clerk."

"Oh, that one," Vati chuckled, "He is a scamp! He is the one who played that trick with Prosser's goat-herd. You know those goats of his kept knocking down the fence of their pen, and roaming around and eating from people's garden-plots."

"What trick with the goats was this, Vati?"

Prosser's flock of goats had been the bane of everyone like Hansi and Liesel, trying to grow vegetable gardens along Creek Street. While all had sympathy for the Prosser family and their determination to build a fine herd, such sympathies had gradually become muted. The Prossers were incapable of keeping their animals from eating other families' cherished gardens and had been unsympathetic to complaints about it. Everyone had been secretly relieved when the herd had diminished to two or three animals and not inclined to inquire closely as to what had happened to the rest.

Vati chuckled, and explained, "You must not put it around, Magda, for if Prosser finds out, he will be extremely angry. It is no more than what he deserves for being so careless with those goats. Young Nimitz caught the billy-goat and dressed him up in a suit of old clothes. He even tied a hat on the top of the billy's head and turned him loose, and the sight of it panicked the rest! They scattered up-hill and down-dale. Such a ridiculous spectacle, seeing the billy scamper down the middle of the street, running and trying to pull off those clothes! I don't think Prosser got more than a few of them back.

I suppose," he added, wisely, "that the Indians had some very fine meals! Certainly none of Prosser's neighbors grudged them a bite, once their gardens were free of the menace."

"Well, he certainly has taken care of the ones he has left," Magda observed. "From the way people hated those goats, I only wonder that none of us had a meal of them, as well."

"You never know," Vati said, slyly. "The Indians often bring us meat to trade, some of it very strange tasting indeed."

"Oh, Vati!" Magda covered her mouth with her hand, and began to laugh. "I should like to think I could have told the difference, but if it were already skinned and dressed . . ."

"So," Vati bent over his task again, "this young man amuses you? I think he amuses us all. Would it please you if he visits us now and again? As a friend, of course, nothing more."

"Vati, you are incorrigible," Magda told him severely.

"My dear child, you should have friends, especially young men who make you laugh." He set down his mallet and froe and looked at her with great affection. "We—I forget sometimes, how much we all depend on you, and what a great burden that must be. We have all had such hard times! Perhaps now you may allow yourself to take a little time to be happy with the company of friends. Think on it, Magda— this house full of friends and laughter and singing!"

"We'll need a roof over it, first." Magda leaned down and kissed him affectionately on the forehead. "Before we can even think of hosting friends, with laughter and song. Enough of this idle chatter, Vati; invite Charley Nimitz if you like. He is funny and clever and the children will love him. He will tease Hansi, amuse the boys by talking to them as if they are men, flirt with me, and talk to you of the Old Country ... but in the meantime, your house is still unfinished."

"To work then, my dear child." Vati took up his froe and mallet and began splitting off shingles with vigorous enthusiasm, while Magda carried her basket into the little cabin and thought on how wonderful it would be to bake bread over a fine stone hearth. She was wearied of cooking and baking over an open fire, as were all the women. But still, there was excitement in doing as she and Vati and the boys, and Hansi and Liesel were doing: building their new lives and new homes, just like everyone else who had believed the Verein promises and signed a contract. In spite of all the hardships and uncertainties, and the death of Mutti and the baby, there were still so many things she was glad for having seen and experienced. The world around her was larger, the horizons were more generous, and she thought that she might be happier than she had ever been before. She had nearly put Carl Becker out of her mind. She thought of him only as she thought of some of the men who had tentatively courted her back in Albeck, someone who was part of her past, not of the ever-expanding present. She briskly dismissed any such thoughts as being of no consequence as soon as they occurred; if he had any serious intent towards her, she was sure that would have heard from him long since.

Chapter 10 – *San Saba*

Margaret Becker Vining married Doctor Williamson the day before Christmas, standing up before a Justice of the Peace in the private parlor of her house. The parlor was adorned for Christmas with a tall cut pine tree decorated with candles and garlands of bright-red mountain-laurel seeds, drilled through and strung together, and a number of fragile blown-glass ornaments.

"Mr. Ernst had a box of them sent from the Old Country," Margaret told her brother, when Horace and his younger brothers had settled the fine tree in the corner of the parlor the week before. "He was kind enough to send me some. It is quite the fashion now to celebrate Christmas this way."

Garlands of evergreens and brave red ribbons adorned the rest of Margaret's comfortable parlor. The Justice was one of her boarders and performed the brief ceremony before an audience of her other boarders, the Vining boys, and Carl. He kissed her cheek fondly and shook the hand of his new brother-in-law, all the while feeling profoundly grateful that he was present, well-dressed, and strong enough to stand as a witness for the brief ceremony without passing out.

"They all look regretful," he whispered to his sister, "your other boarders. As if they had their shot and missed it clean."

"I do not know what you are talking about," his sister answered sedately, embracing him. "Be happy, little brother. Be happy for us, and for yourself. Only please do not encourage the boys to do that riding trick—where you hang by one hand and foot from the side of a galloping horse and shoot from under your horse's neck?"

"That one?" Carl whispered innocently. "It is a very useful maneuver, very useful in some circumstances."

"None the less," Margaret sighed, very deeply. "I suppose it is fortunate that I have married a doctor. Try not to break too many of their bones, or your own. I love you very deeply, little brother." She embraced him again, and lightly kissed his cheek, "You should come home more often."

"I will," he answered, realizing with some astonished wonder that he meant it. This time he had truly felt as if he were home, instead of just passing a few restless days in a more than usually comfortable camping place. He had never stayed long enough in Margaret's warm and undemanding orbit to feel he had a rightful place in it, never long enough to partake of the gentle routine, until forced into it by a lengthy convalescence. By the time he was well enough to sit at table for meals and spend evenings in the parlor with Margaret, the Doctor, the boys, and whomever of the boarders were desirous of sharing their company, he was halfway to thinking it was not a bad sort of way to spend an evening: playing cards, or sharing interesting bits from the newspaper with each other, telling yarns about his friends in the Rangers to the boys, while Margaret shook her head in mild disapproval over her mending. When Doctor Williamson bought a piano as a surprise wedding and Christmas present for Margaret and asked for Carl's help in installing it in the parlor, he felt that his place in the family circle had been established.

They only talked of Vati Steinmetz and his oldest daughter once when Margaret was trying out the piano the first evening that it was hers, and fell into playing the first bars of "Joseph Lieber, Joseph mein". She began to sing the words and Carl joined her, singing the half-forgotten words, quietly as everyone in the parlor hushed to better hear them:

> "*Joseph, lieber Joseph mein,*
> *Hilf mir wiegen mein Kindelein!*
> *Will es wiegen und singen ein:*
> *Nun schlaf in Ruh, Die Äuglein zu,*
> *O Jesus!*"

"That's a beautiful song, my dear," Doctor Williamson looked up from his medical journal, as they finished. "I have never heard you sing it before . . . is it new?"

"We used to sing it when we were children," Margaret answered. "Oh we knew so many songs, songs that I almost never sing myself, now. The boys were never very interested in learning the old songs. Their father didn't speak German, and all their friends speak English."

"You haven't taught them songs like this? Like 'Christmas Tree'?" Carl asked, almost incredulously. It seemed that they had never stopped singing, when he was a boy and Ma was still alive. Margaret looked melancholy, as her fingers moved over the keys. "Oh, little brother, it is one of those things that one lets go, almost without thinking of it. And it's not like you spent much time singing old songs at Christmas, once you left home. I don't know how you could expect anything different of me. Things do not stay the same, as much as we would wish them to."

"I know that," he answered.

She looked at him shrewdly and said, "She would know all the old songs, little brother. That one you spoke to me of, when you first came home." His face became very still. Margaret wondered briefly if she had gone too far in making mention. She lowered her voice and asked gently in the German which she so rarely spoke these days, "You have not sent word to her, or a letter? We knew in October they had gone with a large party to Mr. Meusebach's new settlement on the Pedernales. Have you taken any thought to what you should say or do?"

"No." he answered, softly.

"Why not, then?"

He was so long in answering that she began to think he would not, that he would quietly leave the room with it unanswered, but he finally said, "There has been so much sickness among them—at the coast and in the Comal settlements. And she might also be married by now. I would rather not know for sure. And just go on thinking her alive and free. This is so, as long as I do not know otherwise."

"You are an idiot, little brother," Margaret said finally, half stern and half compassionate.

"So Pa always said," he answered, ruefully. "But it's how I wish to let it lie. I will do something when I am better fit. Just not now."

Margaret shook her head and said, "Don't leave it wait too long, then."

He didn't begin to feel restless until a grey and blustery afternoon in the middle of January. He was splitting firewood in the yard at the back of the house, rejoicing in the feel of returning strength, knowing that he would be tired by the time he had split another stack and his shoulder would ache like a bad tooth. It would be a good tired, though, and not that bottomless pit of exhaustion that made his knees tremble and his head spin. He paid hardly any attention, hearing a pair of horses coming up the drive from the road: people were always coming and going at Margaret's house. Presently his youngest nephew came out to the back veranda.

"Uncle Carl, there's a man come to see you. He didn't want to wait in the parlor. He's around front, waiting for you."

"Did he tell you who he was, Peter, or give a message?"

Carl thunked the ax into the splitting block and left it upright, unhurriedly dusting woodchips from his clothes.

Peter answered, eagerly, "Colonel Jack Hays, he says. Is it really?"

"I never tell fibs, young fellow." Jack himself emerged from around the side of the house. "And my message was for your uncle to put down that teacup and knitting and come have a drink with me. I decided I was in too much of a hurry to wait."

"As long as you're buying, Jack," Carl answered, with unalloyed delight. "What brings you here?! The war's not over, is it?"

Jack was sizing him up, in that quick assessing way of his and he shook his head, "No, just a flying visit. Gen'ral Scott's heading for Vera Cruz soon, and I had some business to attend to. You look better'n I expected you to. Bill thought sure you were near to a goner. He figgered you'd be better off with the home folks, even if you didn't make it. It was a gamble, Dutch, but it paid off."

"So what's the job this time?" Carl asked, skeptically.

Jack looked wounded. "Why has it got to be a job? We could be just celebrating your full recovery."

"It's a job, when you're buying." Carl dusted off the last of the sawdust.

"Observant . . . that's what the Rangers pay you to be."

"We get paid?" The old and well-worn jest had a familiar taste to it. "So, where are we going, Jack?"

"Spicer's Tavern, of course. Isn't that the usual haunt?" Jack answered, casually. "I brought a horse for you to look at. A friend of mine is selling him. Thought you might like to ride for a bit, anyway."

Peter Vining listened to this exchange, hanging on every word in open hero-worship, and now Carl said, "Peter, tell your Ma I've gone with this gentleman, but I'll be back for supper."

"I know you favor grey nags," Jack said, as they walked around to the front of the house, "but this one has a good size to him, and amazing stamina. Good blood line; sire was half Kentuck thoroughbred. Could go all day at a dead gallop and never break into a sweat. If he suits, let me know."

The brown horse had three white socks and a blaze the length of his nose. Carl let him nuzzle his hands. Then he looked at the brown horses' teeth and said, "Young enough. Well broken?"

"Needs a bit of gentling, but my friend had no complaints."

"Have a name?"

"None that matters. I just called him Three-Socks." Jack swung up into his own saddle, and Carl adjusted the stirrups on the brown horse's saddle and followed suit. It felt good to be back on a horse, almost as good as coming home. Jack would take his time, getting to the point. Carl knew this from long acquaintance.

They rode along the gentle slope of the road that ran past the Becker place, past houses and town-lots that had once been part of their farm. Carl didn't recognize them any more, except for occasionally a particularly large tree. Alois Becker had sold off everything but the couple of fields closest the house, and the town crept closer and closer every year to the old home-place. The remaining land still surrounded it like a moat. Margaret's sprawling house sat at an odd angle from all the others, amidst its trees and fenced paddocks.

Two cups, a quiet corner at Spicer's and a bottle; Jack poured two fingers for each, and Carl waited quietly as was his habit. They talked for a while about the fighting before Monterray, and what had happened afterwards, and the progress of the war, the withdrawal of the Rangers, and what might happen when Scott moved inland from Vera Cruz. Jack finally confessed that the progress of his courtship of Miss Susan Calvert had been more or less successful. Before Jack went to rejoin the Scott in Vera Cruz, he planned to marry her. Only then did he finally move around to his purpose.

"You recollect Prince Fancy-Trouser's successor, I think. Red-bearded hoss and seemed like a more sensible man. We met him after you finished playing the beau ideal, back along the Guadalupe last spring, when we were out recruiting."

"So I do. And?" Carl had endured a quantity of heavy-handed japery from the other witnesses to that occasion, including Jack who had been humorous about it for days.

"Meusebach. Had the sense not to throw his aristocracy at us three times a day and five times on Sunday. Moved heaven and earth to get his people up-country; those of them left alive, that is. I give him credit; he took a bad hand and did better at it than many," Jack owned honestly, and poured another two fingers. "He's a good enough man and a well-intentioned one, he shouldn't have been left in the position that he was, but what the hell—he volunteered. But it's in my mind now to do him a good deed. God knows, he deserves one, the poor bastard."

Carl swallowed from his own cup and waited. All in good time. He kept his own bland expression, the one that Jack swore made him so good at cards. Seeing that he wasn't going to rise to the bait, Jack continued, "He's been talking about going into the Llano country in a couple of weeks, to make a truce with the Comanche that he hopes will protect his folk. Most people are thinking its just talk; they remember Prince Fancy-Trouser's grand plans. Myself, I think he's going to do it—and it has a chance of working."

"Will it?" Carl asked, mildly.

"It might. He has one thing going for him; the Comanche know his folk ain't our folk. They might be persuaded to go lightly on them for a time."

"Time." Carl poured another two fingers for himself. "I remember they went easy on us, compared to the Mexes, until the newness wore off. Then they lost all respect. How much time?"

Jack shrugged, that young-old face riven with weary and hard-bought wisdom. "Two years. Maybe as much as ten, depending on how much authority the chiefs he palavers with hold over their ambitious young bucks. Whatever time Meusebach buys for his folk is to the good, even if it don't last. They'll need that time."

"My interest in all this?" Carl asked mildly, and Jack smiled.

"Besides that black-haired Dutchwoman you had such a shine for? To ride with Meusebach into the Llano, and keep a quiet-like eye on developments. I think he'd appreciate an extra hand, someone who knows the score, just in case it goes bad all of a sudden."

"You think it might go down the wrong way?"

"All it would take is one wrong word, and he'd have hisself another Council House fight," Jack answered, and poured a little more for himself. "I'll give you a letter to take to him, asking for you to accompany his party. You in, Dutch?"

"You didn't have to ask, Jack." Carl sat back, thoughtfully nursing his drink, and Jack reached into his coat-front and extracted a white envelope and put it on the table.

"Didn't think so, but figured I'd at least do you the courtesy, then. Here's the letter. I heard Meusebach is fixing to leave from New Braunfels in the next week or so and head towards that new settlement first."

"If I miss him, there's plenty of trail where I can catch up." Carl let the letter lie on the table for a moment, before picking it up and folding it double. "There's one thing I'd best let you know, Jack. This'll be the last time. My enlistment already ran out; this is just a personal favor. I don't think I'll be back, either."

"We'll purely miss you, Dutch," Jack didn't sound much surprised. "You sure about that?" He topped up Carl's drink with the last of the bottle and waited.

"I've been doing this a long time," Carl answered, finally. "Ten years since I signed up with Smith's company, and near eight years off and on riding with yours. And I was in the militia before I was old enough to grow a beard, near enough. I think I need to be doing something else, now. Settle down, have a place of my own."

Jack signaled for another bottle, and said, "Well, it is a game that most can only play for a couple of years. You don't need to apologize to me. You been at it for longer than most I know. Surprised it took you this long, though. That pretty gal have anything to do with it?"

"No, not much, no more than your Miss Susan would keep you from going to Mexico again. I had a lot of time to think, this winter. See, that's the longest time I ever stayed in one place since I left home and joined the militia with my brother. I came around to forgetting in all that time what it was like, having a proper home, your own folk, and your own place. Staying with my sister reminded me of all that. They're nice things to have, Jack. I'm of a mind to want them now for myself, before it's too late."

"Too late?" Jack opened the new bottle. "You were just unlucky at Monterray, that's all. They say it makes a man think, taking a wound like that. You'd never taken one that bad before."

"Not that kind of late." Carl traced a circle on the tabletop in a bit of spilled whiskey. "Remember Wilks? Rode with Tumlinson for a while? Used to talk books and philosophy around the campfire. I always got some powerful amusement out of listening to him, with his belt stuck full of knives and a beard of hair down to his elbows, talking Latin and such. He said once that we should have a care. After a while, we'd run the danger of becoming who we fought. I just don't want to go all the way towards being something I don't want to be, that's all. Living like nomad, no particular place to go, no real kin of your own to mourn after you're gone. I want to stay a civilized man, Jack, while I still can remember what that is. I don't want to finish up an old soak like Trap Talmadge, not really fit for anything much any more."

"No law against it." Jack topped up their cups again. Carl reminded himself that he had not drunk whiskey for a while and his carrying capacity might be not anything like it was before. But Jack wasn't given to drinking as much as some. With luck, he'd still be able to find his way back to Margaret's. "A toast, then; to a place of your own, as long as you can get away and drink with old friends now and again."

"To a home," Carl echoed. "Which reminds me; would you come to supper? Margaret keeps an open house for any friends of mine. You would be welcome."

"I would like that," Jack looked a little abashed. "If she truly would not mind; I have a hankering to see a home as would make you consider giving up the freedom and adventure of the trail."

"Then we should be away soon," Carl stood, slightly swaying, "while we can still remember the way, and Margaret has time to set an extra place."

"You've lost your head for strong waters, Dutch." Jack swayed himself only a little less. "It's probably best for you to settle down soon, anyway. About the horse …"

"We left them in front, didn't we?" Carl looked around, vaguely puzzled.

"To the best of my recollection. I was about to say," Jack hiccupped slightly, "if you like him, pay me for Ol' Three-Socks when you get back from the Llano. And you're invited to the wedding of course. Sit up front and thump any of our old friends who might get humorous on a solemn oc…oc…occasion."

"Damned generous of you, Jack, spotting me the use of a horse."

"Least I can do," Jack waved a hand, dismissively. "God knows, you can't get anywhere in this country without a good one."

Late that evening, after a dinner which was very merry and passed in quite a pleasant blur for Carl, Margaret tapped gently on the door of his room.

"Come in," he said, quietly. He was cleaning and loading his Paterson revolvers. They had lain unused in a dresser drawer for much of the winter, save for that one day, almost the first that he had been well enough to venture far from the house. He had practiced shooting until his arms felt like bags of lead and he was so tired afterwards that he had been ill again for several days. Margaret had been very put out over that. The extra barrels and all the tools were spread out on a square of flannel in the middle of the bed. His knife and long carbine lay next to them, along with the meager contents of his saddlebags and the buckskin coat and moccasins that he wore for long patrols.

She opened the door, and took it in with one glance.

"You're away again?" She didn't seem surprised. Margaret very rarely was.

"Early in the morning, yes."

"You were planning to say goodbye to us, this time?"

"Of course." He sounded vaguely offended. Margaret sighed.

"Jack Hays snaps his fingers and you come running. At least linger tomorrow long enough for a good breakfast."

"I have to get an early start. I've a need to catch up to a party who may have left from the Fountains already."

"So," answered Margaret with asperity, "it will be an early breakfast. You need not steal away from my house like a thief. And I'll pack some supplies for you, also."

"I'm traveling light . . ." He looked up from his polishing, as Margaret sat herself down on the edge of the bed opposite him, and surveyed the assortment spread across the counterpane. ". . . and not taking much."

"You have room for an extra shirt," she observed. She shook it out and neatly refolded it; the mended shirt which had come home with him from the war in Mexico. "I see you have room for a little hope in your heart, little brother. Good for you." She took a small bottle out of her apron pocket, and rolled the shirt around it. "I put a portion of opodeldoc liniment in a small bottle... the Doctor advises its use when your shoulder aches. He says you have complained of it once or twice. Where are you bound this time, or is that something you may not say?"

"I may," he answered. "John Meusebach is going into the Llano country to make peace with the Comanche and buy a little time for his settlers. Jack is sending me as—a sort of body-guard, I guess—and to keep an eye on things."

"A spy, in other words," Margaret said, and he shrugged obliquely.

"It wouldn't be for the first time. Meusebach is supposed to be going to the new colony on the Pedernales first, and gathering his party. Then he intends journeying to San Saba to meet the Comanche chiefs at a large encampment there."

"Be careful then," Margaret said gravely, as he threaded a full-loaded cylinder into the Paterson, re-attached the barrel, and secured the wedge and small screw that held it all together. He smiled thinly, as he carefully slid it into the waiting holster.

"I always am, Margaret."

"One more thing; your friends went to that colony, did they not? I believe it is now called Friedrichsburg. Will you search for her there?"

"I might," he replied simply, offering nothing more, and Margaret sighed.

"Should you find her and discover that things with her are as you wish—and if they work out as you seem to hope, you must let me know."

"Why is that? Do you need to approve of her, first?"

"That might not be a bad idea," she answered fondly. "But no, there is a gift I have for her, a little broach of Ma's. She intended it to be for your wife whenever you married, but died thinking you and Rudi were both killed at Goliad. She gave it to me then, to hold for my boys. She meant it for you, though, and you shall have it. Just let me know."

His head bent over his work, and she could barely hear his answer.

"I will, Margaret. Thank you."

"Good night then." She stood up and went to the door, but as she slipped out she whispered, "It would have made Ma so happy to know you lived. Take care, little brother, until you return again. Don't wait until you are near-killed, next time."

"I won't." he promised, and Margaret eased the door closed.

In the morning and well before dawn, he ate a swift and silent breakfast in the kitchen, already dressed for the trail. Margaret and Hetty, her cook, plied him with food, which he wolfed as if he didn't expect to eat another good meal for weeks. Then he hugged Margaret and slipped out the back door, a ghost in the grey winter fog and the hooves of Three-Socks tap-tapping down the road. From the porch, Margaret could hear them for some little time after he was gone from sight, away towards the river and the road to the south, leaving only the faint dripping sound of condensation falling from the branches of the apple trees onto the ground underneath.

Then she wiped her eyes on the corner of her apron and went inside, reminding herself to tell the hired girl to turn out his bedroom and put into a box for storage any of his clothing and boots that her brother had left behind, until he returned again. Until that day she might have need of that guest room.

Upon riding into Neu Braunfels, Carl discovered that the Verein expedition to the Comanche had already departed for the west some days before, but Mr. Meusebach had been delayed with other urgent business and had not yet gone. He went to the Verein headquarters, a rambling log-built palace on top of a hill with a wide verandah overlooking the growing town and said to first person he saw coming out the main door, "I've a letter from Colonel Jack Hays for Mr. Meusebach, if he is within. He might also remember meeting me before. I also worked for Prince Solms when he was in Texas, two years ago." He dropped onto one of the benches which lined the verandah, waited quietly and without impatience, until his messenger came out to say that he was summoned into Mr. Meusebach's presence.

John Meusebach worked in a room that looked as if it once had been a small dining room, with an elegant table and many dainty gilt chairs. There was a sideboard full of fine china and glass, but all of that was covered deep in dust and cobwebs. Not so the boxes of books and papers piled everywhere. The table was also covered with more papers, orbiting around a stretch of blotting paper, ink-bottles, and pens. Jack's opened letter sat in the middle before John Meusebach, who pressed his fingers to his eyes as if his head ached just as Carl was shown through the door. He stood up, though, smiling a very real welcome, "Sit, please, sit—wherever you wish, and there is a clear chair. Of course I remember you, Sergeant Becker. Do you wish to speak in English or German?"

"Whichever you favor," Carl answered. "It makes no difference to me,"

"Nor to me either," the former baron confessed. "We should conduct it in German, although I should be more practiced in English, since it is the language of my new country. No, this is a Verein matter—and this letter from Colonel Hays," he tapped it with his finger," presents me with a dilemma."

Carl said nothing, waiting patiently with his face in that amiable and slightly sleepy expression which deluded so many. Behind it, he was thinking that John Meusebach was another one of those like Jack, with that same cool judgment in sizing up people and situations, but lacking some of Jack's utter cold ruthlessness. Jack would have made up his mind before speaking; this man was temporizing.

"I have a fear, you see," Meusebach continued, "that in making a separate peace with the Comanche—if I am successful, that is—it may rather—what is the word? Show up your own authorities. It may show too much of a contrast in our way of doing things, if we meet with a success which has so far eluded you. And we—certain of us fear that our efforts might be sabotaged, in order to make your own failure in this regard somewhat less . . . marked, shall we say."

"Colonel Hays has nothing but the best wishes for your success in this venture," Carl said woodenly. "As do all of us." He didn't add the rest of his thoughts. *We just don't think it will last very long, that's all. And the odds of losing your hair in the effort are pretty high.*

Meusebach held up his hand, placating, "Please understand I have no doubts regarding Colonel Hays, in this regard. Or yourself; through your family, you are all but one of us. I have the greatest regard for you both; I merely felt I had to make clear some of my apprehensions. Against that is weighed certain of our own shortcomings." He sighed, very deeply. It looked to Carl like he did have a headache. "In the main, we—the Verein, that is, were not very well informed about certain conditions and situations existing here. We paid too little attention to those few who were well-versed and experienced and too much to those who only thought they were. Given the gravity of our situation here, and how much depends on the success of this mission, I dare not turn down this offer of assistance. I must be able to call on the expertise that one such as you possesses for the success of this venture."

"You won't regret it," Carl answered, stolidly, and Meusebach answered:

"All that I ask is that you accompany us, not as a Ranger, but as a Verein soldier, as one of us. I would not like to have my talks— disrupted, should you discover an old enemy among the Comanche, perhaps one which you encountered before."

"Not much chance of that." Carl stood up. "Just about all of them are dead."

"Oh." Meusebach looked momentarily startled, and then recovered himself. "You relieve my mind, on that score, oddly enough."

"And about the other thing—as a Verein soldier?" Carl added, firmly. "I refused to wear the Prince's livery, or whatever clobber you have your troopers wear these days. I don't care for uniforms, 'specially not out in the Llano. I'll follow your direction or those of whoever is in charge of your troopers, but only if I think they are sensible under the circumstances. Deal?"

Meusebach looked at him, with just a bare hint of a smile under his beard.

"In all the time that you were commanded by Colonel Hays, were you ever disciplined for insubordination, Sergeant Becker?"

Carl shook his head. "No. Speaking my own mind worked just fine for him. When do we leave?"

"I expect it shall have to content me as well," Meusebach answered wryly. "I hope to leave for Friedrichsburg tomorrow."

To his relief, they rode fast the next day: himself and Meusebach and a handful of mounted Verein troopers. They did not push as hard as Jack would have pushed them, but they did not need to. It startled Carl to see that there was already a well-made road threading up into the hills. With stone causeways of river-rock over boggy ground and gravel-paved cuts into and out of creek beds, in some places it came very close to being a fine highway.

"It's the best established road in Texas," Mr. Meusebach allowed with considerable pride.

They splashed through the last ford on the Pedernales very early on a Sunday and approached Friedrichsburg at about midday. Meusebach drew rein as they approached. It appeared that some of the land about had already been put under plough.

"You look surprised," Meusebach said to Carl. "Our people have accomplished much in a year; almost everyone has a house, of some sort. They were obliged to build themselves. Alas, we could not build so many houses as promised. We were misinformed of the actual costs."

"Another of your inexpert experts?" Carl said, and Meusebach laughed, sardonically.

"So much was squandered, wasted! It was enough to make an accountant weep, going over the books and reports. I have scoured clean what I can." His face got a hard look to it, and Carl thought, *Maybe he does have enough ruthlessness in him.* Meusebach continued, "And I will have a little more scouring to do here, after we arrive. I will have about a day's work here. You are at liberty, until we leave. Look around at our town. Do you have friends among those here, who might show you hospitality?"

"I might," Carl answered cautiously, "The family of Christian Steinmetz was most particularly cordial to me, when they encountered us on the road last year."

"As so they should have been," Meusebach answered, with amusement. "Hans Richter worked last year as a wagon-master for the Verein; he told me that he says a prayer of thanks, every time he passed that place on the river. He is very fond of his daughter. It was most gallantly done, by the way." There was nothing to be said, especially after having endured many coarse jests about the incident, and Meusebach added, "Steinmetz has a town lot at the corner of Market Square. He has a fine beamed house half-built. I would look for his family there, if I were you."

Carl bided his time until he was free, leaving Three-Socks corralled in the compound by the Verein storehouse and headquarters and Meusebach gone off with a very purposeful expression on his face towards a fine lumber house nearby.

"I must speak with Doctor Schubert," he said only. "We'll leave Tuesday morning, at sunrise."

Carl watched him stride up to the house and shrugged; none of his business, after all. He set about finding his way to the Market Square and a half-built timber-beam house, himself being equally torn between anticipation and apprehension.

It proved to be very easy to find, among a brave assortment of dog-trot log cabins and garden plots fenced with planks upright into the ground. The whole of it was laid out between straight broad avenues wide enough to turn two yoke and a wagon, a little town longer than wide and centered in the middle on a vast open square. The plaza was empty of almost anything but a quantity of stumps, a tangle of timbers piled up in the middle of it in a manner that suggested purpose and a greybeard laboring away with an ax and shovel around the foot of one of the stumps.

"I am looking for the Steinmetz house," Carl asked the elder, who straightened and wiped his forehead. It was warm for early February: shirtsleeve weather, which coaxed folk out of doors in late winter into summer-mild temperatures for a few days or hours. The old man waved his hand towards the south-east corner.

"You're too late for the christening," he said, "but I think they will still be celebrating."

"Christening?" Carl said, blankly.

"Grandson for Steinmetz. About the first child begotten here, so they say; nine months to the day after they got here. Marvel they had the stamina to go at it, after the journey, but young folk these days!" He bent to his shovel again with a grunt and a groan.

Carl asked, "And why do you not celebrate with them?"

"Oh, I will, as soon as I get this one pulled."

The house that his guide pointed out was indeed half-built: a skeleton of square beams, braces and window frames delineating where the future walls would be. It sat close to the street, like some of the houses in the older Mexican parts of Bexar. The far half was finished, the space between beams filled in with unbaked clay bricks and plastered over. Shutters covered the window openings, and a drift of smoke rose lazily from a chimney; it looked as though they had finished enough of it to move in. Carl walked towards the unfinished corner, drawn by the sound of happy voices, children laughing, and a chorus of men's voices, raised in song. He could walk through the framework of beams, towards the yard in back of the house, where two huge post-oaks shaded what might be a pleasant and sheltered garden someday.

Today, the mess of construction in back had been pushed to one side to make way for tables and chairs moved outside for a meal. He recognized the song that three or four of the men were singing, and whispered the words, suddenly hesitant to just walk any farther. This was not Margaret's house, where he would be certain of welcome, day or night.

> *'Today I had to wander*
> *Along in deepest night:*
> *I closed in night-time darkness*
> *My eyes from any sight*
> *And there its twigs were rustling*
> *As though they called to me*
> *Come here to me, my fellow*
> *Here's rest and peace for thee ... '*

Some of the folk scattered in casual groups within he recognized, or thought he did, old Steinmetz in deep conversation with a tall old man in black and a churchly white frill around his neck, all under a fine haze of pipe-smoke. His stocky son-in-law Hans glowered like a bullock under his brows at something one of his friends said. His wife had been haggard and ill, back when he first made their acquaintance. Carl barely recognized her as the pretty round-faced woman with her lap filled by the baby, all dressed in a froth of lacy white. Most of the women hovered over her. So did the little girl Anna, taking a proprietary and protective air towards her younger brother.

That made him smile, suddenly wondering if Margaret had been like that when he was born. He rather suspected now that she had been. He lingered by the angle of the new wall, half out of sight from the happy gathering and suddenly wistful. He thought he picked out the twins, those two bad boys, romping with a small pack of their kind but he did not immediately find that one of the Steinmetz family which he hoped most to see, until she emerged from the house, laughing at something said by the man she walked beside in the way of old friends who were comfortable with each other.

They were both carrying trays, piled with bread and platters of meat. The other man was fair-haired, with a merry face split by a wide grin. For a moment Carl thought he would much rather walk empty-handed towards a Comanche war party than move forward from where he stood. Margaret was right. He had been a fool, and left it too late. Better that he had not come with Meusebach; best to ride away into the Llano with him, without ever looking for a certain spirited, black-haired girl.

But as he stood there, half-decided to turn and walk back to the Verein blockhouse, a little hand stole into his. Startled, he looked down into the dark, morning-glory colored eyes of a little girl who stood there, swinging their linked hands and laughing with confident friendliness up at him. Rosalie, the littlest daughter, the one with red-blond strawberry curls, tugged him forwards; before he could take a step either forward or away, Old Steinmetz called her name and she answered happily, "Here I am—I found him, Papa!"

After that moment there was no possible escape, for she pulled him towards the gathering, and Steinmetz rose from his chair with an expression of happy welcome on his face, exclaiming, "Sergeant Becker! What a joy it is, to see you again! Hansi! Magda, look who is here! You'd never guess! Welcome, my boy, welcome! What a surprise, eh? Come and meet our friends. Such a day this is!"

Carl listened to him without quite hearing, as his eyes met Magda's. They seemed very wide and dark—and he had not the least idea of what she was thinking behind them, but her fingers on the edge of the tray were nearly white with the force of her grip.

Seeing him, Magda felt as if she had been struck a sudden blow. She had not forgotten him, but had put him into the back of her mind, a memory worn with overuse and finally put aside. With finishing Vati's house, and caring for the boys and Rosalie, she was constantly busy. Any romantic attachment in her life bent itself towards Charley, whose persistent charm made her laugh. Suddenly he appeared again out of the blue, that diffident and soft-spoken man who said so little and looked so much, who had been kind but also mocking, who had ridden quietly away with his Colonel, towards the war in Mexico, leaving behind nothing but silence and a tumult of questions in her own heart. All of them had been put to rest, but now they were revived. What had brought him back? An interest in herself, as Vati and Liesel had seemed to think? He looked the same as ever, she thought—the same rough travel clothes and Indian moccasins—but on closer look, she thought he looked tired, as if he had been ill. But when he looked at her, as he did when Vati spoke her name, his eyes held a question. But what the question might be and the answer to it, Magda had no idea at all.

Chapter 11 – *Comancheria*

"I just rode in with Mr. Meusebach," Carl said, by way of explanation, as little Rosalie swung their linked hands and laughed up at him.

Vati and his friends surrounded them, half curious and but warmly welcoming as Vati exclaimed, "We thought you were in Mexico with your Army still! Well, never mind then, you are welcome! Magda, look who is here! You are with Mr. Meusebach's party? We had heard he was expected! This is our friend, also newly come to Friedrichsburg."

"Charley Nimitz." That was the brash young spark who seemed to be on such good terms with Magda. He shook Carl's hand with firm grip, "So you were in Mexico - what news of the war, then?"

"No more than you would know yourselves from the newspapers," Carl answered. "I took hurt in the fighting before Monterray and spent the winter convalescing at my sister's house."

"But you must be recovered, if you are venturing into the Comanche country with Mr. Meusebach?" Vati said, looking deeply concerned.

Carl said, quickly, "Oh, yes, quite recovered."

Vati patted his arm in a fatherly fashion, adding, "Then have something to eat—oh, there you are, my dear." He blinked affectionately at Magda, who silently handed Carl a full plate. "Show him to a place where he may sit down and . . ."

"Come tell Peter and John and I about the latest talk then," Charley Nimitz offered. "All of that doesn't make it into the newspapers." He added in a lower voice, as Magda moved away towards the house, "And we can offer you a good drink, too. Although Peter swears he could make better. He's a stonemason with delusions of being a brew master! John Hunter here - do you know him? He's another American like you. With you and Mr. Meusebach, the number of people in town who speak English has more than doubled."

Since he couldn't work out what to say for himself, Carl let himself be drawn into the knot of younger men, at ease under the second tree, a little apart from the women and families. As he and Charley joined them, one of them was saying, ". . . so, Doctor Schubert ordered that the cannon be fired, since Mrs. Specht seemed so upset. 'Boom!' it went off, everyone covering their ears, and then Mrs. Specht cried out, "But my husband is deaf!""

The audience for the story fell about laughing, all but Carl, and John Hunter who only smiled uncertainly. Charley explained, switching seamlessly between English and German, "We have this little cannon, in front of the Verein storehouse. You might have noticed it as you rode in. Or maybe not, as it is very small. Aside from overawing the natives, when it is fired mostly it is because people are lost in the woods and by hearing it they might be guided back."

"Lost . . . in these woods?" Carl said in blank disbelief, shaking his head as both he and Charley laughed.

"You forget; to most of these folk, a mile or two is a great distance and a grove of trees is a mighty forest."

"They'd better catch on, quick then," Carl said only, thinking regretfully of how it might have been better all the way around if he had simply killed Prince Fancy-Trousers when he had the chance and spared all these amiable, well-meaning farmers from being dumped into the wilderness like a basketful of unwanted kittens. "And your Mr. Meusebach better be the slickest sharper ever to come down the pike when he goes out to pow-wow with the Comanche."

"He's done well so far, "Charley pointed out. "He did a good job of negotiating with the Huaco chiefs, at Neu Braunfels. He's trained to be diplomatic. And when it comes down to diplomacy not being of any use, the rest of us are not all that helpless. Most of our men have had some kind of military service or training. It was required."

"Conscription," one of the other men put in, contemptuously. "For the officer class to play at soldiering with."

"Still—getting lost in your own woods is not terribly reassuring," observed one of the other young men. He was a thin, intense fellow with an unnervingly direct look. He passed the bottle to Carl. "Peter Berg, stonemason. I don't get lost. I pay attention."

"So he does," Charley said, "So do I. It comes of having been to sea."

John Hunter exchanged a glance with Carl and they both laughed as John said, "The sea may be the only bigger thing than the wilderness out here."

"Pay attention to this one, rather," advised one of the other young men, pointing at Charley. "Let me tell you why!" and he began an account of how Charley had dressed up someone's billy-goat in clothes and sent the poor beast skittering through the streets. Charley listened with a broad grin on his face and capped it with an account of how he and some of his shipmates had set a tavern in Le Havre on fire, thru the medium of a contest as unspeakable as it was ridiculous.

"Shot out a blue flame from his bung-hole, clear across the tap-room, and set fire to a leaking brandy-cask!" Charley shook his head. "Before we could move, the whole wall was well alight and we were all trampling over each other in our hurry to get out the door. I swear, we would have all been arrested, but that the tap-keeper couldn't be sure who had done it and the watchman was laughing too hard when he heard the story."

"We've wrecked many a thirst-parlor," Carl said admiringly, when he and the others had stopped roaring with laughter, "but we never thought of doing it that way. We did have a fine old time, once, at this fandango . . ." he passed the bottle to Fritz Lochte, and began the story. The afternoon passed for him more comfortably than he expected. On the whole, it seemed hardly any time at all before the afternoon sun was slanting warm and golden through the bare branches, and people were making leisurely farewells. John Hunter went to hold the hand of a pretty girl with curly dark hair, and Charley said, "John came here on other business, caught sight of Sophie Ahrens and has been here ever since. At least he can speak a bit of German to her now. One look and—pifft!" He waved his hand, expressively and Carl said:

"Happens all the time, I reckon."

Hansi Richter and his pretty wife took their leave, the baby well-wrapped against the first evening chill and Anna clinging sleepily to her father's shoulder.

"It is good to see you again." Hansi Richter shook his hand. "We never thanked you properly for your advice, last year. It was good. So—are you on your way to another war, this time, or are you going to bide for a while?"

"He's going to bide with us for a day or so." Vati appeared at his elbow. "And then go off with Mr. Meusebach to make peace with the Comanche. Always to the rescue, eh? I won't hear you say no, of course."

"Otherwise, you would have to stay at the Verein bunkhouse," Charley added, "and there is barely room for another, with the other men in Mr. Meusebach's party. The only other choice is Doctor Schubert's house, which is not recommended . . ."

Hansi Richter's wife sniffed disapprovingly and murmured, while Hansi and Charley exchanged a knowing look, "That women is more than just his housekeeper, I know it!"

"And his name isn't Schubert, either. Nor is he a doctor!" Charley added.

"I have left my traps and such at the Verein . . ." Carl started to say, and Vati beamed and replied,

"Well then, you should go and bring them back here. I wouldn't hear of having you stay anywhere else!"

Charley suggested, "Look, I shall issue you some rations from the commissary, it's all to the best, anyway. There's no room, and you may as well take your meals here until you leave. I'll authorize it, don't worry."

"What will Doctor Schubert say about that?" asked Vati, polishing his glasses in a worried manner.

Charley smiled blandly. "Probably a lot, but after today, it will not matter. Not after what Mr. Meusebach is planning to tell him."

"Ah." Vati looked rather smug. "I knew he would overreach himself. The chickens have come home to roost, have they? Knew it would happen! Magda, my dear, Sergeant Becker is going to stay with us for a few days. Charley is going to issue his rations to us. Why don't you walk with them to the storehouse and show him the way back."

Carl opened his mouth to say that he was perfectly capable of finding his own way back to the Steinmetz house from the Verein headquarters. There was a flash of bemused exasperation on Magda's face and an exceedingly bland one on Vati's, and he seemed to hear Margaret's gently chiding voice, *"Little brother, that is called an opportunity for a little time with her. Do try and think of something gallant to say, then."*

"Let me get my shawl from the house," Magda said quickly. She kissed her sister and Anna, as they took their own leave, and met Charley and Carl by the door. They walked in companionable silence for a little way, with Magda between them.

Presently Carl asked, "What was it that your father meant about Doctor Schubert? Who is he?"

"He's the Verein authority here," Magda answered, with a face that suggested she smelled something bad. "My brother-in-law has had words with him. We are afraid that when the farm lots are distributed, those families who have not danced to his tune will receive the worst and most distant lots. He plays favorites, and he sacked Mr. Bene, when he had done so much for us at the first. We don't know why he was sent here; he is a repellent little man who looks like a toad," she added, in tones of intense dislike.

"He has not offended you with discourtesies, Miss Vogel?" Carl ventured. It had been his somewhat limited experience that when a woman spoke of a man that way, she often had good reason.

"He wouldn't dare," Charley answered, cheerfully. "Miss Vogel would dice him up with the most killing of looks. I have seen her do it. No, I think he was sent here because Mr. Meusebach was desperate for someone who was one of us and yet knew the country. But he didn't work out, and it seems that he is not a qualified doctor, nor even that Schubert is his real name, so Mr. Meusebach is cutting his losses and giving him the sack before he does any more damage. You know," he looked sideways at the two of them, "there was much criticism of the Verein for their bad management. He is attempting to pull something from the wreckage with this business of peace with the Comanche."

"It will take some doing," Carl said, and Charley answered, confidently:

"If it can be done, he's the very one to do it." But Magda stayed silent. Carl thought she looked worried. Perhaps she was worried on his behalf, which gave him no small encouragement. He fetched his bedroll and saddle-bags from the blockhouse, feeling considerably cheered. At the storehouse, Charley unlocked the door with a great flourish of keys, and allowed them to step inside. He fussed around for a few minutes, pulling items from shelves and boxes, and then presented Magda with a small bundle of them, saying, "I shall tell Mr. Meusebach that you are staying with friends and where to find you if you are needed before Tuesday morning. It was a pleasure to meet with you, Becker . . . Miss Vogel, always a pleasure." He kissed her hand with what seemed to Carl to be quite unnecessary enjoyment, showed them out, and locked the door. He departed in the opposite direction, whistling cheerfully, and Carl silently offered Magda his arm.

He still hadn't thought of anything much to say, except for asking about Charley, which he thought might not be such a good idea, but she saved him from deeper waters by saying abruptly, "I heard you tell Vati that you had been wounded in the fighting in Mexico. You must be fit again, if you are going with Mr. Meusebach's men."

"Yes, more or less."

"We . . . that is, my father worried about you." She was looking sideways at him, as they walked. "He thought that we might have heard something of you, before this." Was that some kind of reproach, Carl wondered? Then she added, "Hansi said the Army has a way of taking men away. We did not know you had been wounded."

"No way for you to know of that," Carl agreed, and by way of extenuation, added, "I got sick with the ague and lung-fever, too."

"And your sister cared for you, then?"

"All winter. It's about the longest time I ever spent in one place since I left home. And then I heard of Mr. Meusebach's parley with the Comanche, and thought I might ride this way ..."

"And pass the day with Vati and our friends?" She looked sideways again, very shrewdly, and he thought of how he had nearly walked away from their house. He had spent all winter, torn in two parts over whether he should look for her among the Verein settlements. "Vati was most glad to see you. I had thought of you as a sort of comet that flashes across the sky and then is not seen again for a hundred years."

He meant to say something about returning in less than a hundred years, but instead he blurted, "Is Mr. Nimitz a particular friend of yours?" and regretted it almost as soon as the words were out. But she shook her head, laughing a little.

"No more than any other," she replied, this was, he thought somewhat reassuring, and a little safer ground for conversation. "He is a very popular gentleman, and accounted to be good company, although he is very inclined toward jests and practical jokes."

"He is that," Carl grinned, remembering Charley's account of the tavern. "He reminds me of my brother, in that way. Wherever there was a crowd of people laughing, there was Rudi in the middle of it."

"You talked of your sister," Magda said, curiously "who lives in Austin, who nursed you when you were ill. She who has the same name as I do? But you never talked of your brother, before. Where is he now?"

"He is dead," Carl answered simply. "Since ten years ago. It is not a good memory, Miss V . . . Miss Margaretha."

"No, it would not be," she said, sympathetically. "How my mother died—that is not a good memory either. Vati told us that we should rather try to think of her living, and remember that."

"Your father is very wise," he said.

Magda answered, "And your own was not so?"

"No," Carl said, for Alois Becker had been a hard and bitter man.

Magda seemed to wait for him to say more than that, but with another one of those shrewd sideways looks, she said, "So then, tell me of the good memories. You must have some. Your father had a farm, and your brother played jokes—unless you would rather not," she added, hastily. He shook his head, oddly relieved to have something to talk about.

"This winter with my sister, I was reminded very much of the good memories, even if it is all greatly changed. The settlement nearest my father's place was called Waterloo. That was before the government bought up all the land thereabouts to make the capitol there. It looked very much like this—on the far edge of the wilderness as it was then. There was always danger. My father ploughed his fields with a rifle slung over his shoulder. Later on, when he and Rudi were out ranging, my mother and Margaret put on men's clothing and carried guns when they were outside the house, so if any Indians were watching they would not think we were unguarded."

"It sounds terribly hard, living that way," Magda said, with a shudder. "Thank god; we seem to have nothing to fear from the Indians and may have even less, thanks to Mr. Meusebach."

Carl shrugged, "It did not seem so, then. We did not know any other way to live so we were quite happy with it. Rudi and I, we roamed the woods as we liked."

"Didn't you go to school?" Magda asked, and he shook his head.

"No, Ma taught us at home from her books. There was a school, off and on, but hardly ever any teacher. I can read, though. And do sums," he added, vaguely defensive. Ma had always felt rather badly about how he and Rudi ran wild, rather than go to school. "I didn't mind much. Those I knew later who went to a proper school pretty much hated it."

"It all sounds very odd," she said at last.

He shrugged, "We liked it."

"Tell me some more, then," And so he did, walking and talking up to the very threshold of Vati's new house, on the doorstep without quite realizing how they came to be there. With a slightly panicky feeling, Carl realized that he would have to say something soon, something now to make his intentions clear. As soon as she opened the door and they went inside, there was no guarantee of ever being alone with her again in the next day. She reached toward the latch, and he stopped her hand in that moment.

"There's something I want to tell you," he began, already feeling that he was fumbling badly, but determined to plunge ahead regardless. "I plan to ask your father's permission—"

"My father's permission for what?" she asked, suspiciously.

"To come courting you. If it is something that you would welcome. If you would be pleased..."

"To give you fair warning," she answered, sighing a little, "I really have no intention upon marriage with any one suitor or another. Not Charley Nimitz or Fritz Lochte or any of the other young men who might double their farm plot thereby."

"I'm not any of them. And I'll have my own acres for service, no matter if I am married or no." His spirits rose irrepressibly. At least she hadn't said no. He was in the running, hadn't completely dealt himself out. "Miss Margaretha, all I want is an opportunity to talk you into changing that intention. Might I ask for that, at least?"

"You may." Her eyes were huge in the shadows, and she whispered. There were voices in the house, behind the door. "But I make no guarantee."

Was there something else to be said, or done? He couldn't think of anything. He still held her hand; instead of kissing it as Charley had done, he turned her hand over, and gently kissed the inside of her wrist, that soft bit of flesh where the veins ran blue under her skin.

Just at that moment, Vati opened the door, saying, "We'd wondered what was taking you so long—I thought I heard your voices, and wondered why you did not come in." He blinked at them in vague puzzlement. The two of them stepped into the barely furnished parlor, their hands falling guiltily apart. Vati shut and latched the door after them.

"Sergeant Becker was telling me about how his family first lived here in Texas," Magda answered. Carl thought her voice sounded faintly unsteady, but Vati seemed to take no notice.

"How very interesting," he answered, "There must be so much that is new to us, that you take for granted—please don't find our curiosity tiresome."

197

Magda silently vanished into the nearest doorway; it sounded like the children were in there, in the kitchen near to the warm fire, leaving Carl to face her father.

"No, nothing like that—sir, there is something I would like you to know."

"I know." Vati polished his glasses. Not a nervous gesture, Carl suddenly realized, but a thoughtful one, giving Vati time to construct an answer. "You wish to ask my permission to court Magda and you have it. After all, it is her decision in this matter which counts. She would pay no attention to my opinion, if she wished to encourage the attention of a man of whom I did not approve." He held up his hand, as Carl started to speak. "No, no, you do have my approval, for what it is worth. She is a sensible girl—but not appealing to every man's taste, not like her sister. Magda is sharp and clever, with a will of her own. Most men do not appreciate that in a wife. Ordinary beer will do for most, but there are some who appreciate a finer brew or some rare vintage. So, knowing that she is not to every taste, she thinks she is not to anyone's taste at all. Or so I deduce. It will not be easy -"

"Most things that are easy," Carl observed, "are usually not worth the trouble of getting—or keeping."

Vati's eyes lit up happily, "Yes, that would be the spirit! I should say no more, for she will know I have talked with you about this!"

He started guiltily as the door at his back opened. Magda put her head around it, saying briskly, "Vati, surely you are not going to talk in the hall all night? Come into the kitchen by the fire. I have asked the boys to put a pallet upstairs. You should show our guest the rest of the house, since you have become so proud of it!"

"You see?" Vati said, fondly and Carl followed him, thinking with astonished relief, '*Well, that went much better than I expected!*'

Four days later, he stood with Three-Sock's reins in his hand, waiting at the top of a low rise, and observed in a dryly ironical voice as he watched smoke gushing up from the fast-moving grass-fire:

"This is not a good start."

"No it is not," John Meusebach agreed, in tones of deep gloom.

"How did the fire get started?" Carl asked.

"Von Roemer said the campfire got away from them," Lieutenant Wilke explained, glumly. He was the young officer now in command of the Verein troopers; able enough, but not accustomed to the frontier.

Carl sighed. "We could let off fireworks, I suppose. Just to make sure that everyone and his brother know we're on the way."

"I do not intend to be secretive about approaching the Comanche encampment," Meusebach retorted, "but you are correct. This is … unsubtle."

"Three wagons," Carl ticked off on his fingers, "a couple of Shawnee hunters, five Mexes, a passel of surveyors and thirty troopers—and a crazy man with a little hammer who keeps wandering off to look at the rocks. Me, I can't think of any way to be more unsubtle."

"Von Roemer is a scientist," Meusebach answered, reprovingly, while Wilke scowled. "He has his enthusiasms."

"He's gonna be a hairless enthusiast, if he isn't more careful about wandering off," Carl warned, mordantly. "You know how I am accustomed to travel into this country? Fast and light, no baggage, no passengers. We light a fire for a meal and then move on for another hour or so before spending the night—without a fire."

"You can always turn around and go back," Wilke commented, somewhat acidly, and Meusebach looked pained.

"Enough, Herman, enough."

Carl did not take to Lieutenant Wilke or Wilke to him. Meusebach's officer took a particularly Prussian view of authority and military discipline. Carl's refusal to wear the Verein uniform, or follow those of Wilke's orders which he thought nonsensical, were a particularly sore point for him.

"That was for the purpose of making war," Meusebach answered, patiently. Meusebach had given up any pretense of Carl being a Verein trooper after about three days, just to keep some sort of truce between Carl and Wilke. "My journey is for the purpose of making peace. They have no reason to receive us with hostility."

"Yet," Carl said. He had become better acquainted with John Meusebach in the last week, enough so that he could speak his mind openly, as he would with any man he respected. "And I am in favor of having four men on watch at night—all night."

Meusebach smiled a little grimly, "There is no argument with you on that score. Take note, Wilke. Do you have any more words of warning for me, then?

"Yes. Don't get sucked into playing monte with those Mexes around the campfire of an evening. They'll have your shirt, boots and horse before you even know what happened."

"I had not considered that particular hazard." Meusebach raised his eyebrows, "Your presence is an education, as always."

"Doing my best here, doing my best." Carl sketched a casual half-salute, intended to bait Wilke, who looked particularly sour.

The party moved slowly over the next few days, with what Carl felt to be ponderous slowness. Meusebach and the scientist, Von Roemer, marveled at the beauty of the hills and the plentitude of game, which the Shawnee hunters brought back to camp of an evening.

"They say we are watched," said the young Mexican man who had been hired by Meusebach as interpreter and guide to the party. His name, so he told Carl was Lorenzo Rozas. He wore his hair long, in plaits like an Indian. "From the hills . . . they know we are here. Many tracks they have seen." Carl grunted acknowledgement. He and the three Shawnee hunters and Lorenzo sat around the hunters' fire. The three hunters were smoking their sumac-tobacco.

"A blind man could see our tracks," he said morosely in Spanish and Lorenzo nodded agreement. "So ... how long did you live with them?"

"Long enough." Lorenzo answered, enigmatically. "But not long enough to forget all of who I was. We will reach the Llano tomorrow, or near enough. Then I think they will do more than watch."

"As long as they don't do it tonight," Carl said. He ached all over, from weariness. It had been necessary to fell trees and cut a ramp through a creek-bed for the wagons, a labor at which all but the

Indians were called to perform. They had not moved very far that day, and had pitched tents for the night not far from where they had camped the night before. Half a dozen tents and three wagons formed a circle, with the horses and pack mules confined to one end, while campfires were scattered within the remainder.

"I wish we didn't have to truck with those damned wagons," he said, and Lorenzo shook his head.

"No. It is worth the effort, since they are full of gifts for the Comanche chiefs."

"So . . . tomorrow, then?"

"Or the next day," Lorenzo answered. "Me, I wish this business was finished. I feel like a mouse, watched by a hundred cats. Señor Meusebach, he says we must seem to be calm, unafraid."

"Follow his lead," Carl advised. "I'm pretty sure he knows what he's doing . . . he's the only Verein chief I've met who does, which must count for something."

Lorenzo looked at him across the fire. "You do not like this also. But you are here, anyway. Why is that?"

"I promised a friend I would see this through," Carl answered. "And the lives of a good few friends more... they're all at stake here. I owe it to them." *Including the life of a certain feisty black-haired girl,* Carl added to himself silently.

Lorenzo was right: on the morning of the second day, as they were finishing breakfast and preparing to break camp, one of the American surveyors, a man from Gonzales named Roberts suddenly straightened and looked keenly out into the stony prairie. He finished tightening his horse's cinch and said calmly, "Lookee there, Becker. I b'lieve we have company."

Carl followed the direction he was looking towards: a scrap of white, bouncing and fluttering on the end of a staff, held by a horseman. A small party of them now became visible over the scrub and tall grass. When they were still some distance away, they stopped and sat waiting patiently He turned to look for Meusebach, talking quietly over his breakfast coffee with Von Roemer.

"They're here," He said quietly. "Right on time, according to Señor Lorenzo." Meusebach stood up, pitching the last of his coffee into the fire. Lorenzo appeared silently, and Meusebach nodded to him. Tension crackled like summer lightning around the camp.

Lorenzo swung up onto his horse, riding bareback, and unarmed with anything but an air of casual arrogance. He flashed a grin down at Carl and said in Spanish, "See . . . I show them I have not forgotten everything I learned from living with the Honey-eaters."

"Just tell them we wish to parlay with their leaders," Meusebach said, in the same language, and everyone watched as Lorenzo's horse pranced toward the Indians and their white banner, until Meusebach said, in German, "Best finish breaking down the tents and packing, while we still have time."

In a few minutes, Lorenzo returned, unhurriedly. It had seemed like an hour, watching them from a distance, and Carl was willing to bet practically anything that they themselves were being carefully watched by more eyes than those of the white-flag bearers. Lorenzo rode between the wagons, and slid down from his horse, saying, "They want to see you then, Señor Meusebach. They're Comanche, and their leader is called Ketumsee."

"How many should I bring with me?" Meusebach seemed quite unruffled.

Lorenzo answered, "As many as are needed to be thought courteous; four or five. No more."

"Right then, yourself, and Becker. And two volunteers, if you please." At a nod from Wilke, one of the Verein troopers brought up his horse, as did Roberts, the surveyor who had first spotted the truce flag. They rode out of camp, two and two, following Meusebach, with Carl doing his determined best to be unobtrusive and unnoticeable. Just an ordinary fellow, part of the scenery; much harder to do so after having been accustomed for so long to be the large and menacing presence at Jack's elbow. Just riding out across the Llano on a chill winter morning under a sky the color of dirty pewter, he told himself, and under the gaze of a thousand hidden eyes . . . plus those of the mounted truce party. He looked sideways at Lorenzo, serene and confident; the translator had managed to put his nerves aside. With a trickle of unease, Carl wondered how much the man really had forgotten about living among the Penateka, the honey-eaters of the Comanche.

The Comanche waited patiently for them, the man with the truce flag a little in advance of the others, who had spread out at his back, to the right and left. Meusebach drew rein ten or fifteen feet distant, and gestured Lorenzo to come up next to him. Carl, Lieutenant Wilke, and Roberts the surveyor ranged themselves unbidden, mirroring the Indian party. Meusebach waited calmly. He seemed to be watching them with polite interest, and Carl was aware of his own heart hammering in his chest. This was the chancy part, for they were arrogant and touchy bastards. Carl suppressed a grin at the sudden thought of Prince Fancy-Trousers parlaying with the Comanche: two of a kind, in that case.

Now the Indian . . . what had Lorenzo said his name was? Oh yes; Ketumsee. He was speaking, clearly announcing his words to all those unseen listeners as well as to Meusebach and his party. A youngish man, lean and weathered, as all Comanche warriors were, with long plaits trimmed with silver ornaments, and a length of red cloth around his shoulders.

"They have been watching us, since crossing the river," Lorenzo said neutrally, as befitted a translator. "They believe we have come to make war, so they have sent their families away, and surrounded us with many fighters. They have sent word to other tribes. Now, they want to know, have you come with peaceful intent, or to wage war. Either is agreeable to them."

Meusebach must have thought out at least something of what he intended to say, Carl thought, for his words were composed, and thoughtful. He waited patiently while Lorenzo translated each phrase.

"We have come here with only peaceful intentions. We traveled from across the great ocean to build new homes and live among the Americans. We have built two cities . . . where we intend to show the same hospitality to you, as we expect you to show us. We come as neighbors, to visit and bring presents for your chief. All we ask is that you meet us with honor and integrity . . . and refrain from stealing our horses."

That last made Carl snort with suppressed laughter. When Lorenzo translated it, he thought he detected a ripple of amusement among the Indians, too. Horses were their weakness. Asking that they keep their hands off horses might be about as fruitless as asking an old tippler like Trap Talmadge to keep his hands off the bottle. Meusebach added sternly:

"Observe also, that we are well-armed, and well-able to defend ourselves, if necessary."

Wilke looked quite smug; as well a man might be who had a pair of heavy dragoon pistols on his saddle.

Ketumsee's reply was brief; Carl thought he sounded amiable, or at least as near enough as was possible.

"You have appeared well, in their eyes. Open and honest, he says, as great a chief as the sun. He has invited us to his camp, which is two days distance from here. He will send word to the other chiefs, to come to a great council to consider a treaty of peace with your people." Lorenzo added, "It would be well to offer them some of our food."

"Well, then, invite them to breakfast," Meusebach sounded quietly jubilant. "There's a good first step."

"Many a slip 'tween the cup and the lip," muttered Roberts. It made Carl's skin fair crawl to turn around and ride back to camp following Meusebach with the Indians at his back. He kept reminding himself that it was all going well, so far, and Meusebach looked to have struck the right note. Well, so did it look to the peace commissioners who kicked off the Council House fight, his inner cynical voice reminded him—right up until the knives came out.

At the camp, he tried his best to lurk in the background, to watch Ketumsee and his party without calling attention to himself; somewhat of a challenge, since he was near to being the tallest men in Meusebach's party. Their Comanche guests ate with great gusto, attended by Lorenzo and a deeply fascinated Von Roemer, who scribbled notes madly.

"You are bristling like a well-trained mastiff who has been ordered not to chase the cats," observed Meusebach with quiet amusement. He and Carl sat a little apart, drinking the last of the coffee. "You do not care for them . . . it is against your nature, yet you obey."

"I've seen too damn much of their calling cards," Carl answered a little grimly, "but whatever works to put a stop to them. I don't much care, as long as I never have to see any more of their leavings, after a raid on one of our settlements."

"Never fear," Meusebach sounded almost jaunty. "New minds to an old problem . . . that may have a solution at last. Really, Von Roemer and I are most interested in seeing what we can of their camps and people."

"I can't for the life of me understand what brought you out here," Carl shook his head. "Folk like Steinmetz, like Berg and even Charley Nimitz, them I can understand. No land, or bad land, no way to get something better, even just excitement. Not you. You had a high place, property and connections back there. And you don't strike me as the excitement-hunting type. Pretty much the opposite, at that."

Meusebach looked thoughtfully into the tin camp cup in his hands.

"You would think so, and they would seem like fine things to you. But they are burdens; all unbearable burdens placed on you by something else. By your family, by your name, by centuries of honorable service, steadfast in purpose, always. Do you know what my birth name and title is? Ottfried Hans, Freiherr von Meusebach." He said it as if it tasted bad. "Offspring of the honorable and ancient houses of Baron Carl Hartwig Gregor von Meusebach and his lady, Ernestine von Witzleben Meusebach. Four hundred years of nobility and obligation, thundering down upon my head in one awful blast. Mind you, I love and honor my parents..."

"I'd have left, because of the name alone," Carl said, after a moment.

Meusebach laughed uninhibitedly, like a schoolboy with a merry jest. "Awful, wasn't it? That's why I had it changed to plain John. You might think," he added, "that sorting out the mess of this Verein business is a great burden and obligation - and it is, I won't deny. But it is a duty I freely chose. My own chosen name is on everything I have done here for our people. Not my family title, and not out of tradition, as something which is only to be expected from the Baron von Meusebach." He wrapped his fingers around the tin cup again, and looked at it again, as if it were some sort of oracle. "Besides," he added softly, "I despair of seeing things in Germany getting better. You do not follow political matters back there; you would have no need . . ."

"Keeping track of political doings here is enough of a chore for most of us," Carl agreed. "I don't see any need to poke my nose in another set of affairs, just because my grandfather came from there. Any more than them over there should be poking their noses into ours."

"Still, one should be aware in a small way, even if to sense the direction that the next storm comes from." Meusebach shrugged, adding, "I thought much about these matters, as they affect Germany. To be truthful, I could not see things improving. The political liberals, the free-thinkers; they yearn for a constitutional form of government. It would be a good thing, as long as those who work to that end do not go overboard, as they did in France with their revolution and wind up a rule by the mob. Or what is more likely to happen, such a revolution of our own- even were it completely peaceful, would still be repressed by our monarchs—by the monarchs and conservative interests . . ." Meusebach smiled a little wryly. "See? I still speak of these things as mine, and ours. I might have left Germany, pledging true faith and allegiance to another, but Germany has not left my heart, not entirely. I considered what the future might hold for Germany, Becker, and all I could see was revolution or repression and war—or one following the others. I could not see anything in the future changing for the better, so I chose to come away, before a choice was forced upon me. It seemed only sensible to drop my title. There wasn't much need for it, when all is said and done."

"Most folk here don't need barons and that, in fine coats to look after them anyway," Carl said, and Hans Rahm's words came back to him again, what Hans had tried to tell Prince Solms, back when this all began at a tavern-table in Washington-on-the-Brazos. "Texas has a way of making equals of us all."

"So it will," Meusebach said, "so it will, and the sooner the better, to my way of thinking. But I owe them peace with the Comanche and time enough to find their feet."

Chapter 12 – *El Sol Colorado*

Ketumsee and his men accompanied Meusebach's peace-making party on that days march farther into the San Saba River Valley, after stuffing themselves full and providing the hovering and quietly excited Von Roemer with copious pages of notes on their dress, appearance, and behavior. They departed in the early evening, after another full meal.

"They return in the morning to lead us to Ketumsee's camp," Lorenzo reported to Meusebach, who appeared mildly elated. Von Roemer would have followed after the Comanche delegation, if Carl and Wilke had not quietly dissuaded him from doing so.

"I'd say they were eating us out of house and home, if we had a house," Carl remarked. "Just how often are we supposed to feed them, Lorenzo?"

"Whenever they hunger," Lorenzo answered. "Do you still regret bringing the wagons, Señor Becker?"

"No, but we might have to start hunting for ourselves, soon."

Meusebach shook his head, "I should rather wait until we have their permission to do so,"

In the morning, a larger band of Ketumsee's men appeared for breakfast.

"Our formal escort," Von Roemer said with transparent delight.

Meusebach looked at Ketumsee's delegation and observed quietly, "Imagine such, accompanying King Friedrich-Wilhelm on a state appearance." Von Roemer snickered and allowed, "I am sure the Highest would insist on trousers, which would spoil the picturesque appearance considerably."

"Our hungry formal escort," Carl observed, sourly.

They traveled that morning at a leisurely pace, across the rolling grasslands towards the San Saba, where a range of low rolling hills rose above a long valley. A white flag fluttered from the top of a tall staff on the highest hill, above an ever-shifting mass of rich color, with the morning sun glittering in small flashes on silver ornaments and spear-points.

"For what we are about to receive . . ." muttered Roberts, the surveyor who rode closest to Carl. Carl nodded, his mouth suddenly too dry to speak. That ice-cold detachment that possessed him in moments like this, magnifying every tiny moment, allowing him to see and judge everything in terms of death and survival had descended as soon as the Indians began moving towards them. He stuck close to Meusebach. The man was his charge, his duty to protect, as Jack had asked of him. The tiniest sound seemed to ring crystal-clear; the jingle of harness and horse-tack, one of the Mexican teamsters humming tunelessly and nervously and the rustle of wind in the grass between their horses. Three-Socks whinnied nervously, and ground his teeth on the bit in his mouth. Carl patted his neck soothingly, with an assurance that he most definitely did not feel. He didn't think it convinced Three-Socks, either.

As they approached the valley, the great mass of Indians began moving slowly down the hill, resolving from a shifting mob of horses and people into one long mounted line, centered on the white flag. To one side rode bands of men and warriors, each with their war-chief leading, bristling with shields and lances at the ready. On the other side, a long line of women and children, blazing in their finest clothes, their horses adorned and painted as splendidly as the people.

A voice called from the Indian lines, when they were still some distance apart and Lorenzo tilted his head to listen. Then he said, in that neutral voice he used when he translated,

"The chief of you, the Red Sun and his chief warriors ... is to ride forward alone towards Ketumsee." And he continued in his normal tone, "If you should fire your guns until they are empty, it would make a good impression." Seeing the reaction in their faces, Lorenzo added, "They will do the same. It will indicate trust. It is a courtesy."

"I'd sooner count on a full load for courtesy, myself," Roberts spat into the dust.

Carl said, very calmly, "They could kill every one of us right now, four or five times over and not break a sweat whether we have loaded guns or not." He said nothing about the two extra Paterson cylinders in the pockets of his leather jerkin, hard metal lumps against his ribs. In the event of having to load them . . . always a chancy business on horseback, since he would have to detach the barrel, change out the cylinder and then tap the barrel hard enough to fix it in place—and he doubted the Comanche would be sitting around letting him do this, if Meusebach's peace conference all went suddenly bad. Still, he would have to try, even if there was no chance to fight his way out of this mob. He knew too damn well what the Comanche liked to do with live captives. So did every one of them, even Von Roemer the scientist although he most likely didn't believe it.

Meusebach collected them with a glance and a jerk of his red beard: Carl and Von Roemer, Lorenzo and Roberts. "As soon as we empty our guns, have the troopers do also," Meusebach instructed Lieutenant Wilke. Wilke looked as if he would dispute that, and Meusebach added very gently, "Do so, Herman. We gain nothing without trust." And he wheeled his horse and walked it sedately towards the Indian lines. Carl and the others followed, and when they were close enough to pick out individual faces, Meusebach reined in his horse and sat for just a moment, looking across the space between at Ketumsee. With a quick gesture, he unshipped his shotgun from the long holster on his horse's saddle, and emptied both barrels into the ground. Lorenzo and Von Roemer were unarmed. Carl drew both his Colts and also emptied them, as Three-Socks jibbed slightly from the noise of it.

"This had better be a good idea," Roberts said in a low voice, as he un-holstered his own revolver. Behind them, a crash of shots echoed against the hills from their own party, answered by a ragged fusillade of musketry and puffs of black powder from the Comanche ranks. Carl let out his breath very slowly, hearing that; he had not realized he had been holding it. So far, so good; Ketumsee and his chiefs advanced, and Meusebach heeled his horse's flanks. Within a very few paces, they were intermingled, a slow pavane of horses and men revolving around the knot at the center: Meusebach and Ketumsee.

A pony burdened with a handful of giggling children—Carl couldn't tell if they were girls or boys shot under Three-Socks' nose, making the horse startle and step back. They were calling something at Carl, and Lorenzo looked over his shoulder to say in Spanish, "Take off your hat, Señor Becker! They want to see your hair."

"Figuring to decorate, already?" he asked mordantly. Lorenzo laughed.

"They had heard that many of the Allemands were colored like you, that is how to tell." Carl took off his hat, and the children shrieked happily like magpies. Their pony veered away among the crowd, squeezed like a melon-pip between two larger horses.

"Certainly dressed up fine, today," Roberts observed, as they rode together. "As splendid sight as I think I have ever seen ... and after we are done with this, I don't think I ever want to see again. How many do you think there are?

"Five, six thousand," Carl answered.

"Where are we gonna camp?"

"Off to one side, I hope. I'd like to be able to put something down with the guarantee of picking it up again."

With a great ceremony, Ketumsee and his men led Meusebach's party toward their own camp, a field of skin lodges stretching as far as they could see along the mesquite plain by the riverbank. Roberts whistled quietly between his teeth when he saw that, and Lorenzo said carefully, "Ketumsee invites us all to stay as guests within his village."

Carl was relieved to see Meusebach shake his head, with grave and regretful courtesy and reply, "We wish not to impose, for our horses and mules are very hungry. If it pleases Ketumsee, we will set up our camp where the grass is deep and green, across that little stream from his village, and exchange hospitality without imposing upon his pasturage."

With some trepidation, Carl waited for Lorenzo to relay Ketumsee's reply, but apparently this was the correct note to strike.

"The Red Sun is the most considerate of guests," and so they were conducted to a broad meadow, a little apart from the city of conical skin tents, where they set up their own camp and lit fires.

Most of the men couldn't help but keep looking apprehensively over at the Comanche camp. Von Roemer was so intrigued by it all that he tripped over an abandoned prairie dog mound and fell flat while walking along the stream bank, trying to estimate how many skin lodges there were. Characteristically, he was distracted by the burrow itself.

"It's a sort of marmot," Carl said patiently. "They bark, rather like puppies."

"Remarkable, most remarkable," Von Roemer mused, thoughtfully.

It seemed that evening that almost the entire Comanche village came by to visit, which proved to be very trying for them all, except for Von Roemer. There were children everywhere, skittering like tiny brown lizards between the wagons and under the tent-canvas flaps. Carl found himself particularly plagued by half a dozen bold little boys who keep trying to sneak up behind him to cut off a bit of his hair, to the vast amusement of their elders. When the brashest of them came whooping by on horseback, leaning out with his little knife in hand, Carl whipped around and caught him by one ankle and around his middle, peeling him off his pony.

"I have had just about enough of this game," he announced, and Meusebach half-started up from where he sat. He relaxed once he saw that the Comanche watching didn't seem particularly concerned as Carl carried the boy by the ankles - at some length because of the knife and the fact that the brat was squirming himself practically double – and dropped him headfirst with a mighty splash in the stream.

The adult Indians fell about laughing, and Lorenzo commented, "Señor Becker, I think you are his godfather now. They may even call him 'Dropped in the River'." The boy clambered out of the river, scowling and Carl said,

"Look, if they want a bit of my hair, all he need do is ask for it politely . . . go ahead tell him . . . but sneaking up on me like that is gonna get someone hurt."

Still laughing, Lorenzo relayed the message, and the boy replied curtly. Lorenzo said, "He says it is more fun his way."

"Tell him he'd better get used to cold water."

In the morning, they unpacked the chests of gifts which had been brought with such effort: lengths of cloth, knives and hatchet blades, beads and buttons, fine woven blankets, and presented them with formal ceremony to Ketumsee. In the afternoon, Meusebach and Von Roemer strolled towards the Comanche camp with Lorenzo and some of the others. All went ostentatiously unarmed, but bundled against the late winter chill and a bitter north wind. When they returned to camp some hours later, Meusebach appeared as composed as always, but Von Roemer seemed a little rattled.

"I must admit," Meusebach said, rubbing his hands together over the fire, "their skin lodges were a much more comfortable shelter against the cold then what we have. I almost regret not accepting Ketumsee's invitation. A warm fire inside the tent, with the smoke going up through the top . . . most practical."

"That poor child was cold," insisted Von Roemer with real indignation, "And half starved as well. Did you hear how he said it? As if he spoke of trapping an animal! 'I caught him on the Big River'."

Carl looked sharply across the fire at him, and Lorenzo said quietly, "Señor, there is nothing we can do. The Honey-eaters sometimes treat captives as their own children."

Von Roemer indignantly replied, "But he was a white man, not a savage! And he did not want to come with us! We asked him to come away with our party, but he refused most firmly. He wished to remain, insisting on it with great vigor."

"He?" Carl asked, and Meusebach sighed, heavily.

"We saw a young man among Ketumsee's men—a white man, one of your people. He had a little boy, a Mexican boy as his... slave. I suppose that is what we would call it. But the white man could speak some English, and he told us his name. Leon, I think it sounded like."

"Lyons," Carl said. "So this is where he finished up." Meusebach and Von Roemer looked astonished.

"So you have heard of this—this white Comanche?"

"I think I know who he might be—might have been. Warren Lyons, took about ten years ago from his father's farm in Fayette County, on the Colorado River. He was about eleven years old then."

"That age would be about right," Von Roemer nodded, still puzzled and outraged.

Meusebach asked, quietly, "You said 'he might have been' this boy. At first you said 'might be'. Why is that?"

It was Lorenzo, who answered sadly, "Señor, because the children they take from the settlements, some of them. They forget. They forget everything if they remain too long. They forget their own blood, their own home. They put on the ways of the Indian, and they are lost."

"Some folk count it the cruelest of their ways," Carl added, soberly, seeing Von Roemer and Meusebach's shock and disgust.

"Crueler still than the outright killing, and that's crueler than you can imagine. Captives get made into slaves or whores, mostly and either worked to death or sold back to the right customer for goods or foodstocks. But sometimes, when they're the right age, especially boys—they'll keep them and raise them up as their own in the tribe. 'Less we get them back right away, we don't ever really get them back. That Parker girl was taken about the same time, and from the last I heard tell, it's probably too late to get her back, too. Lyon has a ma and two brothers in Fayette County who may think he is still alive … but not as they knew him."

Lorenzo nodded somber agreement. "It is true … so have I seen."

"But what would make someone raised in the proper way still choose this?" Distressed, Von Roemer waved his hand towards the Indian camp, "To choose this primitive kind of life, willingly?"

"To some, it's not all that bad a life," Carl pointed out. He was made more uneasy than he liked to admit by living, even briefly among the Comanche. *To live in the Llano, free as a bird, under a blue sky with cloud-shadows rippling over the endless meadows of sweet green grass. To hunt and tame horses, to spend jolly evenings with your fellow warriors, gambling and telling tales around the campfire… what was it he said to Jack, about becoming what you fought? Carl could see the appeal of living the life the Comanche did, clearer and more attractive than he liked to admit.* "Weren't you just saying how much better and warmer a skin lodge with a fire inside might be?"

Lorenzo added, "For a man, it's a very good life, señor. Ride where you wish, hunt what you will, take what you want, if you are strong enough to take it."

"Barbaric!" Von Roemer hardly looked mollified.

Carl asked, curiously, "You did not forget who you were, Lorenzo … how was that?"

"I was taken as a small child and my father was able to pay ransom and take me home before they could train me as a warrior," Lorenzo answered, quietly. "Still—I went back and forth several times."

"So are we reminded," Meusebach added softly, somberly "of how much it means to us to have peace. I would rather that we learn of each other ways without losing our own, or see our children torn away from us, to forget the ways of their fathers. We should not continue importuning young Mr. Lyons, Ferdinand. He has made his choice."

The following morning, eating breakfast among the usual crowd of curious Indians, they were astonished to see two men in proper clothes ride towards their camp. At first they believed they were all seeing things, a pair of riders in frock coats among the brilliantly adorned but usually half-naked Comanche.

Carl was still being stalked by the most persistent of the group of small boys; he fixed the nearest with a scowl and gestured meaningfully towards the creek, as Meusebach asked with mixed curiosity and indignation, "Who is this?"

"Looks like more company for breakfast." Carl squinted at the riders. "By God, its Jim Shaw and Major Neighbors . . . you, what are you after!" He scowled at the small boy who had stolen closer, tugging at Carl's trouser-leg and brandishing his little knife.

Meusebach hid a smile in his beard and said, "It would appear they enjoy being thrown in the creek. I know Chief Shaw; he went with us to search out places for our new town, but who is this Major Neighbors?"

"He's an old friend. He used to ride with Jack, but now he is the state Indian agent, and answers to the Governor. He's the best friend the Tonks ever had—and he would like to make peace with the Comanche also. He has friends among every tribe living in Texas." The boy plucked at his trouser-leg again and looked up, hopefully. "Right," Carl sighed. He scooped up the child, carried him squealing towards the creek and pitched him in as the two riders splashed through the shallow ford. "I suppose I will have to do that with all of them! Bob, what brings you out this way besides a damned long nose?"

"I could ask the same of you, Becker. What in hell you are doing in the middle of Comancheria with all these damned Dutchmen, throwing little children into the creek?" Robert Neighbors was a lean and rangy man of about thirty, with a lively and intent gaze, who had gone from fighting Indians to fighting for their interests.

"Jack sent me, of course. Did you forget that I am one of these damned Dutchmen? The little brats kept trying to sneak up and cut my hair."

"That so?" Robert Neighbors scratched his jaw, with a rasping sound. "Better than lifting it entire, I reckon!" The dark-faced man who rode with him grinned and called out a humorous-sounding observation to the little boy who was scrambling out of the water. Another small boy came hurtling down the creek bank, screeching like a banshee. Carl scooped him up on the run and pitched him toward the center of the creek. The child landed with a terrific splash and a squeal. Neighbors added appreciatively, "Very good, hoss! The smaller ones go a little farther!"

"Damn your eyes, Bob, what are you doing all the way out here?"

"Yes, what is your purpose in following after us?" Meusebach asked, intently. He had followed Carl a little more slowly to the creek-bank "And why would it be your business? Good day to you indeed, Mr. Shaw. I had not expected to see you again so soon. Good day indeed."

"The Governor sent us." Major Neighbors dismounted and took off his hat. "Once he had heard you were really intent on this scheme and on your way into the Llano. Me, I'm here in my capacity as Indian Agent and Chief Shaw, because he is a natural gentleman and a scholar, and one of the damn-finest scouts and translators around." He looked at Meusebach with great seriousness and continued, "We were sent to warn you—to beg you not to go into Comanche territory in pursuance of this insane plan of yours, Mr. Meusebach, sir. We were horrified to get to Friedrichsburg and find that you had already departed. Please believe me when I say you are in deathly peril, all of you are, every moment you remain—" His impassioned plea was interrupted by another small boy, shrieking a treble war-cry and tearing down the creek-bank at a dead run.

"Sorry." Carl scooped up the boy and launched him stream-wards. He landed with a whoop and a splash.

Meusebach said gravely, "Deathly peril, I believe you were saying, Major Neighbors?"

Jim Shaw grinned broadly, and observed,

"I b'lieve you ain't doing too badly at that, Mister Meusebach. Not too bad at'tall. Put a little more back in it, though," he added to Carl, who answered sourly:

"You throw the next one then."

Jim Shaw slid down from his own horse: he was incongruously dressed above the waist in an impeccably tailored broadcloth coat and buckskin leggings below it.

"All comedy aside," Meusebach cleared his throat, "I appreciate and understand the Governor's concern, and your concern also. I even profoundly appreciated Colonel Hays's concern and at his urging I allowed Sergeant Becker to accompany us. But I do not believe we are in any physical danger at this time. Your apprehensions are somewhat misguided."

"Our most pressing danger is of running out of supplies." Carl pointed out, and Bob Neighbors grinned, a little reluctantly.

"Come around for meals, do they?"

"Like a plague of locusts," Carl answered. "Take it off your plate before you can lift a bite to your mouth. I thought sure Von Roemer was going to stab an old woman with his fork last night."

"Ferdinand would never be so ungentlemanly," Meusebach allowed. "Although I think he would own to a certain temptation in the matter."

"You ever thought of walking up to their lodge and helping yourself? By custom, you can claim hospitality," Jim Shaw suggested in enormous amusement.

Both Jim Shaw and Carl came close to laughing at the bemused look on Meusebach's face, before he answered, "I should not like to press any advantage through something so petty, gentlemen. We have already gained a great concession. Ketumsee has sent messages to Santanna and others such as Mopechucope and Ponchanarkip. We cannot now withdraw, having come this far without mishap. I believe the Comanche people are ready to listen to reason, and I believe they are halfway towards seeing the advantages that would accrue to them if there were a peace between us. I cannot leave with such a duty laid clear before men, gentlemen, especially since we have already dared so much."

He looked directly at Bob Neighbors. Carl realized that Meusebach already knew that Bob was the one to be persuaded. And he was not just arguing for their mission to continue, as if Bob could do much of anything to prevent it. No, Meusebach was pleading for the two of them to continue with his party. He had cunningly hit on Bob's weakness: his conviction that the Comanche could be tamed, to settle down like the Shawnee or the Delaware.

"We must have peace with the Comanche for the good of our settlements, gentlemen—and the Comanche must be at peace with us for their own benefit. If our two peoples can mingle in peace, it could be that the Comanche might be drawn towards our ways, be more amenable towards giving up their constant warring with others."

Not very likely, thought Carl, *But it's what Bob wants to hear.*

"You have great authority, and Sergeant Becker says you have wide experience and many friends. You want a peace treaty as well. Join your efforts to ours and help us make it a reality."

"You put it that way . . ." Bob scratched his jaw thoughtfully again.

Jim Shaw shrugged and added, "Nothing ventured, nothing gained. You can count me in, Mister Meusebach. But take my advice and move your camp, if you can."

"I intend to." Meusebach shook Bob's hand and led the way up to their camp, saying "Your assistance in this enterprise will be invaluable, Major Neighbors, and most welcome. No, I plan to journey on to the San Saba Fort, while we wait to meet with the other chiefs. The Verein had reports that the Spanish found silver in the vicinity. If such reports prove true it may defray our expenses. If not," he shrugged. "Von Roemer wishes to collect more curiosities and I must see a great deal more of this grant which Prince Solms saddled us with so thoughtlessly. The surveyors must also commence work. And we must hunt, lest we run out of food entirely."

They consulted around the fire that morning and worked out the next steps to be taken, in pursuance of a grand council with the chiefs. It relieved Carl considerably to have Bob Neighbors and Jim Shaw along for this venture, men of known repute and established qualities. Perhaps they could fill in some of the gaps in Meusebach's experience. It wasn't as if the man had much truck with Comanche Indians before, no matter how practiced he was at diplomacy. Carl liked Lorenzo and trusted Meusebach, but one had a murky background and the other was near to green as the grass when it came to Texas. Although, he reminded himself again, Meusebach's relative inexperience meant that he could see it with new eyes, unhampered by old feuds and jealousies. In the morning, they broke camp and sent Jim Shaw and Lorenzo to bear word to Ketumsee that they would return after traveling as far as the old ruined fort.

"How did they take it?" Carl asked of Jim, as they rode away from Ketumsee's camp with a certain amount of relief.

Jim shrugged, impassively. "As a matter of small interest. The Red Sun and his men may go as they please, since he has pledged only to seek peace."

Some days later, they left the wagons and a large part of the company at a campsite in a wide and pleasant side valley. The land became broken and rough, and being in agreement that the company halved was at no more risk than all of them together in one place, Meusebach ordered the surveyors and most of the Verein troopers to remain there, surveying and hunting while he and Von Roemer, with Bob Neighbors and Jim Shaw and the rest rode ahead, along the river valley. Leaving the wagons behind relieved them of much labor, and allowed the smaller portion of Meusebach's party to move swift and sure as birds. After five days, they came upon it: a nearly square masonry enclosure of crumbling double walls in a grove of mesquite trees. Von Roemer marveled at the plants growing out of window embrasures.

"For how long has this been abandoned?" he asked of Carl, who shrugged and ventured a guess of about eighty years or so.

"There was a mission to convert the Lipan Apache close by," he added, "Until the Comanche massacred them all. Folk in Bexar still talk about it. They about gave up on converting the Lipan after that."

"Such a heroic effort, to build this!" Von Roemer looked around at the walls, some still standing to about twenty feet tall, "You would think there was a strong purpose, but I can find no evidence of mines or smelting operations."

"There was always talk among the Mexes about silver and gold mines," Carl said, "but I haven't ever heard about actually finding any here."

"I also doubt it," Von Roemer said, decisively "The native rock is all limestone and chalk. The fossils are very interesting, though. Did you know that all this land was once at the bottom of an ocean?"

"No," Carl answered, skeptically. "Never heard anything about it, unless it was Noah's Flood. How can you tell otherwise?" This kind of information had not been included in any of the school books that his patient and exasperated mother had tried to drill into her reluctant sons. In turn, Von Roemer himself looked exasperated.

"The fossils! You know what fossils are? Living things, buried in the mud of ageless time and turning to stone; in this case, sea shells and ocean creatures."

"Gospel truth?" Carl asked. Von Roemer looked even more exasperated.

"I will show you, this very minute! Such marvels as you live amongst, all blind and unknowing! Did you know there are creatures and plants here that are unique, that scientists in Europe have never seen before and ignorant men like you think nothing of them! It is enough to make a saint weep!"

"Considering that men like you can barely find their way to such wonders without the help of men like me, I'd say that saint has a lot more than weeping to do!" Carl retorted, and Von Roemer looked abashed.

"I regret, I did not mean what I said to sound as it did. There are no proper schools in this country, are there?" he asked apologetically.

"There are ways to learn what we need to know out here ... it's just that it isn't in any classroom or book!"

No, learning to track a war party over a stony trail for three days wasn't taught in any books, nor was snatching up a coat from the ground, leaning down from the saddle of a furiously galloping horse, and he didn't think he had to think any less of himself for that. It still rankled with Carl after all this time, how Pa always said that he was a dunce next to his brother. He took a breath, and forced himself to calm down; it did no good to be angry at Von Roemer or Pa.

"Show me those fossils, though, if you wouldn't mind."

"But of course!" Von Roemer's face brightened, and for the rest of the day, he led Carl on an exhaustive trek to every chalk and limestone ridge, every clump of grey-green foliage topped with a brilliant corona of blossom. A vastly amused Jim Shaw trailed along for a while, eliciting a lengthy quantity of notes in Von Roemer's ever-present notebook, for he proved to know the Delaware names and qualities of many of the plants which Von Roemer was particularly interested in. That night at their campfire, kindled in the center of the disintegrating parade ground of the old presidio, Von Roemer waxed euphoric over their sharp eyes and observational skills: Carl and Jim exchanged a commiserating and humorous look over the campfire, for they had been dragged over every inch of the country around the crumbling walls.

Still, it did feel a little like a holiday, even following after Von Roemer everywhere. When they explored the ruins the next day, looking for remains and names and carvings into the crumbling stone walls, they found the names of a couple of Mexican officers, and a couple of others which Carl thought he recognized. At the campfire that evening, Meusebach sounded regretful as he told them they would and must return on the morrow.

"Time to talk peace with the great men," he said with resignation. "Enough of your stones and plants, Ferdinand; we must apply ourselves to our purpose, now."

Oh, good, thought Carl. *Let's get this over with. I think if I look at another stone sample of sea shells, I will brain Von Roemer with it and take the consequences. I should like to find a book about this all, though. When we get back—if we get back, I will ask Mr. Steinmetz about this all. He's a clever man; he would know.*

The peace talk took place in a grove of trees, around a great fire. A ring of buffalo robes was laid upon the ground around the fire for fifteen or twenty of the great chiefs and for Mr. Meusebach. Jim Shaw stood behind him, to translate to the council. Von Roemer and Lorenzo stood back in the ring of trees, with Carl and Bob Neighbors, all watching intently with Herman Wilke and the others of their party. Nothing much seemed to be happening, save for a long and ornate pipe being passed around.

"Don't look for anything to happen in a great hurry," Bob advised. He leaned his back against a tree, taking out his penknife for a bit of whittling. "Those three, they may be big chiefs and hold a lot of authority over their people, but if their warriors aren't for something, it doesn't happen. They will go back and palaver with their folk before they give us an answer. But still . . . it's no small matter to have gotten a hearing."

"Which among them are the great ones?" Von Roemer asked, greatly curious. "I cannot tell their rank from their dress and accoutrements."

"The very old man, in that cotton jacket—that would be Mopechucope. Means 'Old Owl' or so they tell me."

"He does indeed appear most wise and venerable," Von Roemer said dubiously, but the word Carl would have used was more along the lines of 'crafty' and not a man to play cards, or otherwise engage with in a friendly gamble.

Bob continued, "Now, the war-chief, Santanna—that would be the big, strong-looking hoss, immediately opposite us."

"He has most lively and benevolent features," Von Roemer noted. "Of all, he appears to be the most open to social converse." And Santanna had been the most interested in hearing about the Verein settlements, asking many questions about them, and about their people. Carl profoundly hoped his curiosity had a benevolent purpose, rather than otherwise.

"Of all of them, he looks like he'd be good company over a bottle of whiskey," Carl ventured.

Bob nodded agreement. "Now, the last gentleman, Ponchanarkip—which translates among the polite as Buffalo Hump— he appears as if he'd just as soon cut your throat as say hello." Of the chiefs, he was the only one not to affect some element of civilized dress. He had a buffalo robe belted around his waist and bracelets of copper on his arms, and stared sullenly into the fire. "In fact, he probably <u>has</u> cut throats sooner than say hello, but not so many of them of them of late."

"Plum Creek," Carl said, and Von Roemer looked puzzled.

"Had you met Chief Ponchanarkip before?"

"Not as such," Carl answered, "But we might have run into each other once. But all I rightly saw of the Plum Creek fight was a cloud of dust and ash with a lot of screaming Comanche in it."

"Such curious names," Von Roemer mused, after some minutes of frantic note-taking. "Really, it seems that some names are . . . well more of a joking reference to some incident."

"Some of their names are so forthright you can't say them in polite company," Bob Neighbors pointed out. "Buffalo Hump, for one."

"How very singular . . ." murmured Von Roemer. "Still, it says much in their favor, having such a robust sense of the comic."

"In his case, it's a reference to his enduring prowess with the ladies," Bob Neighbors enlightened Von Roemer in a stage whisper.

"Oh, they got a real sense of the comic, all right," Carl said. "One of the captives they took when they sacked Linnville had the soles of his feet skinned clean off, and they made him run ten or fifteen miles before they shot him full of arrows. A real gut-buster, that was."

Bob let out a snort of laughter and said, "Dutch, you sure got a way of killing the mood," while Von Roemer looked horrified.

"They start now," Lorenzo whispered, and sure enough, Mr. Meusebach had begun to speak. His voice carried clearly to the outer circle.

"Lawyer fellow was he?" Bob whispered, in admiration. "Damn, if I'm ever arrested and charged, I'll hire him in a heartbeat."

"Brothers, I have come a long distance to meet with you to speak peace," Meusebach spoke with gravity, leisurely uncoiling an intricate web of words, while the chiefs listened impassively but with great attention. "I hope you listen to my words, for they are true and sincere, as we Germans are accustomed to speak so. Our ancestral people are warlike, and courageous, and as you have seen, accustomed to bearing arms. I have been sent with some of my people from across the wide water. We are united with the Americans, as our brothers, and live under their law and the authority of the President."

He paused for Jim Shaw to relay his words, and then embarked on a description of where the Verein settlers had set up their lodges along the Guadalupe and Pedernales rivers, and how they intended to settle also along the Llano, to bring their wives and children, to raise corn and cattle.

"We do not fear war," he said, "but we love peace, and if you are willing to walk the path of peace with our people, our hearts will be made glad. It is our hope that you may leave the path of war and walk the path of peace, to visit our people and our cities, villages and homes. If we are friends, we shall always share our meals with you when you are hungry. If you walk the path of peace with us, you will ever be able to obtain corn, flour, sugar and other foodstuffs . . . your wives and children when they are hungry, will know where they will receive support and that will make their hearts happy!"

Another pause, for Jim to relay those words, and then Meusebach outlined what he wanted: that his settlers be able to travel freely in Comanche lands, without fear of harm, and the Comanche to do the same among the Verein settlers, that the two peoples be allies against attack by others. He asked for permission to send surveyors, so that they might know exactly where it was permissible to till the soil.

"My people will build houses among you where the soil is most suitable for planting corn and other crops, and we shall live as a family of brothers. We need only a small amount of land for our gardens! You raise no corn or animals for yourselves; you depend upon hunting, and set your tents here today and somewhere else on the morrow. When the buffalo move to the north, and the deer to the forests, when the grass dries or is burned . . . when you are unable to hunt and the cold north wind keeps you in your lodges and your horses are thin... then come to my people and barter for what you need. I have seen that many of you must now go hungry for days... yet you would have plenty to eat, because our people will grow on those small lands much more than we need for ourselves."

"A hit, a very palpable hit," Bob murmured appreciatively. "If they can see the sense of letting people grow crops, season after season, instead of coming in and raiding the lot . . . "

"Shush!" Von Roemer flapped his hand. "He is speaking again, and I am trying to take down every word!"

"I hope that we can come to an agreement," Meusebach said, with an air of conclusion. "I call upon our mother Earth, to witness that I have not spoken falsely. I have nothing more to say to my brothers, and listen now to what my brothers will answer."

"Now comes the proof of the pudding." Bob had reduced his whittling to a pile of small shavings. The chiefs seemed to be

225

speaking quietly, one to another, but finally Old Owl spoke, grave and thoughtful words to which they all listened with courteous attention and Jim Shaw relayed them.

"We must consider with our people the words that our brother the Red Sun has spoken. We shall meet tomorrow to convey our reply. I have spoken."

"Well," said Bob, after a moment, as Meusebach and Jim Shaw withdrew from the council circle, "the knives aren't coming out. That's a good sign, I expect."

Chapter 13 – *In the Time of Two Peoples*

They gathered in the morning around the council fire to hear the chief's decision. These things happened at a seeming leisurely pace, but Carl was well aware of the undercurrent of tension. It showed in different ways for all of them: Bob's ceaseless whittling, Meusebach squinted against the bright sunshine as if he had a headache, and Von Roemer paced nervously. Only Jim Shaw seemed completely unaffected. He and Meusebach took their places among the chiefs as before, ringing the council fire, with Carl and the others watching from under the trees.

"What do you think?" Carl asked softly, and Bob looked up from his whittling to look around the circle.

"Can't tell—they're playing it very close to the chest."

Moments trickled quietly by. The elaborately ornamented pipe went from hand to hand, until it reached Old Owl, who puffed quietly for some moments, while Bob whispered, "Oh, he's playing this out for all it's worth, the old villain. Tell what he is saying now, Lorenzo."

"The usual courtesies," Lorenzo shrugged. "Some nonsense about a black rim under his fingernail yesterday that is white today. His heart is glad to see those who have come so far across the wide water. He has spoken to his people, taken counsel with the warriors and old men—Ah!" Lorenzo's face brightened. "They will do it! He is saying 'we shall leave the war path and walk the white path of peace with your people as was proposed—and I shall do everything I can that we shall remain upon it, once agreed upon'."

"Glory, glory and hallelujah!" breathed Bob. "The damned stiff-necked Dutchman has done it!"

"Shhuush," Von Roemer hissed, "I wish to hear the rest of it."

"He wishes to consult with some of the distant tribes before settlers are allowed along the Llano . . . they are at war or hunting buffalo, but he says that by spring—when the grass is well grown, he will have resolved this. He has spoken, and has nothing more to say."

"My brother has spoken," Meusebach answered, formally, "and I have heard and considered his words. The hearts of our people will be made glad when they hear of the words of peace spoken by my brother. His people have no objection when we now build our houses and set up our tents. My brother wishes to follow the path of peace with our people, and will confer with the other warriors of his tribe. My brother speaks of a division between our peoples. I do not scorn my red brothers because they are of a darker color, nor do I regard my white brothers as noble because they are lighter in color. If our great father and president wishes to draw a line of distinction across the land, then let him do so. We shall not see the distinction because we are brothers and wish to live together as brothers; our warriors delight in combat and we are accustomed to war. Our weapons are not corroded, and we do not wish a peace treaty with any other than our brothers, the brave Comanches of the west. I have spoken."

"Always a good thing to remind them of that," Bob grunted, "about the weapons and all."

Old Owl spoke again, very briefly, and Jim Shaw translated his words so that all could hear.

"My heart is glad at my brother's words. I shall come to his town after the second full moon with my people. Send a messenger we know and can believe that he was sent by you and we shall come and conclude the peace treaty you have wished. I have spoken."

"Now, let's hear what the others shall say," Bob added, as the old man passed the pipe to the burly and gregarious Santanna, whose words were relayed again by Jim Shaw,

"My brother, we have listened to your words. What we as chiefs decide in this matter, our people will obey. We hope that you have spoken truly. This will become clear when what has been promised is delivered. I believe that you and your people mean to deal as honestly as brothers should. I hope that my brother of the Germans has a great heart for all of our children. We shall walk the path of peace and keep it with our people. That path will be broad and wide and lead to his gates, to the hearts of his people, so that my people may enter and stay among them without fear and betrayal. I have spoken."

"Well said, well said," Bob complimented in a whisper. "He sounds as if he means it. Now for Buffalo Hump. He looks as sour as if he just bit into a pickle."

"He's not the chief of as many as he once was." Carl observed, "Not after Plum Creek."

"Greedy for horses," Bob shook his head, sadly, and explained to Von Roemer, "He led his entire tribe into the lowlands seven years ago raiding and looting as far as the coast, in revenge for the Council House Fight. They took more horses than you could shake a stick at, every one of them loaded with loot. Slowed them down, gave the militia and the Army time enough to catch up."

"Shush!" Von Roemer hissed again, for Ponchanarkip had finished speaking, and Jim Shaw was translating his very brief words.

"Do not think that there is anything I do not approve because I do not speak. My friends, the chief commanders of peace have spoken. My chiefs and my warriors have held council. I am in agreement with all that Mopechucope and Santanna have said. I have spoken."

"Not much for the flowery words, now isn't he?" Bob commented. Von Roemer looked vaguely disappointed, and Carl said, "Comes as a relief." He turned to Lorenzo and asked, "What now?"

"We feast them, of course," Lorenzo answered. "You are not surprised, Señor Becker?"

"No, not much."

* * *

Letter from Christian Friedrich Steinmetz: Written on 15 March 1847, From Friedrichsburg in Texas, to Simon Frankenthaler, Goldsmith of the City of Ulm in Bavaria

My Dear Friend: Such splendid news that I have to relate! The Commissioner for the Verein has with great perspicuity and daring negotiated a peace with the fearsome and warlike Comanche. Mr. Meusebach departed with a company of men nearly two months ago, intending to meet with their leaders and chiefs and to secure our continued safety from war and continuing depredations. We had heard nothing of their progress, although two emissaries dispatched by the Governor came to us a week after their departure. They expressed great fears for the continued safety of Mr. Meusebach and those with him. I found this to be particularly distressing since our very good friend Mr. Becker was among them. Of this young man, I have written several times before. This is the same who has asked my permission and approval to court Margaretha, which I most willingly granted. He is sober and responsible and seems much taken with her, although he speaks very little . . .

* * *

"It won't last," Carl remarked quietly to Meusebach, as they came down over the last heights, on their return journey. Another detachment of Verein troopers had ridden out to meet them, dusty and excited about Meusebach's return, but nervously looking over their shoulders at Santanna's wandering camp at their backs. It was Sunday morning; they could just see the roofs and smudges of smoke in the distance. "It will hold for a while, I mean. But it won't last."

"I don't see why not," Meusebach replied. He knew at once what Carl meant. They had talked many times of the Comanche and their ways, over the past two months. "I feared so, at first . . . but they strike me now as honorable men, as men who keep their word, once given. There is no reason why we both cannot live peacefully, each of us living as we do, and coming and going in each others lands. I truly believe now that a lasting peace is possible."

Meusebach had come away from the peace parley appearing as if a crushing weight had been lifted off his shoulders. He seemed to be younger and more carefree, jesting light-heartedly with Von Roemer and Carl, and buoyed by a genuine if inarticulate friendship with Santanna. Carl shook his head.

"Men die. This agreement of yours is personal—and it's only between you and the southernmost Comanche. Not the others, not the

Kiowa, the Apache and all the rest who raid through these parts. I heard lots of talk about our two peoples, and nations and whatever, and it's likely to only mean something permanent on your part. On the Penateka—maybe as long as the lives of the chiefs. Ten, fifteen years at best."

"How do you reason?" Meusebach asked. He looked as if he had a headache, as if a little of that weight were laid back on his shoulders again.

"Old Owl—he is old, even as they reckon age. Santanna and Buffalo Hump, they are strong now but they also aren't exactly young. They lead and the young warriors follow, for now."

Bob Neighbors was listening, as he rode on Meusebach's other side with Herman Wilke. Now he spoke up, saying, "They hunt, and they raid. You said so yourself at the conference fire. It's how they live, and how the young warriors acquire merit and horses. They don't farm; they don't weave, or make fancy pots, or herd sheep and goats, as some tribes do."

Carl continued, "Their leaders have given their personal word, and they'll keep the ambitious young bucks under control, for a time, anyway. But when Old Owl dies, who will take his place? Will it be someone who honors his words? When Santanna and Buffalo Hump grow weak and frail, there will be rising young bloods who'll see the easy pickings in your settlement. They probably won't be able to resist temptation, especially if they are from the Northern Comanche tribes. They are men who haven't given their word of honor to El Sol Colorado."

"You're getting chatty, Dutch." Bob Neighbors remarked, "Listening to all that Comanche palaver must have rubbed off on you. I b'lieve that's about the longest speech I ever heard you make."

"I still believe we can make a lasting peace," Meusebach insisted stubbornly, meanwhile. "They can learn from us, we can do each other good."

"You people may be able to stick to that," Bob Neighbors answered, "and I hope to hell you can, but they know damn well that our leaders have a hell of a time constraining our own ambitious young bucks from trespassing on Indian Territory. What was it that

General Sam said once—that if he built a wall fencing off the Indians, he'd then be plagued by white men climbing over it? I'll do what I can, of course." He sighed wearily. "Sufficient unto the day are the evils thereof. You did good enough for this day, Meusebach. Perhaps that's about all we can count on."

"Then we shall have to make the most of opportunity," Meusebach sighed, and turned to Wilke. "Have you any thoughts on who among us should go and live among them, as an emissary?"

"Or hostage," Bob Neighbors said, under his breath as Wilke answered:

"I have asked among the troopers. Of course, it must be a man without family here."

"Not a hostage," Meusebach interjected firmly. "Our agent, to the Indians."

Bob Neighbors replied imperturbably, "Well, calling a cow-pat a rose sure as hell won't shoo the flies away."

"Would you volunteer for such a venture?" Wilke asked Carl, who shook his head soberly.

"No."

"Why not?"

"I got too long of a history with them to entirely feel real friendly. And also—once I got past wondering if they were going to scalp me just for the hell of it, I might get to enjoy the life all too much."

"Like young Lyons," Meusebach looked thoughtful. "I take your point. Still; we have until May to find the right man for this service. There may be some daring soul among the men who went to serve in your Army in Mexico. Most of Captain Buchel's men have now returned." As they approached the first houses, he asked, "Will you be continuing on with us and returning to New Braunfels?"

Carl shrugged.

"I'll need to go to Bexar and report to Colonel Hays, first. I might be staying on, after that."

"Good." Meusebach smiled with real pleasure. "You know, as one of my final acts as commissioner, I have recommended that other settlers be made welcome to our grant and settlements, not just those that we brought from Germany. I know that Prince Solms thought it best to keep our folk separate, but he was in error about that."

"I would add that to the end of a very long list," Carl said wryly and Meusebach continued.

"I do not think it does our people any favor, to keep apart and separate from others. Besides," he added, as a shadow seemed to pass over his face, "I don't think the Verein can afford to charter any more ships. If we fill up the grant, it must be with settlers who come on their own. You would be welcome, Becker, you and any others who care to join us."

"Appreciate the offer," Carl began to say, thinking that he might very well stay, but it would all depend. But looking ahead, over Three-Socks' ears, he saw Vati Steinmetz and his family standing among the settlers in Market Square, and Magda Vogel lifting her hand to wave towards him. And in that moment, he knew that he would stay.

* * *

Mr. Meusebach and his party returned on Sunday last, triumphantly escorted by a cavalcade of Indians, the particular tribe led by a Chief Santanna, with all their women and children. They are encamped in fields by the river, just outside town, and come and go as freely as welcomed guests. Such a magnificent sight they presented, riding into town, with lances and shields at their sides, as with the knights of old! I shall write to you more about this as we come to know them well. Mr. Meusebach says that we have agreed to mutual hospitality, and to come and go among each others' dwellings as if we were indeed one people!

Some two weeks ago, we were deeply frightened by what appeared to be portents of disaster: bonfires burning on the peaks of hills around about town. It took some little time to realize they were lit in response to the custom of the country in Saxony and Westphalia for Easter-Eve. We were able to celebrate Easter under the roof of the Verein-Church, which is now about half-complete. Dr. Schubert designed it before his departure: a pleasingly proportioned octagon structure with a dome like a coffee-pot patterned after the cathedral in Aachen. The church is situated in the center of Market Square, and will serve all denominations for worship and also as a school, town-hall and fortress, being stoutly built of timber and stone plastered over.

* * *

"Look, Magda, isn't it a magnificent sight?" Vati was staring at the cavalcade of Indians thronging Market Square. "They have brought their skin-lodges with them! Fritz Lochte says they will be camping in the open meadows by the river!"

"They look very fierce," Magda answered, while Liesel gasped apprehensively and clutched Hansi's elbow with one hand, while she held tightly onto Anna's hand with the other.

"Never fear, ladies," Charley said reassuringly. "We shall protect you, won't we, Hansi?"

Liesel's husband looked very dourly upon the scene.

"We'd need more than what we have to cope with that lot," he answered. "If this is their friendly face I hope never to see their warlike one."

Market Square, with the roofed timber skeleton of the Verein-Church in the middle of it presented a spectacle, a mass of color and constant movement. Strong browned limbs and dark hair, painted in strange designs, colored with cinnabar and white and red on cheeks and bare chests or on the flanks of horses. Streamers of ribbon flowed gaily from their horses' manes and tails, from the long hair of men and women, from the heads of long lances. Johann and Friedrich watched in round-eyed delight, and Rosalie pointed at everything and shrieked with excitement, pulling at Magda's hand.

"I am looking for our friends," Vati remarked, peering across the crowd. "Alas, they are very dull in appearance and dress by comparison, rather like sparrows in contrast to peacocks. Do you see them at all, Charley?"

"I cannot," Charley Nimitz replied. "Can you, Magda?" He had been sitting next to them at church that morning, and came away at once when a Verein trooper came down from the blockhouse to say that a messenger had ridden in from Mr. Meusebach's party.

Being taller, Magda could see a little farther: she had spotted Mr. Meusebach's flaming red beard against a wagon-cover by the last buildings in town, where the three Verein supply wagons creaked slowly up the north-road.

"There," she said, "at the bottom of Market Street."

There was Lieutenant Wilke and his Verein troopers who had ridden away with the wagons two months ago. There also was a familiar buckskin coat and Carl Becker's fair hair, as pale as ripe wheat under the spring sunshine. She lifted her hand to wave at him, and then felt she would look like an idiot doing so. He had seen them, though. Without hurry, he urged his horse into the crowd, and was in front of them in a moment, slipping out of his saddle with a groan of relief as his feet hit the ground,

"Hello, little miss," he said to Rosalie, and he picked her up and swung her around in the air, her skirt flaring like the petals of a peony, while she laughed excitedly. He kissed her cheek with an enthusiastic smack, and set her on the ground again. He did the same to Anna, coaxing a giggle out of her as he swung her up, the ribbons on the ends of her short plaits flying. And then, with a grin, he did the same to Magda, swinging her clear of the ground with his strong hands on her waist,

"Put me down!" she pleaded, startled and pink with embarrassment,

"Certainly, Miss Margaretha," he answered serenely. But he kissed her cheek as he did so, and his eyes were laughing at her, as if daring her to do anything about it.

"You're all bristly!" she said, her feet on the ground again,

"Two months on a long scout will do that to a man. Hello, sir," he shook hands with Vati, who had just stood there, beaming. *Really, was that all he was going to do about it?* Magda thought. "Hullo,

Charley! Set anything on fire, yet?" he asked, and Charley laughed and slapped his shoulders.

"Good to see you, whole and entire, but did you have to bring the whole tribe back with you?"

"They came of their own," Carl answered, and turned to the boys, who clamored with questions; who was the chief among the Indians, what did the inside of their skin tents look like, had he been there helping Mr. Meusebach all that time, and a thousand more.

"Boys, boys, a little decorum, please! Welcome home, welcome home!" Vati was bursting with excitement and a thousand questions of his own. "A triumphant return, I can see. So Mr. Meusebach was able to negotiate a truce . . . splendid, splendid! Isn't it, Rosalie, yes, yes, please behave like a proper little girl! You must tell us all about it, then. I know Mr. Von Roemer, from Berlin was with you! Such a clever man, he has been traveling across Texas for months! He did me the courtesy of sharing one of his monographs—extraordinarily learned, most stimulating company."

"He talked about fossils," Carl said. "Quite a lot." He tilted his head and looked at Vati thoughtfully. "Do you know anything about them?"

"A little," Vati admitted, modestly. "I believe I have a copy of the Comte Buffon's Epochs of Nature, but it is in French. I can translate the most interesting extracts for you, of course."

"I'd like that," Carl answered, and his horse nudged his shoulder, as if to ask if they were going to move along, soon. "If you don't mind," but his eyes went to Magda, who wondered if it truly were fossils on his mind. She thought not.

Vati said, "You must stay with us, of course, unless you have commitments elsewhere."

"No, I haven't," he answered simply. "I'd like that." And Magda saw that his eyes, the color of the sky, were lit with such transcendent joy that she could not bring herself to object. It would have been like beating an innocent child. And anyway, most of the house was finished.

"Come, come," Vati urged. "There is so much that has happened! As you can see, we have begun work on the church building! And Old Mr. Wahrmund has managed to clear so many stumps."

Many years later, Magda told her youngest daughter, "Except for the years of my marriage, this was perhaps the happiest and most contented time of my life."

"How was that, Mama?" her daughter asked, curiously.

"It was rather odd to feel it so, Lottie, but it was true. Even though there were many people falling ill over the summer, and many deaths— oh, no we did not escape hardship. But we ourselves— your uncles and aunts and your grandfather— we had come safely through so many dangers and discomforts. We were at last delivered to a safe harbor! We still grieved for your grandmother, and little Joachim, but we had begun to build anew. John Meusebach had negotiated peace with the Comanche, so we did not need to fear them any more. The Verein was finally delivering many of their fine promises. The farm lots were distributed at long last, and your Uncle Hans was over the moon with joy. He had good lands although they were a little removed from town, adjacent to your grandfather's share, near to where Live Oak is now. He made many grand plans for the management of them both and finally began to build a good house on his farmland for your Aunt Liesel and the children, the house that he had promised her when we came away from Albeck. Your grandfather's house, where you were born was finished over that summer, also. Your Grandfather had many clever friends who shared his interests, so he also was diverted from his cares. But your Onkel Fredi was not so happy, for he and Johann were obliged to have regular lessons when the school began. Still, they managed to have many amusing adventures. When I think on that time, it seems as if everything had a golden glow to it, as if that summer were preserved in amber.

"And the Indians truly came and went, as they pleased, even into your houses, and were welcomed?" Her daughter asked disbelievingly, and Magda answered:

"Oh, yes. Some of them more welcome than others, of course. They used to bring meat to trade, and fruit and nuts gathered from the woods, and for a while there was an Indian woman who used to mind

your Aunt Liesel's babies, while your aunt worked in her garden. One of Chief Santanna's wives even bore a child under Mr. Specht's roof, and the Chief made out afterwards that Mrs. Specht was the child's god-mother. Emil Kreiwitz—you know, old Doctor Keidel's friend, who has a ranch near Castell? He went to go live with them for several years, to learn their ways on behalf of the Verein. He had many adventures while he was with them."

"Once, they had a grand parade, chanting and dancing all the way down Main Street as far as where the Nimitz Hotel is now, jingling tambourines made out of cheese-boxes. Oh, that was a sight; your Grandfather was as pleased as a boy at the circus. And they were there also when the Verein-Church was finished and consecrated, but I think they did not know what to make of such a thing."

"It sounds wonderful," said Magda's daughter, with a wistful sigh. "Almost too good to last."

"We knew, I think, that time was fleeting," Magda said. "And so that summer had a special luster. We were moved to enjoy it ever more deeply, having that knowledge."

"And you married Papa at the end of that time?"

"Oh no, Lottie, it was not as simple as that. And there were times also, when the presence of the Indians made us very nervous. I am still angry about my baking of bread!"

High summer, and the tall window shutters stood open, back and front, to admit a breeze into Vati's house, for the kitchen was very hot from the cook-fire. It was late afternoon, the hottest time of the day. Magda wiped sweat off her face with the corner of her apron and surveyed her work with satisfaction and no little triumph; three plump golden loaves of bread. Peter Berg and his brother had done fine work in stone: the chimney drew every speck of smoke out of the house, and the bread-oven was a marvel, save that the fire needed to be built up so much that it turned the kitchen into one large oven. Or so it felt to Magda; she went to the window that overlooked the back, and drew in deep breaths of slightly cooler air. The two great oak trees cast a moving and speckled shade underneath, where Johann and

Friedrich had finished making bricks for the day. Before summer's end, Magda thought they would be able to finish the other half of the house, filling in the timber frame with bricks. Most of the outside walls were already filled in to the top of the ground floor.

Now the boys were helping Carl by trimming the shingles he had split that day, the three of them working industriously away at that task. It astonished her to realize how seamlessly and unobtrusively he had slipped in among them when he returned from reporting to Colonel Hays, down in San Antonio. He moved his few things into the old cabin at the back of the lot, built a corral for his horse, and worked with Vati and the boys on the house, as quiet as one of the wood creatures. By mid-summer of their second year in Friedrichsburg, it seemed to Magda as if he had always been there. He read Vati's books, and talked long with him into the night. Waking at midnight, sometimes Magda would look down from her window and see a light, glowing behind the oiled paper window of the little cabin. He constructed a swing for Rosalie out of a wide plank and two long lengths of rope, and hung it from the branches of the oak tree nearest the house, and never seemed to be in a hurry for anything. Magda often forgot he was there at all, being so quiet, except when he was asking Vati about something in a book.

In the next room, she could hear Vati in conversation with Pastor Altmueller and a couple of other friends, deep in an abstruse discussion which kept them enthralled but left anyone listening to them completely baffled. This time it sounded as if they were talking about politics in what Magda and the younger element had begun to call "the Old Country". This was probably why Carl was still cutting shingles. He wasn't interested in it either; that was the country which they had left behind. Magda turned away from the window and let out a small cry of astonishment. She was not alone in the room after all.

A tall Indian warrior stood next to the kitchen table, looking intently at the fireplace, and furnishings. He had entered so noiselessly she had no idea of how long he had been there, and her heart fairly jumped into her throat. He would have had to have walked in through the parlor, where Vati and his friends were still talking, undisturbed. Obviously, they had not noticed the Indian either.

"What do you want?" she demanded, but her own voice sounded high, and nervous. The Indian paid no attention at all, not even glancing in her direction. Magda didn't feel frightened, nothing more than a trickle of unease. He had a knife in a fancy leather scabbard attached to a narrow leather band around his waist, which except for a short leather kilt was all that he had on in the way of clothes. Black hair hung down his back, and in the midst of it all, she noticed that he had no eyebrows or eyelashes, which made his appearance quite unsettling, inhuman.

Magda told herself, her father and his friends were in the next room, and Carl and her brothers were just outside. And Mr. Meusebach had said, over and over again, they had nothing to fear from the Indians, but even so Magda wished very much that he would leave. And just as she thought that, the Indian abruptly scooped up all three of her loaves of bread and spun on his heel.

"Put those down!" she demanded. He paid her no more attention than he would a bird twittering at him from a bush which was infuriating, and moved towards the door. She ran after, calling, "Give those back to me! Vati, Vati—stop him, he is taking my bread!"

But the Indian was already gone, swift and silent through the front door left standing ajar, and so was her bread baking, nothing of it but the smell of yeast fading in the warm afternoon air, and Vati saying distractedly, "Magda my dear, was there someone here? What has happened?"

Pastor Altmueller and the other men looked just as puzzled, as she cried, "There was a big Indian here, he walked into the kitchen and took my bread!"

Vati looked astonished and said, "What Indian?"

It was now her turn to be astonished, for of the five of them, not one had seen the Indian walk twice through the room.

"Vati!" she said, exasperated and angered. "That was for our supper, now what shall we do!"

"Oh dear," said Vati in distress, "Magda my dearest, he did not offer you any insult, or take anything but the bread?"

"No, Vati, nothing like that, but that what I worked all day to do, and he just walked in and took it! I have no flour left but that wretched stuff ground from corn!"

"You will think of something," Vati replied confidently, but then he looked at her again, with concern. "You are quite all right, Magda? You look very pale."

"Don't fuss, Vati, I am quite recovered." she answered; bad enough to have been so frightened, now to have her father frightened as well. That wouldn't do at all.

Vati still looked skeptical, and he said in an aside to Pastor Altmueller, "Alas for the bread! It is a mystery, how to make edible bread with the corn-meal which the Verein gives to us!"

"I can show you," Carl offered diffidently. She started a little, for he had come inside from the back, as silently as the Indian had. "If you like, that is. It's very easy."

"You can make bread?" she asked in surprise, and he looked surprised himself.

"How else to feed ourselves on the trail?"

And for that, she had nothing to say, as he followed her into the kitchen, and searched out an iron skillet. He asked quietly if there were any salt-pork, for that was best.

"No, only some bear-grease that Mr. Specht traded from the Indians." She still felt unaccountably shaky from the encounter with the Indian, now that her fury at losing the bread loaves had worn off.

"That'll do," he said, and calmly directed her to measure out so much of the corn-meal flour, with a bit of salt, and one or two other things that she had never thought necessary for bread, and pour the whole liquid mess into the hot skillet with the melted grease rolling around in the bottom. All the time, she felt him watching her.

"And it isn't kneaded and set to rise, before baking?" she asked, baffled, and he looked amused.

"No, it isn't."

She dusted off her hands against her apron and observed, "Well, that explains to me why it has always come out so disastrously. I made a stiff dough, and treated it as I would wheat-flour—don't you dare laugh!"

241

"I'm not," he protested mildly, but he did indeed look very amused, and when he added, "Your way would make good bricks, though!" she snapped:

"Out of my kitchen, then!"

"Yes, Miss Margaretha," but he was still laughing. He leaned against the doorjamb, just outside the kitchen. Obscurely, she was glad of him being there. Her heart still jerked oddly in her chest, from fright at the Indian's sudden appearance; she would wake up in sudden terror, over the next few nights, thinking that he was in the room with her.

"Miss Margaretha?" Carl asked presently, and she started; so typical, he was so quiet that she forgot he was there. She was setting out plates for dinner, and the one in her hands clattered noisily against the table as her hands trembled. "You should not be frightened. We are supposed to be at peace with them."

"Yes . . . I know. I mean, I am not frightened."

"Yes you are," he answered evenly. Without another word, he came back into the kitchen and put his arms around her. He felt solid, comfortingly steady, like she was leaning against one of the oak trees. His shirt smelt of fresh-cut wood chips, and wood-smoke, and vaguely of horses. He held her close against him, while she thought with mild surprise how really quite pleasant it was to be held so, as if taking a rest from a task too exhausting. When she stopped shaking, he loosened his arms and said again, "You should not be frightened. I think I must teach you how to shoot."

"What?"

Startled, she stepped back a little, and he answered seriously, "It would be a useful thing for you to know. You might be alone, next time and they might want more than bread."

"But didn't you just say that we are at peace with them?" She felt better, but embarrassed for her reactions, first to the strange Indian invading her kitchen, and then for finding comfort in being embraced.

"For now," he answered, inscrutably, "but it is really a thing you should know how to do. Like cornbread," he added, with a very solemn face.

"Out!" she pointed at the door.

"Yes, Miss Margaretha."

He didn't press the issue of teaching her how to shoot, and did not bring it up again. Several weeks later, it came to mind again. This time she thought better of it. In the cool of morning, she knelt in the tangle of the family's vegetable patch, just outside of the little cabin they had first lived in. She was picking early beans, and thinking that the little fluted green squash would be ripened over the next few days. She loved the vegetable garden; it rewarded all the effort and hopes put into it. From where she was knelt among the beans, she could look out onto San Antonio Street, where children were dawdling past on their way towards the Verein-Church for school. There were the Strackbein girls, Elizabeth and Christina giggling together. Magda waved to them, thinking that they both had grown so much, blooming like flowers, since coming with the first train of carts to Friedrichsburg.

The girls were walking on the far side of the wide street in which a couple of Indians from Santanna's camp cavorted on their horses. They were, she slowly realized, showing off for each other, and also for the school children, most especially for Elizabeth and Christina.

She sat back to watch, diverted and amused. Carl was cutting shingles, under the oak tree a little distant and he watched also, but in a way that made her blood suddenly run cold. The Indians were young men and proud of their show of horsemanship. This was town, where they had been made welcome as brothers. Surely no harm could be meant by this, but the tension in Carl Becker was unmistakable and tightening like a coiled spring, as he carefully set aside the froe and mallet, never once taking his eyes from the two Indian horsemen.

One of them wheeled his horse with a shrill cry, and leaning from his light saddle snatched Elizabeth Strackbein around the waist, drawing her up onto the horse in front of him. He went galloping down the street with her, shrieking with laughter. *It's a game,* Magda frantically told herself, kneeling frozen among the cabbages. *It's only a silly game of showing off, the girls are laughing!*

Carl moved silently from under the tree, out to the street-edge with the trimming knife in hand, fixing the other Indian with a cold, intent look. It seemed to Magda that their gazes locked tight on each other, a look as hard as iron shackles and full of dreadful meaning. There was a message being passed right in front of her; below the ordinary surface, beyond and underneath the sight of a reckless pair of young men showing off and a third young man wordlessly warning them not to let it go any farther.

The horseman came galloping back; he had gone no farther than the next street. He reined his pony savagely, in a cloud of dust. Elizabeth slid to the ground giggling, and then the two Indians rode away without a backwards look. Carl watched after them for a moment. When he walked back to where he had been working, Magda thought he looked his calm and oddly gentle self again; the cold intentness already gone.

Did all men have that capacity for violence deep in them? Or in most of them, was it disciplined with such steely self-control that one almost never saw it come to the surface? It shook Magda deeply, knowing that he had in him, and yet she had never seen it until this day. Something of that tendency ought to show, she thought but chided herself at once for being so surprised. He was a soldier. For the first time she wondered exactly how long had he been one, for he had never said. She stood up from the vegetable patch, feeling that she had been there for hours and walked towards the house.

"It was only a game," she said softly, as she passed Carl, already returned to splitting shingles. "There was no harm intended, I am sure. The girls were laughing."

"I didn't like to see it," he answered, simply. "Things can get out of hand."

"Perhaps you should teach me how to shoot, then." Magda answered, and he took her hand, grubby with garden dirt, and kissed the inside of her wrist, just as he had done once before.

"I will have some business in Austin, in the fall," he said. "I will teach you before I go. I promise."

Leaving in the fall? She walked back to the house, thinking that she would regret that departure, regret it very much indeed. And Vati would be heartbroken, losing his favorite pupil.

Although Charley Nimitz might not mind, terribly, for all that he and Carl were friends. All summer, Charley had openly sought her out for company; walking home with her after church, and calling at the house, ostensibly to speak with Vati, but spending the time with her. She found it rather flattering, for Charley's company was much sought after. Having other women envy her on that account was a heady feeling.

"He also has serious intentions, my dear child," Vati said, one evening, after Charley had gone whistling up the street towards his quarters in the Verein compound. Carl also had said a quiet goodnight, and slipped out of the back door. "No, do not turn down the lamp, I will stay and read for a while. He does not wish to speak openly of his plans, but I thought you should be aware. Young men sometimes become rather silly when they are rivals for the same girl, even if they are friends."

"Vati! I am not doing anything to set them against each other?"

"Certainly not, my dear," Vati agreed, peaceably. "You are sensible, but there are silly thoughtless chits who would be very flattered to have two men fighting each other over her; who perhaps would even be jealous of their friendship for each other and think nothing of breaking them apart." He polished his glasses, and put them on again, and said very earnestly, "I merely thought you should know of this, so that you could guard against any inadvertent words or action."

"Thank you, Vati," she stooped and kissed him on the forehead. "Consider me warned, then. I only wish that you could tell me which of the two I would prefer!"

"Oh, dear," Vati looked amused. "That is a matter for your own heart to decide."

So, at least she had an idea of what was in the wind, the following Sunday after services in the Verein-Church, when Charley asked her to go for a walk along Main Street.

245

"I'm looking to buy a town lot, to set up a business," he said carelessly. "And I wanted Miss Magda's opinion, if you can spare her for a little while."

"Of course," Vati said, heartily, "Of course - may we expect you for supper, then?" Carl looked to have not heard anything at all, or reacted as if it was not any matter of concern.

"Certainly," Charley answered, cheerfully. "I'll see what I can bring to make it all merrier, eh?" They walked along Main Street in companionable silence for some little way, before Charley confessed, "I own that part of the reason I take such happiness in visiting your father's house is his house! It's not the main reason, though - but I do envy it."

"Why? I am sure there are finer houses," Magda answered. "And sure there will be built finer still."

"Yes and I will have one of them, too. No, your fathers' house is comfortable and welcoming. Especially with the garden, out in back. When I build my hotel, as many rooms as possible will look out on the garden."

"A hotel? Is that the kind of business you want to have here?" That intrigued Magda, startled her even, although when she thought a little more, it didn't seem so surprising at all. Charley was gregarious; he loved a crowd of people. The more there were, the better he liked it.

"You are surprised? Didn't I ever tell you? My parents have a hotel in Charleston. Not one of the fine modern ones, but a very respectable, comfortable place. I'd have been quite happy staying in Charleston, and helping them run it, but for two things."

"Let me guess . . . too close to the sea would be one reason?" Magda ventured and Charley laughed, delightedly.

"That would be it! And the other would be that there were I-don't-know-how-many other hotels just like it. One or another more or less wouldn't make any difference to Charleston at all. But a good, comfortable hotel in a place like this? It would be a gold mine, especially in comparison to anything in competition. I know the business from the ground up and I know just what to do to make it better than anything else for miles around. So, what do you think?"

"I think it sounds like what you should do," Magda answered seriously; "I could never picture you as a farmer, like Brother Hansi."

"With no one but the cows to make conversation with? I'd go mad after a week!"

"Where were you dreaming of building your hotel?" Magda asked.

"Main Street, of course; this is the place I was thinking of, on the corner. I look at it every day from the front of the commissary."

They had nearly reached the Verein compound, where Magazine Street intersected with Main, and the town-lots had been distributed to the first settlers.

"I'd buy this one first with the house on it, and the one next to it when I could afford it," Charley looked thoughtful.

Magda said, "It looks rather small, for a hotel."

"Four rooms. I'd build on, of course. It'll be a lot of work. And here's the thing, Miss Magda," He took both of her hands in his and looked very earnest. "This is the sort of business where it helps to be married. I can't speak out plain for myself yet, but I intend to. I've always intended to speak up; we hold each other in affection, or so I have thought. I can't afford to buy this place and set up a household just yet, but I thought I would let you know my feelings. Should you be intending to accept another—well, come and tell me first! I beg of you most sincerely, so that I can kneel at your feet and earnestly plead for you to consider my suit. Let me prove it!" and he knelt on both knees in the street and clasped his hands together, with a look of comic yearning on his face.

"Dearest Miss Magda, please don't marry anyone else without giving me a chance!"

"Charley, get up, people are staring at us!" Magda began to laugh, "I promise—now get up!"

"All right, then," He sprang up and kissed her hand with great energy, "See then, I have a hope of success, for I can always make you laugh!"

To herself, Magda groaned, thinking of what Vati had said. It was all very well for Liesel to talk of fish in the sea, but what did a woman do when she had too many caught in her net?

Chapter 14 – *Affairs of the Heart*

Letter from Christian Friedrich Steinmetz: Written on 20 August 1847, From Friedrichsburg in Texas, to Simon Frankenthaler, Goldsmith of the City of Ulm in Bavaria.

My Dear Simon: Such a multiplicity of events to report in this letter! With the war in Mexico coming to an end, many of the young men who enlisted to fight in it last year are released from service, among them a Dr. Keidel who has been hired by the Verein to replace Dr. Schubert. We are greatly relieved at the presence of a man well-practiced in the medical arts, remembering how we feared for the health of my dear son Friedrich during our journey here. (NB: were you ever able to learn anything of the properties of the leaves I sent you, with which a kindly-intentioned Delaware Indian treated him?)

We hear most distressing accounts of epidemics of illness at Karlshaven, and among those of our people traveling from there to Neu Braunfels, which makes the presence of a doctor here most comforting.

With the assistance of our friends, the walls and roof of my house are at last completely finished. I have now a shop with a workroom behind it, with its own door to the street. We hope one day to afford glass in the windows but for now, we make do with stout wooden shutters. There are four rooms on the lower floor, with five rooms upstairs. How my dearest Hannah would have loved this house, so simply but comfortably fitted! Behind the house we have made a small paved terrace around a well and two fine oak trees, the first of which supplies water to our household and garden and the second provides shade on the hottest of days. Daughter Margaretha grows many herbs there in pots and raised beds. Behind that is the vegetable garden, and at the very bottom of the lot there is a small corral and the shelter where we lived at first, while building the house. Our dear friend Mr. Becker lived there over the summer, but he has gone to Austin on business of his own, which he did not say anything of to me. Margaretha seems to look on him with favor. She has another admirer *whom I like hardly less. He has also asked my permission to court her, so my dear child is rather spoilt for riches in this matter. Both are honest, honorable and hard-working; she would, I believe be quite content with either.*

But if she is not so inclined, I am confident she will reject their suits of marriage so tactfully that they will feel nothing more than gentle regret, unlike the sad recent case of Peter Berg, the stonemason. He worked tirelessly this year, saving for a house of his own, and to send money to his intended so she could join him. She came as far as Galveston but hearing so many unfortunate stories about conditions in the Verein settlements that she changed her mind and most hurtfully sent him a message saying she would marry another, instead. He has taken himself off to the hills to live alone, as a hermit . . .

* * *

Butterflies, tiny white and sulfur-yellow butterflies danced in the warm summer air, over the row of small thyme and rosemary shrubs, and where the lettuces and cabbages had begin to bolt and send up flower stalks. Magda thought she might as well uproot the stalks and throw them onto the compost pile, but she liked to see the fair of butterflies orbiting them, and so did Rosalie.

"Miss Margaretha, might you have some time, this morning?"

Startled, she glanced up. He moved so quietly that she never heard him most times. Unlike the Indian who had taken her bread, this did not frighten her, and she wondered why. Perhaps she sensed his presence, on some other level. This was rather a disquieting thought.

"I might," she answered. "But to do what?"

"I want to go to Austin soon. I said I'd teach you to shoot before I went."

"Oh." She sat back on her heels. She thought of how deeply frightened she had been by the silent thief of bread and how Hansi had bought a new shotgun, when he went out to live on his farm plot on Live Oak Creek and build a house out there for Liesel. "Yes," she said, finally, "I'd like that. When?"

"Now."

"I'll tell Vati."

He took her elbow as they walked away from the house, down Market Street; past where the cabins and garden plots straggled out into open fields south of town. He carried his coat, rolled up under his arm. The street dwindled to a rutted track and then to a footpath, across a grassy meadow, where the wind bent the grass-heads in deep ripples. Someone had pounded three wide stakes into the ground until they stood about waist-high.

"If I really wanted to task you, I'd make you do this from the saddle," he said. "At a run."

She stopped dead still.

"I'll go straight back to the house unless you stop teasing me."

"No point," he answered, solemnly. "You'll probably never have to do it from a horse, anyway. Right, then. I'll show you how to load, first."

He unrolled his coat onto the ground. One of his Patersons was rolled up into the middle of it along with a pouch of shot, a metal powder-flask, a small lidded jar that smelt faintly of tallow, another which rattled and an odd little metal tool about the length of her hand. One end of it was a bulb about the size of a large grape, with a narrow milled band around its equator, and the other flattened into the shape of a leaf with the tip broken off. There was a shorter finger-span metal rod hinged into the middle of the tool. Nothing about it resembled any of Vati's clock-making tools.

Carl took up the Paterson and said quietly, "It's a close-in weapon. I can't see you needing to sharp-shoot." He held it out to her, by the barrel." Here, take it. Right hand . . . but be careful where you point it, even if you think it's not loaded."

"It's heavy," she said, experimentally holding it as she had seen men do, "And where is the trigger?"

"It slides down when you pull back the hammer to cock it. Actually, this model is rather small, but you'll probably want to brace your right hand with your left under it. That's it . . . straight out in front of you. Pull back the hammer with your thumb, and sight it by lining up the sight on the end of the barrel with the notch on the hammer—just like that. We have three rules, Miss Margaretha. Don't carry a weapon unless you know what to do with it, and don't take it out unless you mean to use it."

"What is the third?" she asked, as he took it back from her, and began working the leaf-end of the tool on a tiny screw on the side.

"If you take aim, you better hit what you're aiming at." The screw loosened, and a dull-metal square wedge with a shallow groove in it slipped out. He set it neatly aside, adding, "You don't want to lose that, it holds the whole thing together. First, I'll show you how to load and after you shoot, you re-load." The leaf-end of the tool slipped into the space where the wedge had been. "You'd best not lose this, either," Carl explained, with a grin. "Among other things, you need it to pack the charge and ram the bullet in." They sat on the ground, with the coat between them; he showed her how to measure the precise amount of powder into each cylinder as it rolled past the hammer and the exact amount of force necessary to pack it tight. Then a lead bullet, also packed against the charge with the little hinged tool levered against it.

"A little seal of grease . . . something to keep a spark from setting off any loose powder," he added, as he opened the little box which rattled. "You really don't want more than one cylinder to fire at a time."

"You make it sound as if this could be more dangerous for the shooter than those to be shot at," she said.

He looked a little amused and answered, "Not if you're careful, every time. Care should be a habit, Miss Margaretha." A little brass cap, like a tiny top-hat fitted over a little nipple at the end of each cylinder. "Right then, now you're ready." He stood up, reaching down to assist her to stand.

As she did, she asked, "Does it take this long, every time?"

"No. You'd be surprised how fast you can re-load, sometimes. I have extra cylinders, already loaded, but then I must take the barrel off, and put it on again, which takes nearly as much time. Now go on —take it and aim at the nearest post. Hold it in your hand like this with your arm out straight. Don't be frightened of it, Miss Margaretha, it's only a tool." He stood behind her, his hand over hers with the revolver in it, making her hold her arm out straight from her shoulder.

"It's too heavy," she said almost despairingly, for the long barrel wobbled as her hand shook from the exertion of trying to hold it steady.

"Brace it with your other hand, like I showed you . . . that's it, underneath your right. If you can't reach the hammer with your thumb, use your other hand." He stepped away from her, almost reluctantly. "Now, the trigger will come out as soon as you pull back the cocking lever. Line up the notch in the hammer and the sight on the barrel and see if you can put a shot though the first stake." She could just barely reach the lever with her thumb. It slid smoothly backwards until it locked into place with a click, and his steady voice continued, "Hold it steady, and pull back on the trigger... gently!' he added as she pulled too hard. The crash of the shot, and the recoil almost made her drop it out of surprise. "Again." He didn't seem surprised. "Just a gentle pull will do it. Don't flinch. Cock it again, with your thumb if you can. Take aim—and again." He was an unyielding taskmaster. Patiently, relentlessly, he took her through three more shots.

"Now, reload; this time, you try it." He watched her intently, as she fumbled with tool and powder-flask and shot, the little rattling box of caps, correcting the tiniest slip until her hands were dirty with powder and tallow and she was ready to shoot again. His patience began to feel slightly inhuman and she finally cried out in frustration:

"I don't know why you're doing this!" All three posts were left un-chipped. She had reloaded the Paterson twice, making mistakes at every step and feeling like an idiot. Her arm ached all the way to the shoulder and her ears rang. She could taste the black powder on her lips, her hands were filthy and her head hurt.

"Because you need to learn it," he answered, unyielding. He took the Paterson out of her hand.

"I'm not used to this." She plumped down onto the grass, half crying "This isn't my idea. It wasn't my idea to even come here!"

"No?" He sat down, next to her. His hip to her knee, her knee next to his hip, close but facing in opposite directions, so that he could look at her face and she could look into his. "But you are here now. And there is something . . . no, two things I should tell you." His eyes were very intent, close to her and as blue as the sky. Around them the tall grass whispered in the wind, the wind that blew off the Llano, that endless plain just beyond the hills. "The first is that there have been women whose men thought to leave them with a gun in the house but when there was a need to use it, they didn't know how and they were afraid. Or they were afraid to fire it, because they didn't know how to reload. They had always counted on their man being there and so they died. Or they were taken and then they died. You must know how to do this and you cannot be afraid, Miss Margaretha."

"I'm not afraid," she answered, cut to the quick.

"Good. Then act like it." As if to take the sting out of it, he reached out and awkwardly pulled her shoulders towards himself. "I am sorry I cannot make this easy for you to learn, but there is no other way." His voice rumbled comfortingly against her ear, the way Vati's did, when she was a little girl, and he held her close. She thought, as she had on that day when that Indian had stolen the bread baking, when Carl stood in the doorway into the kitchen afterwards to keep anyone else from coming in and startling her, that it was an amazing comfort to lean against someone so calm and solid. This time his shirt smelt of gun oil and black powder, and she rested her aching head on his shoulder for a while, under the sky and the wheeling hawks and the tall grass that rustled around them.

"What is the second thing," she asked, presently, having gotten over the urge to cry as if she were no older than Rosalie. She sat up straight, linking her hands around her knees and resting her chin on them.

"I was paid for some of my enlistments with certificates for land." he answered, "You understand, it was all they had to pay us with. I saved my certificates until I should see some land that I wanted."

"Land! I think it is all that you men ever think of," Magda sighed, and he smiled very slightly.

"Not always, Miss Margaretha. We think sometimes of other things. But I have finally seen the land that I want. So that is why I am going to Austin—to secure it for myself."

"Where is this land?" she asked, curiously. She was a little downcast, for it would probably mean that he was going away. Vati and the boys would miss his presence, and that she would also – quite vexing, now that she was accustomed to it.

"Not too far," he replied. "Just over the hills, about a day's ride from here, in the upper valley of the Guadalupe. It's pretty empty country, still, but I would like to build a house there. And . . ." he looked down at the grass, and spoke quickly, as if he wanted to say it before he changed his mind. "When I have finished the house, I will come back and ask you if you would like to share it with me. As my wife." And then he looked straight at her again, with that calm blue gaze, as blue as the sky. "You need not answer yes or no right now. I thought you might like to think on it for a while. That's all. I will understand if you say no—if you don't want to leave your father, and your friends here. It's a hard life for a woman, and lonely, too. All I can promise is that I would do my best to make you happy always, Miss Margaretha."

"I know that," she answered, being overtaken with a sudden surge of affection for him. "And you have always been so very kind to us. And you continue to be kind by not pressing me for an answer right away. It is a big decision."

"And it should be your own decision. You should not allow someone else to make it for you—and also," he got to feet and held down his hand for her, "You should try some more with the aiming, Miss Margaretha. It does no good when your shots go wild."

"You are a heartless taskmaster!" she complained, half relieved to be back on steadier ground, and he handed her the Paterson again.

"Yes. Now aim—that's it. Remember, if you should have to shoot at a person, aim for his breadbasket. This weapon tends to go a little higher, but it'll at least be a bigger target than the stakes. Even if they are moving toward you, you should be able to hit something vital. Don't bother for a head-shot. Good. Now again." And the lesson continued, his quiet and remorseless voice directing and lecturing, until her arms trembled from the effort of holding the long-barreled Paterson steady. She had sent a bullet through all three stakes at least once before he was finally satisfied.

"I'll show you how to clean it all, properly, too." He rolled everything up in his coat again, and took her arm as she complained:

"And I thought the lesson was over!"

"Not until everything is as clean as your kitchen." And he added, as they walked sedately back towards the rutted track that led towards Market Street. "There is another thing you should know. If there should be a time when you have a sudden bad feeling about a person—if something makes you frightened, uneasy, and you begin to think that something is not quite right—you should pay attention to that feeling."

"I thought the lessons were over."

"No, this is another one. You see, Miss Margaretha, most people would not pay attention. They tell themselves that they have imagined something; they are jumping at shadows and they don't want to be thought a fool. But what I really mean to say is that your mind has put them all together at once without you noticing any particular one. It could just be important to pay attention. It could save your life or someone else's."

"Whose life was saved because you paid attention?" Magda asked, bluntly.

"I didn't pay attention. None of us did." There was that curious stillness in him that she had sensed once or twice before.

"I see. Then someone died." She ventured. He was silent for so long, she thought he wasn't going to answer.

"Yes, many—including my brother Rudi. But I lived because of him."

Ah, so that was the bad memory that he had spoken of once before, when he had talked of his brother who loved to play jokes and laugh. Goliad was the name that made him go still and silent that time when they had first met. Vati had asked—oh, yes, now she remembered. There was something that had happened there; she would ask Vati.

"He must have loved you very much, to make sure of that."

"So he did. I don't think that our father ever forgave me for that." Shocked, she looked up at his face to see if he were joking. But he half-smiled, adding thoughtfully, "My firstborn son should be named after him. Unless you have a name you like better."

"You're very sure of me, aren't you?" He was teasing her again, she thought and stopped in the middle of the path, where the grass still grew tall. He stopped with her as she half turned to face him. The sun was a little short of noon, dazzling in her eyes as he suddenly leaned down to kiss her, full on the mouth, and she was so surprised she kissed him back. His mouth tasted a little of coffee and black powder, and suddenly there was nothing at all in the world around them, the air going out of her lungs with a gasp as his arms tightened around her. Her very bones turned to water and fire, she desired nothing more than his embrace and the totality of that conviction shook her. If he hadn't been holding her, she would have fallen. To her shock, her arms were around him, pulling him closer, feeling his ribs under her hands; her heart pounded and she felt dizzy, light-headed. His own heart thudded; they were pressing so close together it felt almost like a single heart. She was never entirely sure how long they stood in the path, locked together wordlessly. When they pulled apart, gasping slightly and staring with astonishment into each others eyes, he was nearly as shaken as she was.

"When I return from Austin," he said, finally. "I would like another one like that."

They returned silently to Vati's house. He was away very early in the morning, without saying much else to anyone but conventional pleasantries. Magda did not mind, for her thoughts were left as tangled as one of the grape thickets in the uncut woods along Town Creek. In any case she could not think of what she ought to say to him when the memory of that kiss left her feeling warm and flustered, all at once. Would it feel like that if Charley kissed her? He had kissed her a thousand times, although not as Carl had, without any particular reaction that she could remember. She supposed she could ask

Charley to kiss her, by way of an experiment, but she cringed from that notion after a moment's consideration.

After the children had gone to bed she lingered in the parlor with Vati, knitting a pair of socks for Johann. The shutters hung open to an evening breeze, which gently rustled the oak leaves in the garden. Occasionally a moth blundered into the room searching for the light. The room seemed very empty, unaccustomedly so and Vati in a somber mood. He put down his book and looked across at her, as if almost expecting to see someone else.

"You seem very quiet tonight, dear child. Might I presume to venture a guess as to the cause? If it is any comfort, I rather miss him also."

"It is not that, Vati." Magda sighed. "Oh, yes it is, in a way. He told me that when he returns, he will ask me to marry him."

"Most splendid news, my dear!" Smiling with happy interest, Vati set down his book, and polished his glasses. "What will you say then?"

"I don't know!" It occurred to her that the foot of the sock she was working on was too large for Johann. What was she thinking of! She pulled out the needles and began to unravel the excess, "Charley has said he wishes to marry me as well and I don't know what to do! I mean that I think I could be happy with either, they are evenly balanced as to their qualities and I care for both, and I don't know what I should say!"

"Well, yes, to one of them." Vati tried to look serious but he kept smiling, almost mischievously. "You cannot marry both of them! Do you fear that if you say no to one or the other, or to both that they will be so heartbroken they will both go off like poor Peter? So sad, to imagine that behind every hill and tree there may be a lovelorn hermit, some sorrowful Werther thinking melancholy thoughts about you, dear child!" Against her will, she giggled, picturing either of them, Charley the irrepressible or the level-headed Carl, pining away or shooting themselves out of unrequited love of her or any other woman..

"But which one, Vati?" she asked. "Which one would you rather have for a son?"

Vati polished his glasses again, answering seriously, "In all fairness, I cannot say, my dear. I like both of them equally well. It is not my place to say which I could best endure as a son. You must decide which you can best live with as a husband." He sighed and put his glasses on again, looking at her over them. "I don't know. Perhaps your dear mother might have given you better advice. She so wanted to see you happily wed, with children and a household of your own."

"I should ask Helene Altmueller." Magda ventured. "She has so often had wise words for us all, in Mutti's absence."

"Yes, of course!" Vati brightened. "Why did I not think of that? A woman's touch, just the thing! In any case, my dear, I am sure you will make a good choice."

"I wish I could be so sure," she sighed, and rolled up her knitting. "I think I shall go upstairs now, Vati. But," she hesitated, "There is one thing. What do you know about a place called Goliad? You said that a dreadful incident happened there, once."

"Ah—that," Vati closed the book he had been reading. "It happened in that year when the Mexican General Santa Anna tried to take back Texas with a great army. Too late, of course; he had already lost the hearts of those who lived in the settlements. There were two forts which the Americans and Texas settlers held. One was taken over the bodies of its defenders and the other surrendered thinking they did so under the rules of war. That was the citadel in Goliad. General Santa Anna wanted to cow the populace so he gave orders that all those taken at Goliad were to be executed. And so they were. His soldiers marched them away in groups and turned their guns on them, as soon as they were out in the fields. There were some who escaped, but most of them . . ." Vati looked at her very sadly. "Some of their bodies were burnt, but most lay out in the fields where they fell for months, until one General Rusk and his men came to take the citadel and bury the murdered garrison. It was, as a wise man said of another such deed, 'worse than a crime, it was a blunder', for it united the settlers against him as nothing else would have done. Why do you ask, my dear?"

"Only that someone spoke to me of such a thing and I wondered." She began to put away her knitting, but Vati put on his glasses again and looked at her over them, saying, "He was there, you know. He was barely older than Johann and Friedrich. So cruel, to make a soldier of a boy that age! I fear the harshness of this place sometimes, and what it might make of us, yet."

"What did he tell you of it?" Magda was startled and curious, and Vati sighed heavily.

"Nothing. And I would not pry. I merely remembered reading an account of that horrible event, written in an American newspaper which Simon saved for me years ago when I was clipping and saving everything I could glean about Texas."

"Your scrapbook?" Magda asked, and Vati sighed again.

"I have read many of my clippings over and over, and I have a good memory for names. Such accounts of the killings came from those who were kept safe by a compassionate officer, taken out of the fatal march, or who escaped in the confusion. One such came from the younger son of a Mr. Becker, who had a farm at Waterloo on the Colorado River. That is where he is from, is it not?" Vati interjected, and Magda nodded.

"I tell you, it took me some considerable racking of my memory to connect that account to our friend. Most tragic, it was. He saw his brother and all his comrades being shot down, all around him, just as his brother pushed him out of the way. He escaped to the river but dared not show himself, since there were Mexican soldiers everywhere. He made his way home by stealth, traveling at night and hiding during the day. I am not surprised that he doesn't wish to speak much of it," Vati sighed and removed his glasses once more.

"Some do, of course. There was likewise a long account from a Mr. Ehrenburg, who wrote a book about his narrow escape from the same dreadful massacre. But I do not think our friend is one to speak lightly of his experiences to anyone, even to those he holds in affection."

"He spoke of it in a little way to me." Magda said, "But now I fully understand what he was saying." She put away her knitting, and set her workbasket in the corner behind her chair. "Good night, dearest Vati."

In the morning, she picked some beans and considered a cabbage from her garden before relenting: the cabbages were not large enough yet. She put the beans and some snips of herbs into a basket and set off towards the Altmuellers with Rosalie. They had drawn a town lot on Austin Street, in the back of where Charley hoped to set up his hotel. With only their own labor, the Altmuellers had not been able to plant as large a garden, although their old parishioners and some of the folk they had tended to at the beach encampment had helped Pastor Altmueller build a two-roomed cabin. Helene Altmueller was sweeping the little porch between the rooms, but set the broom aside as Rosalie scampered up, calling happily, "Auntie 'Lene, Auntie 'Lene, we picked some greenies for you!"

"Good morning to our little rose!" Helene set aside her broom. "Good morning, Magda! What is this?"

"Just some beans from our garden," Magda explained to Helene, "and also a dilemma of my own, hoping for some of your advice."

"Mine or my husband's?" Helene took up Rosalie in her arms, adding, "He is really rather more qualified than I," and she cooed at Rosalie, "Who is getting to be a big girl then? You have done so very well with her, Margaretha. She does indeed blossom like a rose."

"No, it is your advice—in the place of my mothers," Magda answered.

"Oh, that manner of advice; I shall do my best, although I may be in a bit of a rush shortly. Come and sit down. Does this concern a matter of the heart, then?" They sat in the little porch between the two rooms of the cabin, on some rough chairs of cedar with leather seats, which Helene had made comfortable with some cheerful calico cushions.

"It does," Magda began, and then looked at Helene sharply. "Does everyone in town know of my own business, in this?"

"No—your father has often opened his heart to my husband and myself, regarding his hopes for you and one or another of your admirers. So, I take it that one of them has asked for your hand?" Helene encouraged.

Magda sighed, "No, both of them have, in a manner of speaking. The problem is I feel a regard for them both. I shall be obliged to give them an answer soon and I just do not know what it is to be. The more I think about them, the less I am sure!"

"Just so that I understand completely," Helene shifted Rosalie to a more comfortable position on her lap, "the one of them is your father's friend, Mr. Becker is it? Who was helping him finish the house? And the other is?"

"Charley Nimitz, the commissary clerk."

"Very personable and hard-working young men," Helene nodded in approval. "What of their ambitions and prospects?"

"Mr. Becker has gone to Austin to secure a quantity of land on which he intends to build a house and farm. Mr. Nimitz intends to buy a town lot and open a hotel on Main Street."

"And you do not favor one over the other, particularly?" Helene asked.

"No, and that is why I am so in need of help!"

"Perhaps if you made a list," Helene suggested thoughtfully, "a list for each, of all their qualities. Both the good ones, and those things which you think might eventually grate and . . ."

"Decide for the one with the longest list of one, and shortest of the other?" Magda asked. Helene said, "Don't be flippant, dear girl. No, I thought that making a list might help you to organize your thoughts, sort out how you really feel about what each of them offers you. For instance, Mr. Nimitz wishes to open a hotel. As his wife, you would expect to take some little part in his business; there would be strangers incessantly coming and going at all hours. Would you thrive in such an atmosphere as that? Now, Mr. Becker, he intends to have a farm . . . somewhere around here, I take it?"

"Not too close by," Magda answered.

"Well, then, he would offer you a quieter life, with perhaps not quite so many strangers traipsing in and out. You see? Construct your list, and consider it carefully and think on this, dear Magda; which of the two gentlemen do you wish to grow old with?"

"Mrs. Helene," Magda was struck with a sudden thought. "You have not considered it an affliction, with many strangers traipsing in and out of your house—have you?"

"Oh, no," Helene answered firmly and kissed Rosalie on the forehead. "For that was one of the things I considered! Oh, such a long time ago it seems, when Doctor Altmueller first stated his intentions! I could bear it with considerable equanimity, I decided. Really, one meets so many different people, and one hears so many extraordinary things! I would have never considered anyone else. My husband is as comfortable to me as a pair of old shoes. Marriage to some excessively romantic young gallant always struck me as rather uncomfortable. That sort of excitement is vastly overrated. Perhaps the young thrive on it for a time, but there is a lot to be said for comfortable steadiness after a certain age. You must excuse me, Magda dear; there were some folk newly come to town last week. My husband thought that I should look in on them."

"I understand." Magda took Rosalie from her lap. "Thank you. I don't think even Mutti could have given me such sensible council." She embraced Helene and took her leave, reflecting that Helene had at least suggested a way to think rationally about her dilemma. She was no closer to a decision, though. Almost the biggest decision of her life, she realized and her heart quailed within her. So much depended on this; not just her own future happiness, but also Carl's and Charley's.

She did as Helene had suggested, that evening after supper, in the upstairs room that she and Rosalie shared; not much different from the little gable-end room that had been hers and Liesel's when they were girls in Albeck, although out of the western-facing window the sky was painted in fantastic colors, orange and purple and gold, arrayed around the setting sun. With a shiver, she realized that she had begun to think of that time as something that was quite some time ago: Liesel had a daughter and a son, had lost a child and was now— so she had confessed with many blushes this last week after church services and a pleasant dinner in Vati's garden—expecting another. Hansi had taken possession of the many fine acres that he had always yearned after. Mutti had been gone from their lives nearly two years, without having ever met the child who was now accepted as hers and

Vati's daughter, or either of the men who jousted with each other for the hand of her own oldest daughter.

What shall I do, whatever shall I do? Magda thought despairingly, some weeks later, *I am back where I started from, no closer to an answer than ever!* She had written out a long list, and scribbled it over with lines and question marks, and gone over it every evening and still nothing she could add to it banished her fatal indecision. There was no more to be done for it tonight, she decided sadly. Daylight from the upper bedroom was nearly gone and it was almost Rosalie's bed-time. Time to see to her washing her face and putting on her nightgown, to tell her a story, listen to her goodnight prayer, and to tuck her into the bed that they shared, making sure that the raggedy blanket that was Rosalie's favorite was with her, all wadded up in a bundle at her side. It was too hot in these summer nights in their new country to sleep with it over her.

"'Nite, Auntie Magda!" Rosalie favored her with a joyously suffocating hug, and scrambled into the bed.

"Sleep well, little dear," Magda answered. "Church tomorrow, remember!"

"We'll see Anna and baby Jacob?" Rosalie asked, happily.

"Yes, we shall. Go to sleep, little Rose." She kissed the child's cheek and wondered what it would be like to have her own children. Would she care for them as much, or more than Rosalie and Anna? Perhaps she should ask Liesel, and while she was at it, ask what she thought about the other matter. If anything at all, Liesel loved romance.

"How delicious!" Liesel clapped her hands, that Sunday afternoon when they had gathered with their friends in the garden, for the men to talk and smoke and the women to gossip and sew while the children played. Magda and her sister sat a little apart, while the baby slept in his cradle at Liesel's foot, attended by an enchanted Anna and Rosalie. Magda had just laid out her dilemma to her sister. "So he has spoken at last! And Charley has also made his intentions clear? You are spoiled for choices, Magda! Hansi—listen to us, you are about to have a choice of brothers-in-law!"

"Am I?" Hansi asked, cheerfully and hoisted his mug in salute. "Prosit! Congratulations, Magda! Although I hope you were kinder to them, than you were to me, when I asked you." He had taken off his coat, and loosened his neck-cloth. The Lochte brothers had produced a couple of stoneware jugs of beer, over which the men were being quite merry.

"You were entirely not serious, then!" Magda told him, firmly.

Hansi kissed her cheek in a brotherly manner and answered, "Well, I thought I was, but you told me not to be ridiculous and to go ask Liesel at once, before you had to listen to any more tears and vapors!"

"I did not have the vapors!" Liesel insisted, laughing and blushing pink as a rose.

Hansi continued, "She said you did and also she was tired of stepping over apple peelings in the morning. Did you really believe that tossing apple peelings over your shoulder at midnight will spell out the first initial of your intended?"

"If I thought that would work, I'd do it, save for they both have the same initial!" Magda sighed.

Hansi kissed his wife, just to make things fair and asked, "So which of them is it to be, Lise?"

"That's the problem," Liesel answered, "She can't make up her mind between Mr. Becker and Mr. Nimitz."

"Indeed?" said Hansi, in surprise. "All else being equal, she should marry the one with the largest . . . property." And he leaned down, and whispered something in Liesel's ear.

She giggled, blushing and whispered back,

"Hansi, you are awful! I can't tell her that!" "No, perhaps not," he agreed, grinning broadly. Then he looked at Magda, with a serious and brotherly affection and offered, "Either of them would be an agreeable addition to the family, although I think Charley is jollier company by a far stretch. They are both good eggs though, so it wouldn't matter either way to me. Different for you, of course."

"Oh, yes," Magda agreed sadly, "I keep hoping that I will wake up in the morning and just know, but it hasn't happened so far."

That night, she dreamed a vivid dream of a river as clear and green as emerald glass, slipping quietly over a bed of white marble pebbles and gravel. In places, the water splashed over little rills, running between larger rocks cushioned with velvety moss, making a sound like a child chuckling. Grass grew on the banks of that river, starred with flowers, gold and white like daffodils, and golden leaves fallen from the branches of trees. The trees were large, with thick grey and white trunks, and in her dream Magda walked along the river, thinking she was following after someone, a fair-haired man but so distant and half-seen among the trees that she could not tell if he were tall or short, wiry or broad-shouldered.

"Wait . . . wait for me!" she called once or twice, and she thought he half-turned towards her. But no, she was alone again, walking by the river and enchanted by the cool green depths and the splash and sparkle, as the water tumbled over and over. Brilliantly colored dragon-flies with jeweled eyes darted and hovered over the froth, and the water-drops that glittered like diamonds, and she came to a stone seat, set by the side of the deepest pool, into which the loveliest of the waterfalls tumbled. In her dream, she seemed to be tired. She sat down on the stone seat, reveling in the lovely sight of the waterfall and the deep and placid green pool.

Here was the waterfall, splashing and chuckling to itself, throwing a rainbow mist around the rocks and where it fell into the pool, and it came to her that it was like Charley, ever moving, turbulent, and bubbling with activity. And the green and tranquil-seeming pool, through which moved a powerful, unknown current; that was Carl, of course. Quiet and calm, always there. Helene's words came to her then: *Which of the two gentlemen do you wish to grow old with?* And in that moment, dreaming and awake, she knew the answer to the question. It seemed then that she turned around, for there was someone standing behind her, under the trees at the edge of the golden wood, smiling a gentle half-smile, with his eyes as blue as the sky.

Magda woke up at that moment, pale grey dawn seeping around the edge of the shutters. She thought she had been wakened by something, a horse's shod hoof clinking against a stone, perhaps. The room was dim and next to her in the bed, Rosalie curled in her nest of blankets. Moving quietly, so as not to wake her, Magda slid out from the covers. She thought Vati and the boys were awake, for small noises carried so far in the stillness of morning. She opened the shutter to the cool morning air and breathed it gratefully. She knew, knew the answer to the question that had been vexing her for weeks, knew the answer so certain and sure that she couldn't see how she had not known it plain as soon as he asked it of her.

Something moved in the yard below, something beyond the oak leaves down at the end of Vati's town lot. A horse, a brown horse in the corral, a brown horse with three white feet; her heart leapt within her. She found her wrapper and pulled it on, caught up her shawl and ran barefoot down the stairs, flinging the back door open. She ran across the terrace, the stones cool to her feet as he was fetching a bucket of water from the well. He turned at the sound of the door, with the same half-smile from her dream.

"Yes," she said, simply. "The answer is yes."

He set down the bucket, and if she had thought he had looked to be blazing with joy on that day that he came back from the Llano with Mr. Meusebach and Vati asked him if he would like to stay for a while, then that was a candle-flame next to a bonfire. In the next instant, she was in his arms and he in hers, as if there was nothing else in the world.

"I did want another of those," he said, finally. Wretched man, he was still amused at her expense, but she didn't mind, didn't mind in the least, for this was the man she would grow old with. At her back, Johann commented interestedly from the upstairs window:

"Vati, Magda is kissing Mr. Becker in her nightgown in the garden!"

"That is none of your business, Johann," Vati replied, from inside the house, "And I am sure he is not wearing Magda's nightgown. Close the window, and go downstairs for breakfast." But in a moment, Vati was at the window, calling distractedly, "Magda dearest child . . . is that indeed Mr. Becker with you? You should be more circumspect, your dear mother would not approve. And the children are hungry . . . are you going to come in and fix breakfast?"

"Well, at least he does not have a shotgun," Carl whispered, and they hung onto each other, laughing for the very joy of it as if there were all the time in the world.

Chapter 15 – *In the Time of the Full Moon*

"I have my land," Carl told Magda's family over breakfast, after a thousand questions from the boys and Vati "But I will need to build a house and that will take some time. We would like . . ." and he looked very shyly at Magda, ". . . to marry in the spring. That should be enough time to settle everything."

"That should more than enough time," Vati answered. "Are you sure you wish to wait that long? I am only considering that you might wish to begin your lives together sooner, not that I am in any sort of hurry to lose my dearest Magda, but still, it does not take six or eight months to put up a house."

"It will, to build one worthy of her," Carl said earnestly and looked a little surprised at himself. Magda thought fondly that he seemed more at ease, more open and content. Only now did she see that before, he had always seemed to hold himself in reserve, a little apart.

"But who will take care of our house?" Johann asked, worriedly. "And us?"

"We will take care of ourselves," Vati said stoutly, "Never you fear."

That was something she had never considered, Magda realized with a sinking feeling. Who would cook and mend, and bake bread, and make sure that Vati did not spend all his time reading abstruse books, and the boys went to school? And what about Rosalie?

"There is time enough to work out that sort of matter," Vati added. "Between Liesel and Madam Helene—and it's not as if I am entirely helpless,"

"Yes you are, Vati, dear," Magda said, fondly. "You would boil your socks with the soup, and forget to plant cabbages."

"None the less," Vati insisted, "you have given your word to Carl. You cannot go back on it, I will not hear of any such thing. The wages of a housekeeper are a small thing, next to your own happiness, Magda my heart. Six months is more than enough time to work out a solution."

268

"It might have seemed an age to wait,' said Magda to her daughter, many years later, "but strangely enough, the time did not drag on my hands. It all did work out, though. Madame Helene knew of a dear lady among the recent arrivals who was a widow—Mrs. Schmidt, that is. She would come from her house every morning during the week, and fix meals, and keep things straight for Vati and the boys. I loved your grandfather and your uncles very deeply, and Rosalie was as dear as my own child. I did not wish to go into marriage, thinking that I had abandoned them, and your father respected that." Magda sighed, and tears threatened to overflow onto her cheeks. "Rosalie, my dear little sister! Your aunt said something to me once; that she was given to us as a gift. She feared that the powers who gave her to us would take her away just as she had been given." Magda dabbed at her eyes with a delicate linen handkerchief.

Her daughter said gently, "I just barely remember Auntie Rosalie: beautiful and always laughing, showing Grete and I how to make flower-garlands on a summer day in the woods by Town Creek."

"It was such a tragedy. A horrible, horrible tragedy and you also were nearly caught in it, Lottie. But I did not want to let you go with them, that day. Liesel chided me then for always keeping you by me; she thought I was being terribly hard, not to let you have a pleasant holiday away from the house where your grandfather was dying."

"She screamed so, when Uncle Hansi came and told her," Lottie said with a shiver. "I was frightened of Auntie Liesel, then. She stared at me as if she hated me. She was angry at you and Uncle Hansi, too."

"Your aunt was not well, for a long time," Magda said, gently. "And perhaps it was wrong of me to be glad I had not let you go with them. But I couldn't have borne it, to have lost you. I couldn't have borne it!" Magda lifted her gaze, staring out the window to the sweep of the walled meadow beyond the orchard, stretching down towards the riverbank, streaked and dappled with late afternoon sunshine. 'He built me such a beautiful house and I had so counted on growing old, with him!"

At some time and soon, Magda would have to tell Charley—a task she rather dreaded. She was fond of him, valued him as a friend and would have been happy with him if her dream-made insight had turned otherwise. It was not his fault he wasn't the man she wished to grow old beside and that her own soul cried out for the tranquility of the deep water in the current of life and not the sparkling waterfall.

She walked along Market Square on the afternoon of the day that Carl had returned, the day that she promised to marry him. She turned the corner to walk with heavy footsteps along Main towards the Verein commissary, realizing again as she looked along the street how much had changed since the first wagons had brought them to the oak wood between two creeks in the valley of the Pedernales. Charley's American friend John Hunter had built a log house at the corner, where he traded goods with the Indians, and the settlers. He courted Sophie Ahrens under her mothers' benevolent and watchful gaze, and there was talk of electing him as the clerk of records when elections would be held. After all, he spoke English and knew how the Americans did things. A sober and hard-working young man, although he did have a hot temper when provoked; those first qualities made older men like Vati look on him with favor. He would do well here, Magda thought, as well as Charley himself. She almost wished that Charley did not care for her as deeply as all that, because if he did he would be hurt, like poor Peter Berg over his faithless girl who came all the way across the Atlantic to marry him, and then changed her mind at the last minute. On the other hand, if he was able to treat his dismissal lightly, perhaps he did not really feel all that much for her. She set her lips and hurried towards the commissary, past the forge, and Mr. Specht's store, and young Mr. Wahrmund's establishment, ornamented with a pair of bright-flowered shrubs in wooden tubs out in front.

The commissary was empty of all but Charley, who looked up at the sound of her footsteps, and greeted her with a happy smile, "Miss Magda! Always a joy—I'm afraid there is nothing new today; the supply wagons have not been arriving as often of late."

"Charley, I have something to tell you," Magda blurted out. Everything she had planned to say went out of her mind entirely. What to say, first? Charley himself came to her rescue.

"Ahh, my dear Miss Magda. Will it do any good to get down on my knees again?" The good cheer had already gone from his face. Magda shook her head wordlessly. Charley came from around the counter, saying, "You know, it has been my own experience that when anyone says 'I have something to tell you' it is usually something one doesn't wish to hear. Let us go outside, and sit under the trees for a while. Never mind, the storehouse can look to itself for a few minutes. There's little enough in it anyway."

He took her arm, and they walked a little way, to where a stump of a tree felled to build the storehouse afforded a shady seat. Magda thought it might have been one of the trees they had used for a table, on that evening when they finally arrived from Neu Braunfels and all the town was just one rough clearing and a half-built blockhouse.

"So who is the rival that I have lost you to?" Charley asked. He sounded jaunty, rather than sorrowful. "Might I still have a chance to sweep you off your feet?"

"No," Unexpectedly, Magda laughed, softly. Charley had that effect. Nothing with him was ever tragic for long. "It is Mr. Becker, Vati's friend. We will be married in the spring. You are not heartbroken, are you?"

"Like poor Berg?" Charley answered, philosophically. "No, only bruised a little. I don't much mind losing out to him so much, when all is said and done. He's a good sort, a worthy rival. Now if you had chosen some other chaps I could name, I'd become a hermit out of pure chagrin and bafflement. Still," he took her hand and kissed it gently, but he held it for a moment longer, and his eyes were unusually sober. "We could have been very happy together, Miss Magda. Of that I am certain."

"I believe so, as well," Magda answered. "I wouldn't have encouraged your attentions otherwise. May I ask that we can still be friends?"

"Of course, like a fond brother and sister." They sat companionably for a moment, and then Magda laughed.

"The last suitor I turned down did become my brother, after all. Hansi thought he wanted to marry me, but my sister loved him very much, so I told him to stop being silly and ask my sister instead."

"Do I need to wait for Miss Rosalie to grow up, then?" Charlie scratched his cheek, thoughtfully.

"No, but Sophie Miller looks after you so very yearningly. She always looks as if she is about to cry, when she sees us walking together." Magda said briskly, "And she is very pleasant and sensible."

"Can she keep accounts, and cook for a large number of people?" Charley asked, with a bit of renewed cheer.

Magda shoved his ribs with her elbow, "Faithless man! I wouldn't know about that. You'll just have to ask her yourself!"

"I hope her elbows aren't as sharp, then." Charley answered, and then he sighed and looked thoughtful. "You know, I am thinking of taking another position. There is a lumber-mill with a need for a good bookkeeper. I have begun to think there is not much of a future with the Verein."

"What? How could that be, Charley? We depend on the Verein and their good offices. What of Mr. Meusebach?" Magda was a little shocked. Although the Verein had certainly not come anywhere close to delivering on all the promises they had made, those promises that had drawn Vati and Hansi from their comfortable lives in Albeck, they had been the strong pillar around which their new lives had been built. The Verein had brought them here, put food on their table, mapped out their futures and given them land, made peace with the Comanche on their behalf. Surely it could not just cease to be, as Charley seemed to think.

"He resigned as commissioner in this country, having done all that he could do to make us secure from the Indians, and repair all the damage done from bad advice." Charley pointed out, "But there is a limit to what one man can do."

"Vati said something of the same," Magda said. "He had been listening to gossip, after the *Apollo* brought us to Galveston, but I did not really understand. How could the Verein go so badly wrong?"

"They were not men of business, most of them," Charley explained. "They had their heads among the stars, and they listened to bad advice and saw only what they wished to see. This enterprise was supposed to turn a profit, you know. But they had such big dreams! I think they wanted to fulfill them all at once, make one glorious philanthropic splash and appear noble and generous to all."

"I did think at first," Magda ventured thoughtfully, "that what they promised was a little too good to be true. But they did bring us here; they did give us land."

"But where do you think the money came from?" Charley asked, somewhat impatiently. "Oh, I know they took fees from everyone who signed a contract, but it wouldn't have met a tenth of the projected expenses. The Verein members all put forward their own money, as investors. They expected to make a profit, eventually."

"From us? How could that be?"

"No, not from you all directly, not like slaves from Africa or something of that sort; they expected to make a profit from the land. The land that is all Texas has, and which folk who have none hunger for. Did you know how they worked it... sharing out the land?" Charley asked, and Magda shook her head, thinking that Charley, with his head for business must still have a better idea than Vati, with his always in the clouds.

"They always wanted people to come settle here. First the Mexicans, and then it seemed to work, so that the Texans did it in the same way. An investor, an impresario they called him, would sign a limited contract for a tract of land and guarantee that he would bring in so many people to settle on it. For every family or single man who came to settle on that grant, the settler would get a portion of land, and the investor would receive a portion for himself. You follow me so far, Miss Magda?"

"So, the Verein would have property for itself, and the more of us brought to settle on their grant, the more property of their own?"

"Very good," Charley nodded. "Which they would then own free and clear, as soon as an equivalent portion was settled. And once it was settled, that Verein-owned land would become even more valuable, especially if there were a town, with commerce and trade, to attract even more settlers. In selling that land, the Verein would recover their expenses incurred by bringing people to settle on it in the first place. Always good to have a bit of profit; not much point to running a business, otherwise," he added with a mock-solemn expression.

"So, what has happened, then?" Magda asked, keenly interested in spite of herself. This affected her family; everything the Verein had done in three years had affected her family. Charley rubbed the back of his neck, thoughtfully, "I don't know for certain. Being a lowly clerk, I am not privy to the doings of the high and mighty. But I can listen to gossip, as your father did and make my own guess. First, they listened to every sort of bad advice they could, drained their funds and landed themselves with huge and useless tract out in the Llano country—which wasn't even good for farming! And secondly, with great trumpeting in the newssheets and showers of pamphlets they began to bring settlers over by the shipload, before there was a place to put them all."

Magda nodded her head, remembering the folk living on the beach at Karlshaven, and asked, "But isn't this part of their grant?" she asked. "It can't be useless to them; Vati says there are nearly a thousand people living here and around."

"No," Charley replied. "In fact, this piece of land, and the land where Neu Braunfels was built, was purchased outright, which expense drained their budget even farther and stretched their credit past the breaking-point." He shook his head. "There was so much money wasted at first and then so much money spent to patch up the damage from a bad decision. A sensible, steady businessman would have secured a small grant of rich and good land first, settled just enough settlers on it, sold enough of their own share to recover expenses and then some, and used that to bring over more settlers for another grant, and repeated the process. It's the way I would have done it, and I think Mr. Meusebach and others of his mind would have preferred such a method, but they were overruled by those who wanted a grand splash and a great profit all at once."

"Is there a reason why it cannot still be done?" Magda asked. Charley shook his head soberly.

"No. First, the Verein is now deeply in debt. Those who funded it at the beginning may not wish to pour in any more, since they have lost so much now. And secondly, the reports of mismanagement and the appalling sufferings of many of the Verein-sponsored settlers are common knowledge across Germany. No one reading accounts of plague and hardships and how people were left to suffer in the cold and in the open would think of risking the same by signing a contract with the Verein. So, no more settlers to bring onto a Verein land grand. No investor, no matter how philanthropic, would wish to pour more of his own money down a dry well. No more money, no more credit." Charley looked at her very steadily, "And no more supply wagons arriving."

"So we are cast on our own devices, then?" Magda asked, with a shiver.

"As far as anything that costs money? I'm afraid so. But do not look so downcast, Miss Magda. I think the Verein, or whatever form it takes, and friends like Mr. Meusebach and Mr. Bene and others, they will continue looking to our interests. It is just that we can't look to them to do all for you, as everyone seemed to expect, at first. We shall have to begin sorting out matters for ourselves." Charley laughed, "Like me, walking away from Verein employment. I'd sooner work out my destiny for myself, thank you. After seeing the hash that they have made of things, I am sure I can do better. And if I can't? Well, it is only on my own head, no one else's!" He took her hand and raised it to his lips and added, "You are sure I can't change your mind? This is the last time that I'll ask."

"No, Charley, my mind is settled on this."

"Very well, then," He kissed her hand, magnificently, "Then all my best wishes to you, the soon-to-be Madame Becker."

* * *

Letter from Christian Friedrich Steinmetz: Written on 1 January 1848, from the Friedrichsburg in Texas, to Simon Frankenthaler, Goldsmith of the City of Ulm in Bavaria.

My dear friend: Greetings and best wishes for this New Year! We have experienced so much in the year just gone, but it appears that we must expect just as much in the year to come. Please set aside the concerns that you have regarding our situation here; so many of the stories you have read, which contain a certain element of truth are inflated by the grossest sensation into something I hardly recognize! I freely confess that we have experienced some hardship, but nothing greater than others have experienced in coming to this country. We arrogantly assumed that with proper German organization, we would easily avoid the woes experienced by others, but pride goeth before a fall, as the saying goes, and we are chastised and humbled by experience. But in no way discouraged, for our labors are just now beginning to be rewarded. I would not hesitate to invite any of my old neighbors in Albeck, or even yourself and your family to join us, now that we have a firm foothold established here. In fact I do urge you to consider emigration, my dear friend, for just as you read of troubles here and worry for us, we hear of troubles afflicting the country of our birth, and worry for those we left behind.

Be assured that from our vantage point, our future appears very bright. My dearest Margaretha is engaged to marry; Son Hansi and daughter Liesel's family will increase once again; the boys are growing sturdy and vigorous, and our little Rosalie blooms like the flower that she is, in the freedom of this country. We thrive, my dear old friend, have no apprehensions on our account. We have seen the beginning of construction of a fine wagon road, from here to Austin, and Mr. Ransleben has opened a grocery and general store. Mr. Leyendecker regularly holds classes for the children in his home. We are becoming accustomed to addressing the concerns of our community, and arranging for our affairs to our own satisfaction. Those of us who have the interest to become involved in public affairs and contrary ideas fear no knock at the door, no officious interference in our lives . . .

* * *

"Your father would ride in from his farm every two or three weeks," Magda told her daughter, many years later. "He would plan to arrive on Friday or Saturday, to do business as he needed, stay the night and go to church with us on Sunday . . . then set out to return to his property. Your aunt and uncle did the same from theirs, although they had not the long way to travel which he had. Your Uncle Hansi sent for a wagon-load of lumber about this time, and built that little cottage on his town lot, for them to live in over Sundays. Such a pretty little house . . ."

"I think it looks like a doll's house," her daughter said. "I've always loved it."

"So did I," answered Magda, "for we spent our wedding-night there."

"Mama!"

"Well, we did!" Magda smiled impishly. "Never think that your elders were always that way, Lottie dearest . . . above flirting and stolen kisses in the shadows when we thought no one was looking!"

"Mama! For shame!"

"Really, Lottie, you would not be so missish about these things if you had grown up on a farm! Besides, although I longed for your father's company before we married, I had to share him with my brothers and your grandfather! All that winter, your grandfather gave him books to read, and he would always want to quiz him about those. Your father had not much of an education, for the frontier was still so wild when he was a boy. He educated himself when he was a man grown and much better able to appreciate it. Your uncles admired him enormously, for he had been with Mr. Meusebach when he went to make peace with the Indians and ridden with Captain Jack Hays for many years. That was something that was made much of, even then. He was a hero to them from the very first, and when he taught Johann and Friedrich how to ride, and follow trails . . . well, they *were both over the moon with worship. Friedrich even behaved himself, which was a marvel itself, for he was a very imp when he was a boy."*

"Indeed?" Magda's daughter said, doubtfully. "He seems very grave and important, now."

"Sobered somewhat by experience and responsibilities, Lottie dear. If you want to tease him out of that solemn face he wears now, ask him about some of his and Johann's merry pranks." Magda smiled, fondly. "Those were such lovely days. It was just as well that we couldn't see into the future."

All during that winter and spring Magda felt that she lived in a bubble of happiness, floating a little off the ground. The feeling intensified toward the end of the week, around Friday or Saturday, knowing that at any moment she might hear his quiet voice in conversation with Vati in the parlor, or look out of a window at the back of the house and see his horse in the corral. Carl never made a great show of his arrivals, just quietly put up his horse and slipped into the house, silently appearing with as little fuss as if he had never been away at all. On a day in late winter, he came in through the back door as she was carrying a basket of clean laundry upstairs. She dropped the basket on the landing and ran downstairs to his arms. Hearing the door open and close, Vati came out from his workshop to see what was going on.

"Oh, my," he was giving a vigorous polish to his spectacles, as they pulled apart, laughing a little breathlessly, "This is early . . . we did not expect to see you until later. Did you know you had a message from Mr. Ransleben, at his store? He has received..." Vati stopped himself, as Carl said:

"Oh, good, I'll walk over and get it." He smiled very shyly at Magda, "It's for you, anyway. A sort of present."

"And he has a box of window-glass for us, also."

"We'll go together, Vati," Magda could hardly bear to let go of Carl's hand. "Window glass? Can we afford this?"

"I have been busy at mending watches this winter," Vati sounded very pleased with himself. "I have even had them sent to me from Neu Braunfels! And I thought I could afford glass for two or three windows, at least. It is warm with the shutters closed, but so very dark. Oiled paper does not let in enough light for me to work by. So glass for my workroom window and then one or two others. We'll talk when you return, eh?" And he retired to his workroom, and Magda kissed her husband-to-be fleetingly and pulled her shawl closer around herself, for the day was chill but bright with sunshine.

"I am not close enough to having glass in the windows," Carl said, as they walked out into Market Street, "but Berg thinks to have most of the walls finished by early summer."

"I can live with shutters and oiled paper," Magda said, firmly.

"It almost looks like a real town, now," Carl said, as they skirted the edge of Market Square, where the sound of a men's chorus came from the coffee-mill shaped dome of the Verein-Church. Magda turned her head and listened; oh, yes "Linden Tree". That song would always remind her now of the evening under the trees when they feasted on Conrad's bear, the day they crossed the river and arrived at their new home under the oak trees. Carl added, "I almost hate to take you away from it. What are they singing for? That doesn't sound very holy!"

"As long as we come back often," Magda said firmly, "my place is with you, wherever you choose to live. That is the Sangerbund - they have just started a singing society."

"Have they?" Carl brightened. "Can anyone join?"

"As long as you know the songs and carry a tune, I expect you can. Vati would know, his friend Pastor Altmueller started it."

"We used to sing—just our family, though. All our close neighbors, they weren't German, so it was just us." They turned the corner, and walked along Main Street. Here, many of those who had town-lots had also begun to build stone or fachwork houses like Vati's, close against the street, with an eye towards doing some kind of business as Mr. Ransleben, young Mr. Wahrmund and Mr. Specht had done. There were still enough spaces between them that someone walking along could see other houses behind, the fallow gardens of last year, and those trees which had been left standing. But Main Street itself was relatively busy.

"I see Santanna's folk are still visiting," Carl added, as a straggle of Comanche men on horseback rode by, feathers and red togas fluttering in the chill winter breeze.

"They're not as forward about coming into the houses now," Magda remarked. "I think they are uneasy about being within solid walls."

"Not half as uneasy as I would be, visiting their skin tents," Carl answered. He seemed about to say something more, but they were nearly to Mr. Ransleben's store, where he had carefully paved the space in front with slabs of stone, to make a sidewalk above the level of the street, and to keep his customers from tracking in too much mud. A couple of saddled horses were hitched up to posts in the street. Just as they reached the door, a man erupted from it, shoved violently by Mr. Ransleben himself, who was shouting,

"Don't you come back, neither of you! I don't need customers like you any more than I need your damn counterfeit money! How much a fool do you think we are?"

The man stumbled on the threshold, nearly falling from the force of Mr. Ransleben's thrust. His hat fell off, a tall black felt hat with a narrow brim. He spun around bristling like a wild-cat, shouting and snarling English words that sounded like a curse and a threat, scrabbling for his hat on the ground with one hand and the wicked long knife thrust through his belt with the other. Magda didn't recognize him; new people came to town all the time, but this man wasn't one of their own. Not a German, rather one of those rough Americans. Another man followed him out of the store, catching his arm as they both saw Carl. Magda was immediately aware of two things as Carl stepped in front, gently setting her aside: he knew those two men, grubby and unkempt as they were, and they recognized him. He had gone all cold and watchful, the way he had when that Indian boy had caught up Elizabeth Strackbein and taken her on a short ride. For a long moment, the hatless man seemed to half-crouch, as if tensing for a fight and glaring at Carl. Then he swung his head towards the doorway, from which came the sound of a gun being cocked, very loudly in the dangerous stillness.

Mr. Ransleben stepped into the doorway, with a shotgun leveled, and the second man dragged his companion away from the door. That moment seemed drawn out to infinity, long enough for Magda to look at the hatless man. He had a feral face, like a fox or some other vicious animal, twisted in a furious snarl, and his eyes didn't match. One was light blue and the other looked grey, no color at all.

It was just a moment, a breathless moment after all, and the other man tugged at his arm, saying something in English. The odd-eyed man then spat at Mr. Ransleben's feet, and let his friend pull him away. They flung themselves onto their horses, and were away in a great splatter of mud thrown up by the horses' hoofs.

Mr. Ransleben lowered his shotgun, and Carl asked quietly, "What did the Waldrip brothers want?"

"You know them?" he asked, as they followed him into the dimness inside. "They are ruffians, Becker, the worst sort of ruffians! They wanted whiskey, they wanted that and the other, and then they tried to pay me in counterfeit coin! I ask you, pot-metal castings with the gold beginning to rub off! Do I want them around my place?! I do not! I can't think which is a worse insult, that they should try to cheat me or they should try to cheat me with such an obvious fake! Who are they, then - Not your friends, in which case you should pick better friends, Becker!" Mr. Ransleben went behind his counter and put away the shotgun, as Carl answered.

"No, not my friends. I know of them, that's all. They're squatting on some land downriver a good piece from my place."

"They are farmers?" Mr. Ransleben said, disbelievingly.

"No, they do a little of this, and a little of that." Carl answered. "They are not liked or trusted. I expect they were trying their luck where no one knows them,"

"Well, we know them now!" Mr. Ransleben said with great satisfaction, "Ruffians and cheats, which is how we know them now! Best to not think on such trash once it is swept out the door, is that not so? I expect you are here for . . ." and he contorted his face in a sly wink at Carl. "It came in a shipment this week. Worth waiting for, believe me. You're a lucky woman, Miss Magda, a lucky woman indeed."

"If you say so, Mr. Ransleben," Magda answered sedately, as Mr. Ransleben produced a flat pasteboard box, about the size of a thick folio book from under the counter. "My father actually sent us for the window glass that he ordered."

"It's in the back; I'll fetch it," Mr. Ransleben excused himself, and returned, staggering slightly under a much larger wooden box. "It's quite heavy, I fear."

"I'll carry it," Carl answered. He gravely handed the baseboard box to Magda, saying, "You may as well have this now. It's yours anyway," and hefted the box of glass.

They took their leave of Mr. Ransleben, and as they walked back towards Vati's house, Magda asked, "You know something more about those men—more than you told Mr. Ransleben. What is it?"

"And I know something? How can you tell," He smiled sideways at her, the gentle and teasing smile that she thought she could never see too often.

"I know you, and when you are very quiet. You thought those men—the Waldrip brothers were dangerous. I saw how you watched them. What did you know of them, that you did not tell Mr. Ransleben?"

"It's not what I know," he answered. "It's what I suspect, but there is no proof. I don't even know if what I think can be proven, so I can't really say to anyone but you, and maybe one or two others that I trust. There was a man who rode in from one of the shingle-makers' camps further up on the river to buy supplies in Bexar. He was carrying money, notes and coin, and riding a grey horse. Berg and I passed him, on the trail, and I particularly noticed his horse. Dark grey, darker mane and tail, white star on the nose. Looked a lot like the horse I had during the fight before Monterray, that's why I looked so close. Three, four days afterwards, that man was supposed to have been killed by renegade Indians. Killed by a spear in the back, found scalped and with his horse gone . . . what else will folk think?"

"We are supposed to be at peace with them," Magda said, firmly.

"Just the Comanche," Carl reminded her. "And there are plenty of renegades, from all the tribes. There are even some white men who don't mind letting an Indian take the blame." He was quiet for a moment and added, "I am afraid the Waldrips might be that sort."

"Why?" Magda shivered suddenly, and not from the chill winter breeze whipping up dust in the street, and sending icy drafts up underneath her skirts.

"The money was gone," Carl answered quietly. "All of it. Which is very odd. The Indians wouldn't have any use for it, they'd be more likely to scatter it around on the ground. They might take gold or silver, to make into ornaments, but paper money? Never known it to happen."

"But what makes you think that Waldrip man might have something to do with it?" Magda asked.

"About a month after that, I was in Bexar and I recognized that horse. It was the same horse, I'd swear to it. And when I asked the man riding it where it came from, he said he had bought it fair and square from J.P. Waldrip not a week past. I didn't like to say much, he looked like an honest man. But that was enough to make me think that those Waldrips might be trouble and Mr. Ransleben did himself a favor by throwing them out of his store."

"Can't you go to the officers—o your magistrate with this, with what you think?" Magda asked, and he shook his head.

"Not on a slight bit of suspicion like that. Waldrip might have come by that horse honestly, and that man might have been robbed by the only Indian in the country who knows what to do with paper money."

"What can you do, then?" Magda demanded, "There must be something!"

"Keep a wary eye on them," Carl answered and he looked amused. "The thing to keep in mind about that kind of pest is that they have a way of making lots of enemies, all on their own. One day, one of those enemies will shoot him down like a dog in the street and save everyone the fuss of a trial."

"And so that is what happened with J.P. Waldrip," Magda told her daughter, with immense satisfaction.

"Oh!" her daughters' eyes rounded. *"So* <u>*that*</u> *was the man. I'd always wondered how you recognized him again."*

"The eyes, Lottie—there was not another man in the country with odd-colored eyes, a man who held a gun to my child's head. He was a fool to think I would have forgotten such a deed." Magda looked as if she were grimly savoring a memory. *"Yes, he was a fool. He had made enemies of many men, but he never realized until the very end that he had made his worst enemy in a woman."*

But on that day, the man in Ransleben's store was forgotten as soon as Carl and Magda returned with their boxes. Vati received the box of glass with as almost as much joy as if it had been a box of books, and carried it away into his workroom, talking excitedly of window frames and the fall of light. Both Carl and Magda looked after him with affection, and Carl said, "I hope that your present makes you as happy."

"Should I open it now, or wait?" Magda asked.

"Whatever would please you most."

So she took the box into the parlor and opened it carefully, as he watched.

"Oh," she said, "They're beautiful!"

Inside the box, padded in a nest of silk brocade was a silver hand mirror and a fine hairbrush that matched it and Carl said, "I meant them for a Christmas present. I thought you would like something like that."

"I do," she answered, "They're so lavish—now I feel that my Christmas gift to you was rather paltry in comparison."

"No, it wasn't," he said, shyly. "You know, I think we should set a date for marrying, now that the house is nearly done. Since you and your sister have found someone now to keep house for Vati. That is, if you are ready."

"Yes," she answered, "Yes . . . I would like that."

Chapter 16 – *A Fine Stone House*

Letter from Christian Friedrich Steinmetz: Written on 30 March 1848, from the Friedrichsburg in Texas, to Simon Frankenthaler, Goldsmith of the City of Ulm in Bavaria.

"My dear old friend: Happy news from my family to yours! Daughter Liesel has born another fine son to her husband. The baby is christened George, and is healthy and vigorous. Son Hansi is as delighted with this new addition to his household as I am with the impending subtraction from mine; or not quite a subtraction, since I gain another son by this miracle of mathematics. My dearest Magda goes from my roof, to that of her affianced and my good friend Mr. Becker at about the time that you are in receipt of this letter. . .

* * *

Up until the very middle of her wedding-day, Magda thought very little about the event itself except in the most perfunctory way, and more about how Vati would host their friends at a wedding feast in the garden afterwards. She had said yes in a distracted manner to Liesel's suggestion that she wear Liesel's own wedding-dress, while her mind was busy with thoughts of baking pies and roasting meats and wondering if they could borrow enough plates and chairs from the neighbors. Vati had commissioned William Arhelger to build a fine wooden brides' chest for her. Earlier that morning, she had packed her wedding chest with linens and quilts, folded away all her clothes, and her treasures such as the silver hairbrush and mirror. She had thought no more of the matter, other than that a little while later in the day when she was finished with the baking, she would put on Liesel's white silk dress and they would all go to the church together, herself and Carl and the family. Pastor Altmueller would say the words of the wedding service over them, and then they would be married. Carl would take her to his new house; it would all be quite straightforward.

Magda could not imagine why there should be any great fuss made over such a simple matter. But hosting the party afterwards, for all their friends . . . she felt a much keener interest in that. She was rolling out pie-crust on the kitchen table and thinking that she ought to see that the boys brought in more firewood, when Mrs. Schmidt came in through the garden door, carrying several baskets filled with bread and cakes. She set them down, exclaiming, "Miss Magda! You should not be working like this, on your wedding day!"

"Don't worry, Elizabeth, I'll see to her." Mrs. Helene appeared behind Mrs. Schmidt, in the kitchen doorway. She carried a small valise and an oval pasteboard hat-box.

"But the pies!" Magda protested, and Mrs. Helene said firmly, "Not another word, dear. It will not be proper to have you smelling of cooking on your wedding day. Let Elizabeth oversee the rest of the cooking. I saw Hansi and your sister just coming in to town. Liesel is bringing the girls' dresses, as well as the wedding dress?"

"Girls' dresses?" Magda asked, in bewilderment and the two other women exchanged knowing looks.

Mrs. Helene answered patiently, "Anna and Rosalie; we agreed that they should be your attendants, remember?"

"No," Magda ransacked her memory. She couldn't remember having agreed to anything of the sort. Perhaps this was one of those things that Mrs. Helene and Liesel had agreed on between them. She could hear a wagon coming along the road and voices coming from the garden: Hansi and Liesel's voices, greeting Vati and the boys. Carl was not there; Charley and his friend John Hunter had taken him to stay elsewhere before the wedding. Magda could not help thinking that this was becoming all too complicated. Liesel came through the door with her arms full of Baby George and something long and bulky, wrapped in a length of calico. Anna followed, directing Jacob's tottering footsteps. Liesel stopped in the doorway upon seeing Magda with her hands still dusty with flour.

"You haven't even begun to get ready?" she exclaimed in astonishment.

"No . . . should I be?"

Liesel said one of Hansi's favorite oaths, then.

"There's no need for that!" Mrs. Helene remonstrated, as Liesel scowled at her older sister.

"Upstairs, Madga. Now!" she snapped. Mrs. Helene gave her a gentle shove towards the door. Reluctantly, Magda dusted flour off her hands and took off her apron. Mrs. Schmidt deftly took it from her, and nodded as Liesel added, "Is the water hot? I'll come down for a jug of it in a minute. Anna-lovey, go find Rosalie, and bring her upstairs."

Outmaneuvered on every front and sternly dragooned by her sister, Mrs. Schmidt and Mrs. Helene, Magda climbed the stairs to the room that she and Rosalie had shared, and which was now stripped bare of all her own things. Without quite knowing how this could be happening, she found herself standing in front of the washstand in her shift, washing in a basin of warm water into which Mrs. Helene had decanted a small bottle of rosewater. Meanwhile Liesel and Mrs. Helene dressed Anna and Rosalie in pretty blue dresses and tied up their hair in matching ribbons.

"Now, go sit down and behave," Liesel told the girls, and they sat on the bed and watched with happy interest, as Mrs. Helene unpacked her little valise. "I've brought three petticoats," she said.

Magda said in astonishment, "Whatever for?"

"For you, dear," Mrs. Helene answered. "Are you finished washing? Then come and stand here . . . oh my, nearly half-past. We shall be late."

Liesel said, "It's not as if they can start without the bride." And then the two of them set to work on Magda, as if she were some kind of large doll, incapable of dressing herself.

"Breath in," Liesel commanded, standing behind her, "Now, out!" and as Magda did so, Liesel pulled her corset-laces so tight she gasped.

"I can't breath!" she protested.

Mrs. Helene said calmly, "Yes you can, dear," and dropped another petticoat over her head, and another after that—so many of them Magda feared she could hardly take a step without having her skirts knocking over small children and pieces of light furniture.

"Stand still, dear, you're fidgeting." Mrs. Helene powdered her shoulders and décolleté with sweet-smelling orris-root powder. Magda sneezed, resoundingly.

"Good health again," Mrs. Helene added, and Liesel unwrapped the dress from its calico shroud.

"I let out the hem as much as I dared, but I fear it is still too short for the current fashion," Liesel said. She pulled the heavy skirts straight, falling into a bell-shape over layers of rustling petticoats. Mrs. Helene held up the bodice for Magda to slide her arms into the sleeves, and settled it on her shoulders. A series of little hooks fastened it to the skirt, and Liesel busied herself with those, as Mrs. Helene fastened up the back.

"It is beautiful fabric," she murmured appreciatively "And a lovely dress . . . it will not matter, for otherwise it will trail in the dust, and I don't think we want that."

"I can't breathe," Magda gasped, "and I cannot bend down for my stays poking me in the ribs." The other two paid her no attention at all.

"I took in the sleeves, also," Liesel continued. "The silk was a present from Vati's friend Simon. He had a relation in the trade in Marseilles and Mutti and I made the dress together." She sighed, and her eyes met Magda's. Some tears trembled on her eyelids and she dashed them away with the back of her hand and said, "Don't you dare cry, Magda; it will make your eyes red. Mutti would have loved this. She would have been so pleased! I hope that the fashions won't have changed so much that we can't remake this dress for Anna, when her time comes."

"Will I wear that dress?" Anna said from the corner, with deep interest.

"Yes, dear heart when it is your turn to be married," Liesel answered.

Magda added bitterly, "They will stand you up in the middle of the room, and primp and truss you up, and stuff you into it as if you were some kind of human sacrifice!"

"Shushhh!" Mrs. Helene told her, with unaccustomed firmness. "It is the custom for the bride to be dressed on her wedding day, Margaretha!"

Liesel added in tones which were supposed to be reassuring, "It won't be that bad, Magda. He seems very kind and considerate. It won't hurt that much."

"What won't hurt!?" Magda said with alarm and Mrs. Helene looked at the wide-eyed little girls in the corner and again commanded, "Shussh!" while Liesel whispered, guiltily:

"Afterwards, silly. Tonight when you go to bed. What he does to you do after you are married."

"Liesel!" Helene said warningly, and she took Magda's hands in hers, saying, "What your sister means is that after you are married, your husband will pay . . . certain attentions to you. In private, when you are alone together. It is nothing to be worried over, Magda my dear. Most wives come to welcome those attentions, very much."

"What attentions?" Magda said, frantically.

Helene answered, "Your husband will explain to you, I am sure. Now, dear, sit down. Let us do your hair . . . very soothing, I think, to have someone brush out your hair. Bring over the small stool, Liesel and help her to sit so that she doesn't wrinkle the back. It's just brides' nerves, Margaretha. Everyone getting married has them."

Mrs. Helene draped a towel over her shoulders and talked to her calmly as she drew a hairbrush through Magda's loosened hair. Liesel opened Mrs. Helene's pasteboard hatbox, and took out a length of veil edged with lace, as delicate as a spider-web.

"French silk," Mrs. Helene said, happily. "It was quite the fashion when I was young . . ." she went on talking, but Magda heard not a word of it.

Certain attentions? Which might hurt? What else was this about this business of marriage that she didn't expect, didn't know? She racked her mind, hastily turning all that she knew of marriage. Oh, of course she knew that married couples slept in the same bed and that certain things went on; that was not a great surprise. Two months of hearing whispers and the half-stifled moans and cries from the bunks of the married folk on the Apollo had been enlightening—obviously, they had been doing something. She had never wondered much on exactly what, and to suddenly be told now that it would be painful at first? As painful as bearing a child? Liesel had howled something awful when she bore Anna. Magda felt rather as if she had sleepwalked into a great, yawning pit. To her horror, she thought she might be trembling. She forced herself to sit very still under Mrs. Helene's gentle ministrations and to think of nothing. That effort carried her all the way through the business of Helene pinning up her hair and dropping the gauzy fog of veil over her head. There was a wreath of silk orange-flowers and leaves to be pinned down over that, and the pins scraped her scalp.

"All ready," Helene said finally, with happy satisfaction, "Go tell your father, Liesel."

"I can't see," Magda said, distantly.

"Don't worry; we'll see you safely to the church, my dear."

And so they did, and Magda obeyed mechanically, walking where they led her, taking Vati's arm, kneeling when they told her to kneel, and repeating the words that Pastor Altmueller said. Her voice did not sound like her own, but she heard another quiet voice repeating the same words and when the veil was lifted from her face and laid back over the wreath and she could see again, it was Carl's face, lit with triumphant joy. She looked at him and thought, *Please get me away from here,* as he kissed her gently on her cheek and led her out of the church.

At that moment, she suddenly felt as if she awoke, with her feet firmly on the ground, walking out of the Verein-Church on Carl's arm. The shimmering bubble in which she had floated for months had suddenly burst, and she faced the reality of what was happening . . . and wondered with a sudden rush of panic, if it was the right thing to do and if not, was it too late to go back?

It wasn't a dream; this was truly herself, walking through the middle of a crowd of friends, tightly laced into Liesel's wedding-dress, Mrs. Helene's ivory-silk and lace veil falling back from her face and halfway down her back. She felt like a prize cow, groomed, polished and pomaded and led before everyone's admiring eyes. The weight of her hair pinned up made her head ache fiercely. Everything she had said in front of Pastor Altmueller, everything that Carl had answered, it was all in a blur and it couldn't possibly be real. But it was . . . the heavy weight of Mutti's wedding-ring on her hand. Vati had insisted. It was a way, he said fondly, that Mutti could still be a part of their lives together in some small part.

"Are you all right," Carl whispered, very softly. She couldn't help noticing that he also looked a little dazed. And also like her, he appeared to have been dressed and polished by other hands and pushed forward to be looked at. Clad in a good broadcloth coat and fine linen, he contrived to appear both younger and awkwardly uncertain.

"We're married," she replied in dumb incomprehension.

He patted her hand that lay in the crook of his elbow in a way meant to be comforting, and answered happily, "So we are."

Magda felt as if she were drowning, as they walked back to Vati's house and the wedding supper in a garden lit by lamps hanging from the lower tree branches amid a great crowd of their friends, everyone in town it seemed like. The noise of their happy clamor sounded to Magda like the sea-surf, washing back and forth while she sat stiffly in the place of honor for hours and answered mechanically but sincerely. She couldn't breathe, with her laces pulled so tight. She had to dance and was obscurely grateful for Carl, moving with her, his hands on hers. There was singing and music. She picked at the food on the plate in front of her, noticing that Carl did not seem particularly hungry either. Perhaps he was feeling the same sort of panic, now that it was done.

Was that a couple of curious Indians among the crowd of wedding guests? Frankly, it wouldn't have astonished her in the least. John Hunter held hands with Sophie Ahrens, while Mrs. Ahrens beamed at them all impartially, and Mrs. Lochte was laughing at something her oldest son was saying. There was Charley, with his new wife on his arm, Sophie Miller that was. She looked to bloom with happiness, so being married couldn't be that awful. She held Magda's hand and said something gracious, and Charley kissed her cheek very respectfully, and then Carl laughed over something Charley had said, which was only to be expected.

As Charley and Sophie moved away from them, Carl whispered, "When can we leave? We have a long way to travel in the morning."

"Now?" Magda answered, pleadingly, "Can we leave now?"

She needed that pool of stillness, to pull that quiet around herself like a shawl, to lean against him as if he were a sturdy tree and try and convince herself that this was not a mistake, and perhaps he sensed that, for he answered, "It's turning into a very fine fandango; I hardly think they would miss us. We'll just slip away." He looked mischievous as a schoolboy, as carefree as Johann or Friedrich in the light of a couple of swaying lanterns hung from the lower branches of the oak trees.

"I'll need to find my sister, to help me change out of this wretched dress."

"I'll find her." Carl promised, "I'll tell her you've gone upstairs." He kissed her very gently and helped her to stand. How did women of fashion truly manage those unwieldy skirts, she wondered to herself? It was easier for him to slip unnoticed through the merry crowd than for her, having to accept kisses and congratulations, and best wishes from folk whose faces all passed before her in a single blur. At last she gained the house, and Liesel met her on the stairs.

"Hansi has already gone with the wagon," she whispered conspiratorially. "Everything is ready at the Sunday house. You two may just go out through Vati's shop and no one will be the wiser. In the morning, just leave the key on the ledge over the doorway."

"Just unlace me, before I burst," Magda begged her and Liesel smiled, happily.

"We thought you might wish to slip away, without making a fuss. No one will know but us... so embarrassing, having all of his friends making a chiviaree under your windows. Is that what they call it here, making a rude orchestra under your bedroom windows at night?"

"I can't imagine anything more horrid," Magda said, breathlessly.

Upstairs, in the room which had been hers, Rosalie and Anna were already tucked into the bed, with Jacob a little lump in between them and baby George in a cradle at the bed's foot. Liesel swiftly pulled out the hair pins and divested her of the wreath and veil.

"It really will be all right," she said kindly. "It's a bit awkward at first, but I am sure he will know what to do . . . men do. They rather like doing it, and he's handsome enough to have had many opportunities. Besides, it's what you have to do to get children." She moved around and began undoing the hooks at the back of the dress bodice.

Magda asked, in a strangled sort of voice, "Do what, Liesel?"

Her sister answered, sounding quite exasperated, "What married folk do in bed . . . really, Magda, did you not notice the way of things on the farm? The bull with the cows and the stallion with the mares, and all?"

The heavy silk sleeves fell off her shoulders, but Magda hardly noticed, until Liesel untied her corset lacings.

"It's . . . like the animals?" she said blankly, and gasped, as the loosened corset let her breath again. *Man and wife carried on like the animals did?*

"Duck down, let me take lift the skirt over your head," Liesel answered briskly. "No, not quite. Just think on what they need do to make colts and kittens and calves. How many petticoats do you still want . . . just two, then? Here's your dress."

Gratefully, Magda pulled her plain dark Sunday best dress over her head and let the extra petticoats drop, still thinking blankly, *Like animals?* Liesel gathered up the shimmering folds of silk while Magda did up her own buttons, considerably relieved to be doing so for herself for once.

"Hurry," whispered Liesel as one of the outside doors opened and closed downstairs. "That will be Hansi. Here is your shawl and bonnet. Everything else is already there for you. Now if you want to be away without any more fuss, this is your best chance."

Hansi and Carl waited in the hall downstairs, by the door underneath the stairs that led into Vati's workroom. The happy sounds from the party outside floated into the house through windows left open to take advantage of the cool night air.

"Just go, before anyone comes in and sees," Liesel whispered. "I've left my presents for you in the Sunday House!" She kissed Magda on the cheek as Hansi quickly handed a key to Carl, and shook his hand firmly.

"Welcome to the family," Hansi looked pleased and somewhat amused. He kissed Magda on the cheek and added, "I told you to choose the one with the biggest property!" Liesel made a clucking noise and slapped at his arm.

"Hurry!" she said, "There's someone coming!"

It was Vati, tip-toeing like a conspirator, and whispering.

"Am I too late? No? Then my blessings on you both!" He embraced them, saying, "We'll see to the guests; so many people, no wonder you wish to be by yourselves. I'll latch the outside door after you, and make excuses."

Vati led them through his workroom and let them out through the shop door; a last embrace and the door fell shut behind them. For the very first time that day, they were alone. Market Street, and the square beyond with the bulk of the Verein-Church squatting in the middle of it, stood dark against the stars and a wash of moonlight. There were pin-pricks of lantern-light in the windows of other houses. Carl's hand closed around her icy-cold fingers, and they walked in silence a little way along Market Street, down towards Creek.

After a moment, he said, "You looked so very beautiful, in the church today."

"I felt like a doll, all dressed up like a lady of fashion," she answered. "I couldn't breathe. I was afraid I would faint."

They had walked this way in this manner so many times before, comfortable in each others' company. Queerly, Magda felt reassured; this was the tranquil, quiet pool. She had made a good decision, but what had Liesel had said about the other thing? Her heart hammered in her chest. Both Liesel and Helene had been—well, not exactly forthcoming. But they had said it was not so bad. She wished she could bring herself to ask Carl about it all. Apparently he was the one who was supposed to know, and tell her.

There were lights behind the curtains of Hansi's Sunday house, a tiny one-room cottage on the front of his town-lot. The hut where he and Liesel had first lived served as a stable now. Three horses moved restlessly in the corral next to it, and the light farm wagon which Carl had driven from his place was parked close by. All of the things that had been thought appropriate for a new wife to take to her husband's roof were packed in it. In the morning, they would hitch up the team and go home, over the hills to that place which she had never seen and begin that new part of her life, joined to his life. But between now and then was tonight.

In silence, he unlocked the door, and gallantly held it open for her. The inside of the little house was golden in candlelight, and Magda looked around, touched by the kindness and care with which her sister and Hansi had prepared the Sunday house and left it to them. A plate of bread and butter, cold ham and cheese was left on the little table by the window, covered by a napkin. A clutch of brilliant red and golden daisies filled a pottery cup . . . oh, yes, Anna had been part of this, as well. There was no fire in the tiny stove, for the summer evening was warm enough, and the candle-light cast a warm glow on the dishes in the tall cupboard.

More candles cast a flickering light from the washstand in the corner, and another ragged knot of flowers bloomed from a vase on a shelf over the bedstead, in the corner next to the door. Pink primrose petals had been scattered across the bed, where the sheets were turned invitingly down on both sides. On the spotless linen pillowcase on one side lay a crisp white nightgown, trimmed with drawn-work and embroidery, and on the other a man's nightshirt, similarly ornamented. She recognized Liesel's handiwork; obviously the wedding presents she spoke of. Her silver hairbrush and mirror were laid out on the upper shelf of the washstand, and the cloth valise of her clothes was set down next to it.

Carl cleared his throat, and she jumped at the sudden sound of it; he had walked in behind her, and was looking at the bed, from over her shoulder.

"I'll see to the horses, if you would like time to . . . um, wash and change." He sounded as nearly uncertain as she felt, which was not comforting. He was the one who was supposed to know what to do.

"All right," she said. The minute the door fell closed behind him, she was wrenching at the buttons of her dress with shaking fingers, pulling all the pins out of her hair, divesting herself of petticoats, stays and shift, hastily pulling Liesel's beautiful gift over her head, and doing up the buttons of it. All of her clothes were hung up and she was sitting on a wide bench at the bed's foot brushing her hair, when he returned. She heard his footsteps on the porch, outside, and the door being closed and latched, and then his quiet footsteps as he crossed the room.

She didn't dare look up, as he paused for a moment and then walked around to the side of the bed with the nightshirt on it. Her hands felt like ice. She held her shawl tight around her throat as she pulled the brush through the long black spill of her hair. Behind her, she heard the rustle of fabric, the sounds of small movements as he hung up his coat on the hook next to her dress, and sat on the bed to take off his boots. Her very heart hammered against her ribs as if it wanted to leap out of her throat. *Why are you frightened?* She chided herself, *This is Carl, who has ever been so kind and gentle, how could you be afraid of him now?*

But she was fearful. Possibly only thing that kept her from jumping up and running out of Liesel's Sunday house was embarrassment, embarrassment and pride. When he came around the end of the bed and sat next to her on the bench, she nearly leaped out of her skin. She stole a look at him, sideways through the veil of her hair; how gawky and ridiculous he appeared with long bare legs and feet under the nightshirt.

Oh, good, she thought as she tugged savagely on a snarl, *Now there's two of us to die together of embarrassment!* Silently, he took the brush out of her hand and began stoking it through her hair, unhurried and gentle as always.

At last, he said, "You look terrified . . . what did they tell you would happen now, Margaretha?"

"Practically nothing," she answered shakily. "Mrs. Helene, she said that my husband would pay certain attentions to me . . . attentions that I might eventually welcome . . . but my sister said it would hurt at first." Her voice dropped very low, "But that it was how we would get children." Her face felt hot with blushes of embarrassment. "And that you would know how."

"Ah." he said, and went on, brushing her hair. Oddly enough, it was as soothing as Mrs. Helene had said, this very afternoon. "So I do. I'll be as careful as I can. I don't want to hurt or frighten you, believe me, Margaretha!"

"I believe you," she answered sturdily and he set aside the hairbrush. So tiny was the space that he could reach the washstand without moving from the bench.

"You should know," he looked at her earnestly, taking her hands in his, "that the bodies of men are somewhat different from women."

"I knew that!" she answered, indignantly. *Did he think she was an idiot?* "I looked after my brothers when they were babies and more!"

"But men differ again, from little boys," he said, somewhat flustered. "And you would not have seen . . ."

"Then how so are they different?!" she demanded.

He looked flummoxed, and answered, "Right, then." He stood up and so did she, facing each other at the end of the bed. He pulled off the nightshirt, over his head and dropped it carelessly on the bench, in a gesture that had more than a bit of challenge in it.

"Oh." she said. "I see," Embarrassment scorched her cheeks for seeing and not being able to look away as she ought to do, but at almost the same moment she thought, *But he is beautiful, as fine as a drawing of a Greek statue in one of Vati's books! I ought to be able to look at him, if I want to—after all, he is my husband now!* Lean and hard-muscled, pale on those parts of his body normally clothed; she was amused to see that the hair in other places was darker than that on his head, light brown and curly. The only marring was a tangle of livid and ugly scars on his upper left chest, and across his left arm.

"Yes," he said. For a moment, she thought he looked rather smug and that there was a challenge in his gaze towards her, as well as a measure of approval. She lifted her chin. Never let him think she was truly afraid. He liked courage; well then, she should be courageous. Her shawl slipped from her shoulders and her hands went to the buttons at her throat, and at her wrists. In seconds the nightgown lay on the bench, and she stood veiled only in her loose hair, meeting his challenge with her own.

The Sunday cottage was so small; they stood only a little apart. He touched her face with one hand, sweeping aside her hair from her shoulders and cupping her breasts in his hands, as reverently as if he were touching something worshipful and holy. He took her wrist in his other hand and put it on himself, saying, "It is all right to touch me."

Then he drew her into his arms and she went to him, thinking that her skin felt like ice, but her face was still flushing with embarrassment. His body radiated warmth, like the stones on the river-bank after a day of sunshine. So they stood pressed together, and that part of him which was not like the body of a woman, that part which was wholly male, poked against her belly as if it were a live and separate thing.

"I'm cold," she whispered at last.

"Then we can lie down under the covers," he answered. The sheets seemed cold against her flesh, but he was warm, whispering endearments, caressing her with sure gentleness, and patterning her skin with kisses. It seemed to her that her very bones had turned to water, when he said with a funny catch in his voice, "Let me in now, Margaretha!" She meant to tell him yes, without knowing quite what he wanted, but his hand was already *there,* as he rolled onto her, pressing her thighs apart. His body already pinning her underneath him, she let out a small cry of astonishment. That blunt male part of him pushed at her, seeking an admittance that she could not deny. Something within her gave away with a tearing sensation. It did hurt, just for a moment. She wanted to bury her face in his shoulder to hide her expression and to muffle her cry of astonishment and pain.

"Sorry!" he gasped, and dropped a kiss on her forehead, and her arms went around him; it was not his fault, she was not afraid, and to her astonishment the thought came into her head that this was how man and wife became one flesh. This was how they came so close, for one to be allowed inside the other, tenderly and with all consideration, for all the awkward indignity of it. She held him close, pulled him down on her body as he thrust into her, again and again. After many minutes of this, he suddenly fell flat on top of her with a shudder and a groan, gasping as if he had just run a long footrace.

"So this is what married people do," she said finally and judiciously. It had not been as bad as she feared. And if Mrs. Helene was correct—as she undoubtedly was—she would come to welcome the attentions of her husband. In fact, she rather thought she might welcome them again, very soon.

Carl laughed breathlessly into her hair, broadcast across the pillow and answered, "So I am told . . . although sometimes the unmarried do so also." He rolled off of her and a little to one side, although they lay very closely entwined. Magda lay quiet, thoughtfully looking up at the ceiling over her head. So that's what all the fuss had been about—really, how silly she felt now. She turned her head on the pillow to find her husband looking at her intently, a question in his eyes.

Are we really married, he seemed to ask, *are we now truly bound to each other—lover, dearest friend, partner and helpmate?* She tenderly cupped his face in her hand. It seemed that this might be where their marriage really began, not when they repeated the vows or when Pastor Altmueller had pronounced them so, but here and now, naked and vulnerable and seeing each others' soul in their eyes. With the strength of a man, he might have the capability to hurt her with his bare hands, but her husband had his own vulnerability. Someone whom he loved could hurt him with a word. The death of that brother whose name he could still hardly bring himself to say had hurt him dreadfully—she stood by his side now, and such would not happen to him if she could prevent it. *Yes,* she answered silently; *we are bound to each other always, my love—always.* Seeing that, he smiled, and turned his head so that he could kiss her fingertips.

"My confession, Margaretha; I had dreamed of doing this, ever since the first time I saw you, knee-deep in the river and furiously angry with me, and your brothers and everyone else. Have I a chance of doing it again?"

"Well, of course," Magda pulled his face to hers, and kissed him most lovingly. "It's what married people do. "It was not . . . quite what I expected. It was not considered something I should know about. Until today, I had never wondered at all. I thought that married folk just slept in the same bed. Although," she added, "now I know what Hansi and Liesel were up to, before they were wed, back in Albeck. They used to appear from different directions, almost at the same time, she with bits of straw in her hair, and he had a most smug expression." Then she began to laugh in delight. "Oh, my, I just thought. Herr Pastor Doctor Altmueller and Mrs. Helene, they are married also!"

Carl lay back and whooped with laughter himself, for the imagining of the terribly dignified and elderly Altmuellers doing as married folk did in bed.

"Now, that's something to think of in the middle of his next dull sermon!" He said at last. Magda nestled herself contentedly against his scarred shoulder, thinking to herself that perhaps the best thing that married folk did in bed was to laugh together, at things that no one else could know about. He held her close, while his breathing gradually became slower and easier, stirring her hair a little where it lay loose across the pillow. She wondered if she ought to get up and put out the candles, but that his arm was around her and she didn't want to disturb him. Much to her surprise, the last thing she was aware of before sleep claimed her, aside from a peculiar raw ache *there* in that place between her legs, was that Carl had already fallen deeply asleep.

Last asleep and the first to wake, Magda opened her eyes to a room not entirely dark. Over the top of the calico curtain veiling the eastern window there was a strip of paler sky, with a pearly look to it that meant fog. Dawn was coming, if not here already; Magda wondered if she should get up and fix breakfast for them. She was hungry now, and there was the food left for them last night, which they had not touched.

Good . . . she would get up and make sandwiches of bread and cheese, for had they not escaped last night on the excuse of wanting to make an early start on their journey? But she was arrested by the weight of him, lying on her hair. He lay on his side, and in sleep one arm had fallen across her waist, and she did not think she could move without waking him, nor after a moment did she want to. She studied his features, relaxed in sleep, thinking that she would be well content to wake up like this, every morning for the rest of her life. He looked very young, slumbering like this, as serene as a child. And just as she decided there was nothing for it but to go back to sleep herself, he stirred a little. The arm lying across her waist tightened, and he announced drowsily, "Oh, good, I didn't dream it all."

"Do you want me to pinch you, to prove it?"

"No, but you can give me a kiss and that will do for a start."

"You'll have to let loose of my hair, first," she said. He sat up, freeing her hair. The morning air struck chill on her shoulders and breasts as the covers fell back with him. She kissed him most lovingly, but he captured her in both arms and bore her down to the pillows again.

"Good start," he said breathlessly and she protested, as little shivers of excitement rose from inside her.

"You said we should get up early, since we had a long way to travel."

"Did I? We'll make it up," he answered confidently. He smiled down at her, his body already moving over hers, and Magda was lost. "We must make sure we are not dreaming, Margaretha."

Some considerable time later, they dressed in a great hurry, for it was nearly sun-up, and light enough to see without a light. Magda did not feel any of the embarrassment she had felt the night before, and their glances met with amusement and fondness as they struggled with buttons and laces. He even helped her with her stays, dropping a kiss on the back of her neck as he did so,

"I don't know why women bother with such contraptions," he commented.

"Because we must," she answered, and sat on the bench to pull on her stockings and shoes. He was already dressed, "I'll go and hitch the wagon . . . is there anything else?" His look took in the whole of the tiny Sunday House.

"Liesel said not to bother; she'd take care of everything."

She gathered up those last few things of theirs, thinking of how terrified she had been the night before, how ridiculous such fear seemed in the morning. She thought with new affection of how Liesel had arranged things for them; how very considerate to give them the Sunday House for that one night. And now she might understand her sister better, now that she was married as well. She found a knife, and made sandwiches of the cheese and ham, and brought her cloth valise with the nightclothes packed on top out to the door.

There was a fog hanging close to the ground this morning, especially in the creek bottom, shreds of it swirling through the tree-branches, combed out like bits of wool through teasels; a quiet grey morning, with moisture dripping from tree branches and beading the blades of grass and the shreds of last year's garden. The horses jingled their bits impatiently as Carl stepped inside, to find Magda wrapping up the sandwiches.

"Let's be away home now," she said. "We'll eat on the way."

"All right then." He took the valise, and locked the door after them. Magda thought, as he handed her up to the wagon seat, that for the first time in three years, she was utterly content to be setting out on a journey. But at least this time, it was not a venture into the unknown.

They drove through town, past households just beginning to stir, with Carl's saddle-horse, Three-Socks, tied to the back of the wagon. They followed the cart-road southwards, towards San Antonio, and the fog began to lift at mid-morning, revealing a golden, promising day.

Sometimes she caught him looking sideways at her, as if he was reassuring himself that she was really there, next to him on the wagon-seat. She knew this because she sometimes did the same, wanting that proof that it was not all a dream; her husband indeed sat next to her with one foot propped on the wagon-box, whistling happily to himself and handling the reins with careless assurance.

"You can drive?" he asked once, "There are places where I might want to ride ahead."

"I've driven a light cart with a team of horses," she answered.

"Good enough. These fellows are well trained—try it for a while." He handed her the reins, but kept his hands on top of hers. She wondered if it were just an excuse to touch her, and decided that it didn't really matter. Now and again, he climbed down from the wagon to unhitch Three-Socks and ride ahead for a while, leaving her to drive the wagon. The road climbed a long gentle range of hills; they were most of the day at it, since they had started so late. Early in the afternoon, they came to a place where the road went down to a wide green valley, with a river running east to west.

"Bexar . . . San Antone is down that way." he waved a hand towards the south. "My place—our place is to the west, on this side of the river. It's another couple of miles, if you want to stop and rest."

"No," she answered, although she ached from the constant bumping of wheels over ruts and gullies. "I just want to be home. You've not said very much about it."

"I'm not much good with words," he answered. "I didn't want to make it seem like a palace. But it's a good stone house. Berg did some fine work. There was a cabin on the place when I laid my claim —the hired men live there now. We built a stable for the horses at night." He looked as if he were searching for the right sort of words. "It's not settled country, Margaretha. I'm not telling you any lies about that. It's not as wild as it was, when Jack and I began riding long patrols into the hills, but it's still not anything like what you've been used to. We put up a palisade wall connecting all the buildings, just in case we ever got in the way of a war party looking for trouble. I don't think we would!" he added hastily. "But looking like we are set for trouble is a good way of getting trouble to pass you by. All of us who live along this way, we ride our lands pretty careful, and keep a weather eye out." He looked at her anxiously and asked, "So, are you thinking of telling me to turn this wagon around, and take you straight back to Friedrichsburg?"

"Of course not," she lifted her chin. "That wasn't settled country, when we first came to it. And if you think I came all the way over the ocean in winter, just to turn around and run because you tell me 'it is not settled country', then you should think again. Really, my heart's love, do you think I am made out of glass?"

"No." He appeared distinctly relieved, "I did not think that, but—"

"Good," she said, crisply, "Then it is settled. Let's go home."

Chapter 17 – *Journal of the Plague Year*

"It's a fair open road along here," Carl said, as they traveled west from the river ford and the track to the south. "But too much cover between the trees for my liking. There used to be an Indian village, a little way along a creek we're coming up to. If you want to take the reins, I'll ride point until we get closer."

He swung down from the wagon and went around unhitching Three-Socks from the back. Magda settled herself in the center of the wagon seat. The track ahead followed the river, leading in a long smooth curve into a wide valley wooded with oaks and sycamores.

"How much farther?" she asked, as he rode level with the wagon.

"Five or six miles," her husband answered. "Not far." He spurred Two-Socks to a trot and Magda slapped the reins on the backs of the team animals. She would be glad to reach the end of this journey and see her long-promised home. Here were the last miles of a long road, the road she had first set her feet on three years ago, when Vati and Hansi had led them away from Albeck, dreaming under autumn skies. Now it was summer, on the other side of the world in a country empty of everything but promise.

Carl rode a couple of lengths ahead, easy and relaxed, as Vati had once observed, as if he had been born on horseback and only occasionally dismounted. But Magda also saw how he looked carefully to the right or left and sometimes went farther ahead and drew rein, holding still to listen. She herself heard nothing but the harness jingling, and the sounds that the wagon made, bumping over the track. Once, he struck off the track a little way, circling around behind a clump of trees and brush several times, and once he rode up to the top of a low rise and spent many minutes looking at the land ahead.

That time, he circled back to the wagon, and rode alongside, saying, "There are three or four men, riding down the track towards us . . . not Indians. One of them is Waldrip; no one else has a hat like his."

"Is there so much more danger here?" she asked, "You are taking so very much more care than you were before."

"No, not so much," he answered, cheerfully. "It's just that the Comanche war parties used to come along here, fairly often. It's also close to where that man was found, the one I told you about."

"That one that you wonder if Waldrip had something to do with?" she asked, and he nodded.

"That's it. Just keep the wagon moving." He sounded quite jaunty, which reassured her enormously, until the moment that she observed him resetting the Paterson revolvers in their holsters. By then it was too late to do anything more than lift her chin and carry on.

Three men on horses came around the bend ahead; as they came closer, Magda recognized the odd-eyed man whom Mr. Ransleben had thrown out of his store, the man with the tall black hat, which looked very fine, as if it had once belonged to a much more important person. She was fairly sure he recognized her; Carl spoke to them casually in English as they went past, for they all touched their hats to her courteously enough but still she did not like the way their eyes went over her, as if their gaze left slug-trails of slime, or the greedy way they looked at the well-laden wagon.

After that encounter, Carl rode close to the wagon, and she put it out of her mind, for she began to see cattle drifting under the trees, those wide-horned beasts that were as nearly as wild as deer. Her husband said, with a faint note of apology. "I know you must want to see the house, but I think I should have you meet the Browns, first. The track goes past their place, and they'll be watching for us anyway."

"Who are the Browns?" Magda asked.

"They're Americans . . . our closest neighbors. They've been in Texas for years—came up from Gonzales and settled here. It's one of their boys who works for me. Mrs. Brown, she's about the only other white woman for a good few miles, this way."

"So you think we should be friends?" Magda raised her eyebrows.

Carl answered, "It's not as if you can pick and choose, Margaretha."

She sighed, thinking of how he had warned her so many times of how distant his property was from Friedrichsburg and her family and friends. Each time, she had reassured him that it did not matter, but only after the journey that day did she realize he meant exactly what he said—it was a considerable distance, and very empty country.

"Then we should pay a call," she acquiesced, "but a short one, dear-heart."

"The Browns aren't much for formal calls," Carl answered with amusement which Magda did not fathom until they came a little closer to their house. Which Magda realized with horror and surprise was not really a proper house at all, but several squalid and ramshackle log cabins a little distant from the track which ran along side the river. The largest cabin was raised a little way off the ground, and chickens ran in and out of the space underneath. The clearing around the houses and the ragged field of tall maize plants was studded with tree stumps. When her husband drew rein and called, "Hello, Brown! Anyone at home?" nothing moved, save for a cloud of flies hovering over the immense hog, which slumbering peacefully in a muddy wallow at the end of the porch where obviously the dishwater and garbage were emptied regularly. Magda felt her skin crawl. A pig and all that filth and smell, right at the front of the house?

She whispered, "There is no one at home, dear-heart—must we linger?"

"They're around," her husband answered, just as a woman appeared in the doorway, wiping her hands on a grimy towel tied around her waist.

"Howdy, neighbor!" she called. "That be your new missus, I reckon!? Well, I'll be! Come up and set a spell!" She turned and cupped her hands, shouting stentoriously "Paw—boys! It's Dutch Becker and his missus!"

"We can't stay long, Miz Brown," Carl answered, very studiously not looking towards Magda, although the corners of his mouth quirked upwards in quiet amusement. He was teasing her again, the wretched man! He solemnly handed her down from the wagon and saw to tying up Three-Socks and the wagon team to a convenient stump, while she faced their hostess and attempted to hold a gracious expression on her countenance when faced with a slatternly woman of no particular age, whose bosoms slumped un-corseted beneath a faded calico dress. Her cheeks also slumped in, for lack of teeth, and her feet were bare and dirty. So was the hem of her dress. She smiled warmly at Magda, irregardless of the missing teeth, as Carl said, "Miz Brown—my wife, Margaretha, Miz Brown."

The ragged woman took Magda's hand, with rough grace, exclaiming, "Welcome, Miz Becker! Nate, he wuz always sayin' Mista Becker, he was off a'courting, but I done tol' him, I'll b'lieve it when I see . . . an' so holp me, now I do! Whur did he pick you from, honey, an' then drag you out hyer all this way, jus' lik' a man?"

Magda looked helplessly at her husband; she understood spoken English, but not in the uncouth way Mrs. Brown spoke it.

"My wife's family settled in Friedrichsburg on the Pedernales," Carl came to her rescue; sky-colored eyes dancing with suppressed amusement. "But they have not been very long in Texas, so she does not speak English very well, yet."

"Ne'er mind then." Mrs Brown patted Magda's hand, "You'll soon be right at home—Brown!" she shouted suddenly, over her shoulder as a man appeared at the edge of the corn-patch, a thin man as ragged as a beggar with a rifle slung casually on his shoulder. "It's Becker an' his new missus! Now, you jes' come and set a spell, let the menfolk talk!" Mrs. Brown towed Magda after her, across that wretched excuse for a farmyard and up onto the sagging porch. She showed Magda to a seat on a crude wooden bench with the air of a duchess welcoming a queen to her grand salon, and there Magda sat for some twenty uncomfortable minutes, while Mrs. Brown hospitably brought her water in a cracked cup. In the yard, her husband talked long with Mr. Brown and three or four lanky young men who appeared slowly from various directions. They laughed among themselves and slapped his shoulders approvingly as if they were old friends—which they undoubtedly were, Magda reminded herself.

She was secretly appalled at the dirt and the comfortless squalor of the Browns' farmstead; it was as if they did not care to put any more care into it than was strictly necessary. There was no vegetable garden, no flowers. The chickens and the pig wandered where they pleased. From the bench she could look a little way into the cabin. What she could see of it was as bare as a prison cell, and as cheerless. How could they live this way, like the meanest beggar in a ramshackle, dirty hut? And Magda now wondered with horror—surely Carl did not expect her to live this way? And she looked at Mrs. Brown, in her dirty dress and bare feet, with lank strands of hair falling out of the bun that it had been indifferently combed into and wondered if this was what she would become.

Presently, her husband excused himself from the circle of men. He came up to the house, speaking in English to Mrs. Brown, thanking her for the hospitality, meager though it had been. Magda did not care what he said, but took his hand as if he were saving her life again.

"We'll go home now," he murmured quietly in German to her, while Mrs. Brown patted her cheek and admonished her cheerily.

"Don't be a stranger to us, Miz Becker!" Magda forced a smile and thought it fortunate that she kept herself from saying *If only!* out loud. Carl gravely handed her up to the wagon seat and took his place beside her, having once again tied Three-Socks to the back. Magda said not a word, until they had left the Browns' behind. Carl looked sideways at her, with the corners of his mouth quirking upwards again.

"You'd best let it out, Margaretha, before you burst."

She cast over a couple of remarks in her mind, before she blew out her breath and asked, "Do—all the American settlers live like that? How can they bear to live so poorly!?"

Aggravating man, he had done that deliberately; now he answered gravely, "Many do even if they have a choice, when their wealth is in land, or cattle and horses. Brown has as large a holding as my own, but with many more cattle on it. You wouldn't know to look at him, but he's about the richest man in these parts. Him and his kind, they just care little for what Miz Brown calls the fripperies.

Give them a little land, a horse or two and a patch of corn, they're as happy as lords."

"A cock on a dunghill, rather! They live worse than the Indians!" Magda said, and unexpectedly her husband nodded in agreement.

"They're good folk, for all of that," There was just a hint of reproof in his quiet voice. "All they ask is that other folk let them be. They're our closest neighbors, too—it's good to get along with them, otherwise we might have to put up with the Waldrips more than we need do already."

"True," Magda sighed, and she thought of the other dread. "Your house . . . our house—surely it is nothing like theirs . . . is it?"

"No," and he looked sideways at her. "As I promised—for you, I built a fine stone house. But would you have married me, if all I had built was a cabin like theirs?"

"Without the pig," she answered, after a judicious pause. "Assuredly, without the pig. Or the stumps in the yard." He laughed, and held the reins with one hand long enough to embrace her with the other arm. A stone house, she reminded herself; a fine stone house, not shabby and temporary cabin, but a house which would last longer than themselves.

"The house is on a knoll, just around the bend," her husband told her at last, when they had cone three or four miles from the Browns. "You should be able to see the chimney from here."

"Where does your holding begin?" she asked.

"We've been on it for half a mile or so."

"That is a princely property!" she said with a gasp, and he laughed.

"No, not as we measure things! We'll be leaving the track here. Porfirio thought it a fine idea to mark it by nailing a bull-skull to the tree. He's the Mex boy who works for me. We round up the cattle every year, take them down to the market in Bexar. Truth to tell, it's more suited hereabouts to grazing, than anything else."

"How many people work for you, then?" she asked, curiously.

"Three for now, but they come and go; there's Porfirio and Nate Brown—he's one of Brown's younger boys. They have more young ones than wants to live at home, seems like. And Trap Talmadge; I've known him a long time. He was in the first troop that Jack and I rode with. He used to ride with Jack, too. Broke his knee in a bad way a couple of years ago, but he can still work . . . jack of all trades, more or less. I met up with him again after I came back from the Llano with Mr. Meusebach. When I took up my land, I hired him to work on the house with me, as much to keep him off the bottle and out of the gutter as anything else. And just for the record," he added, with the air of a man laying out more bad news, "Porfirio stabbed another Mex in a fight over a girl down in Bexar. The other man has a lot of friends, so Porfirio is dodging some angry Mexes and the magistrates and waiting for the ruckus to die down."

"What about young Mr. Brown?" Magda asked disapprovingly. "What are his faults?"

"He's only sixteen, hasn't had enough time to accumulate any yet." He looked at her, almost anxiously. "But they're all gentlemen. There's nothing you need worry about with them."

"I hope not," she said. Men and their friends, she thought with a sigh. Such friendships made them indulgent, or so Vati had told her more than once.

Now, they came to a place where the wagon-tracks diverged, at the base of a gigantic oak tree. As Carl had described it, the trunk of it was adorned with the skull of one of those wild Texas cattle. The track led away from the river, climbing a gentle slope. More cattle grazed among the trees, sunshine dappling their hides. A split-rail fence enclosed a large field filled with half-grown maize. Another fence, a crude affair of timber poles zig-zagging back and forth surrounded a meadow in which some more cattle grazed.

"Trap and I have a thought to improve the cattle bred hereabouts." Carl told her. "When we finish fencing some more pasture. It'll take a couple of years to get it the way I want it."

The track curved around the edge of that field, and beyond, at the top of the knoll Magda could see a chimney topping a shingled roof. Clean new limestone walls gleamed like ivory, here and there between the trees, and Carl was looking anxiously at her face. A man on a horse emerged from between the trees and waved his hat at them, and from a distance she could hear dogs barking.

"That's Porfirio." Carl lifted his hand, and the man waved his hat at them, and whistled shrilly. A pair of large tan-colored dogs burst out of the field, their tongues lolling and tails up, and bounded alongside the team barking in a friendly manner. "Down, damn you, down! Those two flea-bags are Chief Dog and Little Dog. I keep them to bark at strangers, and they bark at everything that moves. Dogs are good things to have, out here." He looked at her sideways. "They don't live in the house, by the way. They would like to live in the house, but their job is to guard the stock."

The stone house perched on the edge of the knoll, overlooking the distant river, as Carl had said, a palisade the height of a man, built of raw upright timbers connecting the other buildings behind it. A stout gate of sawn timber stood open, giving access to the farmyard within. Two other men . . . no, a man and a boy waited for them there, and Porfirio clattered through the gate after the wagon and slid down from his horse like an otter slipping off of a stream bank, while the dogs gamboled clumsily around them.

Home. This was home, and her domain. She was aware of all four of them looking at her anxiously; even the dogs looked anxious as her husband reached up to help her down from the wagon. She tried to smile reassuringly at him, saying, "It is larger than I thought. And it looks very fine from the outside. Much finer than I expected." His face lightened, which reminded her piercingly of how much he wanted to please her, with the house, with everything. He spoke to the men, in English. In turn, each of them took her hand. She thought she understood what they were saying. Vati had tried to teach them all English, but like him she could read it but barely understand it spoken.

I shall have to ask him to teach me this, also, Magda thought, *He steps between English and German so easily, and so must I, now.*

Nate Brown was half-grown and skinny; he barely touched her fingers and mumbled shyly, "Pleased, ma'am." Then he added something else, which she couldn't understand, and her husband noted her puzzlement.

"He and Porfirio worked up a wedding present for you," Carl explained, sounding amused. "They rounded up a young cow with a calf. You'll have a milk cow, as soon as she's tamed a little more." Magda contemplated milking one of those feral, long-horned beasts and quailed.

"How much more tame?"

"Well, she kicked down the stall three times, knocked everything to splinters the first time. It wasn't in splinters the second or third time, so we are making progress."

"Thank you for the cow," she said carefully in English and the boy looked nearly as happy as her husband did. Porfirio the Mexican boy was little older than Nate, stocky and round-faced, with a broad grin that reminded her of Charley. He had all the worldly assurance that Nate Brown lacked. He kissed her hand gallantly and addressed her as "Señora" but all the rest of it was in Spanish; she could see why he could woo a girl away from another gallant, just from the sound of it, and the wholly admiring look in his eyes.

"He says you will be the grandest jewel and ornament to my house. He hopes that we will have many fine children, and prosper mightily."

"That had the sound of a most flowery compliment," Magda observed to her husband, who answered wryly;

"He has a way with them—which is what tends to land him into big, big trouble. This is Trap Talmadge, a gentleman and adventurer of South Carolina." With his weather-scorched face, at first glance Trap Talmadge looked nearly as old as Vati. He spoke in a soft, husky drawl. A slight man with a ragged mustache, he walked with a limp and a lurch, and took her hand with as courtly an air as the Mexican boy did. There was a faint sour smell of old drink about him, and his accent was impenetrable. Magda thought of those sorts of Americans that Vati had noticed in Galveston, who looked like beggars but had the manners of a courtier.

"He is honored," Carl translated. She said, "It sounded like he said more than that," Carl laughed.

"He confesses that he is astounded I was ever able to court and win such a fine and gentle lady."

"Pleased to make your acquaintance," she said carefully in English to Trap Talmadge, and asked Carl, "Exactly how old a friend is he?"

"Old enough to still think of me as being about Nate's age. Now, he thought to appeal to Mrs. Brown and to get a laying hen and a dozen eggs for a wedding present. He even built a house and pen for them too, which from Trap is the height of chivalry. He doesn't much care for farming."

He took her hand, and led her towards the house, saying eagerly, "Let me show you the inside. I think you will like it. Margaret sent a wagon-load of furniture from Austin, with a message to say that it was her gift to us. Otherwise she was afraid I would think a bedroll on the floor in the corner would be good enough."

"That is very generous of her," Magda was touched. "Almost too generous—I know she is your only kin-folk, can we accept it?"

"We may. She keeps a boarding house and has more furniture for it then she has rooms to put it in. Besides," he kissed her very lightly on the forehead, "the men would be very annoyed at having to pack it up again. And we would ourselves have to sleep on a bedroll on the floor if we did." The house was shaped like a T. In the angle of it facing the farmyard was a long covered porch, with three steps leading up. A line of a dozen or so wooden boxes and troughs were lined up along the edge, where they would catch the sun, and in each was a small, spindly sapling.

"What are those?" she asked. "They look like apple trees."

"Apple, persimmon, apricot, and cherry . . . the start of an orchard," he answered proudly. "Your father's friend Mr. Lindheimer sent me some of them. Came all the way from the East, they did. I took up the persimmon from where they were growing, two or three miles away. Trap thinks I'm a fool for bothering. He's another one like Brown—grow a plot of corn and kill a hog, and move on when they get restless." He shook his head. "Folks like him and the Browns never tire of sowbelly and cornbread, but my folks had a real farm."

An orchard; he planned to build an orchard. Magda's heart lifted; he was indeed thinking of the long future, not just the next harvest, not like so many of the other Americans. There was a carving over the doorway, and her husband said, "Peter's idea—he thought it would mark the occasion suitably."

Magda looked up; in the stone lintel over the door was carved the date 1847 and a tree branch; the branch of an apple tree with leaves and two apples, and a bird in a nest.

"For Miss Vogel," he smiled proudly, "Miss Bird, you see. I had to explain it to Trap and the boys."

"It's a lovely idea," she said, so moved that her voice was hardly steady.

He opened the door for her and stepped back as Magda walked through it and took possession of her kingdom, the fine stone house that he had build for her and for their children, the stone house that would be a replacement for the kind of house she might have had, if she had stayed behind in Albeck. Like Vati's house, the windows were covered with wooden-shutters, which now stood open to the air, and afternoon sunshine, slanting in from the west. She stood in a narrow hall, with a stair in it and a door on either side.

"Parlor," Carl opened one. Here were riches and comfort indeed: a stone fireplace, and a rag rug on the floor, four spindly chairs around a circular table, on which stood an oil lamp with a fine glass bowl and shade. Two windows looked outwards towards the river, two inwards at the farm-yard. He opened the other door, "Kitchen . . . dairy and larder through there. There is a cellar underneath the kitchen. The stair to it is through the dairy. It stays cool down there through the summer. Peter thought you would like that. I've been mostly living in the kitchen, since it was the first room finished. There's another door out to the yard. I had him build the fireplace as much like the one in your father's house as he could."

"It's beautiful!" Magda's voice shook. "It's beautiful, but there is stone-dust all over."

"We did our best." Carl sounded defensive, and Magda put her arms around him and drew his head down towards hers,

"Of course you did," she said, and kissed him very firmly "You are men, and have no idea how to keep things as clean as they ought to be. Just show me where the broom is."

"Broom?" said Carl blankly. "One moment." He went to the door again, and called out into the yard. When he came back, he looked happier. "Come and see the upstairs, first."

There were four rooms upstairs, but only two with furniture in them: two small beds with their mattresses innocent of any bedding and a chest of drawers in one, but the other beautifully set with a large bed, a wardrobe and a dressing-table fitted with a mirror. There was a washstand in the corner, with a pretty blue-glazed pitcher and basin on it. Magda surveyed the room with approval. Her own bedding and linens should suit very well.

"I think I like your sister, very much," she said, impishly. "Everything she has sent is perfect. She must be a very practical German housewife, to know exactly what would be needed."

"That she is," Carl laughed with relieved delight. "She would also—or so she told me—scratch your eyes out, if you would ever treat me unkindly. But there is something that she gave me for you to have. I meant to bring it with me for the wedding, but then I thought you should have it now."

Downstairs she could hear the door opening, and the men carrying in something heavy; they were unloading the wagon of the brides' chest and those boxes of things she had brought with her for her home, for their home. Vati had presented them with a clock of his own making, which would go very nicely in the parlor.

"Tell them to bring the big painted trunk upstairs," she whispered. He went to the open window and called out to the men outside, in the yard, seeing to the horses and unloading the wagon. Then he went to the dressing-table and opened one of the tiny drawers. He took from it little leather bag, and spilled something small into his palm; a cameo broach of pink and white stone, set in gold with a tiny rim of seed-pearls around it, barely as large as his thumb.

"It belonged to my mother," he said, as he pressed it into her hand and closed her fingers around it. "Margaret said that she wanted it to go to my wife. I don't know where she had it from. Maybe her mother. I never paid much attention until it was too late, but now it's yours."

"So many gifts!" Magda took it, and her eyes came close to overflowing. "From people we can never come close to thanking! What we shall do for them, then?"

"Live a happy life!" Carl drew her close to him, heart to heart. "Live a happy life and be generous to our children." She would always love this, standing close, feeling that their hearts were beating together, knowing that he would love and shelter her, and that she would love and protect him always. And then he whispered, "It's a very nice bed, Margaretha. When will we see if it is as comfortable as it looks?"

"Tonight!" she answered, as they separated hastily at the sound of heavy footsteps on the stairs. "There is too much to do!" That was the boys, staggering awkwardly under the weight of the painted dowry chest. They placed it where she pointed, against the wall under an eastern-facing window. When they had gone downstairs, she kissed him again and pinned the little broach at her throat. "Whatever else is needful, I have brought with me. Let me see to unpacking..."

"You don't need to do everything in one day," he protested, and would have kept her close, but she slipped under his arm.

"I will have to set up the kitchen if you want any dinner tonight!" She ran lightly down the stairs, just as Trap Talmadge came in through the door with a new-made broom in his hand. She took it from him with thanks, and set to work organizing her kingdom.

* * *

Letter from Christian Friedrich Steinmetz: Written on 15 August 1848, from Friedrichsburg in Texas, to Simon Frankenthaler, Goldsmith of the City of Ulm in Bavaria

My dear old friend, such joys and sorrows have come upon us since I wrote you last! Although my family and my business thrive and prosper, our larger circle of friends is beset with troubles. An influx of new arrivals to our town and to Neu Braunfels, straight from the hardships of the voyage, and those sad events attendant upon the death of our hopes for true

317

reform have brought fatal epidemics of disease. The cholera and other afflictions have visited their full horrors upon us. Our burial ground is now sadly filled; on some recent days the graves could be scarcely dug fast enough. Among the recent and much-mourned dead is the wife and helpmate of my very good friend, the Reverend Altmueller. That is he who had bravely shared the travails of our own crossing and comforted us, as much as one can be comforted after so grievous a loss upon the death of my own dear wife. A courageous and selfless lady, struck down in the midst of caring for others so afflicted! He bears up as well as can be expected. It is not only our own folk who have been so stricken. The Indian tribes have also been grievously affected; among those so stricken was Chief Santanna, almost our best friend among the Comanche with whom we have made peace. I have taken some precautions as regards my own nearest and dearest, as long as these epidemics rage. My dear little Rosalie is sent with son Hansi to live with my daughter Liesel upon their holding at Live Oak some little distance from town. I beseeched him to keep them all away from town until this monstrous epidemic has been sated with enough lives. Rosalie bore up very well, for I told her many tales about the wondrous times she would have with Anna and the other children. She is so attached to me; I feared that our parting would go badly. But son Hansi passed it off as an adventure and carried her away on his saddle-bow, and she waved a cheery farewell to her dearest Vati.

As for the boys, I sent urgent word by messenger to Margaretha's husband, asking if they could stay with him. She has always taken a much firmer hand with the boys than Liesel, who is much distracted with her own children. Son Carl and one of his men came for them straightaway, riding straight over the hills on horseback as was his former custom. They stayed only a short time, just long enough for Johann and Friedrich to put on some stout clothing and to pack some small luggage to take with them. I own to missing them very much. The house seems almost deserted with only myself in it. I have asked Altmueller if he would like to stay with me for a time.

Mrs. Schmidt comes in most days to see to the household matters . . .

"Auntie Magda! Auntie Magda!" shouted Friedrich, when Carl and Trap rode in, about midday of the next morning, heralded by the barking of the dogs. "We saw some Indians last night, some Indians but there was a white man with them . . ."

Magda put aside the rake, and ran, holding onto the wide-brimmed straw hat which shaded her eyes against the sun. She had been preparing the soil for an expanded vegetable garden, tucked into the corner of the palisade between the house and the sagging and much-weathered cabin where Trap and the hands lived. The chickens scratched energetically in the turned earth at her feet, seeking bugs and earthworms. Her husband had planted only a small garden in the spring, before their marriage, and she had ambitions for something larger in the next year.

"What Indians?!" she gasped, as she ran up to them. The boys had been riding doubled behind the men. Carl let Friedrich down, his face looking most comic as his legs nearly gave way underneath him.

"Last night. Six or seven of them, and a man in white clothes riding with them!" Friedrich hugged her, exuberantly. "I thought at first we might fight them but Uncle Carl and Mr. Talmadge, we went behind a thicket, and Mr. Talmadge went off a little way and watched them."

Magda hugged her excited brother and looked over his head at her husband.

"What is he talking about?" she demanded, "What were you intending to do . . . and who did you think they were? Oh!"

Trap Talmadge had let Johann down from the saddle, but when he let go of the boy's arm, poor Johann was so tired, his legs wobbled and collapsed underneath him. He sat woefully in the middle of the farmyard, looking as if he were about to cry. Magda flew to him, and tried to help him stand but it was Carl, who lifted him and set him on his feet, saying, "Sorry, we had to push so hard on that last stretch. Trap did not like the look of those Indians. Walk a little way, and

319

stretch out your muscles, Johann." He looked over the boy's heads at Magda, and said very low, "Later."

Magda had been just long enough married to know that he would tell her the rest of it privately, so she hugged Friedrich to her and asked, "How is Vati—what other news is there of Liesel and Hansi and all of our friends. What has been happening?"

"A lot of people have been sick," Friedrich said, very soberly, "and Mrs. Helene died. I think that is when Vati decided to send us all away, until winter comes."

"Mrs. Helene? Pastor Altemeuller's wife?" Magda stood stock still in the yard, petrified with shock and grief. How could this be, that kind and indefatigable woman gone, cut down like a stalk of wheat under a sickle-blade. She could almost feel the scrape of hairpins against her scalp, hear Mrs. Helene's fondly chiding voice as she and Liesel had trussed her up in Liesel's white silk dress, and when she asked *'Think on this, dear Magda . . . which of the two gentlemen do you wish to grow old with?'* She and Carl had returned to Friedrichsburg since their wedding, but she had never had a chance to tell Mrs. Helene how right she had been.

But at least, thought Magda, *Mrs. Helene must have seen that we were happy. She must have seen that! I have to believe that she did see it. I so wish that I had told her! This is almost as awful as Mutti dying.*

"Yes, Mrs. Helene," Friedrich said, and now he looked downcast. "Doctor Keidel said she had been caring for some new people, who came in a wagon from the coast, and then she was sick herself. There were so many people dying that a cart came around to take them to the burial ground. Vati said it was like the plagues, and Doctor Keidel said it was because there was something in the air or maybe the water that caused it, and one day the burial cart tipped, and one of the bodies rolled out, all in its shroud and it fell in front of Mr. Ransleben's shop before some women who screamed and screamed!"

"Friedrich," Magda sighed, "We didn't need to know that!"

"I know that," Friedrich said, and hugged her around the waist. "It just slipped out . . . we're glad to be here, Auntie Magda. You're not going to make us go to school, are you?"

"There is no school out here," Carl ruffled his hair, affectionately. "But you will have lessons, and plenty of work, enough to keep even you out of trouble."

"I like school!" Johann spoke up bravely, and his twin stuck out his tongue at him. Carl said something in English to Trap Talmadge, who looked amused. He limped away, leading their horses as Carl and Magda took the twins into the house, with the dogs following hopefully after. He briefly embraced her as they went inside.

"She was a very good lady, Margaretha . . . a very good lady indeed."

"She was," she whispered back. "How could she have died and her friends not know at once?"

"My own mother died, and I did not know it," he answered. For a moment, he appeared quite haunted. "You think you should have known, but somehow it doesn't happen like that. Even when such things happen right in front of you, sometimes it takes a while to really know what has happened." And then, they were inside the house and he smiled at the boys and told them, "Be warned, Mr. Talmadge has plans to teach you both to ride. Not the way you've been raised to think of riding, but to really ride. He says it's a disgrace for a true gentleman not to be able to sit a horse, drunk or sober."

Friedrich's face brightened, but Johann didn't appear nearly as enthused. Magda took them into her kitchen and fed them bread and some of her home-made soft cheese, of which she was really proud. Both of them told her over and over again how happy they were to see her again and to see her house. Friedrich even announced that he wanted to stay forever.

"This is no holiday here," Magda warned them. "You both may very well wish to have stayed in school once you have seen how much work there is for you."

"Oh, pooh, we worked hard enough making bricks for Vati's house," Friedrich said. "Your house is already finished, what else is there to do?"

"Stone walls," Carl answered, smiling impishly. "I am building a small orchard on the slope below the house. In between other chores, we are hauling stone from the riverbank for the walls and your sister is carrying buckets of muck from the farmyard to improve the soil. All this must be done before we can plant the trees, for otherwise the cattle will trample them flat and the deer will eat them down to the ground."

"So, which would you rather do?" Magda asked her brothers. "Pile up rocks with my husband, or carry buckets with me?"

The boys looked glumly at each other, and Johann asked, warily, "Is there a reward for this?"

"In twenty years mine will be to lay on my back underneath one of my trees and eat as many apples as I want," Carl told them. He had that teasing look to him, but at the boys' doleful faces, he said, "As I said, Mr. Talmadge will teach you to ride... and we'll see what other useful things you can learn from him."

"Oh, yes please!" Friedrich said eagerly.

Johann still appeared despondent and Carl added, "I borrowed some books about viticulture and raising fruit-trees from your father and from Mr. Lindheimer, but I have not had time to read them. Johann, if you would like, can you read them for me and make note of anything useful? That would be a very great help." He looked at Johann and added, with an expression on his face so transparently innocent that Magda had to turn away to hide her smile, "There is such a very tall pile of them, I fear I may not be able to finish by mid-winter."

"Oh, yes," Johann said eagerly. "I can do that. Just tell me what you need to know especially." Magda had to step out into the dairy, and press a wadded-up corner of her apron to her face to stifle her amusement. Her little brothers were being maneuvered as deftly as Porfirio worked the cattle into the place where he wanted them, only instead of shouts and a lariat and the aid of his pony, her husband was doing it with words and a cunning appeal to what they were most interested in.

That night, she lay in his arms, in the big bedroom upstairs, with the windows which looked east. She had added many pretty and comfortable things from her dowry-chest; this was the heart of their kingdom. She rejoiced in the possession of a place from which they would never leave, knowing that he felt the same. Their heart, their home, the place which would shelter their children, and their children's children, the place into which they would pour their work, their blood and their love; for he had plans, plans that would take decades and generations to bring to full fruit. This was, Magda knew down to the marrow of her bones, what she had been promised by the Verein and by her husband at their wedding.

"What was it about the Indians?" she asked, her head lying in the angle of his shoulder and chin.

"Mmmm?" he answered drowsily, to the top of her head. "What Indians?"

"The ones you and Mr. Talmadge saw. The ones that Friedrich and Johann were telling me about."

"Oh. Those Indians." He was quiet for some moments, and she finally lifted her head to make sure that he had not fallen asleep. There was just enough light from the moon, slipping through the cracks in the shutters for her to see that his eyes were still open.

"The Indians that you were hoping I would forget about," she said, with sudden acute perception. "Those Indians."

He stirred a little, and answered slowly, "They weren't Indians. White men or Mexes, dressed like Indians."

"Why would they do that?" she asked, dismayed.

"Tell me, and we'd both know. Most likely they're up to some devilment that it would suit for folk to blame the Indians for. Trap couldn't get close enough to recognize any of them and with the boys, we didn't really want any trouble coming after us."

"How could you tell they were not really Indians, then?"

"Followed their trail for a bit. All the horses were shod."

Magda lay still for a time, thinking through the implications of this, before she said, "What are you going to do about it?"

"Not much can be done, all the way out here. Send word to the Browns, and Peter Berg and the others; let them know what we saw and to keep a wary eye out for a party of strangers. Which we do, anyways." He tightened his arm around her, briefly, and added, "Why do you think we have the dogs? And Trap and the boys and I keep a weapon handy to us, if we're very far from the house."

And you or one of them always follows me, in a little while, when I go very far from the farmyard, Magda added silently, and her husband held her close again.

"It won't always be like this, Margaretha. I promise. When I was a boy, it was like this and worse where we lived along the Colorado, but now my sister and her family go about their business as safe as if they were back east. There'll be a time when we can do so as well. Think of how we'll be able to spin exciting stories for our children!"

"More exciting than hauling muck from the farmyard and stone from the river?" Magda asked and he chuckled, a lovely warm rumble in his chest, next to her ear.

"More exciting then that," he answered. "It will make one of Cooper's tales look like a church social." And he tickled her ribs and made her giggle, and for quite some time afterwards she forgot entirely about the Indians that weren't Indians. For the days passed in work, in the slow but satisfactory progress of seeing the orchard wall built, encompassing the gentle slope below the house. Peter Berg came out of the hills one day with his stone-working tools in a pack on his back. He stayed for a fortnight, and helped them to lay out the course of walls, and cut a pair of shallow terraces, to be faced with more stone. He seemed even more odd and abrupt than ever. Secretly Magda sympathized with the faithless girl who had broken their engagement. A man that odd would be most difficult to live with.

On a winter afternoon, Magda leaned her elbows on the sill of the kitchen window, the window that looked out onto the orchard and the sweep of pasture beyond it. It was one of those warm winter days, when the wind didn't blow harsh and icy out of the north, when the sunlight had fallen all day on the stone walls and the sill felt as warm as a living thing.

Peter still worked, chipping away with his hammer and stone-cutting chisel, fitting together large and small blocks, but the others, Carl and Trap, Porfirio and Nate, were in the meadow with her brothers, showing them horse-back riding tricks. That was Friedrich, on Trap's spotted pony, watching as Three-Socks galloped across the meadow with Carl leaning so far out of his saddle that he could snatch up his hat from the ground. At the edge of the meadow, Three-Socks spun around, and Carl slipped to the other side, apparently clinging to his saddle with one foot and one hand, his body entirely screened by the horse. At the other end of the meadow, Carl rose up, and waved his hat at the boys. He was laughing, and Magda could see that Friedrich and Johann were much impressed. It looked like Friedrich wanted to try doing the same. Johann did not seem quite so reckless, for Porfirio was demonstrating how he used a long rope, how he could spin it out and drop an open loop around a long stake driven into the ground. It looked like the long stake Carl had taught her to shoot at. She remembered how patient and thorough he was as a teacher, the day he took her out into the meadow and showed her how use his Paterson pistol… the day that they first kissed as a man and woman. Magda lingered long at the window, fondly watching her husband, so careful and watchful with Friedrich and Johann, keeping the one from venturing into recklessness and patiently encouraging the other.

He would be good with his children, she knew that as surely as she knew that she had good news to tell him, as kind as Vati, but perhaps a little sterner. She had not told him of her glad news yet, being sure of it herself only this very day. There was a tender feeling in her breasts, and a peculiar ache low in her belly, as if there were a tight-clenched lump the size of her fist, just there. It was not the familiar monthly ache which dwindled away with her regular courses; she had felt this for weeks and already fancied that there was a distinct bulge between the sharp points of her hip-bones.

I will tell him tonight,' she told herself. *He will be so happy to know of his child.*

Chapter 18 – *A Price Above Rubies*

Letter from Christian Friedrich Steinmetz: Written on 15 June 1849, from Friedrichsburg in Texas, to Simon Frankenthaler, Goldsmith of the City of Ulm in Bavaria

My dear old friend; You would scarcely recognize our little town, if you had been one of those who saw it from the vantage of our cart-train, three years ago! Then just a clearing in the wilderness, and today, the streets are thronged with travelers and our places of business all thrive mightily. This past winter the American government established a fort some little distance away, housing a detachment of soldiers to see to our protection. We do not feel that we are in any particular danger of the Indian depredations they are supposed to defend us against but the fort does serve a useful purpose, in providing work for our builders and carpenters, and a market for our goods and livestock. Although there is one small scandal attaching to their presence: the wife of Mr. Ransleben, who kept a store on Main Street, eloped with a soldier. Imagine the tongues which wagged over that! He sold his store and moved to Live Oak, near Son Hansi to farm. His establishment would be greatly missed by the town; fortunately, several more stores have opened. Our good friend Mr. Nimitz has purchased a small house on Main Street and made several rooms of it into a hotel and a small tavern, as was his dream. Since the discovery of gold in far California, he has hosted many, who have traveled through town on their way to seek their fortune.

I must admit some of our younger sparks have felt some small inclination to do likewise, but for the main part, we Germans are resistant to the blandishments of the reports we have read. Gold nuggets as thick as pebbles paving the ground indeed! Most of us succumbed once already to this kind of temptation! Having come so far, now to uproot ourselves to follow a willow-the-wisp? It is not likely, my old friend: Son Hansi is adamant that we have already found great riches here and would not chance loosing our grasp on what we have won with great labor. We have already put down new roots; it is not our wont to lightly tear them away again in the same lifetime.

The children thrive: Johann and Friedrich are already grown to nearly twice the height they were when we departed our old home. They grow and thrive in a way most remarkable. I regret to say that only Johann shows any aptitude for books and the intellectual life; such has this country changed my sons! We hope to be able to send him to Germany to study medicine, as he has often displayed an interest, but his brother Friedrich prefers the out-of-doors.

Daughter Margaretha's husband has brought her to stay with me in town to await the advent of their first child, over her strenuous objections. As the most attentive and fond of husbands, he was most insistent on this and had his way in this matter. There is no doctor within a day's ride of his property, and the only available midwife is a neighbor woman of dubious skills. Son Carl feared some dreadful misadventure attending on her confinement. My dear daughter has fretted and fussed for the last month and a half, missing the care of her own household establishment, and the company of her husband! He visits for the Saturday and Sunday, as was his habit before they married, which barely alleviates her fretful moods...

When he rode into Friedrichsburg on a Saturday in late June, and his wife did not come out to the garden as soon as he put up his horse in Vati's tiny stable, Carl knew at once that it was close to that time. He thanked God again that he had made Magda see reason, and spend the last few weeks with Vati. He looked up at the upstairs windows, all shuttered tight and fairly ran across the terrace to the back door. Hansi opened it from the inside as he placed his hand on the latch.

"Good timing," Hansi remarked. "We've just sent for Doctor Keidel."

"Might I see her?" Carl asked, breathlessly.

Liesel leaned over the stair banister with a basket of towels in her arms and answered, "No. Take him away, Hansi."

"Just for a moment?" he pleaded but Liesel was inflexible.

"No! It's just not seemly for any man but the doctor to be present!"

"Please, Liesel," he begged as he came halfway up the stairs. "Just for a moment, so she will know, she can see for herself that I am close by!"

"Seemly!" Hansi rolled his eyes, he seemed much amused. "Let him in for a moment, Lise, then I'll take him to Charley's for a drink."

"All right," Liesel relented, "but only for a moment. And let me go up first." She hurried up the stairs, muttering under her breath and slipped through the door at the top of the stairs. She closed it swiftly after her, before Carl could even see inside. He waited impatiently, hearing low voices inside, until Liesel opened the door again.

Magda stood by the side of the bed, swathed in her wrapper and leaning on Mrs. Schmidt, but she sagged as if she were exhausted and would have fallen without that support. Her hair was raveling out of its' braid and sticking to her face. The bedroom was hot and smelled of sweat and the metallic odor of blood, but he cared nothing for that. She smiled a tired half-smile, as if embarrassed to be seen in such dishabille, taking deep breaths and gasping as if she were in a desperate race.

"You must keep walking," Mrs. Schmidt urged. "It makes the pain less." She shot a disparaging look at Carl who came around and took Magda's other arm, closing his fingers around hers.

"I'm here," he said helplessly. "I'll be here. I wanted to let you know." She was desperately frightened; he could see it plain and it tore at him that there wasn't a thing he could do about it. They would not even let him stay for longer than a minute or two.

"Step, step, step!" Commanded Mrs. Schmidt. "Be useful, make her walk!"

They helped her to totter a few steps, and then her face twisted in a rictus of agony. Carl thought she would have cried out but she bit her lip against the pain and Liesel said, "Enough now… the doctor is here."

He tore his hand from hers as Liesel took his place, feeling that leaving her was some kind of betrayal. Her fingers left red and white marks on his. Doctor Keidel came through the door, opening his bag in a businesslike way and saying, "You'll have to leave, I'm afraid. Go chop wood, or build an ark, or read the dictionary. Whatever it is, go and do it. We'll send for you when needed."

He found himself outside the door, wandering down the staircase and thinking that he would just plant himself on the bottom stair and wait, wait for whatever would be happening. Hansi appeared from the kitchen and said cheerfully, "I'm ready for that drink, if you don't mind."

"I don't feel like drinking," Carl answered, mulishly. His brother-in-law answered, "Well, then walk down to Charley's with me, and you can watch me drinking." And he added with rough sympathy, "Look . . . she might want to be . . . umm, making a bit of noise, you know. Help bring it out. Knowing that you're in earshot . . . it might be a bit of a restraint, if you know what I mean."

That bore consideration and Carl answered after a moment, "Well how long is it likely to be, now?"

He allowed himself to be led out the door into Market Street as Hansi answered thoughtfully, "Now that the doctor is here? Not too long. Not if Magda bears as easily as Liesel." He shut the door behind them, and continued, "Our youngest one came on so fast I didn't even have time to send for Doctor Keidel, or anyone."

"What did you do?" Carl asked, in horrified curiosity, "How did you manage?"

"Tell the truth, nothing much to it." Hansi shrugged, philosophically. "It was rather like delivering a calf, in fact. Only half the mess but nearly twice the fuss. Still, Vati took the children to Sangerbund with him. He wanted to see them diverted and amused, God knows why. Anna's been in the house when the boys were born. I expect he thought that Rosalie would be frightened."

Everyone cherished Rosalie, Carl thought. Everyone loved and protected her. Would he and Magda feel the same way about this child? What if something happened to Magda? He wrenched his mind away from that possibility. But the bad imp in the back of his mind reminded him again that sometimes it did go badly for women in childbed.

The two of them walked a little way down Main Street in companionable silence, while Carl wondered how on earth he would ever manage to be as calm about this as Hansi. He liked children, and knew himself to be good with them, but children were just unformed, small adults. A baby was a different kettle of fish, altogether. Aloud, he ventured, "What do you do with a baby? We've talked all this time about everything else, but that."

"Nothing much, really," Hansi looked at him in mild surprise. "Feed them when they're hungry, change them when they're wet, keep them warm, and cuddle them when they cry—some of them do cry more than others, though. Best not to expect much from them at first, any more than you'd expect from a puppy or a kitten. It's not so hard, really."

"If you say so," Carl answered. Hansi looked surprised.

"Well, I do say so. Anyway, Magda will know all about that, about babies. They really aren't much fun until they're a little older. When you can see that they prefer this or that or are bold or fearful. George is about that age now. I watch him, and I know that he is thinking: planning how he will creep across the floor and that he wants to pull the cat's tail and take away the bit of gingerbread that his brother Jacob has, because he wants it very, very much. Anna now," Hansi continued, looking sideways at Carl, "Anna was very clever, even when she could barely walk. Very solemn like a little nun but always thoughtful—logical, like. Liesel and I never have had to tell her anything twice. Vati thinks she will be a school-teacher . . . something clever, anyway. So, do you and Magda hope for a boy first, or a girl like my Anna?"

"I don't know that we've ever considered that." Carl sighed, "Only that we hope for the child to be born well and straight - and with no harm to Magda out of it all."

"She'll be fine," Hansi said, with sympathy that Carl had hardly expected of him. "Very tired afterwards, of course. But Magda has always been strong. She'll come out of it well and hardly remember the pain of it. The next one will come easier."

"The next one?" Carl looked at him a little wildly. Hansi seemed quite amused.

"So you think now," he answered comfortably. "Just wait."

Halfway down Main Street, they waited while a couple of freight-wagons lumbered by in a cloud of dust and then a long string of pack-mules following after the bell-mare with a string of gently tinkling little chimes on her bridle, and another handful of smaller wagons. Gold-seekers, by the look of them and the mottoes painted on the wagon-covers. "Sacramento or Bust!" Hansi shook his head, "It's as much as your life is worth, crossing the road, some days… ever since the trail season opened."

"Good for business, Vati said," Carl squinted through the dust, settling in the rutted street after the mule string and the wagons had passed by.

"That's for sure. This is the last good place on the road, to have work done on your wagon, and to sleep in a comfortable bed—all those gold-seekers in such a hurry! They pay good money, too, but I think there'll be more gold made off those who look for gold, than those who just look for gold will ever find."

"Some of them may get mighty rich," Carl said as they stepped up onto the raised sidewalk, and Hansi answered with great seriousness.

"And some will die in the desert. I already risked enough following after the pretty tinsel dreams that the Verein held out in front of me. Coming across the ocean cost me my first-born son and nearly my wife." He shook his head. "My gold mine is here; I'd want none other. Neither should you, now that you have started your family."

They had reached Charley's place, already sounding lively on a late Saturday afternoon. Charley had expanded the small timber and adobe house, first to twice and then three times its original size. He had also built on a long room to serve as a tavern, which opened through several double doors on a terrace shaded with trees and hop and grape vines growing over a series of rough cedar pergolas. On mild days, he opened all the doors and business in the tavern overflowed into tables, benches and chairs set outside. The increasing traffic to the west had brought him nearly more business than he could handle; most days Charley barely appeared to have time to breathe. This afternoon he looked to be managing the taproom. Hansi caught his eye and held up two fingers, suggesting to Carl, "We'll sit outside. It's quieter. If anyone comes looking, they can find us easily."

"We shouldn't stay too long," Carl began to say, and Hansi rolled his eyes.

"It'll be time enough to sit and take some ease. Are you going to watch me drink, or have one yourself?" And there was Charley, at his elbow with a double handful of tall pottery mugs, looking unnaturally solemn and considerate.

"They have sent you away to wait it out?" he ventured, assuredly. "No, I don't have a crystal ball. Sophie called this morning and Mrs. Liesel told her." Carl found that he could take Charley's concern very well; after all, besides being a friend, he had also been a serious rival in courting Magda and taken his loss as a gentleman.

"Doctor Keidel is with her, now."

"Good." He set down four mugs with a thump. "On the house— but no more than that! I have to live here, you know! Bad form for a new father to be incapable of walking home, once he is sent for! Sophie would shred me to ribbons if she held me in any way responsible for it."

"You must be doing well, if you can afford to give it away," Hansi observed.

Charley rolled his eyes, "You have no idea. If it weren't for Sophie keeping track, I'd hardly know what day it is. But still, " He looked at Carl with wry sympathy. "I'm sure Mrs. Magda will be all right. Doctor Keidel knows his business. If anyone comes looking for you, I'll send them out here." Someone called him from inside, and Charley hastened away, leaving the two of them contemplating four mugs of beer.

"Good stuff," Hansi said, at last. "Makes it himself. There isn't a business going that Charley doesn't have a finger dipped into it. By the time my sons are men this will be the most civilized town in Texas! To your son, or daughter. Prosit!" They each took a mug and clinked them together.

Carl drank somewhat reluctantly. It went down very well for all of that, and he thought that drinking Charley's very passable beer might as well as anything else to pass the time until he was sent for. Occasionally one of Hansi's friends came over to greet them both and sympathize with their vigil. There was another influx when the Sangerbund rehearsal ended and Hansi was called inside to consult on a matter of ox-doctoring on behalf of one of the travelers passing through. Carl sat alone, moodily staring at nothing in particular. Presently, someone slapped his shoulder and a familiar voice said in English, "By god, Dutch—I thought it must be you! Trust you to be in the only decent thirst-parlor between Austin and San Francisco! Trust a Dutchman on that!"

It was Jack, dusty and smiling delightedly under his ragged trail-beard, with a cup and a bottle in hand and Carl sprang up and answered, "You should know by now, we don't do things by halves! How are you doing, Jack? Oh, damn, it's good to see you again! And what are you doing here? Is there a Comanche war-party hiding under the tables that I missed seeing?"

"Your tracking skills gone that rusty already?" Jack slapped his shoulder affectionately, and stood back to take a good critical squint at him. "Married life agrees with you, I see. You look well, Dutch, very well. And she lets you wander away off the home pasture, now and again!"

"Now and again," Carl said only and Jack looked at him very shrewdly.

"You've got that poker-face on. What's happening with you and that pretty Dutchwoman of yours?"

"Our child." Carl sank half the tankard of his beer. "We're waiting for it to be born. My brother-in-law dragged me down here, since the doctor sent me away from the house. Don't know why they do that. Everyone's being so damned sympathetic . . . makes me want to go and work at something until I am so ragged tired I can't think."

"Oh, that." Jack dropped onto the chair that Hansi had vacated and poured himself a drink. "You could come and ride with me again, if you want to keep your mind off things."

"I told you I was done with that," Carl answered, "back when you asked me to go nursemaid Meusebach and his treaty with the Comanche." Jack shook his cup a little and looked at the liquid within.

"So you said. And so am I," he said, at last and smiled a little crookedly. "You were right about that, you know. About wanting to be a civilized man, while you could still remember what it was? I handed in my resignation to the governor this very year. I'm done with ranging, with hunting down Indians and living on a handful of pecans and my guts. Just like you came around to thinking, Dutch—but leastwise I didn't need a Mex lancer to make it all plain. I just took a bit longer to come to that conclusion."

Carl gaped at him in astonishment; Jack, not at the head of a ranging company? Not out following a trail somewhere in the Llano, living in the saddle? It passed understanding, like seeing the moon and the sun change places. It had always been in the back of his mind, that when Meusebach's treaty eventually collapsed, then he might have cause and need to ride with Jack, to take the trail again with the one captain he trusted absolutely. Looking at his face, Jack laughed heartily and added, "Dutch, I do believe I have finally managed to surprise you."

"That you have," Carl took another swig out of his mug, and asked, "So, why did you do it, then? Best damn fighting officer any of us ever rode with. Why are you letting it go to waste?"

"Couple of good reasons, Dutch." Jack shook his cup gently, watching the liquid in it swirl around. "Besides the one you gave me. Getting married to Susan started me to think along the lines of settling down, being a regular provider, doing something that didn't give my wife good odds on wearing widows' weeds. I . . . well, she's my wife and I love her, you see. I'd love the children I hope to have with her. It's not fair for a married man to take the risks that we used to take. It'd just not. And then, I started thinking—well, about other things. Split up my thoughts in different directions, now. Started wondering what might happen if I wasn't focusing on the duty of the moment, began to think that I might want to go back to surveying . . . and I thought about settling down like you, with a nice little farm or cotton plantation someplace and I tell you Dutch, it just did not appeal. I'm not made that way."

"So, what did you decide to do with yourself then?" Carl asked and Jack beamed.

"I'm going to California. I may strike it rich there but again, I might not. I just might stay there anyway, and send for my wife to join me later. It's a good place for an ambitious man, too."

"You wouldn't come back to Texas?" Carl asked, "Why the hell not?"

Jack shook his head, and answered, "I've been here thirteen years, Dutch. Time to move on." He looked very keenly at Carl and said, "I don't regret the association, mind you, or the stretchers I'll be able to tell when I'm old. I just can't stay in one place, not like you and your folk and that's the truth of it."

"You'll be missed, Jack. You probably already are missed. You'll leave a hole that I can't see anyone else quite able to fill," Carl observed, after a long moment.

Jack answered, "That's where you're wrong, Dutch. I think I trained up enough good fellows, set enough of a good example for them to pick up where I left off. Put your hand in a bucket of water, what happens when you take it out?" He poured himself another two fingers from his whiskey bottle and added, with a decided air of nostalgia, "I can't see them getting up to some of the hi-jinks we got up to, though. That fandango that we ran into, hunting for Cortona, and they invited us to stay around? Even in California, I surely will never in my life again see such tall dancing as I did that night!"

"We did our best," Carl grinned. "Holding up the honor of Texas and our captain's company on more than one contested field!"

"To fine times and tall dancing!" Jack raised his cup, and Carl raised his in response. After they drank, Jack looked at him thoughtfully and said, "You know, you could hit the trail with me, one more time. Come to California and strike it rich! Buy yourself as much land as you want, and never have to lift a finger or saddle a horse again, as long as you live! The newspapers are full of tales, of men just filling their pockets with gold nuggets the size of marbles, and . . ."

For one moment of blazing temptation which he would never admit to a single soul, Carl actually considered it, considered saddling Three-Socks and rolling up his single rough Mexican blanket and following Jack into the wilderness of the Staked Plain, dust and danger and the exhilaration of single-minded purpose. "We're away in the morning," Jack added, "but we could delay a day or so, if you need to square your business affairs, here."

Like a small imp magicked into existence to take that temptation away, Johann appeared by the table where he and Jack sat, with Hansi looming large and worried behind him.

"Opa and Doctor Keidel say for you to come home now," Johann said earnestly. "The baby is born." Magda. He had not thought of Magda for a whole three or four minutes. He sprang up, relief and guilt and worry pouring over him like a waterfall and Jack looked at him with very real concern, saying:

"What is it... what happened?"

Of course, Jack didn't speak German, he wouldn't have understood. With an effort, Carl forced his mind onto the track of English.

"The child . . . the child is born. I'm sorry, Jack. I must go to my wife." The temptation which Jack had put before him vanished like mist in the morning sun; he thought that Jack nodded at him with a look of understanding.

"Of course . . . a toast, then. To you and your family, and your contentment here, always."

"And to yours . . . and your good fortune in California . . . and your safe journey there!" Jack and Carl hastily struck their cups against each other's, and Carl gulped the dregs of his beer. Had he already gotten onto the third, whilst talking to Jack? "Take care of yourself on the trail, since I'm not there at your back." he added, awkwardly.

"I'll do that," Jack raised his cup again. "You do the same." And he added very softly, "Remember Goliad." There were ten years of memories in mind besides Goliad though, beginning on a day in Columbia, when two boys first came seeking for a place in Colonel

Smith's ranger company and one lent the other a good carbine, sizing him up for a good man to serve with.

"Every day of my life," Carl answered, in the same tone. Ten years of comradeship and service, with a brother made by choice and not the chance of blood was not so easy to set aside. "Goodbye, Jack."

"See to your wife," Jack touched his fingers to his hat-brim in a casual salute. "What are you waiting for, then?"

Johann and Hansi fell in on either side, as he hurried through the taproom, past Charley who nodded and called as they passed him, carrying another tray of mugs, "I'll send you something to wet the little one's head with, later!"

"Thanks," he answered distractedly and then they were out on the street, with Hansi puffing at his heels and Johann practically running in his efforts to keep up with the men.

"What did they say about her!?" Carl demanded of Johann, "Did they say anything at all?"

"No!" Johann gasped. "No, they just told me the baby had come and for me to run to Charley's and bring you back. I didn't stop to ask Vati anything else."

Down Main, towards the coffee-mill dome of the Verein-Church and a sudden unbidden memory of Margaretha came to him, of her veiled in white lace, and her fingers feeling like ice in his hands as he slid the heavy gold ring onto her third finger. Her fingers had felt cold today, too, when they sent him away. He walked faster, telling himself that Vati himself would have come if she were in danger. He walked even faster, half running by the time he reached Market Square and swung around the corner.

The front door of Vati's house swung open at a touch; Johann must have left it unlatched. The cheerful voices of children floated in from the back. Obscurely in that instant his mind was relived, for they could not sound so happy if there was death within the house.

Vati's welcomed him, "Carl, my son, come and meet your son!"

It seemed as if he couldn't take a breath, as if something had suddenly walloped him over the head, and the world suddenly burst into a thousand colors of light, of light and wonder and joy.

Vati stood by the unlit fire in the parlor, holding a white-wrapped bundle in his arms, a bundle which stirred just the slightest bit. His own cheeks were sentimentally wet, but he beamed happily at Carl and added, "A fine little boy, and very good-tempered! I think he has the look of a philosopher. Don't you think so, Altmueller?"

"I think he looks like a baby," Pastor Altmueller harrumphed, "and one who will be hungry, soon. But I agree—you have been blessed by our own Father with a very fine little boy."

"And wet, as well," Liesel added. She hovered protectively at Vati's elbow. She looked disheveled and sweaty, her dress-sleeves rolled to the elbow but she had put on a clean apron. She smiled reassuringly at Carl as he asked, urgently:

"What about Margaretha?"

"Very tired, but fine. Doctor Keidel gave her a tiny bit of laudanum in milk to help her rest. She'll want to see you, of course."

"Here," Vati made as if to hand the baby to him. "Take him upstairs to his mother, why don't you? My dear Hannah couldn't bear to have her children taken very far away, no matter how tired she was afterwards, I hardly see that Magda could be any different."

With a look of fond exasperation fairly split between the two of them, Liesel commanded, "Just bend your arm like so . . . there. Vati, give the baby to him. Don't look so panicked, Brother Carl, they are not made of glass. Just be sure to support his little head and shoulders always. Hold him close, or he'll think you're going to drop him."

"Never," Carl stammered. The child was heavier than he thought, a solid and compact lump. He looked down at the baby's face. His own son, his and Magda's firstborn child, and realized to his astonishment that the baby was looking back at him. He was instantly entranced, completely smitten, and Liesel gently shoved him in the direction of the stairs.

"Go, Brother Carl . . . take him to Magda."

It felt to him that he wandered in a fog, up the stairs and into the small hallway on the second floor, barely aware of a breathless Johann and Hansi coming in through the front door down below and of the happy babble of children in the garden: Hansi's own small sons, of Anna and Rosalie shrieking as Friedrich pushed Rosalie ever higher on the wooden-seated swing. Children . . . and now he and Magda had one of their own, to add to the throng; a fat little mite with squarely solid Saxon features absurdly like his own, and blue eyes which held an expression of mixed puzzlement and wonder. One wandering little arm worked loose of the wrappings he was swaddled in, a tiny fist barely the size of his own thumb. Carl tentatively pushed open the bedroom door at the top of the stairs; it was ominously quiet within.

Magda lay motionless and nearly flat in the center of the bed, with the sheet drawn up to her shoulders. She looked as pale as a wax-work, except for bruised-looking circles under her eyes. Her left hand, the one with her wedding-ring on it, lay slack outside the covers, her fingers-half curled. Mrs. Schmidt rose from the rocking chair next to the bed, whispering, "She's just dozed off. But she'll wake in a bit, when this fine fellow wants a little supper. I'll be downstairs for a while, if you need any help."

"No, I don't think so," Carl answered, still in a daze. "Thank you, thank all of you."

Mrs. Schmidt went tiptoe and kissed his cheek very gently,

"My blessing on all of you then; he's a dear little chap. I'm sure he'll grow up and made both of you proud." She closed the door softly behind her, as Carl sank into the rocking chair. He hardly dared touch Magda, fearing to wake her, so he sat with the baby on his arm and they admired each other. He touched the baby's fist with one gentle finger. The soft and boneless little starfish hand closed on it with an astonishing grip: such a tiny perfect little hand, every fingernail an exquisite miniature. Blue eyes, nearly the same color as his own, were fixed vaguely on his face and the tiny pink rosebud mouth pursed and blew a bubble of spit. And he wasn't bald, as had appeared at first; the baby had hair so pale and fine it was all but invisible. He felt a rush of impossible affection; where had it come from, this sudden fierce love for this wondrously new creature, knit from his and Magda's own bone and flesh?

"You have the silliest expression on your face," said Magda, in a thready, exhausted whisper. She was awake, her head turned to one side to look at the two of them, but she was smiling herself. "So . . .

what do you think of our son? I suppose you still want to call him Rudolph?"

"He's perfect, every finger and toe of him," Carl answered, with delight. "And unless you have an objection . . ."

"No . . . as long as we can give him Vati's name, too." Her eyes drooped closed, for a moment, before she added. "I am so tired. I feel like I have been trampled by a cow. Several cows."

"Liesel and Mrs. Schmidt said you should rest."

He stood up awkwardly, with the precious and unaccustomed weight of their son as she whispered, "Don't go. They can't possibly make you go away now. I am so very tired, but if I close my eyes, I'm afraid you'll not be there when I open them."

"Shhusssh, then," he answered, as he set the baby down on the bed next to her, where her arm could curl sweetly around him. "Here's the baby, then. Sleep if you need to, I'll be here." And with that, he carefully lay on his side, down on the bed next to her, on top of the covers, with the baby settled between them, and his arm curving protectively over both.

She sighed a deep sigh of utter contentment and turned her head against his shoulder, whispering, "I want to go home, hearts-love. To our home."

"As soon as we can," he answered, "All of us together."

And the thought of golden California, and all those temptations went glimmering out of his mind; he had no need of them, for all he wanted in this life was in his reach.

Finale: Fourth of July, 1853

Letter from Christian Friedrich Steinmetz, of Friedrichsburg, Texas to Simon Frankenthaler, goldsmith of the city of Ulm, written in the first week of July, 1853

My Dear Simon, I send to you the most happy greetings from my family to yours! I should let you know I wish to hear from you as often as you may write, and your letters to me are received with happy anticipation. To give an honest and complete account of our lives would necessitate me writing to you three or four letters to every one of yours! My business continues to prosper, and the children—the boys and little Rosalie—thrive! I considered your advice as regards additional sundry stock in my shop... which I think I might do, as soon as I have a little more profit. There have been so many new settlers to the county; Friedrichsburg is the crown of the district, amid a constellation of smaller villages. Do not think that we do nothing but labor unceasingly at workbench or plough; we have created our own diversions! Between the City Club and the Sangerbund, Mr. Nimitz' little "Casino" and other revels, we enjoy sufficient diversion from the rigors of life as a settler in a new country!

This week we celebrated the 4th of July in a grand style. Son Hansi and his family and their neighbors from Live Oak Mill joined together and paraded into town on horseback and in many wagons, with a beautifully embroidered banner at their head. They were joined as they approached Friedrichsburg by others from the outlaying district around, and rode in proper order to the Market Square, where they were greeted by the City Club members, with music and many cheers. A little later, the people from the northern settlements arrived, carrying a beautiful Texas flag! This had a large five-pointed star with the words "Club of the Backwoodsmen" embroidered all around. The flag bearer was dressed in a blue denim shirt and trousers, which all agreed was an excellent representation of a true backwoodsman, although Son Carl looked very amused. A welcoming speech was given and then the procession moved *through our city. First the club presidents, then the musicians on a long wagon, then the flag-bearer with the flag of the Live Oak club leading their member, then the City Club flag and their members and the backwoodsmen.*

Everyone was mounted on horseback—or in wagons; a huge parade which made much dust, before we proceeded to an open meadow some few miles away. Many other people had assembled there, for it had all been planned beforehand. We formed a great square, while the Declaration of Independence was read in English first, and then in German. We set up tents, more than thirty of them, where families served refreshments to their friends. The shooting club held a target-shooting match and there was an orchestra for the young people to dance. At odd times during the day there were more shooting matches, foot-races and jumping matches. The winners had to pay for wine, which was enjoyed very much by all. In the afternoon there were more speeches, and after that a grand polonaise.

This happy revelry lasted until nearly sunrise the next morning, when we all drank hot coffee. It was a most congenial gathering; you may be sure, a meet and proper celebration of the anniversary of our new country. In the main and in spite of the tragedies that attended my journey here, I am glad and grateful to have been afforded the chance to see my children and grandchildren build a free and prosperous future.

Your old friend,
C.F. Steinmetz

Historical Notes:
On the Mainzer Adelsverein, Rangers and other Texiana

Of the people in this novel, those members of the Steinmetz and Becker families are characters created by the author, although some of their foibles and characteristics may be based upon people that I knew personally, or historical figures that I read about. Pastor Altmueller and Mrs. Helene are also made up, as are the Brown family, Porfirio and Trap Talmadge.

Just about everyone else whose name is mentioned is real, although in some cases, their character and exploits are so fantastic, so larger than life as to invite suspicion that they are an invention as well. But they were all real, beginning with the Ranger captain Jack Hays, who astounded contemporaries who met him for the first time, knowing only of his reputation as one of the finest irregular soldiers of the frontier. He did indeed look about fifteen years old for much of the first third of his adult life. The Texas Rangers at this time were iteration halfway between being the elite law-enforcement body which they have become, and what they were in the early days in Texas—which was a heavily armed and mounted Neighborhood Watch. Under Hays' captaincy, they became more than just the local mounted volunteer militia, called up on a moments' notice to respond to a lightening fast raid on their settlement or town by Indians or cross-border bandits. They took to patrolling the backcountry, looking for a fight and hoping to forestall raids before they happened, or failing that, to track down raiding parties and recover loot and captives.

There was only one abortive attempt to have them wear uniforms. Ranger volunteers provided their own weapons and horses, and usually their own rations, although the State of Texas did supply ammunition. They were famously unscathed by anything resembling proper military discipline and polish, as the regular Army would discover to their horror during the Mexican War. A contemporary newspaper caricature of a typical 'Texas Ranger" featured a hairy and ragged creature resembling "Cousin It", slumped on a horse and wearing a belt stuffed all the way around with knives and pistols.Just about every healthy, able male in Texas from the time of the War for Independence served as a ranger in one way or another. They all knew each other, seemingly, and they all knew Jack Hays, although he was in Texas for only thirteen years. He was the Kevin Bacon of the Texas Republic. William "Big Foot" Wallace, Sam and Mary Maverick, Jinny, Hans Rahm, Jim Shaw and Robert Neighbors—all these too were real people.

This is the milieu of the character Carl Becker. A note about his nickname "Dutch"; that was the common American terminology regarding "Deutch" or German immigrants. The Pennsylvania Dutch are still termed thus, in spite of being actually German Anabaptists.

Another historical note; after the Irish, German immigrants were the largest European minority immigrant community in the years before the Civil War. German settlers were well established in the colonies; historians estimate that although they were about a twelfth of the overall population, they formed an eighth of George Washington's Revolutionary Army. The Reverend John Peter Muhlenburg preached a fiery Sunday sermon in favor of revolution to his congregation, and then theatrically took off his clerical robe to reveal a Continental Army officers' uniform underneath, and asked for volunteers. He eventually raised a regiment, and led them with distinction. There might even have been some thought given to making German one of the languages of the new republic.

Following upon the collapse of the Mainzer Adelsverein, the failure of the 1848 Revolution in Germany sent another tidal-wave of educated, politically active German immigrants to the United States. German-born and the descendents of German settlers were the largest ethnic component of the Civil War era Union Army—only the Irish came anywhere close. For over two and a half centuries German settlers were a significant presence in the upper mid-west, in Pennsylvania, in Texas and the West.

A lot of what is stereotypically thought to be typically German virtues—hard work, thrift, self-improvement, tidiness—are also seen as American virtues, at least in flyover country.

John Meusebach was real, and so was his peace treaty with the Penateka Comanche. The treaty is held today as one that was never broken, although by the time of the Civil War and it's aftermath, other Comanche tribes and bands of Kiowa and Apache were raiding so enthusiastically among the Hill Country settlers, that one might be forgiven for thinking that a peace treaty with the native Indian tribes was—if not broken, then considerably dented. The speeches made at John Meusebach's peace talks are paraphrases of a near-contemporary account of it .Prince Karl of Solms-Braunfels also was real. He did indeed tour through parts of Texas with a considerable entourage, as described, including two valets to help him on with his trousers. The collapse of the Mainzer Adelsverein land-grant scheme in Texas came about pretty much for the reasons that Charley Nimitz explained to Magda. I have used the original names for the present-day towns of Fredericksburg and New Braunfels—as they were referred to by the settlers who originally founded them.

Charley Nimitz; of all these characters in this book which were based upon real people, he is the most fully-fleshed. In real life, he was the grandfather of Admiral Chester Nimitz; he would have never courted Magda Vogel, since she is a made-up character! The hotel that he founded still stands on Fredericksburg's Main Street, and has been restored to look like a steamboat. He was, by all accounts, notorious for pranks, jokes and tall tales. My imagination took creative liberties with what I read of him. If any of his descendents are offended by this portrayal, than I apologize profoundly.

Many of the other appearances by real people in this volume— the Lochte family, the other early settlers in Friedrichsburg, Neu Braunfels and Karlshaven (which would become Indianola), the Verein soldiers and bureaucrats—are quick sketches of a personality, based on the name of someone known historically to have been at the right time and in the right place, of the right age and having an appropriate background. The final account, of the 4th of July celebration is a paraphrase, taken from a contemporary letter written by C.H. Guenther.

> *If we shadows have offended,*
> *Think but this, and all is mended,*
> *That you have but slumber'd here*
> *While these visions did appear.*
> *And this weak and idle theme,*
> *No more yielding but a dream!*

Wm. Shakespeare, A Midsummer Night's Dream Act 5, Scene 1

Celia Hayes.
San Antonio, 2008

Special Bonus – From Adelsverein: The Sowing

Book 2 of the Adelsverein Trilogy

The adventure continues, with the coming of the Civil War: Murder, war and the notorious "hanging-band" stalk the Hill Country settlements. Magda and Carl, Liesel and Hansi, their brothers and their children have built successful farms and lives – but they are Unionists in a Confederate state.

Chapter One: *Fire in the Night*

"When I came to think back on that matter," said Magda Vogel Becker to her daughter and her great-grandchildren, many years later, "I realized that there had been omens. Your father and I did not see such at the time. All we knew on that morning in summer was John Hunter, on a wearied horse, riding up from the river."

"Mr. Hunter, who was the country clerk for so many years?" Magda's daughter asked.

Magda nodded regally. "The very same, Lottie. He kept a store, like Mr. Specht and Mr. Ransleben . . . no, no Marie," she added sternly to the youngest of Lottie's grandchildren, "Manners, child. Don't tease Mouse. He has teeth and a bad temper."

Mouse the Pekinese only rolled his bulgy eyes upwards at his mistress adoringly from where he lay on his cushion at her feet, amidst the children. He was the fourth of those bearing that name, taking up the mission peculiar to their breed, of being a constant and attentive companion. Marie instantly left off toying with the long fringes of Mouse's ears. She and her brothers and cousins went in terrible awe and worship of their formidable great-grandmother, a tall and straight-backed old woman, who always wore dresses of an old-fashioned style but cut of fine materials in the black of deepest mourning. Oma Magda's bodice fastened up the front with a line of sparkly jet buttons to a high collar at her throat; narrow sleeves buttoned down to her wrists and long skirts brushed the toes of her shoes. *Her hair, still thick and the color of iron, was coiffed by her maid every morning, who pinned a snowy lace and lawn house cap over the complicated weaving of Oma Magda's long braid into a knot that tilted her head slightly back. She spoke with a heavy accent, even after more than half a century in her adopted country.*

She was a being utterly unlike anyone else they knew, completely fascinating, a person from another lifetime entirely. They had never known terror, want, or sudden murder but Great Grandma Becker, their Oma Magda: she did. She was a pioneer and almost the last of the oldest generation, save for her niece Oma Anna, nearly twenty years younger. Marie's older brother Will and some of the boy cousins insisted that Oma Magda still carried a pistol in her valise on those rare occasions when she left the suite of rooms where she lived in her daughter's brightly-painted mansion on Turner Street, as if this was not already the twentieth century! On this day, with Oma Magda being in such in a mood to tell stories, the boys were wild with curiosity about the Confederate cavalry saber that hung over the door of her sitting-room. Oma Magda had never explained how it had come into her possession, only that it belonged to someone who had been a friend to her husband, long ago.

The children had all been raised in comfort and plenty, speaking English and sent to good schools, to cotillion and music lessons. But they prized above all else those rare times when Oma Magda could be brought to tell stories of the early days, of the empty lands and the Llano Estacada, of Indians and cattle-drives, of raging rivers and heroes, of escapes and war. Marie and her brothers, their cousins and second-cousins all agreed that it was much, much better than the nickelodeon. But of all that fund of stories there was one that Magda Vogel Becker would never tell to the children: that of a day on a street under a tree by Charley Nimitz' hotel and a corpse in the dust at her feet.

"I was in the stillroom, pouring milk into pans, so the cream could rise to the top, when I heard the dogs barking at someone coming up the hill. My husband called to me . . . "

Hearing the dogs barking in the way they had for strangers coming up the hill towards the Becker house, Magda came up the stone steps from the cellar with the empty milk can in her hand. Her baby son fussed from his little pen in the corner, standing on sturdy fat legs, while he gripped the top of the pen. He had been christened Rudolph after her husband's older brother. Rudi, dead in the massacre at Goliad fourteen years before, cut down as he shouted at his brother to run towards the river. Magda and her husband had come to an unvoiced agreement to use the diminutive of Dolph for the baby, rather than the name by which his brother had been known, which Carl Becker still called out in nightmares now and again.

She picked up her son, and went to look out of the tall window that looked down the hill towards the green river in the shallow valley beyond. The shutters stood open to catch the cool morning breeze. From the walled orchard below, her husband put down his shovel, digging it into the mound of dirt by the hole in the ground where a small apple tree was to go, and called up to her,

"Who is it, Margaretha?"

Carl Becker was Saxon-fair, a tall even-tempered man who had lived in Texas for all of his life, having been brought as a small child when it was still part of Mexico. He and Magda had married two years before and come to his land-holding on the Guadalupe River, where he ran a few cattle for the market in San Antonio and yearly planted just enough corn to mill for his household needs. He also had ambitious plans for an orchard: walled with stone on the northwest-facing slope below the stone house with the birds-nest carved over the door.

"I'm not sure." From the window Magda could see over the fledgling orchard and its sheltering wall, to the track which wound up long rise from where it branched from the road that ran east and west along the river-bank, past Carl's fields and around the back of the house, into the farmyard. A man rode up from the river, a man whose horse stumbled as if it were weary, head drooping. But as he approached the house, Magda recognized him. "It is John Hunter; from town. He looks tired. You had best make yourself decent for company, my heart."

"I suppose I should," Her husband smiled up at her and took up his shirt from where it lay on the grass next to the young apple tree. As he pulled the coarse cloth over his head, she caught a glimpse of the tangled web of scars on his left shoulder; a memento of a skirmish with a Mexican lancer before Monterray and still livid after four years. That wound had almost killed him. He was a long while recovering and when he was fit again, that war was nearly over and his final enlistment with Jack Hays' Rangers a thing of the past. "You haven't seen Trap, have you?"

"Not since breakfast," Magda answered. Trap Talmadge, who helped Carl run his farm, had taken the light wagon to a nearby cedar thicket to cut poles to repair a fence. Meanwhile, Porfirio the Mexican stockman, young Nate Brown and Magda's younger brother Friedrich had gone off on horseback along the river, searching for mother cows with Carl's brand on them, to mark their calves. They had taken food and blankets, expecting to be several days at it.

Now John Hunter was close to the house, near enough to draw rein while the dogs romped and clamored at a safe distance from his horses' hoofs. "Hello! Becker! Anyone at home?"

"Mr. Hunter," Magda called from the window, "We are here. What brings you so far from town? What has happened?" Down below in the orchard, Carl had picked up his shovel and was walking toward the small gate which gave into the farmyard, next to the house.

"Nothing good," John Hunter answered, grimly.

Carl called out to him, "Come around to the yard. Put your horse in the corral, and tell us what has been going on."

"They've burnt my store," John Hunter said as he nudged his horse forwards. Standing still by the overlooking window, Magda gasped: John Hunter's store was on the corner of Main and Market Street, a short way from her father's house and workshop in Friedrichsburg. Before her marriage, she walked past it often; a long log house with many additions at the back, for John Hunter did much business with friendly Indians, and the soldiers at the fort, as well as the German settlers in the district. Her arms tightened on Dolph. He squirmed, whimpering unhappily.

The men were out of sight now, but she could hear their voices outside: her husband's quiet and level, un-hurried as always. They spoke in English, which she could follow, even though she was still not comfortable speaking herself. John Hunter's voice sounded tense even agitated, for he was a hot-tempered and impulsive man. But losing a home and place of business was a thing which would fray at anyone's good nature. Magda gave her son a hard-baked rusk for him to chew on and amuse himself while in his little pen and busied herself setting out plates. John Hunter would be hungry, if he had ridden all the way from Friedrichsburg. She had bread, pickles, a pot of home-made cheese, dried-apple pie, cold smoked ham and sausages and preserves made from the agarita berries. She thought for a moment, and opened a box of store crackers.

She heard the men's footsteps in the hallway, as she set out the plate of sliced cold sausage. Trap and Carl had butchered a large pig the previous fall which had fed them all winter. This was the last of the sausage they had smoked themselves; Magda would not mind if they ate it all, for they had not the right spices at the time of sausage-making and she insisted that it tasted odd. Carl and John both looked to have washed up at the water-trough by the corral, but John Hunter still had black sooty streaks on his boots and trouser-legs. Even a quick scrub couldn't erase the lines of exhaustion on his face or the blue shadows under his eyes. As they came into the kitchen, he was saying over his shoulder to Carl, "...records lost, all of them! The mob wouldn't even let Mr. Wahrmund and the others get them out, before they fired the building!"

"What of Sophie? Is she safe?" Magda suddenly recollected that John had finally married pretty Sophie Ahrens, and that they lived in back of the store. "Where is she? And my family, what of them?"

"With her mother," John smiled wearily, "Everyone is safe, that I know of. It was only me they were after! Bless you, Mrs. Magda - I didn't know until now that I was hungry. I sent her away as soon as the trouble started. After what happened the last time I had trouble with drunken soldiers from the fort, I thought any risk ought to be on my head, not hers."

"Sit, sit," Magda urged him, "Who burned your store and what risk is this?"

"And do you think anyone followed after you?" Carl added, quietly. He and John sat down at the table, and Magda finished slicing bread. Dolph fussed to be let out, and Magda took him onto her lap and listened to the men.

"No, I don't think so. Can't be sure though. There were a lot of folk in town," John wolfed the food that Magda has set on his plate. "I came away first thing in the morning. Charley Nimitz hid me at his place. He found my horses wandering in the fields above Creek Street."

"How did it start?" Carl asked quietly. John looked sideways at Magda with Dolph in her arms and said carefully, "A soldier from the fort came to the store. I was in the back, taking stock when he came in. He had some friends with him, they were drunk too, but this particular one was much farther gone. He wanted Sophie to sell him more whiskey. She told him no. I came in from the back and told him no again. Then he got ugly. Frightened Sophie pretty bad and then he said…" From the look on John's face, Magda thought the soldier must have said something truly insulting; one of those things that men did not say to women, something that John did not want to even repeat literally in front of another woman. Finally, he said, "He spoke of my wife—to her face, mind you—as if she were a commodity in my store and asked the price."

"Ah," Remarked Carl Becker, in complete comprehension. Magda looked from John's face to his. Her husband had a little of that cold, alert look to him, the expression she had only seen once or twice. For many years he had been a soldier or a ranger, accustomed to dealing in death and casual violence. "What did you hit him with, then?"

"My fist," John answered, "At first. But he drew a knife, and he had his friends at his back. He came at me." John moved his shoulders uneasily, in a sort of shrug, "I took it away from him easily enough and his friends tried to drag him away. But then he broke away from them and jumped on me again and in the melee…" John sighed, "The knife finished up stuck into his chest. Mind you, I think he was dead before he hit the floor. His friends carried him away and I sent for the sheriff."

"It sounds like it was a fair fight," Carl observed.

John nodded, "So it was and there were enough witnesses on my side of it to win an acquittal in a court of law. But a bunch of soldiers from the fort came looking for me that night, 'long with some other toughs. They smashed up the store and set fire to the stock inside. There was enough shooting and hollering to wake the town and everyone else came to see what was happening, of course. The soldiers wouldn't let anyone through to put out the fire, or even let them take away the records," John sighed, wearily, "They were looking close at every man's face, searching for me. It sent them wild, when they didn't find me at the store. Charley had me lay up at his place. His idea, he said they might know where to find Sophie's family, wouldn't be safe for them, if I went there, too. It was a wild night, Becker, men with guns patrolling all over town. The Army is supposed to protect us against the Indians, but who will protect the town against the Army?"

"The law will, if their officers don't. It still doesn't sound good," Carl said, grimly. He had lived in Friedrichsburg long enough to think of it as his town, full of his friends and Magda's kinfolk. "What do you plan?"

"I honest to God don't know," John said, "Except lay up for a while, out of town. Swear to God, if it weren't for Sophie not wanting to leave her family and the humiliation of being run out of town by the blue-coat boys, I'd give a thought to selling up and leaving for good. Charley told me the next morning that there were some tough-looking customers asking after me, all over town. And not in a way that indicated concern for my health, you know, less'n tar and feathers are a patent nostrum, these days." He grinned fleetingly, as if he had just been reminded of something amusing, "I will say this for our folk, Becker—they've clammed right up. As of yesterday morning, there wasn't a soul in town who understood English, if it was a stranger asking questions." He looked at his plate in astonishment, for it was entirely empty.

"Please, eat as much as you wish to," Magda urged him, "I do not let anyone go hungry from our table. Help yourself to as much as you please. You are our guest."

John Hunter helped himself to more bread, and pickles and ham, saying, "Thank you, ma'am. This is first-rate. I haven't eaten so well since the last dinner my wife set before me." He looked at Carl and added, "Nothing like a Dutchwoman for setting a fine table. I'm flat amazed there aren't more like you and I, paying court to the women who came out here with the Verein settlers."

"They have watchful brothers and fathers," Carl answered. He and Magda exchanged a private look of wry amusement. Dolph wriggled mightily and set up a fuss. He wanted down from her lap, but before Magda moved to put him back in his pen, Carl added, "I'll take him— come to Papa, little man." He scooped up his son, lifting him high above his own head.

Magda said severely, "You spoil him! How will he learn proper manners, when you play games like that at the table?"

"He's a baby," Carl answered serenely, "He doesn't need manners yet." He bounced Dolph energetically on his knee and gave him another rusk. The baby settled onto his father's lap, chewing messily and happily. Magda was teased again into smiling at the sight of them. The likeness between them was so marked, it was comic: the same sturdy features and fair hair, the same sky-colored blue eyes, even the expression of mild amusement in them. Dolph adored his father and Carl made much of his baby son. He thought nothing of taking him out into the yard and setting him on the back of his horse. Dolph clutched Three-Socks' mane in his little hands, his baby-dress rucked up almost to his diapers and his fat little legs drumming against the horses' withers, while Three-Socks took no more notice of the child than he would a flea.

"You'll have him riding a horse, before he can even walk by himself?" Magda had remonstrated.

Carl replied, "Not such a bad thing, in this country."

Now John Hunter looked across the table, saying, "That's a fine little youngster you got there,"

Carl looked ridiculously pleased. "He'll be out of the cradle and into the saddle in no time at all. We need another hand around the place, don't we, son?" Dolph gurgled agreeably and his father returned to the business at hand. "Thinking on your problem then—I guess you're planning to stay away from town for a while, until feelings calm down?"

"Not for too long," John Hunter sighed, "I've got a business to run and I'm an elected official, besides. I've got responsibilities..."

"So, you need to make sure you're covered on the flank," Carl chewed thoughtfully on a mouthful of bread and sausage and moved his plate out of Dolph's reach. "No, not for you, son. Stay here and rest up for a day or so and then I think you ought to go to Bexar, into San Antone. Go to the magistrate there and surrender. At least, go through the legal forms and serve notice that it was self-defense. And..." he brightened, as if he had just thought of a particularly good idea, "Go talk to Sam Maverick, first. He's a lawyer, but he used to ride with me in Jack Hays' company. Tell him I sent you, that you're a friend of mine. They're back in Bexar now. Look for a large house on Houston Street by the Plaza. He'll see you right."

John Hunter already looked more cheerful, as Carl outlined this plan. "I like it," John mused. "I suppose it's just far enough away from the hotheads. I can complain to the Army, too, while I'm at it. Damn it—sorry, Mrs. Magda—things are at a pretty pass, when the scum of the barracks can run a man out of his own town." Out in the farmyard, one of the dogs barked but not in the urgent way that they barked at strangers. This was someone they knew. She got up and looked out the window; Trap Talmadge, driving a wagon loaded with cedar fence-poles.

"Not for long," Carl answered cheerfully, "They'll calm down right enough, but just in case, I'll send my foreman with you. He used to ride with Jack as well. If anyone is still looking for you, they won't get past Trap Talmadge. He's about three-parts wild-cat and as wily as they come. Spend the night with us, rest yourself and your horse, and set off in the morning."

"'Preciate the hospitality," John answered gratefully. "Can't tell you how much it means, having a place to rest up and think."

"Any time," Carl said, and tucking his son under his arm, he went out to the farmyard to tell Trap what was going on.

That night, as John Hunter slept the sleep of the exhausted in the guest bedroom, Magda and her husband lay together in bed and talked quietly. The window shutters again stood half-open, letting in an occasional breath of cool air. Such a strange country, Magda thought. Even after six summers in it, she still found it strange that the hottest time of the day was in the late afternoon, not when the sun stood high overhead at noon. And her husband put no credence in the dangers of night air. *"How could that be, since I have slept outside more often than not, and never taken any hurt from it?"* Sleep did not always come readily, when the day's heat lingered after sunset, and her shift stuck to her by sweat. Tonight she thought her husband seemed very quiet.

Presently, she rolled onto her side, and asked, "You are worried about the boys, out looking for our calves?"

He was a long while answering, as was his habit; not a hasty man was Carl Becker, but one who considered his answers carefully. "No," he answered at last, "Not the boys. Porfirio's a good man, and Nate was raised in these parts. The neighbors around here, they're all good folk, apart from Waldrip and his friends. The boys have nothing to fear but maybe an angry mama cow…"

"Then more trouble for John Hunter?" she asked again, and he smiled at her, reassuringly.

"No, he'll have no trouble, once the hot-heads calm down. Their officers will see to that. There may be places in Texas where you can raise an angry mob at the drop of a hat but Friedrichsburg probably isn't one of them. Your Verein-folk take a lot to get their dander up."

An owl hooted in the darkness outside. Carl half sat up, leaning on an elbow and listening. In a moment, he swung his feet to the floor and padded silently towards the window. Magda watched him, silhouetted against the star-strewn sky outside, standing in the darkness a little back from the window-frame, as wary as a wild animal himself. In the heat of summer he slept naked for comfort, like an Indian. The owl hooted again, and Carl relaxed in some infinitesimal way; he must have seen the owl flying. When he returned to the bed, lying down next to her, he said,

"I'm just calculating the odds on Trap being tempted into going on a spree when he gets into Bexar. I'll need him back here, not passed out in a ditch or locked up in the calaboose."

"How did you come to hire him, knowing that he drinks?" Magda asked, for it had long been a sore point. Surely her husband could hire a more reliable man than a broken-down old Ranger sergeant, even if he was a friend.

"Most men drink," Carl answered quietly, "They get a little merry, raise a little ruckus and have a sore head in the morning. But for some of them, they can't stop. It's like a sickness, they can't help themselves. Sometimes they are strong enough to be able to quit entirely. General Sam was one of those." He laughed a little and Magda felt him roll onto his side, stirring the bedclothes a little. It was too hot to sleep comfortably curled into each other but his hand strayed across her shoulder, down to gently cup her breast. It was his way when they slept, to be always touching her as if for reassurance. "He was a legendary drunk before he married. He boarded at my sisters' once, but she threw him out, the morning after he went on a spree and took it into his head to chop down the bedposts with an ax. No one had an idea why he did that, himself least of all. Margaret was furious, though."

Margaret, Carl's formidable older sister, ruled over a sprawling household in Austin, which included her second husband, four sons and a vast collection of boarders, who tended to be grave and sober businessmen, leavened with legislators and lawyers.

"It was her house, she had a perfect right," Magda said, indignant on her sister-in-laws behalf.

"So she did," Carl agreed, "And when he sobered up, I expect he was the first to apologize. As for Trap—he's all right, as long as he's at work. He was all right on a long scout; the best there could be, but whenever we came back to town, I don't think Trap drew a sober breath until we saddled up to ride out again." He sighed, adding, "It was just the way it was. And then he got banged up for good and all, wasn't fit to enlist again. I saw him in a tavern in Bexar, didn't hardly recognize him. Sam told he was still around, and in a bad way. That was the year after I went into the Llano with Meusebach. I was buying the things that Berg needed so's he could build this house."

"What did you do? What did you say to him?" Magda asked. That was also the year that he had courted her, had decided to settle on this land and plant an apple orchard. When he answered, she could tell by the sound of his voice that he was smiling, "He was in a tavern and stinking drunk—not so far gone that he couldn't talk, or not recognize me. He looked up and said, *'Damned if it isn't Dutch Becker. Don't you have a home to go to, boy?'* and I said *'As a matter of fact, I do. I'm going to it this very minute and you're coming with me.'* And then I picked him up by his collar and belt and threw him into the back of the wagon." He chuckled, and added, "Three days for him to sober up enough to say yes, when I asked if he would work for me. He's back-slid a couple of times, nothing serious. If Porfirio and the boys were back, I'd go with him, make sure he stays out of trouble, but you'd be here alone with the baby and I won't have that."

"Mr. Talmadge is a man grown," Magda said, sternly, "You should not have to watch after him like that."

"No?" Carl sighed, "He watched after me and Jack too, when we were both as green as the grass on our first enlistment with Smith's company. I always thought I owed him something—for keeping us from killing ourselves out of sheer reckless stupidity, if nothing else."

"If he cannot guard himself from the drink, what can you do?" Magda asked. "You give him work, a place to live and some kind of purpose. If that is not enough, then it is not enough. Temptation will always be there; he will fall to it every time if he cannot make himself walk away, like your General Sam did."

"Maybe it will be enough," Carl said, but Magda thought he sounded more hopeful than sure of it.

Early the next morning, John Hunter and Trap rode away, along the river towards the shallows and the fording place where the road between Friedrichsburg and San Antonio crossed over. If Carl had a concern about Trap going on a spree, he didn't voice it. On the day following, Porfirio and the boys returned from a calf-roundup farther along the river; dirty, exuberant, and ravenously hungry.

"Twenty-seven," Porfirio reported, as he and Nate and Friedrich turned their horses into the small corral, inside the palisade that connected all the farm buildings together, while Magda gathered eggs in the henhouse enclosure, and listened to her twelve-year old brother chatter excitedly about his adventure, working cattle with the older boys. "Over two days, Señor Becker. I t'ink if we went another day, we would not find any more. They are all close to the river, now that the grass is green in the valley."

"Should be upwards of forty new calves this year," Carl said, thoughtfully. "And all along the river in the usual places for this time of year. I just thought you'd find more than that. When Mr. Talmadge gets back, maybe we should try searching a little further up the river."

"Where is Señor Talmadge, then?" Porfirio asked, with no particular curiosity.

Carl answered, "Running an errand, down to Bexar... he'll be back in a couple of days."

"There is one t'ing," Porfirio uneasily turned his hat around in his hands, "Somet'ing you should know. I did not say to Fredi, but I think Nate saw too. We found two calves, all alone. Their tongues had been split so they could not nurse."

Carl Becker looked very grave; he knew why that was done as well as Porfirio, and what it meant as far as his herd was concerned. "How long ago had it been done?" He asked.

Porfirio shrugged, "Long enough to heal, but not yet long enough to come back and brand. An' before you ask, Señor. I have not seen any new brands, or more than 'dere should be of the old ones."

Carl nodded, a decision made. "Good... then we will go farther up the river, and look for more calves... and soon. Someone's playing a dirty game, and I'm damned if I'll let them get away with it, not at my expense. I'll let the Browns know, too."

"What did he mean?" Magda asked, "About the calves?" as Porfirio tipped his hat respectfully to them both and sauntered away towards the cabin where the hands lived, and which Friedrich had insisted on sharing with them.

"Someone is fixing it so the calf can't nurse and wanders away from the mother cow." Carl explained, "The mother cow which has my brand on it. Once it's wandering off on its own, why then it belongs to the first person who comes along and slaps a brand on it! Unless we actually catch them at it, there's not a damn thing I can do besides be careful about branding my stock ... and yes," he looked at Magda as she was about to ask another question, "My suspicions go the same way yours do. Towards the Waldrips. Naturally."

"Is there any dirty business that they don't have a finger in?" Magda asked, bitterly.

Her husband made a great show of thinking, before answering with a wry smile, "They aren't writing yellow-covered novels, or keeping a workhouse for orphans... but that's about it, that I can think of." The smile faded, and he added, honestly, "Will and Sylvester aren't so very much out of plumb, but J.P. is about two degrees off from being a mad-man."

"He is vicious," Magda said, with a shudder, "He is like a Caligula or a Nero. He would hurt people, for the fun of watching. I think even his brothers are afraid of him."

"Well, I'd not turn my back on him," Carl agreed, "Brother or not. Still," he sighed, "I'd be the first to wish they would just move on, squat a little farther down the trail."

"They are dug in," said Magda, bitterly, "Like a tick, growing fat on others' blood and work, sinking their hooks deeper and deeper. I do not like them, hearts-love, any of them and I am afraid of them, too."

"Why is that, then?" her husband asked, reasonably. "Except for JP, they're no better or worse than most of the settlers who came out expecting better than they found."

"Haven't you seen the way they look so hatefully at this house, this farm?" Magda rounded on him, "Men! You do not see the way J.P. Waldrip looks and envies? He wants it, without the trouble of working as hard as we do and he hates that we have such and he does not."

"Can't say that I ever noticed," Carl said, mildly.

"It's like the heat from a stove," Magda retorted, "His brothers and their friends may be no better and no worse, but he is insane with envy. He would not hesitate to do us harm, if he could do so without hazard to himself."

"Then I will take very good care that he will never have that chance," Carl said, kissing his wife affectionately on the forehead. "Don't worry about Waldrip, Margaretha. He will pick the wrong fight with someone, someday. The world won't miss him when that day comes and neither will his brothers."

"So you say," Magda sounded unconvinced, for she had come to loathe the rabble of Waldrips, especially the oldest brother, the man with the odd-colored eyes whom she had first seen being thrown out of Mr. Ransleben's store in Friedrichsburg. They had moved around the district, squatting on various plots of unclaimed land along the Guadalupe River, building untidy cabins of un-peeled logs and scratching out enough of a farm-plot to grow a crop of corn. Trying to pass counterfeit coin off on Mr. Ransleben was not the least savory of what the Waldrips were suspected of, nor was appropriating unbranded cattle.

Once brought to mind, the thought of the Waldrips were nearly as hard to banish as they were in person. Around the corner of the house that very afternoon, pulling weeds from the larger vegetable garden, Magda heard horses on the road and the dogs making their usual fuss. But since Carl was in the lower field with Nate spreading out a load of well-rotted muck, transferred from the pile next to the stable and she heard Porfirio and her brother out in the yard, she went on pulling weeds. She thought it must be Nate's father or brothers, come to see about the calf-branding and wondered why they had not stopped to speak to Carl, rather than come all the way up to the house. Until she heard a strange voice calling,

"You. Boy, c'mere. There's been a murder done, hereabouts. You seen any strangers hanging about?"

That was not Nate's father. She stood up, bundling the pulled weeds neatly into her apron, and came around the corner, to face the Waldrip brothers. Her brother Friedrich stood nervously in the middle of the yard, by the small corral with a coiled lariat in his hand. The three Waldrips on their horses half-surrounded the boy on horseback; J.P. with his odd eyes, one blue and the other near to colorless, and his brothers on either side of him. They had backed him and Porfirio up almost into the pile of muck with a shovel stuck into it, the straw and waste cleaned out from the stable and chicken house. In the German way, Carl made use of it once it was rotted, in the fields and around his precious trees. They hadn't seen her, they were intent on poor Friedrich who was looking this way and that, uncertain and confused. Magda's brother was twelve years old, grown tall but still a child in many ways. The Waldrips would think it amusing to push both of them into the muck. Magda could see that very well, and knew also that Friedrich would not have understood much of the English that the Waldrips were speaking. Porfirio looked angry; he spat out something in Spanish and stepped aggressively towards the Waldrips, but J.P. only said coldly,

"I asked you, boy! I don't palaver with Mexes," and jerked the reins of his horse so that the animal sidled menacingly close to Porfirio. But Porfirio had spent all of his life around horses and was not intimidated. He caught the bridle with the swiftness of a snake striking out.

Friedrich stammered, "No one. No strangers have I seen." Then he added in German, "And I don't know about any visitors, either."

"Foreigners," J.P. Waldrip looked disgusted, "Suddenly they're everywhere, hereabouts. Like lice on a dog." His parti-colored eyes suddenly fell on Magda, as if noticing her for the first time. "Ma'am," he said coldly. He did not sound polite at all. "Me and my brothers are out to do justice for a murderer. You seen any strangers around here, mebbe in the last two days or so?"

"I have not seen such," Magda answered through lips suddenly stiff and cold, as her heart sank with the realization of who the Waldrips must be after. "We know nothing of a murder. What talk is this?"

It was not two days since John Hunter had stayed with them, saying that men had been looking for him. Had either she or Carl said anything to Fredi and the boys about that? She thought not, for the boys had been too full of their adventure and Porfirio too concerned about calves with split tongues. No, she was confident that Friedrich knew nothing of John Hunter's visit. In any case her younger brother was completely frightened out of the English that he knew.

J.P. Waldrip took off his hat, as if something had suddenly reminded him of what most folk thought of as good manners. "There was a soldier murdered in a knife-fight, three nights ago," he answered. Magda barely repressed a shudder as she looked at him. Curiously, he might not have been so ill-appearing a man, even with the odd-eyes. He had fine, regular features. It was the expression and his manner that made him repulsive. "The man who done it left town in a hurry. We aim to make things right, ma'am. You don't think it's right that someone can kill one of our fine boys in blue an' walk away without justice being done?"

"We don't know anything about a murder," Magda repeated firmly, but with a rising sense of panic. J.P. had an avid expression on his face, as if he were enjoying all this. "My brother knows nothing about any guests."

"What about your pet Mex, here?" J.P. suddenly unshipped a heavy revolver from his saddle holster, and pressed the end of it against Porfirio's forehead. "Him, with his filthy Mex hands on the bridle of my horse?!"

Magda gasped, horrified, seeing Porfirio suddenly turning very pale under his dark-tanned face. He dropped his hand from the bridle and held himself rigidly still save for his lips, which moved silently.

J.P.'s brothers moved uneasily and one of them protested, "J.P., ain't that going a li'l too far ..." as J.P. Waldrip began to laugh. It wasn't a man's laugh, but a high-pitched maniacal giggle that raised the flesh on the back of her neck. She knew why J.P.'s brothers obeyed him; it was because they feared him, and what he might do.

"No, Will, we ain't going far enough!" J.P. laughed again, as if he had made a happy jest, "Jus' not far enough a'tall... and that's..."

"Your brother is a sensible man, J.P. That is quite far enough." Carl appeared like a miracle, stepping silently from behind the Waldrips with a hay-fork in his right hand. Friedrich looked like he had been rescued from drowning and Magda herself went limp with relief. She had not heard him and neither had the Waldrips. He could walk so silently, like an Indian or a ghost; a startling skill possessed by a man so tall. In the instant that J.P. gaped in sudden astonishment, Carl reached up with his free hand and swiftly twisted the revolver out of J.P.'s hand, pulling the short barrel away from Porfirio's forehead, where it had left a pale circular mark. He was none to gentle about it, judging from the grinding sound of hand bones or the way that J.P. grimaced. "You've got no call to threaten my hired man, J.P." he added mildly. "And my wife just gave you an answer. If it isn't the answer you wanted to hear, then that's just hard cheese."

J.P. glowered, and nursed his empty hand against his chest. Magda, with her arm around her brother, saw him look from side to side, unexpectedly cornered like something vicious and feral... and looking for a way out. The manic laughter was gone, but not the dislike in those odd-colored eyes as he looked down at the Beckers and Porfirio, who was cursing in Spanish, below his breath. His brothers shifted nervously, under Carl Becker's unreadable regard. "Didn't mean any real harm, Becker. Jus' having a bit of fun." He grumbled, "You got too many foreigners on your place. I'd be doing you a favor if I cut down on the numbers."

"It's my place." Carl pointed out mildly and shot a look towards Porfirio, "Far as I know, there isn't any rule that I have to get your approval over who I hire or who comes to visit. If you know any different, I'd very much like to hear about it."

"What about when there's been a murder?" Waldrip fairly spat, "You draw any lines about that?"

"'Bout the same lines as you do, J.P, 'specially when I haven't heard anything about a warrant, or any posse being raised lawfully. Until then, I tend to stay at home and mind my own business." Carl answered, and his voice was even, deliberate. Then he smiled a blandly cheerful smile and added, "Now, if you're all het up about doing justice and pursuing the lawful, lately, there's someone going around, along the river slitting calves tongues. I expect in a few days, they might be back to brand them, once those calves get used to getting along eating grass. If you see anyone that don't work for me, branding calves on my land, I'll expect a man of your dedication to justice and the law to let me know—if you see anything of the sort."

"We surely will," one of Waldrips' brothers answered hastily, while J.P. scowled, "We'll surely let you know, we see anything like that."

"Right neighborly of you," Carl's smile broadened to an outright grin. "I expect you'll be moving along, since my wife and brother in law answered your question?"

"I'll take my gun back, Becker," J.P. growled, and Carl turned it over in his hand, as if it were something he had just discovered.

"One of the new Colts," he remarked, sounding almost pleased, "It'll need cleaning though." And he deliberately dropped it into the freshest part of the muck-pile. "Help yourself, J.P. But you might want to keep this in mind, next time you're in Bexar; you just don't want to mess with a dark alley and a Mex with a knife and a grudge."

Magda drew in her breath; J.P. Waldrip appeared almost incandescent with fury, and his brothers looked as if they hardly dared breathe. But her husband still had the hayfork, with its sharp tines, and J.P. was not yet so lost to reason as to forget that. He flung himself off his horse and retrieved his property. They were gone in a thunder of hoofs and up-flung dust as Porfirio cursed after them and Carl said, calmly, "I was going to let you have it, if he let it go," but Magda shivered suddenly.

"You shouldn't have shamed him like that, my heart. Now he has every reason to hate you."

Printed in the United States
138719LV00004B/26/P